Scents of Exile

J. L. Guyer

Also by J. L. Guyer

The Fragrant Trilogy
Scents of War
Scents of Exile

Table of Contents

Chapter One.. 1

Chapter 2.. 13

Chapter 3..27

Chapter 4..38

Chapter 5..52

Chapter 6..69

Chapter 7..79

Chapter 8..87

Chapter 9..99

Chapter 10 114

Chapter 11 125

Chapter 12 136

Chapter 13 149

Chapter 14 158

Chapter 15 169

Chapter 16 180

Chapter 17 191

Chapter 18 198

Chapter 19 208

Chapter 20 218

Chapter 21 229

Chapter 22 239

Chapter 23 251

Chapter 24 261

Chapter 25 268

Chapter 26 278

Chapter 27 287

Chapter 28 299

Character Lists 308

Acknowledgements 313

Dedicated to Stephanie Fink

who came into my life despite the constant moving from place to place in search of homes

and has been a part of my home ever since.

"Remember us, O God of Jedrek! Our scents rot and our homes are gone. We are slaves and orphans. Our enemies surround us and despise us all day long. Restore us to yourself that we may smell your fragrance once more."

—a prayer from Lord Tanish, a priest exiled in Korina

Chapter One

Home. "I'm home, mother," Dana called out as she rushed to one of the many glass cages lining the walls. She pulled out a Kindroot, it didn't matter which one, and took it to the back of the musty cave, barely noticing the scent of her collection of perfumes and ointments.

Coming to the skinnier passageways, Dana took the path to the left and then the right. The passage went quite a long way until it opened to a small room. In the middle stood a stone island. A pale young woman with long black hair lay beneath a cage of amber glass.

Dana hurried to the woman's side and lifted the glass. "I'm home, mother," she said again. "Don't worry. You won't have to wait much longer before you can leave this cold stone behind."

The woman didn't respond, not even to Dana's touch. Even after all this time, it hurt. Dana focused on breathing until she had composed herself. Then she placed the Kindroot on the woman's body, willing its aroma to flow into her mother. The glow around her mother brightened. Dana lifted the slumping Kindroot and replaced the glass, then went back to the front of the cave. She put the Kindroot back in its cage and straightened up.

Breathing in her perfumed scents, Dana refreshed her aching muscles and calmed her nerves. It was good to be back. None of this trying to control armies while on the road and with limited resources. She had her whole cave stocked with anything she could possibly want. Not to mention the essential ingredients she brought home from the coast.

Dana moved to her shelves and began emptying her travel bag. She pulled out a vial and showed it to Manzanita in his glass cage. "Do you know what this is?"

He ignored her. He didn't even shake one leaf at her. Dana turned to look at the rest of her collection of Kindroots. Thankfully, she didn't kill the volunteer this time. He would recover and look like the rest that lined the cave walls on either side. Only a hundred were still alive. She hadn't meant to kill the others, but it didn't matter, so long as she had all the rest together, her plan would work.

She still beat herself up for overlooking the baby Kindroot, but it was too late when she discovered her mistake. No matter what she tried, he continually evaded her. But not this time. Dana walked back through the waterfall to where her horvelina stood grazing on a nearby bush. He still carried her new glass cage on his back, the most important invention she acquired from the puny sea village. Once she had discovered that glass could contain scents from blowing away in the wind, she immediately got more glass to preserve her mother in. Then, the more she used glass, she realized it also prevented magic users from using their magic. That gave her an enormous advantage over her enemies.

She turned to carry it back inside but froze. She sniffed the air again, turning to look further down the river. The scent floating up to her was quite remarkable and not just because it came from her favorite student, but it was unlike any aroma she'd smelled before. He was a miracle, though he didn't know it yet.

"Prince Lucas! I didn't expect to see you so soon." Dana lowered the glass to the ground and stepped around her horvelina so she could greet him properly.

The young prince was dressed in style, as always. He smiled at her as he walked. "My father was going to come and let you know their progress, but I convinced him to let me come instead."

Dana reached out and took his extended hand, pulling him in closer. They smelifed one another, sniffing each other's right cheek, then the left.

"I'm glad you came. I was unloading my supplies from my trip to the coast. Here. Carry this in for me, would you?" Dana walked back to the glass cage and lifted it off the ground. The prince stepped forward and took it from her, disappearing behind the waterfall. She loved that he didn't balk at her commands, but just obeyed. She knew how difficult that was for most royals.

Dana turned to her horvelina with its long tusks and snout face. She reached up and grabbed the reins off his smooth, strong back and led him up and around the top of the waterfall. A stone building lay nestled between a few pines. The river rushed by only a few meters away. "There you go. You're home." She removed the saddle and reins using her mind and the smells of pine nuts to unbuckle and levitate them off the beast's back, something she could not do with glass since it was unaffected by magic.

Then she turned and went back down to join the prince. She reached out to his mind before she made it to the bottom of the hill. "Have you been practicing, like I taught you?"

His voice was clear inside her mind. "Yes. I particularly enjoyed mixing the lemon with the sweet chocolate scent."

"Did it work?"

Lucas hesitated in his reply. "I'm not sure. I think so. Least ways, I couldn't work anymore magic until the smell abated."

"Good," Dana spoke aloud, now that she stood next to the prince at the back of the cave. "I'll send you with a bottle of the blend, a present for our exiled princess."

"Wait. That's what it does? It prevents you from working magic. That's awesome!" Prince Lucas grinned. "That should help quite a bit, in case she isn't cooperating."

"I'm counting on it. You should know that even though she has surrendered, she is still trying to retain some control over things."

"Of course she is." Prince Lucas nodded. "Father said she negotiated the lives of her councilors as part of the surrender."

"Yes, well, that is what I expected. This one seems to be more noble than the others, with the exception of her mother. It's pathetic really. From my brief encounters with her and what I've heard, she'll do anything to save one person's life if she can, even if it means she might lose." Dana thought about that brief battle of the minds over Ithol. While she had wanted to back off and let the girl think she was winning, the girl had been more powerful than Dana had expected. It cost her dearly in resources.

"Do you think she really handed over the Kindroot?" the prince asked.

"No. But that is why your job is to get close to her. He surely won't be far from her. I suspect what she handed Bannon is a fake, but no worries. With her in our grasp, Blackthorn will be home with his family soon."

The prince turned to leave. "My father is expecting me for the evening meal."

"Before you go," Dana plucked a bottle off the shelf, smelled it to make sure it was the correct blend, and handed it to the prince, "please, try to keep your father under control. We wouldn't want him to kill our princess before we've got what we want."

"Don't worry about him. I know how to curb his anger." The prince bowed one more time and departed.

Dana stood near the back of the cave as he left, her parted dress shimmering whenever she shifted into the torchlight. Her dark hair flowed the length of her long back. And she remembered another man who made promises to her before he broke them. Lucas wouldn't let her down. She had her own plans to ensure it. She hated to admit it, but she was exactly like the princess: willing to do anything to save one person's life.

THE WALK TO THE PALACE gates was longer than Agonya anticipated. Her heart raced inside her chest, and she tried to keep her composure. Blackthorn was safe. He was safe. She had a sapling in his place to offer to the Korin Commander. Would he take the bait? He had to. It was her only hope.

She walked with her guards past the murals on the wall that depicted the history of her people. She remembered days of joy and blessings when there were bountiful scents and food and festivals for every occasion. Not since her mother's death had she experienced anything like that. Paradise died the day her mother died. And now she knew why. That was the day Blackthorn's will crumpled. He felt responsible for her mother's death. Had he really been so powerful as to give them all those blessings? No wonder Dana was after him. And her mother's death confirmed his presence in Ithol, which is why Dana's pursuit of him intensified. Yes, the last year made more sense.

"Are you ready, your Highness?"

The large cedar gates that stood before her now would open to the unknown. The Kors waited on the other side. A life exiled from her home and not just her, but all Itholeans would never be the same again. Their lives were not their own anymore.

Agonya glanced at her companions. They knew what surrendering to the Kors meant, and they knew they had given it their all. There was no other choice. Except letting them kill her friend, Lord Commander Huren and all the other brave soldiers whom the Kors had captured. No, there was no guarantee that she could keep the rest of her people from suffering. This was the right decision. She had been too late bringing help back to Ithol. Her mental battle with Dana completely exhausted her. At least Blackthorn would be safe from Dana's clutches a little longer.

Breathing in the frankincense burning in a bracket on the wall, Agonya nodded, and they opened the gates.

Korin soldiers rushed in, surrounding her and the small contingent with her. Then they parted, making way for their commander to approach. But it wasn't the commander. Captain Jaylen Dahel stood on the bridge with a smug look on his face. The kind that said, "I told you so." Agonya had a moment of panic. Had he seen the real Kindroot during their journey together? Would he know that what she offered was a fake? No. She'd been careful. He couldn't know.

The captain strode forward.

Agonya resisted the urge to step back. This man had pursued her constantly since she had the unfortunate luck to cross his path. Sure, he hadn't killed her when he had the opportunity. But he had made her life miserable and now she had to surrender to him? To just give up? It went against every scent in her body.

"Better late than never," he said. "Do you have it?"

She bit her tongue to keep from replying with a retort. Straightening her shoulders, she replied, "I do. Do you have Lord Commander Huren like you promised? I would see him alive before I surrender."

"Ha! You have no right to demand any proof. You must surrender to our terms before we will grant you anything in return."

He hadn't changed. She had hoped that with the knowledge of how the war actually began that he would be a little more sympathetic towards her, but it didn't appear that was the case. Recognizing her defeat, she reached into her bag and pulled out the tiny sapling she had infused with magic. "You have no idea what you are doing. Don't think this is the end because it's not. You're right. I have no other options or believe me; I wouldn't be standing here in front of you, surrendering. But I need you to guarantee that your end of the bargain will be upheld. That there will be no more bloodshed between our people, and that includes my commander and councilors."

"You have my word." Jaylen said curtly. Then he took the sapling from her hands and nodded to his guards. They removed her guards' weapons and tied their hands together. Then he led her out of the gates to his commander's tent.

Agonya let out a sigh of relief when she saw Huren bound up in the tent's corner. He was alive.

Panic returned when Jaylen held out the sapling for Lord Commander Bannon to see. Huren had to mask his response. Thankfully, none of the Kors were paying attention to Huren. If they had, they might have figured out that the Kindroot she offered was a fake.

The Korin commander stepped forward and took the glowing sapling from his captain. "Well done. Now, I've already given the orders to prepare for our journey home to Korina as soon as possible. But I want you to stay here, General Dahel."

Jaylen grinned. "Yes, sir."

"It looked like he got what he wanted," Agonya thought, "a promotion."

The lord commander returned the salute and walked back to his table. Agonya saw him pull out a glass box and place the sapling inside. Blackthorn was safe.

NO MATTER HOW HARD Agonya tried to think about something different, anything different, the monotony of putting one foot in front of the other, day after day, meant it was very near impossible to keep her mind from drifting back to that dreadful day.

After she had surrendered, she'd been forced to march out of the city past the thorny devils and dranks that still roamed free in her city. She'd been back inside a Korin tent, but this time without Maya or Brynn or Blackthorn. And Ashkii hadn't come to rescue her. She was there by choice.

Agonya's foot snagged on a root. She reached for something to hold her, anything. Her hand landed on the soldier walking next to her.

He pushed her away. "Watch it, Princess!" The last word he said with a sneer.

He didn't have to remind her she was an exile now. That she was no longer the queen of Ithol. A captive, a prisoner of war. Agonya lifted her head in defiance.

"If I wasn't under orders not to harm you, I'd have you smacked for that."

Agonya held her tongue. She knew that the Kor would get back at her by hurting a less important Itholean if she argued. She had surrendered to protect them, now she had to restrain herself. Blackthorn was safe and her people wouldn't be dying in battle or starving in their own homes. Surrendering was the best, the right decision.

Horse hooves thumped behind Agonya. She heard its rider speak. "Thank you, soldier. Find someone else to torture."

Agonya stared straight ahead. She knew that voice and wasn't keen on talking to him at the moment. She focused on her Lord Commander Huren, who was walking a hundred paces in front of her. Those soldiers didn't hesitate to club him if he made one misstep.

"There's a reason I made sure you were in this part of the caravan," Lord Commander Bannon said nonchalantly.

"I'm sure there is," Agonya shot back.

"You see, the trouble is, I know how much you care for them." Bannon pointed to all the other captives. "You need to remember; I showed you mercy when you surrendered. I could have killed you right then and there, but I spared your life because I wanted to end the war just as much as you, and if

I'd killed you, then I would have had to kill all your people, too. That's just too bloody."

"If that was too much killing, why did you attack us in the first place?" Why was he telling her this? If their positions were reversed, she wouldn't be telling him her reasoning.

"You, very well, know why. You should have just handed it over when I arrived, and no one would have had to die."

"Not even my mother," Agonya muttered. It wasn't until a few months ago that Agonya learned the true history of her mother's death. How it was her uncle, King Reid, who had killed her in an attempt to kidnap the last Kindroot. Thankfully, he wasn't able to get his hands on Blackthorn, and neither did Bannon. He just thought he did.

"Not going to talk to me? Just remember your place or I will let my soldiers beat sense into you." The commander kneed his horse to go faster, leaving Agonya to her miserable self.

She reached into the pocket of her cloak and caressed the once thick and fleshy leaf, careful to not break its shriveled form. As Agonya felt the dying succulent, she noticed the plants beneath her feet and all around them. The grass was yellow. The flowers were drooping. The leaves on the cottonwoods were paler than they normally were. It made little sense. She knew winter was almost upon them, but something about it was wrong. The plants looked like they usually did when they got ready for the cold, but the smell was wrong. They had no fragrance.

Agonya raised the succulent to her nose. Nothing. She smelled it again. Nothing. She reached for her mother's necklace and breathed a sigh of relief. The scent of her mother was still there inside the silvery locket. The delicate silver bands twisted in such a way that they reminded Agonya of Blackthorn. Maya had been right. Her necklace had fallen on her bedroom floor before she'd had to flee for her life. It felt wonderful to have it back again, but the lack of scents from the surrounding plants was troubling. Was Dana behind it? Surely not. No one was that powerful.

"We need to talk." A deep, familiar voice resonated inside Agonya's mind, breaking her train of thought.

"Blackthorn! Are you okay? Did Maya find you?" Agonya projected her thoughts towards the Kindroot. She could picture him in his little clay pot of soil, his furry leaves with streaks of orange, his colorful berries hanging from the branches. It was almost like old times. Why she hadn't thought about reaching out to him sooner was beyond her, but what was done was done. They were talking now.

"I'm fine. Maya's fine. We made it out of the palace without being detected by the Kors. But that's not why we need to talk."

"Yeah, I know. I've been noticing the plants as we pass by them. There's something wrong. I don't think I can smell their fragrances." Agonya tried to breathe in the surrounding scents, but there was too much dust in the air. She tried not to cough on the soldiers walking next to her, but they made it rather difficult since there were an excessive number of them guarding her.

The guards directly in front of her glanced over their shoulders so they could glare at her, but she just kept walking. What was the point of apologizing?

"Blackthorn?" He sure was taking his time replying.

"That is a problem, but it isn't why we need to talk. You are in danger. I know you always seem in danger, and you are in more danger once they find out you didn't give me to them, but there's more."

Agonya forced herself to keep walking. One step in front of the other. She could handle whatever it was he had to say. She'd faced so many obstacles recently. What was one more? Could it really be worse than Bannon discovering her trick?

"Do you remember the Montane that killed your father?"

Her body shivered, and it wasn't from the cold. Agonya couldn't forget. The Montane that had killed her father and had forced her to flee Ithol.

"He's coming for you next," Blackthorn said quietly.

"How can you be sure? I thought all the Montanes returned to their homes." Agonya still hurt whenever she thought about Ashkii's ultimate betrayal. She had hoped he truly meant his apology. He'd said he loved her, but his words were like perfume that blew away on the wind.

Blackthorn interrupted her thoughts. "Because I smelled him. And Agonya, he isn't just any Montane. If my nose is correct, the assassin is Ashkii's relative."

She heard what he'd said, but it didn't affect her. Ashkii knowing the assassin wasn't news to her. He'd said as much. What difference did it make if they were related or not? At least now, she would have knowledge about the assassin that might give her leverage, because she certainly couldn't fight the assassin and win. He was too skilled.

"Agonya? Are you all right?" Blackthorn asked.

"I'll be okay. I'm glad you told me. Now I will be prepared."

"I must get back to healing the plants. There are many mouths to feed and not a lot of food here."

"Oh right. Do you know what's making them sick?"

"I have my suspicions, but I can't say for sure. I'll let you know as soon as I figure it out. And Agonya?"

"Yeah?"

"Take care of yourself. I would hate to have been wrong about you being able to defend yourself now."

"Don't worry about me. I need you to look after Maya."

"Speaking of Maya, she's coming my way."

Agonya didn't know why she expected him to say more. He always cut off their conversations abruptly, and he had said goodbye in so many ways this time. Somehow, this goodbye felt more final. She might never speak to him again if the assassin found her. In that moment, she was grateful for the excessive guards surrounding her.

"GOOD," LORD COMMANDER Bannon strode through the tent flap, "You're all here. Let's begin. First Division, report."

General Gad stepped forward. "I found some soldiers," he glanced at Captain Lokni, "not adhering to the rules of conduct toward prisoners of war. There has to be a better way to enforce these rules."

"Ha!" Captain Lokni laughed. "Is that the only problem you see? What about our wounded? We are barely keeping up with the caravan and will need several days to rest. Don't worry about the prisoners, but your own people."

"That was going to be my second point. We've only been on the road a couple of days, and they are already struggling to keep up."

"Any ideas?" Bannon asked. He was already getting a headache.

"If I might, Lord Commander," the king's personal warrior and spy, Aekan, spoke up, saying, "We should make the former queen heal our wounded. We know she has healing powers beyond our normal healers. That, or the Kindroot can heal them."

Captain Lokni interrupted. "Kindroot? What is this? Legends from the past?"

Bannon studied Lokni for a minute before ignoring his question and turning towards Aekan. Aekan had been one of the Itholean captives set free. How the Itholeans captured him was beyond Bannon, since Aekan was the best warrior he knew. Aekan also was a heap of knowledge. "Let's talk more after this meeting. But, yes, we should see what she can do."

Aekan smiled. "Of course."

"Good. We will stay here for a day, restocking and letting the Itholean queen try to heal the wounded, and I want a report on any incidents between soldiers and prisoners. We agreed to respect them, and we will. They are not our slaves yet. So far, they have kept their word and so should we. Now, Second Division, report."

The meeting continued for several hours as each division reported on the happenings in their camps. It was much the same: wounded, meeting the needs of their soldiers, food, water, and so forth.

"Finally," Bannon thought to himself. The last of the officers left the tent, and he was alone with Aekan.

"Tell me, Aekan. What do you know about Kindroots?"

"I know Kindroots are the reason we came to war against Ithol. That we need their power to truly be victorious."

"Yes, well, how do you propose we use their power?" Bannon asked. He went to his trunk in the tent's corner and pulled out the glass box with the Kindroot inside. Then he placed it in the center of the table.

Aekan's eyes widened in surprise. "Sir. That is not a Kindroot."

"What? How do you know?"

"I know because I've seen real Kindroots. King Reid was very specific when he told me that the Kindroot we are looking for looks like a cross between a manzanita tree and a blackthorn bush. And that is a chestnut sapling."

Bannon was furious. How come he hadn't been told this information sooner? Who did she think she was, not fulfilling her promises? She was going to pay for this insolence.

Regaining his composure, Bannon addressed Aekan. "How would you like to search our royal princess for the real Kindroot?"

"It would be my pleasure." Aekan's smile broadened. Then he bowed and left Bannon alone with time to think.

Chapter 2

Jaylen took his time exploring the palace now that it was to be his home for the unforeseeable future. He still couldn't believe he'd pulled it off. Lord Commander Bannon had promoted him to general and temporary governor of Ithol until the king could appoint someone else. Apart from the divisions who were now under his control, there were still quite a few Itholeans who had stayed, the poor and unimportant Itholeans. Jaylen had to make sure they didn't get any ideas. Korins were in charge now. He was in charge now.

Jaylen turned another corner. The palace was enormous, even larger than Korina's palace. Jaylen had only been to Korina's palace on two other occasions and as grand as that was, the Itholean palace was grandeur, with murals on the walls and spiral staircases leading to the upper floors. How had such a kingdom like Ithol fallen so far? There were many buildings within the palace grounds, and it was easy to get turned around. On the other scent, Jaylen didn't have to worry about housing his men. They could easily house all the soldiers here and servants as well. The palace grounds had the least amount of damage in the city, and the walls would keep the thorny devils and dranks outside. They'd be safe here.

Turning the corner of an upper floor, Jaylen saw something move. He picked up his pace and neared the place where he'd seen movement. As he reached an arch in the wall, he saw the room beyond. Various plants: small fruit trees, colorful flowers, ferns, and herbs filled every available space. Streaming through the open roof, sunlight dappled the scene with a warm yellow glow. It was a paradise in a sea of ruin. His mother would love it. The yellow sofas added to the room's ambiance. Despite his premonition, the room was devoid of any living creature. His mind must be playing tricks on him.

Jaylen made a note of where the room was and continued his exploration of the palace. He needed to assign rooms to his captains and then they would have to organize a way to corral the wild animals so they wouldn't terrorize the Itholeans who stayed behind. He had promised the former queen there would be no more bloodshed.

The image of Brynn being torn apart by a thorny devil made a shiver run up Jaylen's spine. The devil would have killed him next if the queen hadn't killed the devil first. That had been close. Too close. Jaylen breathed deeply until his heart returned to normal.

He was still alive, and Brynn was the one who had died. There was something unsettling about his death. Jaylen hadn't known Brynn for long and only as an enemy, but Jaylen had seen his character. Brynn was a man of his word and had done everything he could to support his queen and his friends. He was a good man. Jaylen respected that. If only all Kors were like Brynn... but he knew men like Brynn were rare. He knew himself well enough to know that he was not like Brynn. He was selfish and was happy for the promotion when he should have done more for the queen. His father, on the other hand, was a good man. He wished he were returning home to be with his family again, to let them know he was safe and to smell their fragrances, but he had work to do here. There were no thorny devils loose in Korina threatening their lives. The least he could do for her was to protect those that remained.

BLACKTHORN TREMBLED inside Maya's pocket where she stood. They couldn't risk being seen in the palace. He could smell the Kor in the hallway getting closer and closer. "We need to get out of here before he finds us."

"But how?" she replied in his mind.

"Can you get up to the roof?"

"I'm too short."

"Isn't there a ladder in here? I've seen that panel opened to the sky."

"Oh, yes. I think it's over here." Maya crossed the room, opened a closet door.

A moment later, she had the ladder directly under the sunroof.

"Quick! He's almost here."

Maya sprinted up the ladder and was pulling it up behind them just as the Kor entered the room.

"Be very quiet," Blackthorn said in her mind. "Did he see us?"

"I don't think so."

Blackthorn focused on the man's aroma inside the room below them. It was moving further away. That's when Blackthorn's branches relaxed.

"Thank you, Maya! That was close. Now we need to get out of here before we run into anyone else."

The ladder was awkward under Maya's short arms, but she managed to cross the connecting roofs to the gardens at the edge of the palace grounds. "We have to go down into the gardens, but we can use that secret door to get out," Maya said in his mind.

"I can't smell anyone nearby. Do you see anyone?"

"Not a soul."

"Okay. Let's go." Blackthorn felt Maya lower the ladder and then step gingerly on to the top rung. It wobbled beneath her step. Slowly, they descended until Maya's feet were firmly on the ground. The palace garden would have been Blackthorn's choice. If he were to call any place home, it would be there, except for his true home. But he hadn't been there since Dana kidnapped his family. Most of his life, he had lived among the roses and succulents and creeping vines of the palace. The oldest of all the plants in the garden were the peony bushes. While the peonies were a hundred years old, Blackthorn was older. In fact, he was many times older than the peonies, too many to count, yet he loved them. But he knew they couldn't stay there. It was not safe to be in his own home anymore.

He breathed in the fragrances as he passed through his home for the last time, and he tried not to think about his loss. Maya made it to the door behind the vines, and they escaped into the streets of Ithol.

"Where are you going to take me?" Blackthorn asked.

"A few of us have set up a home in the aromatic temple."

"Is there a garden nearby?"

"There is," Maya reassured him.

She was right. And the park even had peony bushes in it. As soon as Maya set him down, he climbed out of his tiny pot and bee-lined for the safety of the closest peony bush. The bush would be his new home for now. Its lush branches hid him well; and when they bloomed, they would emit a fragrance worth smelling. The longing for that scent reminded Blackthorn why he helped Agonya in the first place. To be frank, he was sick and tired of being passed from one human to the next. Yes, he was grateful Maya had come for him, but he wanted his family back. He knew they were only trying to protect him from Dana, and he had no desire to be near the Korin general they'd seen in the hall.

Even when King Azurarus had pushed him into Agonya's arms, Blackthorn had decided he would not get to know her at all. He hadn't wanted to become attached to her like he had to Kanti. A lot of good that did him. Kanti died because of him, lost to him forever. And now? Now that he knew Agonya, her kindness, he had let her go with little chance of smelling her again.

Agonya. She smelled of peonies in full bloom and not just her aroma, but who she was as a person was floral. She convinced him to stay behind because she cared for him more than herself. Then after she left, Blackthorn had smelled the man responsible for her father's death. That man had followed her. She was in danger, and Blackthorn had done everything he could to warn her. There was nothing else to do but rest knowing that she knew how to create a magic shield, and she knew how to heal. That would have to be enough to keep her from dying at the hands of the Montane.

Blackthorn stretched his branches outward. He couldn't afford to dwell on Agonya anymore. He had Maya to think about. She differed from any human he had known in his thousand years of knowing humans. Apart from the fact that they both missed Agonya and worried about her, Blackthorn couldn't figure out how to relate to Maya.

He pulled up his roots and crept across the loose soil until he could peek out of the peony branches. He neither smelled humans nor saw them. "Maya?" He reached out to her mind again.

"Yes?"

"Where did you go?"

"I thought you wanted to be left alone, so I came inside, but I am leaving again soon."

"What for?"

"We need supplies, and there's a report that some traveling merchants arrived today."

"Do you want me to go with you?"

"No, that's okay. Enjoy the sunlight and fragrances. I'll be back in no time."

"Be careful." Blackthorn left Maya's mind. And crawled out of the bush.

Once he was outside of his house, he found the sunniest spot and soaked in the light. He spread his branches out to get the maximum sunlight and dug his roots back into the rich soil. It felt so good to be out of that smelly pot and out of the cramped pocket, to be safely out of the palace.

He would have gladly gone with Maya, but he was grateful for the time alone. He liked that about Maya. She respected his wishes. Of all the human women he'd met, Maya was the sweetest and kindest. In the back of his mind, he worried that he should have gone with her. Thorny devils and dranks still roamed the streets, not to mention the Korin soldiers who were left behind to rule the city.

The biggest problem of all was that Maya couldn't use magic. There had to be a way to graft her into the covenant, to teach her how to use olfamancy. Blackthorn just didn't know how. He barely understood it himself.

Blackthorn soaked in the sun for several hours before he smelled the foreigner. He yanked his roots from the ground and sprinted back under the peony bush. Sprinting, meaning he tried not to tangle his roots and yet moved them as quickly as he could across the ground. The human was getting closer. Perhaps he hadn't been spotted.

MAYA WALKED UP TO THE foreigners at the gates of the city. This was her last hope. That they would be decent this time. The people were starving. Ever since the Kors left with most of the Itholeans as prisoners and taken most of the food with them, it was so hard to find enough for those who were left behind. The guards didn't want to share their food. In fact, the Kors had taken most of the food for themselves. A few travelers, the people she was headed to now, came by periodically, but they always charged too much.

There were never more than twenty travelers at a time. Word had spread about the destruction of Ithol.

"Good morning," Maya addressed the woman talking with a few other merchants. "Which scents do you have for me today?"

The woman stood up to be on eye level, except she was a head taller than Maya. "We have vegetables, wheat, and sheep."

Maya reached into her cart and pulled out the last of the jewelry from the palace at the bottom. "I need as much as you can give me."

"Hmmm. For that, I can give you potatoes, squash, carrots, and these greens."

"I'll take the vegetables as well as twenty bushels of wheat and those sheep over there." How could she be so stingy? They were talking about food! Food was not supposed to be this expensive. How were they going to survive if they sold all their treasures for food?

"The vegetables and the wheat," the woman countered.

Maya reluctantly pulled out a bottle of perfume from her cloak. "Instead of the gold jewelry, how about this perfume for all three?"

"Your scent is pleasant," the woman said, sniffing Maya's hand and taking the bottle from her simultaneously.

Maya loaded her cart with all the food, roped the sheep to follow, and started back to the temple. She heard the men laughing behind her. "Look at the Itholeans now, Lonan. They used to be people I admired. Do you remember the scented feasts they had? Now they have nothing!"

Maya did her best to ignore the ever-increasing laughter. Let them think what they wanted.

"Hey, I've got more for you to buy," one man yelled after her.

Maya turned back. If they had more, she would most certainly need more. But when she saw him, he pointed to his chest and winked. He was just despicable. Maya kept turning and pushed the cart as fast as she could. There was no way she was going to let them see her cry.

"Oh, Agonya! I can't do it," Maya whispered to herself. Agonya's last words to her were to look after Blackthorn and take care of those left behind. Retrieving Blackthorn from the palace had been terrifying. As for the others, most of the Lords, Ladies and soldiers left Ithol with their families. That left the old and the sick, and families that had had no one well enough to fight.

Very few children, only the ones who had the best hiding places, were the ones who weren't dragged off to Korina. Even with most of the people gone, there were still ten thousand people left in Ithol. How was Maya going to help them all? Thirty some days after Agonya left and all their food was practically gone. The food in this cart wouldn't last one day.

There were others who helped, that were strong enough to go out and look for food. Then there were those that made things worse. To Maya's dismay, some of the Itholeans started selling their neighbors to get what they wanted. Maya felt helpless against them. What could she do to stop them? It wasn't like she was scented to be a leader. Misu had joined up with her and many others, but they were in no position to serve justice to ten thousand people. They still had to worry about the thorny devils and dranks who roamed the streets. Maya struggled to wrap her mind around the young man who was killed on his second outing. He had been foolish to think he could fight off a pack of thorny devils by himself. To his credit, one creature died in his attack. One creature... Maya wondered if it was still there? She'd have to discuss its retrieval with Ryker.

Maya searched the streets nearby for signs of the predators and sighed in relief. She'd only seen dranks from a distance on one of her outings. She knew it was only a matter of time before she became cornered. But there was no way around it. They needed supplies. Even if the foreigners sold their food at exorbitant prices, Maya was grateful to buy it, nonetheless.

MAYA SMELLED IT BEFORE she saw it. The sheep bleated as a drank dashed around the far corner. Maya swallowed her scream and pushed the cart at the closest door, a door to an abandoned home. She pushed the cart inside and tried to get the sheep through the door frame. One. Two. Three. Four. A couple of them ran the wrong way. Maya couldn't chase them. She jumped inside behind the fifth sheep and slammed the door shut. A moment later, the drank started to screech and claw the door. Its eerie high-pitched sound was going to draw all the other dranks to her location. If she didn't do something quick, they'd burn the door down in no time at all.

Maya searched the room for anything to block the door. She grabbed a chair and pushed it against the door. The drank screeched again. She tried not to visualize the green acid spraying from its mouth and hitting the door. Instead, an image of Brynn protecting her from its spray so long ago came to her mind. The burning of his legs and back made her gag and gasp for air. She needed to be in control. She pushed Brynn from her mind and focused on the door. The wood beneath the acid was bubbling and disintegrating before her eyes.

Maya's heart raced as she looked for an escape. Then she saw the window in the next room over. She climbed up on a table to have a better look.

"Come on, think, Maya!"

She pushed the shutters open. The drank crouched and spread its jaws wide. Maya looked down the street. She couldn't see any other dranks yet. Quickly, she climbed down and tied the sheep to the cart. Then, she climbed back up and out of the window. Instead of going down towards the street, she climbed up onto the roof. She placed her hand over her heart to slow its pounding.

Then she took a deep breath and crossed over several roofs, keeping an eye out for anything that might help her. A loose board. Perfect. Maya reached down and pried the board free. Then she threw it one street over from the first. Sure enough, the drank heard it and ran towards the sound to investigate.

Maya retreated to the window, climbed inside, and pushed the cart out onto the empty street. Then she forced the sheep to change directions. The long way around was going to have to work.

Several turns later, Maya froze in her tracks for the second time that day. It wasn't another drank but a thorny devil, eating the remains of a young man. It wasn't Brynn. He was already dead. Maya watched the devil intently, hoping he didn't see her. He paused as if he'd heard something, but then continued his meal. That was all it took for her to push her cart down a different road. With no enemies in sight, she entered a different abandoned home, barred the door again, and sank to her knees. All her strength abandoned her then.

Brynn! Oh, Brynn! His face flooded her mind. Only a week ago, a thorny devil tore him in two. Though she had buried him, seeing that poor man being eaten brought the worst images back to her mind.

She loved Brynn. He never knew it! Brynn... Brynn the kindhearted harvester. The man who sacrificed his life for her, for their queen, even though he didn't have to.

Maya slumped on the floor for hours. The others were probably wondering where she was, if she was all right. But she couldn't force herself to brave the streets again. Brynn's face was all she saw.

"Maya," Blackthorn called to her in her mind, "I feel your sorrow. Hang in there. I need you to be brave. Be brave for the children. Be brave for me. There's a foreigner among us. He doesn't smell right. Please, come quickly."

Maya let the tears flow. Blackthorn let her cry but remained with her in her mind. Several minutes later, she rose, wiped her face, and headed home. "I'm coming."

BLACKTHORN SMILED. If you could call it a smile. His face was near the top of his smooth red trunk. The mouths of Kindroots were so small that humans could not see them move. But he knew Maya would make it back. Blackthorn checked the streets she needed to travel and made sure there were no creatures: thorny devils or dranks, waiting for her.

Then he frowned. Not because of Maya, but the stranger was pulling back the door to his home in the peony bushes. Blackthorn froze. The stranger might just see another plant and not know who he was.

No such luck. The stranger snatched Blackthorn around the trunk and pulled him out of the bush. Blackthorn held still. Maybe the man was simply curious. But then Blackthorn read his mind.

"I've found him at last," the stranger thought.

Blackthorn burned the man's hands. The man yelped and let go. "Sticks!"

Blackthorn let his roots soften his fall on the dirt path. The man bent to pick him up again, but his yell brought Misu into the garden.

"Sir, are you all right? I heard a yell."

"I'm fine," the stranger replied, shaking his hand.

Misu thought he was holding his hand out to be smelled and reached to take it. "Pardon, I don't think we've met yet."

The stranger realized what Misu was doing and allowed him to grasp his hand. "I actually just arrived and haven't been able to meet anyone."

"I'm Misu. What's your name? I can introduce you to everyone. I'm sure they would all like to meet you."

"You can call me Skah."

"And where are you from again? What brings you to Ithol?"

"The mountains on both accounts. I've lived my whole life in those mountains, but there are more and more dangers threatening our way of life. I had no idea of the destruction here in Ithol. What happened here?"

"You don't know about the war?" Misu ran his hand through his gray hair. "The Kors had our city under siege. We would have lasted longer, but somehow, they got to our supplies and ruined them. You must have seen the wall they collapsed on your way here?"

"That's terrible. I'm so glad to see that not everything was lost. How did you keep this garden intact?"

Blackthorn inwardly cursed. This man found him because the garden wasn't decaying like the other plants throughout Ithol. Instead of waiting to hear the rest of their conversation, Blackthorn ran for cover. He hopped in and out of bushes until he was sure the stranger didn't know where he was. Then he hid in the vines covering every inch of the temple wall. The men were still speaking, but their voices drifted toward the temple. The old man was going to introduce the newcomer to the rest of the survivors.

"Maya, please hurry! He's a Montane and was sent here by Chief Golar. I need to hide in your pocket, however dreadful that may be."

"I'm here. Don't worry. I'll come straight to you, then join the others and meet this foreigner."

RYKER STOOD UP AND walked over to meet Maya when she entered the sanctuary. She must have looked bad, according to the look on his face. He was a good man. If it hadn't been for him, others would have been lost. Ryker was one of the first that she'd met in Ithol upon her return. He had protected their little group from the dranks and thorny devils and helped them find a home base. Then, he had helped everyone see how important it was to find and help other Itholeans still in the city. Some didn't want to share their resources with others, but he had stood with Maya and Misu the entire time.

"Your smell is pleasant, Ryker! Is Tyler back?"

"I'm here," Tyler said, entering the room behind her.

Maya scanned the hall. There were children in the far corner sitting in a circle while one of the elderly women told them stories. Misu, the one who helped her find the survivors and get organized, met her eyes and left the sick woman's side to join them.

"Ryker, you go first. Were you able to refill the water barrels without any trouble this time?"

Ryker grinned. "Of course there was trouble, but little Jacob came along and together we fought them off. We got about ten barrels filled and carted to the gardens around the temple."

Tyler nodded in appreciation. "I wasn't as successful as you. I've been out in the woods for several days now and it appears most of the wildlife is staying far away from this wretched city."

"About that," Maya broke in. "What do you guys think about salvaging meat from the dead thorny devils and dranks? We need to get rid of them to make our streets safe again, so why not use them for food?"

Misu rubbed his chin. "It's not a bad idea. Not the dead ones, of course. We'll have to kill some for fresh meat. A lot of work, but I think it can be done."

"Good. When you've rested, the two of you can take our newcomer on his first mission to collect meat."

"Newcomer! What? Who? Where?" Ryker craned his neck, but of course he didn't see who she was talking about.

Misu answered, "Yes. He said he arrived here not knowing of the defeat. I showed him a place where he can settle in. I placed him in the room next to yours, Tyler."

"How did you hear about him, Maya? I didn't know anyone besides myself knew he was here."

"I ran into one of the boys on my way here and he told me he saw a Montane in the gardens."

Tyler spit out the water he'd just sipped from his water-skin. "A Montane? Are you sure?"

"I'm afraid she's right. Which is why I don't trust him and put him next door for you to monitor."

"There goes my sleep for who knows how long," Tyler complained.

"I will help you keep watch on him," Ryker chimed in.

"Yes, I trust you to work it out. Now, back to the issue at hand, in addition to the dranks and thorny devils, I traded for ten sheep along with some vegetables and wheat, but it won't last us long at all and our stash of perfumes are dwindling. Oh, and I'm afraid that five of those sheep scattered on my way back. Maybe you can round them up?"

Maya felt Blackthorn enter her mind. "What is it, Blackthorn?" she thought.

"If you plant the seeds of the vegetables, I can help get a garden growing and you should save a male and a female sheep for breeding."

"Yes, of course." Maya thought back. Then she focused on Misu, hoping he hadn't noticed her sudden silence as anything more than thinking about their conversation. "One last thing before I go to meet this fellow, what did you say his name was?"

"Skah."

"Before I meet Skah, I want you to go talk with the cooks to collect all the seeds from the vegetables that we can and set aside a male and a female sheep so we can start breeding them."

"Good idea. I'm on it."

Maya nodded. Her efforts hadn't been completely useless. "Ryker, Tyler, come with me and we shall see who has so graciously decided to stay here with us in this desolate place."

IT DIDN'T TAKE LONG to find the Montane. He was in the garden where he'd originally been found.

"Hello!" Maya called to him.

Skah stood up so fast, she was sure he felt guilty about poking around. "Ah, you must be the beautiful Maya, whom I've heard so much about."

She smiled. "I am Maya, and this is Tyler and Ryker. I believe your room is next to Tyler's and I thought you'd like to meet."

"Pleased to smell you all." The light-skinned man extended his hand.

At least he knew something of their custom of smelling hands upon meeting.

"We've also got a job for you if you're willing."

"I told Misu I would love to stay for a little while and help you get back on your feet. What exactly did you have in mind?"

"A little hunting expedition. It'll be dangerous but between the three of you, I'm sure you can kill a thorny devil or two."

"Thorny devil? Are you crazy? Why not deer or something more pleasant smelling?"

Tyler spoke this time. "Because those are scarce and hard to find, but thorny devils roam our streets unchecked."

Skah nodded. "Have you killed thorny devils before?"

"Only in self-defense. I am curious what they might taste like." Ryker trailed off.

Maya watched for the Montane's reactions. Had she seen him before? She didn't know. All the light-skinned men looked the same to her. He was obviously different from Ashkii and Tse but that was because she knew them. This man was in his thirties, she guessed, a warrior, like most of the Montane men. She noticed an odor bomb poking out of his bag. Ashkii had used those to put the devils to sleep.

Skah continued to ask questions of Ryker and Tyler about their experiences since the fall of Ithol. He seemed genuinely concerned for their well-being. Perhaps he was from a different tribe than Ashkii and didn't have the same duplicitous motives as the Tafkans.

Maya interrupted, "You're a Montane? Where exactly did you say you were from?"

"I didn't. But yes, a Montane from the Imka people."

"Oh. Do you know Chief Golar? I had the pleasure of meeting him not too long ago."

25

"Chief Golar, you say? Yes, the chiefs of all the tribes get together at least once a year to renew treaties and contracts. We don't particularly like Chief Golar, but he is a decent fellow."

"I see. And what brought you to Ithol? It's not too often that Montane folk come to the city."

Skah shrugged. "I don't know. I guess, I was curious. When I saw what had happened here, I wondered if there were any survivors and how they were going to continue to live here. So, I came to smell the scents."

Maya forced a smile, everything about this man screamed lies. "Thank you for your concern but more so for your help. We can use all the help we can muster."

"At your service, my Lady."

Chapter 3

Agonya woke with a gut feeling that she wasn't alone in her tent. And they had given her a tent of her own because of her powers. They hadn't wanted to risk giving her any opportunities to use it. She breathed in the surrounding scents: cardamom, olive leaf, rose oil, and cacao. That was someone's aroma. She just didn't know who. She could hear whoever was searching in her bag.

There were two options: let whoever it was search and hope they went away or confront the intruder. If she let them search, then they would know the Kindroot wasn't here, if that was what they were looking for. But confronting them didn't sound like a good idea either. If it was the assassin, she was no match to fight. As she debated what to do, she heard the intruder set the bag down and move toward her. Confront them, it was.

Agonya yawned and stretched her hand over her head before sitting up.

"Good. Now you're awake, you can tell me where it is." It was a man's voice. She knew it from somewhere.

Agonya scrambled up against the wall of the tent, pretending to be startled.

"Who are you? And what are you doing in my tent?" she stammered.

"We've met before, and I already told you why I'm here. We can do this the easy or the hard way. Your choice."

"I don't understand. What exactly are you looking for?" Agonya composed herself and stood up, but the intruder was too fast. He pinned her against the tent and started patting her all over.

"Get off me!" Agonya glowed as she reflexively tapped her magic, sending a shock into his hands.

The man yelped and let go. "Nice trick. I like a good challenge." He pulled out a dagger from his cloak and approached again. "You know exactly what I'm looking for. I want answers, and you're going to give them to me."

The more he spoke, the more she remembered. This man was the Kor she'd bested in the streets outside of the palace. She barged into his mind and saw his intentions, but he was prepared for her this time and began changing his plans so fast she couldn't form one of her own. She had to think. If he wasn't the assassin, then that meant they had discovered her trick, and she was in more danger than she'd known. What was stopping him from killing her if she didn't cooperate?

Raising her hands as if to surrender, Agonya cried out, "Stop! I'll tell you what you want to know."

But he didn't stop until the dagger was against her neck.

"I've no doubt you will tell me what I want to know. Now, speak!" he hissed in her ear.

"I don't have him," she said, trying to formulate her thoughts. "I gave him to Captain Dahel. If your commander doesn't have him, then you should check with him. Maybe he kept the Kindroot for himself, but I swear I gave up the Kindroot when I surrendered."

"If that were the case," the Kor said, pushing his dagger against her neck, "then why didn't you say so when I first asked?"

Agonya felt her skin break beneath the weapon. He'd called her bluff. What now?

"You know what I think?" he continued. "I think, little miss princess is hiding the Kindroot and knows exactly where it is. I'm curious what you would do if my dagger slipped. Hmm... Do you think the Kindroot would rescue you?"

Agonya breathed in all the scents nearby. The man had an orange in his pocket. She used its scent to put up a shield around her body. The man's eyes widened, and he backed off.

"You are one talented princess."

"I don't know what you mean." Agonya watched him slide his dagger back into its sheath.

He raised his eyebrows. "Oh, but you must. You got inside my mind the first time we met, and you did the same a few moments ago. Now you have a shield protecting you from my daggers. I wonder if you can heal too."

"I thought you were only interested in finding the Kindroot," Agonya stammered, confused by the change in topic.

"Of course I am interested in the Kindroot. But I already know he isn't here."

Agonya gasped. How could he know that?

"See," he grinned, "That's one thing you can't do. You are a terrible liar. Figure out how to heal, if you don't already know."

"Why?"

"Because you broke your promise." His oily voice frightened Agonya. "And since the Kindroot isn't here, I think it's time for me to pay Dahel a visit."

The man left. Agonya was alone with her racing thoughts. The first thing she did was reach out to Blackthorn's mind. She had to warn him.

THIS TIME, WHEN AGONYA woke up, she knew she wasn't alone. Light from the sun was coming through the opened flap. Lord Commander Bannon stood inside, staring at her. It was quite unnerving. A moment later, the man from the previous night came in.

Agonya tried not to cringe away from them. She had to retain her composure. She couldn't show any weakness.

Finally, Bannon knelt in front of her. "I am rather disappointed that you didn't hand over the Kindroot." He tucked a stray hair behind her ear. "Lucky for you, it's not my job to decide your punishment. Which means you get to live... for now. You better pray Aekan will retrieve the Kindroot without any problems. Your life may depend on it. Is there anything that might help him in his search of Ithol? Because he is returning, and he will find the Kindroot."

The beating of her heart sped up at the thought of Aekan capturing Blackthorn. But he was beyond her reach now. She had to trust that her warning was enough, and that Maya was looking after him. "What can I tell you that you don't already know?" she asked.

"Why waste our time with her, Lord? She's just going to talk in circles," Aekan said.

"You don't have to be here," Bannon snapped.

Aekan raised his hands in defense.

Bannon shook his head. "You're right. I requested your presence for her questioning, but now I suggest you go to Ithol. The sooner the better."

Agonya watched the man, Aekan, pull the hood of his cloak over his head and depart. Her body started to relax until Bannon spoke.

"Now, I know you don't want to talk about the Kindroot. The way I see it, you owe us."

Agonya resisted the urge to grab her mother's necklace hanging around her neck. As comforting as it was, she didn't want to draw attention to it lest they take it from her.

Bannon continued. "That's why you're going to heal our wounded. Consider all the things I could do to you before saying, 'I can't.'"

Agonya didn't hesitate. "I can and I will heal them, but I will need access to your perfumes. I can't heal whenever I want."

"How did you form the shield last night?"

"An orange was in that man's pocket."

Bannon stood and turned to the guard standing at the entrance to the tent. "Quick, go catch Aekan. Find out if what she said is true."

The guard took off running.

"If you are being truthful with me, I will provide whichever scents you require."

"Thank—"

Bannon cut her off. "Don't get any ideas. The moment you use scents for other purposes, you will be caged like I caged your fake Kindroot. And rest assured, you won't have any oranges to protect you next time."

A gasp escaped Agonya. How could she have been so careless, giving him that information? And what was this about caging her? He couldn't possibly have that much glass, could he?

"Great. Now that we have an agreement, let's begin."

THE TENTS HELD SO MANY wounded. Agonya's heart ached looking at all the tents filled with people suffering. There were tents for soldiers, officers, and for the prisoners who took ill since leaving Ithol.

Everyone turned toward Agonya and Bannon when they walked into the first tent. Agonya ignored them and walked up to a stretcher. Bannon followed her. He had confirmed that Aekan had had an orange in his cloak. He also discovered that the ripe orange had decayed to a shriveled-up piece of rind.

Bannon addressed a servant nearby. "Get her whatever she asks for, except oranges. She's here to help."

"Yes, sir." The servant nodded and waited for Agonya to speak.

"I'll start with some fresh water and cloth, then I'll need pine bark and orinberries. Do you have a fire for heating water nearby?"

"Yes, ma'am. I'll bring you water right away."

Agonya looked at the man before her. The wound was hard to decipher. Dried blood covered his right leg, which was swollen to twice its size. As soon as the servant returned with water and a cloth, she set to work cleaning it. Then, she moved on to others, cleaning all their outward injuries.

"There. Now, where are my perfumes?" Agonya glanced up and threw the cloth in the bucket.

"Here," a servant proffered a saddlebag, "they brought it in a little while ago."

Agonya pushed stray hair behind her ear and riffled through the bag. "I'll need the fire now."

"Over here." Another guard said, motioning outside of the tent. Agonya stood and followed the guard out of the tent. A fire burned not about twenty paces away. Agonya rushed over and threw some pine bark on the fire and grabbed a pan of water, which she added some orinberries to. She had to figure out how to sneak some perfumes and supplies from the stash they'd given her. It was her only hope to escape. Aekan may have left for Ithol, but the Montane assassin was still coming for her. She had to be prepared.

Agonya watched the water heat up. She had to focus on her reservoir of magic, on the scent of the pine bark burning. She could even smell the berries releasing their fragrance in the water.

"Quick, bring the man with the worst wound here next to me! The water is almost boiling now."

She heard the guard giving orders, but she closed her eyes and breathed in the mixture of scents.

Soon, a man on a stretcher lay next to her. She could smell him. His wound went deep. He must have been important if they didn't leave him behind. He had a huge abdominal injury. Agonya unwrapped the bandages and placed her hands on the wound. Then she willed it to heal. Not too fast. She made sure the magical scent spread from the outer layer of skin down past the skin into the stomach organs. From there, she knitted each layer back together wherever it was ripped. "Thank you, Blackthorn, for giving me anatomy lessons," she thought.

She motioned for someone to stir the water while she worked.

"Amazing! How is she doing that?" Soon everyone was stopping to watch. It probably appeared to them that she sat, hands on the wounded, wafting vapor and scents towards herself.

Agonya requested the next patient to be brought out before finishing the first. As soon as the major damage was repaired, she stopped working on him. He would have to let his body do some natural healing. But now he would be on his feet much faster than he would have been.

Someone took the healed man into the tent, and Agonya started on the second. This time, it was harder. The magic didn't want to cooperate. It liked the fragrances but resisted her attempt to manipulate it. What had changed? She did her best, focusing on getting the patient stable, the infection gone, so that his body could heal on its own.

After the second patient, Agonya rested. It demanded greater strength than she expected.

After her brief rest, she started work on the third patient, then the fourth, then rested again. Agonya worked tirelessly all day long as long as they continued to bring patients to her. People stopped to watch in awe before they had to move on with their own appointed tasks.

At one point, she was aware of Lord Commander Bannon coming and talking with the guards.

"We'll stay here a few more days. Until she has healed all our wounded. The whole caravan will move much quicker."

Agonya smiled to herself. Staying in place for a few more days meant she wasn't further from Ithol, which meant she was closer to escape. She resumed healing the next patient, tuning out their conversation. The faulty magic baffled Agonya. Some were easy to heal, and others were near impossible. There was no pattern, no way to know which patient the magic would respond to.

A guard tapped her on the shoulder. Agonya lifted her hands from the soldier she was in the middle of healing. "Yes?"

"It's time to take a break and eat."

Agonya protested.

"You need your strength. Especially since you will be helping with our wounded for the next few days before hitting the road again."

He was right. Already, she was feeling like her energy stores were draining. She also noticed she was running low on berries and pine bark. She'd have to get creative with her other supplies.

"Lead the way. But first, help this man back inside to rest." Agonya waved at the battle-wounded man.

THE ATMOSPHERE WAS contagious. The soldiers glowed with appreciation and happiness. Even though they were her enemy, Agonya was glad to help. Soldiers and prisoners alike felt drawn to the place where the miracles were happening. So much so that other work of prepping food and water and gathering supplies from the town nearby was being neglected. For that, Agonya was grateful. It meant staying put for longer.

"Hey you!" Bannon barked at a soldier loitering nearby.

The young man nearly jumped out of his skin when he saw the lord commander talking to him. "Yes, sir?" the man replied.

"Get back to work! What good are you doing watching her?"

"Sorry, sir. It won't happen again, sir!"

"This includes the rest of you as well." Bannon glared at everyone nearby.

Agonya tried to ignore the exchange. Instead, she focused on the healing scents rising from the fire and pot.

Bannon approached her when she removed her hands from the patient next to her. "In all frankness, Princess, I'm impressed with the work you've done."

"Well, that's a start," she said, rubbing her forehead. He was softening towards her.

"How did you learn to do this?"

Agonya stood up and looked him in the eye. "I learned to do this because of your people who attacked me. In my moment of distress, I discovered the power I didn't know I had, and it paralyzed me, forcing me to learn to heal. For that I am grateful, even if it was a painful journey."

Bannon looked taken aback by her answer. "You're different from him, your father. I'm sure the king will take your healing of our soldiers into consideration when he makes his judgment on you," he conceded.

He had a backward way of complimenting her. In one breath, he both praised her and condemned her. "Is there anything else, sir?" Agonya asked.

"No, keep up the good work." Bannon pulled out the fake Kindroot and put it on a stone next to her. Then he walked away.

Agonya turned back to her task. The plant was a reminder that she was a prisoner of war and only extending her life by a few days. Her life may be forfeited, but the lives of these people were not. The third day of healing was wearing on Agonya. She wasn't sleeping well, and the more she used her magic, the harder it got. Not to mention her supplies were almost gone. Her people needed her. Day after day they had to march toward Korina with heavy loads on their backs. This was a wonderful respite for them, but many more tireless days lay ahead of them. If she could help those who needed extra strength, she would feel better about the whole thing.

Glancing around, Agonya noticed that for once, no one was watching her. As quick as she could, she snatched some perfumes from the bag and stuffed them into her pockets. No one stopped to ask what she was doing. She started to take more when she saw the fake Kindroot staring at her. No. It was just a tree. It couldn't stare at her. But she felt a connection to it, so she lifted it off the stone and put it in her pocket, like she used to do with Blackthorn.

Then, Agonya breathed in the smoke and vapor rising from the fire. The vanilla smell from the pine bark and the smell of the berries mingled together, filling her up. She willed it to blend with her magic and reached out to the young boy with the arrow wound in his eye. The damage was extensive. If Agonya couldn't fix this, his eye would remain damaged forever. Thankfully, though, the arrow hadn't pierced through to his brain.

Agonya sent the magic to surround his eye and eye-socket. Slowly, they knitted back together. If only her enemies smelled the fragrances she smelled, it would be so much easier to resolve all their problems. But her enemies were many, and they didn't see things eye to eye. Agonya was sure Dana's goals differed from the Kors' working for her. Which made it harder to know what Dana's blindness was.

Agonya's chest constricted, and she gasped for air. She couldn't breathe! Smoke filled her lungs. Agonya doubled over, gasping for air. It wasn't enough. Was she going to die? Darkness blocked her vision. She felt arms around her, lifting her up. Heard voices yelling. What was happening?

Her head lay on a pillow. The pain. Could she breathe again? Agonya tried to suck in the air. It came this time. She felt it enter her lungs. The pain subsided.

"Agonya? Your Highness!" Huren's voice echoed in her mind over and over.

She willed the magic to reach her eyes. The room became lighter and lighter. She could see the shape of someone's head hovering above hers. There were others standing close by.

"Hur," Agonya coughed, "en?"

"I was passing by. What happened? No, don't talk. Just rest."

Agonya closed her eyes. So, this was what it was like not to see things clearly. Did she steal magic from someone? Is that why she lost her sight? Agonya couldn't make sense of it. Then she was asleep.

A SHARP PAIN WOKE AGONYA from her sleep. Something was inside her chest! A knife? Agonya clung to her magic and pushed it through the knife into the hand and then the body of the person holding it. The magic turned into light once it was outside her body. A glow emanated from the knife, lighting up the man's face. Agonya stared at him. His blue eyes were...

frightened? Was he afraid of her? Then she noticed who it was. A Montane. And not just any Montane. That wavy blond hair. Could it be? NO! The thread of her magic dissipated. It couldn't be true!

The Montane pulled his knife out and turned to leave, but not before Agonya whispered, "Ashkii? How could you?"

He gasped when he heard the name, and then he fled.

"Help!" Agonya cried out.

The tears flowed like a waterfall. Her heart wrenched inside of her and not because the blade had almost reached her heart, which surely would have killed her, but because of Ashkii's betrayal. Why did it have to be Ashkii? No, it couldn't be him. She thought he loved her. Then she recalled Blackthorn's words. Someone related to Ashkii. But could anyone look so exactly alike and not be him?

"Agonya! You're bleeding!"

"Assassin," Agonya managed to say between breaths.

A guard called for someone to tell Bannon. Then he pressed his hands against her wound. The pressure hurt. She wanted the pain to go away.

Ashkii. He was supposed to be far, far away. He wouldn't hurt her, but he had. Surely it wasn't him. But he never mentioned a brother. He hadn't wanted to acknowledge that he knew her father's assassin, either.

"Quick! Put everyone on alert. There's an assassin in the camp."

It didn't take long for Bannon to arrive. "What's all this about an assassin?" he barked.

"I don't think it hit her heart. She's bleeding, but not a ton."

"Is it fatal?"

"If the bleeding doesn't stop, yes, sir. She isn't healing herself."

"Why aren't you healing?"

"Can't. Don't have... enough strength," she said.

"How did an assassin get past you, anyway?"

"Sir, he had our uniform."

"Did you let him into her tent?"

"I—I thought he was one of us," the guard stammered.

"You can tell us exactly who it was."

"I'm sorry, sir. I didn't see his face. When I heard her cry for help, I came as fast as I could. The man had vanished. And she was bleeding."

Agonya tuned out their arguing. The guard was in trouble, but she had to focus on healing. But all she could think about was the Montane.

She felt the guard put more pressure on her wound, trying to make the bleeding stop.

Agonya tried to breathe in the fragrances around her, tried to heal herself. Would things have been different if she had married Ashkii?

Chapter 4

Ashkii ran as fast as he could. They were closing in behind him. Any minute that they would catch him if he didn't go faster. He quickly glanced in both directions. All he saw were trees. The village lay behind him now. He could make it to the elephantus pasture. An elephantus could run faster than a horse if it was motivated.

Ashkii broke through the trees into the meadow. An elephantus stood grazing in the field, its long nose scooping up grass and lifting it up to its mouth. Ashkii ran up to it and jumped. He jumped up a good eight feet, grabbed the long fur coat and pulled himself on top. He continued rolling and hit a wall.

Ashkii rubbed his eyes. It was a dream. He sighed. Freedom had been within reach.

"Smells!" Ashkii muttered. His father was infuriating! First, he detained Ashkii, preventing him from warning Agonya about his ambush. Well, actually his father, Chief Golar, had betrayed Agonya first and then prevented Ashkii from helping her escape. His own father tied him up and made him watch the Kors lead her into exile. Golar also made sure the assassin who killed Agonya's father went with her into exile. Was she even still alive? Their assassin never failed, even if he didn't act as fast as Golar would have liked.

"Oh, Agonya! I'm so sorry!" Ashkii ran his fingers through his hair and sat up in his small prison of a room. Even though someone stood guard, making certain Ashkii didn't slip away in the middle of the night, at least his father let him have his own room. He had tried to escape his first night back in Tafka. Yeah. That went well.

Ashkii shook his head. He needed fresh air. Jumping up, he climbed up the rope ladder and pushed open the door in the roof. The moon was low in the sky. The sun would rise soon. Ashkii climbed onto the roof, gave a nod toward his guard, though he couldn't see him, and laid down again. The stars were so brilliant. Not a cloud in the sky. If only he could be like them. Agonya was. She shone so brightly. Whenever she was in a room, she lit it up with her compassion, kindness, and beauty.

Light began to hide the stars as the sun peeked over the horizon. Ashkii sighed and sat up. The start of another day of torture. Every day he had to work the latrine or animal clean up. He was never let out of sight. Sure, he had disobeyed his father, but his father was wrong. Helping the princess was the right thing to do. Yes, he loved her. But it was more than that. His father was wrong about Dana. Would he listen? No. Chief Golar would not listen to his impertinent son.

"Ashkii! Time to work." Niyol hopped from one roof to the other until he joined Ashkii on his own.

"And what does my father have in store for me today? More latrine duty?"

"Uh," Niyol cleared his throat. "Actually, today I convinced him to let you chop firewood with me." Niyol grinned. "I mean, I totally get it if you prefer the latrine to chopping wood…"

Ashkii laughed. "Thanks! I can't believe you convinced him to let me help you! You're amazing!"

Niyol slapped Ashkii on the back. "You smell good too."

Ashkii followed Niyol from roof to roof until they were at the edge of the village. Then they dropped to the ground and strode into the woods, passing several people working on various tasks. They didn't go far, Ashkii could only assume because his father didn't want him getting any ideas, ideas like running away to rescue Agonya.

"Hey now, I know that look," Niyol reproached. "You know it's not going to happen."

"What's not going to happen?"

"You want to leave us again and go off on your adventures. You know it's not bad here if you give it a chance."

"Not bad? Ha! Where have you been? My father hates me. The entire village has turned against me, their next chief! Look at me! I'm a prisoner. And for what?" Ashkii grasped the ax handle and swung at the log. "I did what father asked of me until he went too far. Dana is not the one we should be helping."

"Do you really love her? I thought that was just a ruse to gain her trust." Niyol swung his ax at a different log. "Wow! You have fallen for her! Ashkii, get her out of your head! If we don't help Dana, she'll decimate us."

"No, Niyol, you're wrong. Agonya will defeat Dana, and then what? You think she'll forgive us? We promised her we would help her in her time of need, and we turned on her. We're traitors." Ashkii hit the log so hard with the ax it splintered into pieces.

Niyol thumped his ax again. "Agonya defeat Dana? Don't you know Agonya is dead by now? Kilchii never fails. He will retrieve the Kindroot and Dana will reward us."

Ashkii couldn't believe this! "You don't get it! Even if Kilchii succeeds," Ashkii shuddered at the thought, "even if he succeeds and we give Dana the Kindroot, she will not reward us the way you think she says she will. Dana is only looking out for herself. The moment she wants something else from us and we can't deliver, all that work we did to get the Kindroot will be forgotten." Thud. Ashkii yanked the ax back out of the wood.

"Come on, Ashkii." Thud. Yank. Thud. "I'm trying to help you here! You have to prove you're not going rogue on us before your father will take you back in as his son."

"What does that mean?"

"It means you won't be chief after him if you don't shape up. Kilchii will be chief. Are you willing to risk that for a girl? She's an Itholean, for smell's sake!"

Ashkii dropped his ax, barely missing his foot. "She is not just a girl. She's different. Not like her father at all or those other haughty Itholeans. Why can't you see that? She was here with us. You saw how kind, caring, and thoughtful she was. How wise she was as a ruler."

"Nah, I saw a pampered princess who couldn't walk because she was dumb enough to exceed her magical limits by stealing someone else's magic. I saw an idiot of a ruler who blindly trusted her enemy to do what she said when she was at her strongest because of her newfound power."

Wham! Ashkii's fist flew into Niyol's face. How dare he talk about Agonya that way! Ashkii hit him again. And again, before he felt several hands restraining him. But all he could think was how his best friend was no longer the man he thought he knew. This must be how Agonya felt when she discovered Ashkii had betrayed her. Ashkii couldn't stop it. His body started to convulse. He didn't deserve Agonya. Why had she given him a second chance? There was no way she would give him a third. Not after this.

ASHKII FORCED HIMSELF to sleep. If he didn't, he would go mad, trapped in this room. As he drifted off, he dreamed of another time.

He stood in the center of the village, ready for the other kids to finish their meal so they could go play. Kilchii stood up and sauntered over. "Hey brother, are you ready for me to beat you?"

"No way! I'm faster than you. You're the one that's going to lose," Ashkii retorted.

"Uh uh!" Tse came over. Niyol was right behind. Soon they were all running in the forest, chasing each other.

A drank came out of nowhere. The kids screamed and fled in every direction...

Ashkii, older now, was fighting with Kilchii. "I didn't decide to be born first! Why do you always treat me like I shouldn't be chief?"

"You're a brat, Ash. You don't deserve to be chief. I don't see why I can't be. We're twins, you know, so what does it matter that you were born first?" Kilchii threw the words in Ashkii's face...

Then, Ashkii was watching his brother ride towards Ithol on his mission. Who knew when he'd be back. Ashkii was going to miss him. Turning to see if anyone was watching him, he ran off and found his favorite elephantus and followed his brother.

It was by mistake really that he ran into the king...

Ashkii raced to Korina. If only he could save the princess before Kilchii killed her. He was the only one who could stop Kilchii. It was either Kilchii killing Agonya or Kilchii being killed in the attempt.

Ashkii snuck through the camp. There was no sign of the princess. She must be in the palace. He found her room, climbed into her room through the window. Kilchii was already there. The knife plunged into her chest!

"No!!!" Ashkii tackled his brother to the floor. "No!"

Ashkii left his brother laying stunned on the floor. He went to Agonya's side and wept. It couldn't be true. But there was no breath.

"Ashkii!" a whisper.

"Ashkii!" it said again.

Ashkii bolted out of bed, ready to fight whoever was there.

"Mother? What are you doing here?"

"You're crying."

Ashkii wiped his face. "Just a stupid dream."

Mazali stood up and opened her bag. "I've brought you the supplies you'll need."

"Supplies? For what?" Why was his mother here? She favored Kilchii from the first day they were born.

"For your escape, dear."

"But Father," Ashkii couldn't finish his thought.

"Yes, your father will skin me alive if he found out I was helping you. That's why I can't stay. Here. Take this bag. Go to the elephantus pasture five minutes after I leave. Your favorite will be waiting for you. Be quick. The guards will report your absence soon after you leave."

She jumped out of the room and disappeared. This was his chance. He didn't understand why his mother was on his side now. But she was. The minutes passed. Ashkii jumped out of the room. He didn't see anyone nearby. He dashed towards the forest. Once inside the safety of the trees, he ran like he'd never run before. Faster than he had in his dream. He couldn't be late. Ashkii knew this section of the forest like his own scent. He leaped over rock and limbs and entered the meadow in no time. True to her word, Chestnut was standing near the edge, loaded with traveling supplies. Ashkii jumped on his back, secured the bag she gave him and galloped northeast. It wasn't a dream. He was actually flying through the forest on Chestnut's back, away from his father. "I'm coming, Agonya. Don't die!"

LIFE IN ITHOL WAS BECOMING routine for Jaylen. He was just finishing giving orders to his captains for the day when Aekan arrived.

"General," Aekan said as he sauntered into the great hall.

"Aekan, what brings you back to Ithol? I thought you were eager to return home."

"I would have been more eager if I had witnessed the surrender, which I hear you did a fine job."

Something wasn't right. Jaylen couldn't figure out the reason for his discomfort. "I'm not following."

Aekan wrapped his arm around Jaylen's shoulder. "I know you didn't know. But now that I'm here, we can help each other fix the problem. You see, our little princess lied to us."

It took a moment for Aekan's words to sink in. Oh. She hadn't delivered up the Kindroot. "I see. You believe the Kindroot remains in Ithol?"

"Ah, good, you don't need me to spell it out for you." Aekan clapped his hands together. "We should search the palace. He must have been close to her during that last battle, lending her strength."

"I've already explored the palace grounds and have an idea of where to begin. There was movement near this one room full of plants. I didn't see anyone there, so I dismissed it. I wasn't looking for a Kindroot." Jaylen motioned for Aekan to follow him out of the great hall.

"That smells promising."

The two walked through the arched doorway, discussing the implications of her lie. For some unknown reason, Agonya's deception didn't bother Jaylen as much as it should have. He had hoped he could put this conflict behind him. At least they weren't blaming him for the mistake or stripping him of his promotion. Now he'd have the authority and access to the correct knowledge to get it done properly this time; even if he had to work with Aekan, a man he knew to be evasive and devious.

"Here we are," Jaylen said. "I was in this corridor when I thought I saw something move. There's the room I was telling you about." Jaylen entered the sunroom and grabbed the pole leaning against the wall. He walked to the center of the room, where he hooked the pole to the window on the roof and pushed it open. Light flooded the room, illuminating the potted plants.

Aekan bent over and smelled a succulent. "How are these plants not dying?"

"What do you mean?"

"I mean, all the plants I saw on my way here are dying. Their scents are fading, and the plants are actually dying, not just hibernating. But these... these are thriving." Aekan gestured at the fully blooming peonies across the room.

Jaylen walked from plant to plant, examining each one. Aekan was right. He hadn't given it a second thought before now. Agonya had been careful not to let Jaylen glimpse the package. Even when he had the advantage, the whole thing about Kindroots being magical and all prevented him from touching it, from seeing it. The absence of pain or resistance should have alerted him to the fake. The evidence in this room was overwhelming. The Kindroot had been here.

"This is how we find him," Jaylen said. "We look for healthy plants in the city. We can follow his flight from the palace."

"I like your thinking, Jaylen." Aekan grinned. "How many troops do we have at our disposal?"

BANNON WATCHED HER pass out. If she died now, he wouldn't have to execute her later, but on the other hand, if she died now, then she wouldn't finish healing his wounded and sick. But more importantly, she knew things about Kindroots and one in particular. Bannon made a snap decision.

"Lapu, get as much pine bark and berries as you can find. And the perfumes she was using in the healing tent. Quick!"

The soldier took off at a run. Maybe she could heal herself even in her sleep. Bannon paced the tent while he waited. It made no sense. How had the assassin escaped? He reached the end of the tent and turned. Then he saw a slit in the fabric of the tent.

Bannon pushed the two sides apart and peered out. All he saw were more tents. Bannon knew what his camp looked like. What had he expected to see? Straightening up, Bannon found Lapu returning.

"This is all I found, sir."

"It will have to do." Bannon took the bag from his soldier and knelt next to the former queen. He didn't have a clue how it worked, but he brought out the pine bark and waved it under her nose. Her breathing became stronger.

"Here, hold this for her to breathe its scents." The guard, putting pressure on her wound, did his best to keep pressure on the wound as he removed one hand to take the bark.

Bannon reached inside the bag and pulled out a bottle of perfume. He dabbed it on her upper lip and then waved the opened bottle under her nose.

"Commander! It's working!"

Bannon looked at her wound and could see the blood slow down. He waved the perfume in front of her face again. It was simply amazing. As he watched, her skin began to knit itself back together. "Excellent! You can stop putting pressure on the wound now, soldier."

"Oh, right." He removed his bloody hand and looked for something to wipe it on.

"You may go wash. Give Lapu the bark. He may take your place holding it up. But then return as quickly as you can." Turning to Lapu, Bannon asked, "Why do you think he tried to kill her?"

"Pardon, sir?"

"I mean, why did the assassin want to kill her now? She already has a death sentence hanging over her. As soon as we return to Korina, and King Reid finds out she lied and that we don't have the Kindroot, she's as good as dead. Why would someone want to kill her now?"

"I hadn't thought about that, sir. She knows something the assassin doesn't want us to know."

That's plausible. But why would someone want to prevent her from healing people? He should befriend her. No. She would never divulge her secrets to him, the Lord Commander. However, there were individuals she trusted. It was time to have a little chat with her former councilors.

STINK! AGONYA COULD smell him coming before she heard the horse's hooves. He didn't really smell bad. He had saved her life. It was just that she didn't want to talk to him.

"Good morning, Your Highness." Commander Bannon sounded chipper.

"Good morning, Lord Commander. What brings you to my humble side today?" Why was he smiling like an idiot? "Did you find the assassin?" she asked.

"Sorry." A brief frown crossed his face. "That isn't why I'm here. There's someone here to see you."

The commander pointed at the men guarding Agonya. "Back up, give these two a chance to walk and talk with Her Highness."

Agonya started. Lord Commander Huren and Lord Tanish approached her side before she'd even processed what the commander had said. Wow! What game was he playing? Why was he allowing them to talk with one another now?

"Lord Commander! Lord Tanish! Your smells are pleasant today." Agonya managed her best smile.

"Your Majesty," they both said together.

"I suppose you heard about last night?" Agonya glanced around. Commander Bannon was already a good twenty paces away and getting further away every second. There were others around. There were always people. She was in a huge migration. But the guards were giving them space. "He's here," she whispered.

"Who's here, your Majesty?" Huren looked over his shoulder.

"The man who killed my father and Lord Besnek."

Lord Tanish gasped. "But how? Wouldn't he stand out in this crowd?"

"He's definitely Montane."

"And," Huren frowned, "he tried to kill you last night."

Agonya remembered the assassin's face, framed by the light of her magic. "But there's something I don't understand. The man I saw looked exactly like another man who couldn't have killed Besnek because he was with me during that incident."

"A twin perhaps?" Lord Tanish suggested.

"I didn't think the man I know had brothers, but maybe you're right. I hope you're right because the other possibility is that he has powers of speed or travel abilities. I don't want to consider the implications." Agonya shivered.

Huren nodded thoughtfully. "I have seen many unexplained things in the last month. I won't pretend to understand this magic that you yourself have, but what makes you think he could move from one place to the next in an instant?"

"I can't be sure." Agonya glanced around. Good. They weren't being listened to. "I had a dream," she whispered. "But it wasn't really a dream. I mean, it was a dream about the day my mother died. I was there in the garden, hiding when it happened. A bright light appeared, then suddenly a plant was floating in the air. No one was holding it. I showed it to Maya. She went with me to show my father and, well, the rest isn't important.

"A Kindroot," Tanish said in awe.

Of course, a priest would recognize a Kindroot even disguised in a story. "Tell us, Lord Tanish, do you think this power is something our assassin could possess?"

"The possibility is hard to believe. But your experience confirms the existence of such powers. What do we know about this assassin?"

"He is most certainly a Montane. You, Huren, were the one who informed me of the Montane assassin as the one who killed my father. He may have special powers. I know he can jump insanely high. The man I know can do that." Ashkii was with his father when she had left Ithol. No way was he here.

"My lady," Huren interrupted her thoughts, "I don't know if we will be able to do anything to help you. We are prisoners of war like yourself, but we will do our best to find whoever attacked you. But if he has the powers, you suggest he might have, I don't know how we will stop him from hurting you again."

Agonya rested her hands on her side where the knife had pierced her. It still hurt, even after Bannon let her use fragrances to heal it. Having her own scents would be nice, instead of relying on the Kors. "You might not have to," she said. "If I have enough perfumes, I might be able to protect myself. Do you know anyone who smuggled supplies out of the city?"

"I will ask around," Huren said.

"There's no need to ask, I do know, Your Highness," said Lord Tanish with a sly smile on his face.

"You do? Oh, that's wonderful!"

"In fact, you're looking at him."

Agonya couldn't believe it! Lord Tanish was her savior. "Do you have perfumes now?" Surely that would be too much to ask.

"Indeed, I do." Tanish reached inside his cloak and pulled out a small bottle.

Agonya popped the cork. A most welcoming aroma lifted out. "Mm-mm. This smells wonderful! Let me guess: pine, lemongrass, and sandalwood?"

"Impressive! But the pine is vanilla. I mixed those up all the time." Tanish's whole countenance exuded excitement.

Agonya didn't know he was such an enthusiast about perfumes. "Thank you, Lord Tanish."

She closed her eyes and worked the magic. The perfume released its layers in waves. Agonya drew it into herself and reached out for her wound. Nothing. She should have known these scents weren't for healing. But wait. Something else was happening. Someone was intruding into her thoughts.

"Blackthorn?"

"Agonya?" came the reply in her mind.

"A friend gave me some perfume with—"

"With sandalwood, right?"

"Yes! How did you know? Sandalwood, vanilla and lemongrass."

"Sandalwood is an enhancer for mind communications and since that's how we're talking," Blackthorn hesitated.

"That makes sense. How are you and Maya? Did you get my warning?" Agonya had so many questions. It was hard to know which ones to choose.

"Warning? What warning?"

"Oh no! I tried to warn you days ago. Aekan, that oily Korin spy, is going back to Ithol for you."

"That makes two people hunting me."

"What? Who else?"

"A Montane came to the city. I warned Maya about him, but she has still allowed him to stay. He's helping rebuild Ithol, but he really wants me."

"That sounds like Maya. A Montane paid me a visit too. You were right, he is related to Ashkii if it isn't Ashkii himself. He looked exactly like him!" A tear escaped and rolled down her cheek. She wiped it away and corked the perfume bottle. She still had the scents captured and was doling it out in small doses.

"Are you all right? I mean, he wasn't able to kill you since we're talking now."

"Yes, but he tried his best to kill me. He stuck a knife in my chest. If it had been just a little higher, it would have missed my ribs and hit my heart."

Blackthorn's emotions spiked inside her mind. No words were needed for her to sense his shock.

"I know. I don't understand. When Lord Tanish gave me this bottle, I hoped it would help heal the wound, since my supplies are monitored, but I'm glad you're here with me. I feel so alone all the time. I hardly ever have the chance to speak with my counselors. Speaking of, I need to continue this conversation with you another time. I'm afraid I don't have much longer to talk with Huren and Tanish. Goodbye, Blackthorn! Send Maya my love!" And with that Agonya shut it down and opened her eyes.

"You look happier," Lord Tanish grinned.

"Yes, thank you for that. May I keep this?"

"Of course, your Majesty!"

Agonya glanced around at the soldiers. They were still giving them plenty of space. "Huren? And you too, Tanish, are you being treated well? I saw them beating you the other day."

"Don't worry about me, your Majesty. I'll be fine. Shortly after that, they started to be nicer to me. I don't know what changed exactly."

"They haven't beaten me yet, but I have noticed a change. The food rations are more consistent now, though sometimes spotty."

"Do you know of any prisoners becoming sick or dying?" Agonya feared for her people and the heavy burden the Kors made them carry.

"A few have died, but not as many as you might expect due to the fact that the Kors didn't force the weak to come on the journey." Huren cleared his throat, "It looks like we're out of time, your Highness. I'm glad to see you alive. Please, if you have information about the assassin, that's my biggest concern."

Agonya couldn't see what Huren saw, but guessed Bannon was returning. His scent was getting stronger. "Huren, I'm not sure. I can't say anything in case I'm wrong. I hope to the Patron of Fortune that I am wrong."

Huren didn't reply because at that moment, Bannon dismounted and started motioning for the guards to return to their posts surrounding Agonya. He winked at her and led Huren and Tanish away without a word.

"ALL RIGHT, YOU'VE HAD time with your queen. Now, it's time for you to hold up your end of the bargain." Bannon continued to walk next to his horse so he could keep pace with the two prisoners. What did she tell you?

Huren spoke for both of them. "She says the assassin was a Montane."

"A Montane? What else?"

"She didn't tell me more than that, though I pressed her. She's concerned about how we are being treated. And she asked about supplies."

Huren was a hard man to read. He seemed willing enough to talk, but Bannon got the feeling he wasn't telling him everything. There were ways to make him talk.

The tall, graying man cleared his throat. "If I may, Lord Commander, she needs more than berries. Pine bark is also an excellent remedy, and frankincense goes a long way to relieving anxiety. Perhaps if she wasn't stressed, she might be willing to open up."

Bannon knew little about Lord Tanish, but he seemed like a wealth of knowledge. Maybe he should question him further. "Thank you. I'll look into it. We've passed pine trees along the way. It shouldn't be hard to acquire more bark. As for the frankincense, that'll be harder."

"In that case, letting her mingle with her subjects would also help alleviate her worries. Show her how they are being treated fairly. Yes, that's the best bet. I agreed to talk with you because you saved her when you could have let her die. But the moment you hurt her, the less helpful I'll be."

Bannon raised his brows. How dare he challenge the lord commander? "Is that a threat?"

His answer was quiet and delayed, but Bannon still heard him. "Yes."

Tanish didn't seem like a threat, apart from his words, but maybe it was a mistake to let him talk with her.

"You needn't worry. I want only the best for her, for all of you," Bannon lied.

The seasoned warrior remained quiet. Bannon wondered what he was like. How did the lord commander of the Itholeans fall to such an end as this?

"Well, if that's all she told you, I really am quite busy. Your company is over there, Huren, and yours is that way, Tanish."

The men went to join their small companies where the Korin soldiers would monitor their activities. Bannon mounted his horse and turned back towards Agonya. He'd give her more berries and head back to his command company, check in to see how everything was progressing.

Chapter 5

"Don't let him stay, Maya." Blackthorn intruded on her thoughts. "He's dangerous."

Maya shook her head and thought back at him, "Even if he has ill intentions, Blackthorn, we need him. Before Skah came, we were barely making it to the next day. But now we're able to rest and heal."

"I know you may think that it's better, but I'm warning you. If you don't send him on his way soon, he'll turn against us."

"All the more reason to keep him close. We can watch his every move and be prepared for whatever he decides to do. Whereas, if we let him go, he'll take us by surprise. We don't need two loose leaves floating around undetected."

Blackthorn wiggled from inside Maya's cloak pocket as she walked to the temple for her morning meal. "We need to travel to the other parks and gardens today."

Maya halted mid-stride. "I know he's after you, but you're with me now. He can't just steal you like he tried to do when you met him."

"Skah knows what I can do, and he'll find a way to capture me, anyway."

Maya started walking again. "Then you'll have to stay with me. He thinks you're still in the park. We'll make sure one of ours is always near the park, and we can keep track of who enters. We can start after our morning meal. We need to check how our garden is coming along."

Blackthorn sighed. "Very well, but then we must branch out to the other parks to muddle their searches for me."

When Maya arrived at the garden, the temple park was crowded with people strolling and lounging around, the complete opposite of the streets. The dark green contrasted with the high walls of the temple complex, and the aromas lifted everyone's spirit. The moment Maya stepped in; it was like she entered a new world.

She headed to the freshly planted vegetables. After a few days, the seeds had not only sprouted but were several inches above the ground.

"Blackthorn, look at them. You're amazing!" Maya beamed.

"Hmm. This brown fabric is exquisite." Blackthorn agreed.

Maya laughed. "You know what I meant," she thought back at him.

Several heads turned her way. But hadn't she replied in her mind? They continued to look at her. She pointed at the beautiful garden. They smiled and returned to their tasks.

Finally, they were going to provide for themselves. The only problem was the limited space. Another spot was necessary to grow more food.

"Isn't that what we're doing this afternoon when we help the plants in the other parks and gardens? We can take seeds to plant in them when we go," Blackthorn suggested.

"If we focused on Temple parks, maybe the connection between growing plants and worship could be linked to patrons and gods, not you."

"That could work," Blackthorn agreed. "Then we can create a path out of the city to miss lead the Kors and Skah."

Maya turned toward the kitchens, where she could retrieve more seeds to take with her on her expeditions, but Ryker strode into the park directly in front of her. They smelifed. Ryker lingered near her cheeks longer than was necessary. "Your scent is pleasing this morning," he whispered in her ear.

Maya tried not to blush, but she couldn't be sure she succeeded. "And yours as well."

"I was told I could find you here."

"And why are you looking for me?"

"Skah killed a thorny devil this morning."

"Excellent. Last night's stew was thin."

"There's Skah now," Ryker said, pointing behind her.

Maya whirled around. Skah entered from the opposite entrance, dragging something large and scaly behind him.

"Getting this beast here before being attacked by another creature was tricky." Skah dropped the thorny devil's tail on the ground and squatted next to it. He pulled out a dagger and was about to slice it down the middle.

"Stop!" she yelled. Color rushed from her face. "You can't clean it here. This is where we grow all our food. Ryker, assist Skah in removing that thing. There is a place for butchering animals, and this is not it."

"Sorry, my Lady. That was quite rude of me. Of course we'll go. But I thought we might talk while I worked."

"What did you want to talk about?" Maya itched to be on her way but did her best to be attentive.

"It's about, well, I wasn't sure if I could trust you or not." Skah wiped his forehead even though it looked dry. "I came here looking for someone."

"Oh, I'm sorry."

Skah furrowed his brow. "Sorry about what?"

This time Maya was taken aback. "Um, the person you're looking for isn't dead?"

"What? No! At least I'm pretty sure he's not dead. However, I understand the source of confusion. He's a plant." Skah looked at her and waited.

"A plant? I thought you said you were looking for someone." Inwardly, Maya cringed, and Blackthorn stiffened in her pocket.

"Yes, well, the individual resembles a plant. He really is one. I suspect he is hiding in your garden."

"Now, I'm really confused. You're not looking for a friend who was in the battle, but a plant in hiding. Why is he hiding? What makes you think he's here?" This was a dangerous conversation.

"He hurt our village, and we want justice."

"Justice? What harm can a plant do?"

"It's because of him that these creatures," Skah gestured to the thorny devil at his feet, "came down from the Acrid Mountains and are wreaking havoc on our towns. He is also responsible for the deaths here in this city. So far, I've helped you bury almost a hundred Itholeans. He is the one responsible for their deaths."

Maya tried to look thoughtful. Skah's practiced words were evident to her. And she knew what he wasn't saying. He wasn't saying that the reason Blackthorn was responsible was because he was still free from Dana's grasp. "How can a plant be responsible for anyone's death?" she asked. "The Kors are the ones that attacked our city and brought death here? Look, I appreciate your help. You've been a tremendous help to us, but I can't believe there's a plant in our garden that caused this destruction."

Skah sighed. "I'll start at the beginning. Have you ever heard of Kindroots?"

If it's a long story, we should walk. I don't want that thing here." Maya waved Ryker from his listening perch to come help lift the animal. Together, the three of them carried it out. "Of course I've heard of Kindroots, but they're a myth, something from a child's bedtime story."

"No. They're real, all right. And they allowed not just the thorny devils off the mountains, but also the dranks and horvelinas and whatever else."

The weight of the devil gave Maya an excuse not to answer right away. She struggled to hang onto it. The skin was so smooth and slippery. If it weren't for the longer spikes to grip, she would have dropped it.

Skah lifted his end higher. "I know it's a lot to take in, but please, will you help me look for him so we can give him a trial?"

"You never answered my question about why you thought he was in our garden. Wouldn't that be the worst place for him to be? The garden is our favorite hangout spot." There's no way Skah could know Blackthorn was here. Unless he knew Agonya had him before the exile...

"Yes, well, Kindroots have powers, Maya. They can control the evil creatures as well as the plants. Have you noticed how the plants in your garden are flourishing? Have you seen the plants throughout the rest of the city and beyond the walls? They're dying, while these are living and fragrant."

"I'm not complaining," Maya replied. "If this Kindroot is helping our garden grow, that's a good thing."

Skah started to backtrack. "I get it. You need this, but he's also responsible for all the other plants dying."

"That doesn't make sense, Skah. Either he's healing the plants or he's killing them. He wouldn't do both."

"I'm explaining this all wrong." Skah raked his fingers through his long, blond hair. "Maybe I don't know how to explain it, but he's here. I found him here," Skah insisted.

"Wait, if you found him, then why are you looking for him?"

"He got away."

Silence filled the corridor except for the echo of their boots on the stone path.

Maya wondered about the dying plants. What was causing them to die?

Blackthorn answered after a moment. "Maya, I'm all by myself. I have been for a long time. Jedrek, the first, made a bond with the Kindroots when they burned the contract. As long as one of his descendants was protecting me, the extent of my powers reached much further. Agonya is gone now. And you are not from the line of Jedrek."

"But I don't understand, Blackthorn," Maya replied in her mind. "Agonya left you behind so that she could protect you."

"Part of it has to do with me being here by myself. With my family, we created a paradise but by myself, it is too much for me. The contract is broken, and a curse is on the land and people of Ithol. Not to mention Dana draining my family of life."

"Contract?" Before Maya could drill Blackthorn about what he meant, they reached the butchery room.

"Well? Will you help me?" Skah asked again.

"Yes. Of course, you've done so much for us, how could I refuse?" Maya dropped the thorny devil and turned to leave. "I'll do what I can. But now I have other duties to attend to."

Skah gave a quick bow. "Thank you, my Lady."

"Please, I'm not royalty." Maya continued out the door. She had so many questions for Blackthorn. And she didn't want to stay for the bloody smells that came with slicing open a thorny devil.

"WHERE'S MY BOW?" KRILLIN panicked.

"On your back," his mother replied calmly.

Krillin grasped for his bow, but his mother was wrong. His bow was gone. The thorny devils advanced from both junctions in the tunnels.

Krillin glanced over his shoulder. His mother had her arms wrapped around his sister and their new friend Amber. They were pressed against the dirt wall. Behind them, the stench of two more thorny devils reached Krillin's nose.

"No!" Krillin couldn't lose his family again. He'd made too many mistakes. He couldn't let this be one of them. Krillin searched the floor for his bow, but it wasn't anywhere. He reached for his dagger, the one he kept in a leather holder at his waist. Gone!

A thorny devil growled, baring its teeth. The others joined in.

They smelled like a memory.

Krillin spun around.

He wasn't in the tunnel anymore. Krillin stood on the streets of Ithol and watched, for the umpteenth time, the callous guards beating his brother to death. He was helpless.

Sani called out, "Help me! They're coming. Remember me!"

It made no sense. Sani never spoke during his dreams.

A guard looked Krillin in the eyes, snarled and slammed a club down on Sani's head.

Krillin woke up. His heart pounded so fast; he couldn't count the beats. He tried to breathe deeply, to calm himself. It was just a dream. A bad dream. He wasn't in the tunnel. His brother had died years ago.

Krillin pushed himself off the hard ground and looked around. Sari, Anya, and Amber were all fast asleep, safe. It was true they had run into thorny devils in the tunnels during their escape from the city, but Krillin had his bow and arrows then and shot them all, targeting them by their scents.

Now that he was awake, Krillin heard his stomach grumble. He should have taken the meat from the creatures he killed, but all he wanted was to escape. He didn't think about how they were going to eat when their food was gone. Now he was sick of squirrels. Squirrels didn't go far between four people.

Not once did the girls complain. His mother thanked him every time he handed her a squirrel and got to work cleaning and cooking it. She forgave him, even though he had messed up everything.

A stick poked Krillin where he sat. He stood up. The stars hid behind the tops of the trees, but Krillin knew they were there. A bit of moonlight broke through the branches. It was enough to see his immediate surroundings. He couldn't see the river, but he could hear it nearby. He should follow the river upstream before the ladies woke up. He could scout out the best route. Perhaps it would distract him from his dream.

Then again, maybe not. Thorny devils could be up ahead. Krillin didn't want to lead his family into another trap. They were the ones he needed to fight for. Not his brother or father, despite the injustices done to them. His mother still lived. His sister still lived. Amber still lived. Krillin focused on those thoughts. They were all still alive, and he had to keep it that way. Going back to Ithol or visiting villages on the way to Korina was not an option for them. Aekan would find him, and then Krillin wouldn't be able to protect them anymore. Least of all, he couldn't go to Korina itself. Not to mention the Montanes. He'd smelled their game and wanted no part in it.

The river ran mostly straight here. Krillin noticed that it was starting to wind uphill. It made sense if he thought about it. Water always flowed downhill. He hadn't realized this river came from the Acrid Mountains.

It was time to return. The forest still held dangers, and Krillin hesitated to venture too far. He wouldn't be able to help if they needed him. He still felt guilty about his past decision to fight against the Itholeans in the war. Especially after meeting the king's daughter, the queen now. She was not what he expected. Her Majesty radiated kindness and justice. She changed Krillin. Although he couldn't help her, he knew she wished him well. He had to focus on his family. They, at least, were still with him and remained under his protection.

Krillin found their campsite. Anya and Amber lay curled up together under their overlapping cloaks. Sari was building a fire.

"Good morning, mother," Krillin whispered.

Sari smiled up at him and continued arranging logs for the fire. "You're up early."

"Bad dreams," he admitted.

Sari nodded in understanding but didn't press him to elaborate. Krillin appreciated that about his mother. She was so supportive and wise. If Krillin needed advice, he could count on her to help, but she never pestered him.

"I followed the river to see what lay ahead. We're going to have to leave it soon or we'll be climbing the mountain."

"Perhaps we ought to go up the mountain, anyway."

Krillin shook his head. "Remember those thorny devils in Ithol, in the tunnels? More can be found higher up the mountains. That's not all. There are dranks, horvelinas, other creatures we don't know about. It's too danger-ous."

Sari lit a pinecone on fire with her flint and stone. "We can't avoid all dangers, Krill. If those thorny devils are in the city, perhaps they aren't on the mountain anymore."

"Maybe you're right." Krillin sat on a stump close to the fire.

"Krill? You say Ithol isn't safe. Korina isn't safe. The Montanes aren't safe. The mountain isn't safe. Where can we go? That is safe?"

"I know, Mother. I've been thinking about that. Let's find a place by the river and build a shelter until things calm down. He'd like a cedar home if he could manage. Cedar had the best fragrance.

AFTER THE GIRLS WOKE, they ate what little they had, packed up their few belongings, and followed Krillin upstream through the forest. All morn-ing, the girls challenged each other to identify the plants they passed.

"Name that one," Anya commanded Amber.

Amber didn't answer. Krillin assumed she didn't know what it was. After another stint of silence, Anya spoke up again. "Look! There's a tuberose! Can we stay here tonight, Krill? I want to see it bloom."

Krillin turned back to look. Sure enough, Anya had spotted tuberose. There was also a nice smoothed out section among the trees where they could sleep. He glanced at the sky. The sun was directly overhead. There was am-ple daylight, but it seemed like all they were doing was walking aimlessly. He looked at his mother to see what she wanted to do. Her eyes were shut tight as she took deep breaths. Yes, it was time to stop.

"Of course, sis. It's a good place."

"Yay!" Anya jumped up and down and tagged Amber. "Come on! Let's explore!"

Amber glanced at Krillin. Seeing his nod, she darted after Anya. Krillin still couldn't believe Amber came with them. He met her the very day they left Ithol. But their connection deepened quickly. They understood one an-other, and Krillin loved her spunk. While she seemed more grown up than Anya, these moments helped the little girl emerge.

"Mother? Are you hurt?" Krillin walked over to where she stood, watching the girls climb a fallen tree not too far away.

Sari met his gaze. "I'll be all right. Thanks for letting us stop for the day. My legs are tired from all this walking."

"Why don't you find a place to rest while I set up camp?" Krillin pointed to a few possibilities and took the bags she was carrying.

Before he could pull out their sleeping mats, a breeze blew an unfamiliar scent by him. Krillin set the bags down and sniffed the air again. It smelled awful! Krillin coughed.

"Psst!" Krillin hissed at the girls. "Over here! Now!"

The girls obeyed straight away and were soon by his side. Krillin drew his bow and notched an arrow. Amber drew her dagger, too. Then they waited. Five minutes passed. The smell grew stronger, but they still couldn't see anything.

Something moved, but Krillin couldn't see it. All he saw was a plant moving. The odor was coming from that tuberose. He stared long and hard at it. Finally, it moved a tad later than the wind. The creature's skin blended into its surroundings so well, if it hadn't been for its smell and movements, Krillin would have missed it completely.

"What is it?" Amber hissed.

"Some sort of lizard." Krillin put his bow away and started rifling through his bag for squirrel meat. He tossed it near the invisible lizard and waited. The creature wasn't interested.

"There's another one," Anya cried, not bothering to stay quiet.

"On the pine tree!" Sari chimed in.

Krillin turned around in a circle. He strained his eyes to see the creatures. As he looked, he realized there were not just a few of them, but a hundred!

"Grab the bags! Be prepared to run." Krillin slung a few bags over his shoulders and grabbed his dagger.

All at once, the lizards leaped through the air towards them. "Run!" Krillin shouted. Everyone began waving their arms to ward them off and took off running. The creatures were so fast!

"Ow!" Anya shook a lizard off her shoulder and kept running.

"Cross the river!" Krillin tried to fend off the creatures, to keep them from getting the women. Soon, he had more than he could count attacking him. Whatever smell they emitted slowed his reaction down. He couldn't quite describe it, but he thought it smelled like burning beer. There was no way he could remove them all.

Darting from side to side, he reached the river's bank. The creatures on him dug their claws deeper. The water rose to Krillin's waist. They didn't like the water. Whatever they were, they leaped off Krillin like an arrow from a bow. Krillin dunked his head under the water so that he was completely submerged. When his head broke the surface, he noticed hundreds of lizards lining the bank he'd just left. Krillin swam to the opposite bank.

"Is everyone okay?" Krillin asked. "Where's Amber?"

Sari gave a start. "I... I don't know! Amber!"

"Amber!" Krillin and Anya called together.

"Spread out, she couldn't have gone too far."

"She was right behind me," Sari mumbled.

"Look! There she is!" Anya darted back in the water. Amber was hanging onto a floating log. Krillin dived in after Anya, and they both grabbed hold of Amber and brought her to shore.

Sari was rifling through their bags. "Everything is soaked. We need to build a fire."

"Were any of you bitten or clawed? Any other injuries?" Krillin asked, the memory of the claws piercing his limbs and torso still fresh in his mind.

"Oh! Krillin! What happened? You're bleeding!" Sari rushed to his side and started stripping off his cloak and shirt. His chest didn't look too bad because of the thick cloak he had on, but his arms and legs were pock-marked all over. Sure enough, a few claws had gone deep enough to sprout blood from his body.

"I tried to keep them from you, but there were too many. At least we know they don't like water."

"Yes, and neither does Amber," Anya chimed in.

"Amber, sweetie, what happened?"

Through chattering teeth, Amber replied, "C-c-can't s-s-swim."

"I'm so sorry!" Sari gasped. "I pushed you in! I didn't know. Please forgive me?" Sari wrung her hands.

"It's f-fine. If you hadn't pushed me in, those lizard things would have got me."

"Anya, are you all right?" Krillin peered at his little sister, shaking all over from the cold. He couldn't tell if she was hurt or just wet.

"I think so. One of them bit me, but I got him off."

"In that case, I think we ought to keep moving." Krillin watched the other side of the river. The ground appeared to be moving, but now he knew the truth.

Krillin helped the girls to their feet, and they started off, following the river. The water snaked uphill. The ground next to the river formed little cliffs. Krillin had to climb up them at several points. Each time, he turned and helped the others up.

"Looks like we're going up the mountain. Keep an eye out for a good place to sleep tonight." Krillin racked his brain. Those lizards were completely unfamiliar to him. He suspected they came from the very mountain they were climbing, just like the thorny devils and dranks. This was the reason everyone feared the Acrid Mountains. And here they were climbing up them. Krillin felt helpless. Everywhere they went, he put his family in danger. But they needed distance between them and the lizards. And he certainly didn't want to return to Ithol or Korina. He refused to engage in the Montanes' game or the Korins' war against the Itholeans. So, he climbed.

SOLDIERS STOOD IN POSITION at the city gates and all along the fallen section of wall. Jaylen intended to search all of Ithol in one day. No one would escape if it came to a chase out of the city. Aekan waited for him with his troops on the streets below. All captains were instructed to search each city section for living plants, reporting their findings and locations. Jaylen led his contingent of troops out of the palace grounds and down the steps toward the streets. He sniffed the air, nodded to Aekan, who nodded back and turned his troops to the right while Jaylen led his soldiers straight ahead. They would find that Kindroot once and for all.

Clean streets near the palace made the morning less repulsive. Jaylen still had to wear a scarf over his nose to keep the stench at bay, but he could breathe normally. The scents mostly came from the charred remains of buildings. The dead were buried, and the weapons and other valuables were salvaged here. But the further from the palace they got, the more littered the streets were, and not just with dead bodies but mounds of trash, too.

The first gardens they came across looked dead or almost dead, so they kept pressing forward. Jaylen had his men spread out on several streets, remaining within shouting distance in case they came across any dranks or thorny devils.

It was also early enough that there were hardly any people roaming the streets. Jaylen was impressed with the Itholeans' resilience. Despite being poor and weak, they continued with their tasks, cleaning, negotiating, and living off the land, just as before. Not that the land provided much for them. Which is why he had a few bond-servants who approached him for work. He was happy to provide rations to them in exchange for their service. He wanted to prove living under Korin rule was beneficial to them. They were not the oppressors some claimed they were.

"Sir, there are some green plants in the garden over there."

Jaylen turned to look at the soldier addressing him. He was pointing toward a temple. It made sense that their temples had gardens, where the Kindroot would seek refuge. Jaylen raised his arm and motioned for his troops to follow him.

As they neared, Jaylen slowed his steps and sniffed the air. Blooming plants were a welcome scent. He could almost taste them. Anticipation welled up inside him as they crossed under the arched gateway.

What he saw was more than he'd hoped for. The Kindroot had to be here. Every plant was green and blooming, not just two or three. It shouldn't be possible. The days were too cold. The harvest had ended, but figs still adorned the tree in front of him. Jaylen signaled two men to guard the gate while the others searched the area. "Don't let anyone or anything pass this gate without my permission. Do you understand me?"

"Yes, sir." They saluted him and returned to a resting stance.

Jaylen turned back to face the garden and started walking forward. There were fig trees and peony bushes, orange trees and rosemary bushes, berries and flowers of every scent. Jaylen didn't know half the plants growing in the garden. He should have paid more attention when his father tried to teach him the names of all the plants in their garden back home. In all fairness, he was more interested in his mother's animals than his father's plants.

Movement down one of the smaller paths caught his attention. He thought he'd seen something blue. His men had black and red uniforms, so it wasn't them. Slowly, he crept down the path. There was a hedge all along it, blocking his view of other paths. At the end, Jaylen peered around the juniper and spotted a woman on a bench by a planter. She was beautiful in her own way. Jaylen wasn't used to seeing women with short hair, but it framed her beautiful face. Wait. Was she talking? Her lips were moving, but there was no one else in sight. Could she be talking to the Kindroot?

Jaylen scanned the surroundings but saw nothing matching Aekan's description. He tried to get closer to hear what she was saying, but he stepped on a branch. He cringed as soon as it snapped. The woman's head jerked towards him. He straightened and, leaving all pretense behind, approached the Itholean.

"Good morning, miss," he said, stretching out his hand for a smelif.

She smiled and rose from her seat. Grasping his hand in hers, she smelled it. "Your scent is pleasant. What can I do for you, Officer?"

Usually encounters with Itholeans would go one of two ways. Either they wanted help, or they despised the Kors and didn't hide their displeasure, but she didn't seem to fit either one. She was the one offering help to him.

"Do you come here often?"

"Oh yes," she said. "Isn't it wonderful? I was just recalling a song my mother taught me about Paradise. I mean, if ever there was such a thing, this would be it, right?"

Jaylen restrained his frown. This woman was too happy and carefree. Ithol was not Paradise even if it had a blooming garden in it. "Can you sing me this song? I'd love to hear it."

She blushed and lowered her eyes, but she also started to take a deep breath, as if she were going to sing for him despite her embarrassment. Her first notes were accompanied by distant shouts and clanging swords. She paused. Suddenly, a chilling screech came from beyond the hedge. Her face paled and her tiny frame began to tremble.

"Stay by me, miss. I'll protect you from the drank." How on earth had it gotten past his guards? He shouted for his soldiers to subdue the creature. But it was no use. He could hear dranks screeching all over the garden. He was on his own.

Jaylen dashed forward, glancing over his shoulder to make sure she was following.

"Watch out!" she yelled.

He jumped just in time. Spinning around in mid-air, Jaylen lowered his sword onto the drank he'd jumped over. "Thanks."

Before he could confirm her well-being, he heard another drank approaching from the right. Another soldier was chasing it. Together, they pinned it down and killed it. Even as they killed that one, there was another one upon them. Jaylen fought his way around the garden, gathering his men until all the dranks were gone or killed and everyone was accounted for.

The men he'd left to guard the gates were severely injured. Several men had acid burning them and needed a healer right away. Jaylen gave orders to escort the wounded and to continue the search for the Kindroot. Then turned to find the woman he'd been talking to. She was nowhere in sight. Stink. Something about that woman bothered him, a feeling of something important. The tune she sang was familiar, a song his mother used to sing to him before bed. But there was something else about her he couldn't figure out. If he saw her again, he'd take her aside for more questioning. He should give a description of her to his soldiers so they could find her faster.

MAYA HUFFED UP THE last step and walked to the crenellation on the rampart. Well, what was left of it, anyway.

"Can you let me out of your pocket? I need a little fresh air after that encounter."

"Shouldn't you be hiding? The Kors almost found you!"

"No one will find us here. I don't smell anyone nearby." Blackthorn tried to calm her nerves.

She looked up and down the walkway. Seeing no one, she pulled Blackthorn out of her pocket and placed him in the crenel between two merlons.

"That was too close if you ask me. Who would've imagined being grateful for dranks showing up and attacking? Without them, we couldn't have escaped him. You do realize how close he was to finding you, don't you?"

Blackthorn curled up his leaves and spoke out loud just as Maya had done. His voice was high-pitched, not at all like he sounded in Maya's head. "I know," he continued, "I heard what he said about the garden. That secret he was after was me. But look! We got away, and he didn't even recognize you."

"You're right. He still thinks I'm dead, so why would he make the connection that he'd captured me a few months ago?" Maya looked out beyond the wall and let her heart slow to a normal pace.

"The crenellation pattern was made for us," Blackthorn said.

"What are they?" Maya asked. "I always thought they were different shapes because someone was bored."

Blackthorn stretched out his leafy branches. It took a moment, but then Maya gasped. "Oh! I see it now. The different shapes are other Kindroots?"

"Indeed. Jedrek wanted all of us to be remembered in the city's architecture since we were the ones that helped him get settled here in the Fertile Basin." Blackthorn's limbs slumped over.

Most were destroyed with the wall and would never be remade.

"Did you know Jedrek?" Maya asked.

"He was better than the stories remember him. His scent filled everyone up when he was around. But enough about the past. We need to see what is happening right now." Blackthorn pointed toward the rubble-strewn streets below them.

Maya still saw dead bodies trapped below the stones, homes destroyed, trash piled high everywhere she looked. Weeks of demanding work and yet they'd barely made a dent cleaning the city. The stench had lifted to a tolerable level. Maya wasn't throwing up all the time, only occasionally when she turned a corner or entered a room that still had a strong scent lingering in the air.

"What are we going to do about that Korin captain and about Skah?" Maya rubbed her temples, but it didn't help relieve her headache. "I don't like either of them snooping around our gardens. I think our plan is working. It's working a little too well for my scents."

"I agree. We need to leave Ithol."

"What?! Leave? But there's still so much to do!"

"You said it yourself. It's too dangerous here. There are too many looking for me."

"But I can't leave! Agonya told me to help rebuild the city. Look at it!"

Blackthorn was silent for a long time. "This is also true. You and I can't leave together. We'd be too obvious. They'd track us down in no time. What we need is a team to accompany us to rescue Agonya."

Maya tucked her short hair behind her ear. "I don't know. I don't want to jeopardize your safety. Who can we trust with the necessary skill to pull that off?" Ryker flashed across her mind. She dismissed him just as quickly.

"There's no need to rush. We are not completely helpless here. They didn't find us, did they? But we should be on the lookout for any who might be sympathetic to our cause, including Ryker," Blackthorn shook his leaves at Maya, "and we should start preparing for our journey. Every day we linger is another day for them to discover us and another day separating us from Agonya. I'm afraid she doesn't have long before they execute her, or the assassin succeeds." Blackthorn faced the fields now. Remnants of the Korins' old campsites littered them in the distance.

Maya closed her eyes. When he put it like that, her heart ached to go help Agonya. But Agonya had told her to stay.

"She told me to send you, her love."

"Wait, when did you speak with her last?"

Blackthorn ignored her question. "The Montane assassin was too close to accomplishing his goals for my scents."

"They haven't caught him yet?"

"No."

"You're probably right about needing to go help her," she thought to Blackthorn.

"The sooner the better," he replied. "That Korin captain intended to bring you back to the palace for additional questioning. What might have happened if he had succeeded?"

"And Skah keeps pestering me to help him find you," Maya agreed. "He already suspects me. I'm not particularly good at lying." Maya didn't want to leave Ithol. She felt safe here, despite the dranks and thorny devils and Skah, and the Korin soldiers roaming the streets. It was her home.

"Speaking of dranks," Blackthorn twisted around, "I see dranks being herded around that corner by a group of Kors. We better head back before we have unwanted company. On the way, you can tell me about your family."

"That was a sudden change in topic," Maya thought as she picked Blackthorn up and lowered him into her pocket. "My family? Agonya is my family."

"Have they died, then?" Blackthorn continued the conversation in her mind.

"No. At least, I don't think they have. I haven't spoken with them in years. So far, I haven't seen them lying in the streets, but we haven't reached their neighborhood yet. They don't approve of me working for the royal family. At first, it was a simple request for me to play with the princess. My parents didn't have a choice. It's not like one can refuse the king or queen. I liked it. I love Agonya like a sister and I miss her very much. I still wish..." What did she wish for? That none of this had happened? No. If none of this had happened, she would never have met Brynn. Even though her heart was broken when he died, she did not wish to forget him. "I wish there was an easy solution to all of this."

Chapter 6

Chestnut remained the best elephantus Ashkii knew. Despite a full night and day of relentless riding, Chestnut remained alert and showed no signs of fatigue. Even so, Ashkii pulled on the reins, slowing down to a fast walk. Even the best elephantus would tire if Ashkii didn't pace him better. While Korina was a long journey ahead, he was glad to have some distance between himself and his father.

His mother held true to her word. Ashkii would be forever grateful to her. If only he could undo the damage that he'd already inflicted on Agonya... He left his mind-barrier down every day hoping she would reach out to him. Then he could explain everything, but most importantly, warn her about the danger.

Ashkii relaxed his grip on the reins now that they weren't going at break-neck speeds. It was time to eat. He twisted around in the saddle and un-hooked a bag from the furry beast. Inside there were jerky strips, dried apricots and figs, bread, and cheese. Ashkii decided to eat the bread first because it would become harder and drier over time. He sliced off a piece and put some cheese on top. It was just what he needed. He reattached the food bag and picked up the pace; not too fast, though.

The river ran off to his right. Staying on this side of the river would allow him to bypass Ithol and close the gap between him and Agonya. But he would also risk running into other Montanes, or worse, Dana.

If only he hadn't stolen the Kindroot from Agonya. It was all his fault...

"Ashkii?" an unfamiliar voice sounded in his head. It wasn't Dana's, but a masculine voice, a deep voice.

"I am Ashkii, but what scent do you carry? Who are you?" Ashkii thought back. "Where are you?" Ashkii straightened in the saddle, scrutinizing his surroundings, but all he smelled and saw were the plants of the forest and the river flowing nearby.

"I need your help. I overheard you thinking about helping Agonya. I wasn't trying to eavesdrop on your thoughts, but you did think about me too, which caught my attention."

Ashkii tried to remember what he'd been thinking about. Who else had he been thinking about? He wasn't thinking about anyone he didn't know. Then it clicked. Oh...

"Yes, yes. I'm the Kindroot. You can call me Blackthorn. We need you in Ithol."

"Ithol? That will slow me down. Agonya needs me now."

"Do you even know where she is or the danger she faces?"

"Well, I don't know her exact location, but I know she's being taken to Korina and that a Montane assassin has been ordered to kill her and that he never messes up."

"He messed up."

"What? Impossible!"

"Yes, he tried to kill her several days ago, but he failed."

"How do you know this?"

"I spoke with Agonya in her mind."

"Oh. That is an advantage from which I could benefit. I left my mind barrier down in case Agonya tries to speak with me."

"She won't. You hurt her fairly good yourself. The only reason I'm talking to you is because I know you didn't mean to."

"But you still haven't explained why I should come to Ithol instead of bypassing it."

"Yes, well. You remember the Korin captain you captured in Tafka? He's in Ithol and he is looking for me. I must leave before he discovers me. If I'm found, the Kors will kill Agonya because they won't have need of her anymore."

He had a point about the Kors. Should he go to Ithol? But if he could reach Agonya before the Kindroot was captured, then she wouldn't die.

"I heard that. I get it. You don't know me. Why help me? I used to feel the exact same way about Agonya. I knew the risk, but I helped her anyway because it was the right thing to do. From the start you haven't cared one scent about me, but weren't you just regretting stealing me from her? Will her sacrifice be in vain? She left, so that I might live. Would you let me die only to save her, knowing that you could have saved me, too?"

"Fine. I'll come rescue you, but you better be worth it. If she dies because I made this detour, I will personally deliver you to Dana."

"It's good to know where you stand. Once you're inside Ithol, come to the Temple of Aromatics. There's someone there you'll be happy to see."

Before Ashkii could ask any more questions, the Kindroot had gone.

With a heavy feeling, Ashkii steered Chestnut toward Ithol. That Kindroot better not be disguising his scents. Why the temple of Aromatics? Shouldn't they hide from the Kors at the Temple of Rotten Fragrances? He'd have to convince whoever Blackthorn was working with to change base until they could leave the stench of Ithol. Regardless, he wouldn't stay long.

Ashkii rode at a slower pace. There was no rush getting to Ithol, having no desire to go there, and knowing he wouldn't leave soon. What he needed was to rest, so he guessed it was sufficient for that. Would he get to sleep in a bed tonight and enjoy a steaming bowl of stew? Ashkii was so wrapped up in his own thoughts, he didn't hear him until it was too late.

"Ashkii!"

The sound of that voice could only mean one thing. His father had caught up to him. Ashkii flicked the reins and urged Chestnut into a full-fledged run. They flew through the pines and oaks and didn't look back.

"Ash! Come back! Slow down!"

But why would his father send Tse after him? Ashkii shook his blonde head and kept galloping. Even Tse couldn't trick him.

He heard Tse's elephantus pick up speed. "Ash! Your mother sent me! I'm here to help."

What? Ashkii tried to think it through. If his father had sent him, he wouldn't have risked sending Tse by himself, and Tse wouldn't have known his mother's part in freeing him unless she sent him, but why hadn't she told Ashkii? It didn't matter. Ashkii was tired of being slowed down. Every minute he delayed, Agonya was in more danger. Better to get it over with and trust Tse wouldn't slow him down. Ashkii forced himself to make Chestnut come to a complete stop. Tse rode up, breathing hard.

"My mother sent you?"

"Yes, well, she sent me ahead of you. What took you so long?"

"I wasn't planning to pass through Ithol."

"What changed your mind?"

"A Kindroot. Are you coming with me or just here to delay me so my father can humiliate me again?"

"Whoa!" Tse threw his hands up. "I want to help. Your mother knew how I had taken a liking to the princess ever since I met her. She also heard I disagreed with the rules your father instigated. She reached out to me because she disagrees with him too. Obviously, when I heard her request, I didn't hesitate."

So, his mother didn't like what his father was doing either. But why had it taken her so long to help Ashkii escape? Ashkii shook his head. He would never understand her until they met again, if they met again. "Let's go then. You better not do anything stupid to hinder me or get us caught. I'm praying to the Patron of Life that I'm not making a huge mistake."

THE MONOTONY OF DAY in and day out walking, resting, healing Korin soldiers, sometimes her fellow Itholeans whenever the opportunity arose, was making Agonya sloppy. She needed to be on guard. No one had attacked in days, but that didn't guarantee the assassin wouldn't return. Not to mention, every day nearing Korina brought her nearer to her fate, to her uncle and Dana. Agonya didn't know where Dana was, only that Dana was layering perfumes, and her uncle was under her scent. If she knew which perfume Dana was making, then she might counteract it. Bannon, on the other hand, was easy to sniff out.

The second time he let Tanish and Huren speak with her, they told her what Bannon wanted. They came up with a plan on what they would feed him in order to let them continue talking together. Unfortunately, Bannon was suspecting something. It had been an entire week, and Agonya hadn't seen either Tanish or Huren. She was getting worried. There were rumors of reaching Korina in another week. Agonya needed something to slow down their progress. She almost groaned when she saw Bannon heading her way.

"You're needed to heal another horse injury."

"And you came to tell me this instead of one of your soldiers?"

Bannon raised his hands. "You caught me. Let's have a little chat while I escort you to the wounded."

Agonya had no choice but to let him lead her there. Her guards followed, of course, at a distance. They knew better than to encroach on their lord commander. Agonya wished he would give her a little space.

"Relax, Princess. You must know by now that your friends have fulfilled my purposes. I know what you've been doing, and I want to make a deal."

Agonya shivered.

"Not in a talkative mood this morning, eh? That's okay. I'll do the talking for now," he said. Then he wrapped his arm around her shoulder. "You see, we have a problem. The king will want you killed once we arrive in Korina. Oh, don't be like that. You brought this upon yourself. I may be able to convince him to let you stay alive as long as you continue to provide services to us. So, tell me why the Montanes want you dead, and how to capture the Kindroot if you want to prove my efforts to spare you from execution are worthwhile. I've heard Dahel talk about trying to capture the Kindroot and failing, but I know you know the secret."

Agonya tried to slide out from under his arm, but he held on tighter. "What makes you think I would answer your questions?"

Bannon yanked her to a stop. "See the man lying on the ground there? We're headed to heal him, but I don't have to let you."

Agonya stared at the dying man. Then she saw his face. She tried to run to him, but Bannon kept her by his side. She reached for her magic, breathing in every scent available to her, then pushed her magic toward Bannon's arm. He cut off a cry of pain. For a split second, he lost control, and she broke free of him. She ran as fast as she could to Huren's side. When she reached him, she poured her magic into him as fast as she could. Several hands grabbed her and pulled her back. She tried to make them let go of her like Bannon had when she stung him, but they held fast.

"Thank you. That was very cooperative of you." Bannon's rotten voice echoed in her ear. He put his face right next to hers. "Now I know how to capture the Kindroot."

Agonya wanted to vomit. His warm breath on her ear and neck wouldn't go away. She had to compose herself. Huren was dying right in front of her eyes. To save him, she had to give Bannon what he wanted. "Please, let me heal him. I don't know why the Montanes want me dead."

"You can do better than that." Bannon shook his head and straightened, pushing her into another guard's hands. "Put her in a cage until she's ready to talk."

"No!" Agonya couldn't let Huren die, not like this. But what could she say to convince Bannon to let her heal him?

"Tell me about the Montanes."

"I'll tell you anything you want to know," she pleaded.

"Start talking, or your friend here will die before you can heal him."

Agonya gave in and told Bannon everything she knew about the Montanes: how they'd killed her father because they were looking for the Kindroot too, how they had agreed to help her and then betrayed her, how they were working with Dana but her Uncle was also working for Dana so why weren't they helping each other? "Please, sir. That's all I know. Let me go to Huren."

The commander relented and let her go. "That'll do for now. Hopefully in the future you won't need quite so much motivation." He turned and walked away.

Tears streamed down her cheeks as Agonya knelt next to Huren. He had been a second father to her. A soldier nearby uncorked a perfume bottle and let her breath in its fruity scent and begin the healing process. So much for delaying their progress. All Agonya did was speed it up and give the enemy what they wanted.

AEKAN WAS OUT SEARCHING the city when Jaylen received Bannon's message. Not that it did him any good. Every healthy garden in Ithol was found. Sentries stood guard, but there was still no sign of the Kindroot, nor of that woman. She'd disappeared. The fact of her disappearance solidified her involvement with the Kindroot even more. The only thing Bannon's note said was that his men who wore gloves could keep control of the princess while she used her magic against them. Skin to skin was necessary for the full impact of the magical pain. But for this to be relevant, they needed the

Kindroot first. Jaylen wrote a quick reply to Bannon about Ithol's progress, their food inventory and rounding up of the dranks and thorny devils and a promise to capture the Kindroot quickly. Then he attached it to the bird's leg that had delivered the first message.

The raven flapped its wings and flew up and out of the circular courtyard, heading north. Birds were such useful little things. During war, people paid attention to them and shot down the carriers, but during times of peace they were just like any other animal, blending into their surroundings. That was his problem. His men were not blending into their surroundings. Despite the war's end, they continued to behave as if it persisted. Jaylen motioned for Laniel to join him. Laniel showed promise as a leader when he filled Jaylen's role as captain during the war.

"I need you to remove the sentries we've posted at the gardens and re-place them with men and women dressed in street clothes. They shouldn't guard the gardens but find places nearby to watch the Itholeans without be-ing obvious."

"I'll get on it right away, sir. What should they watch for?"

"I want reports on everyone who enters and leaves the gardens, how long they stay, how often they visit, what the garden looks like before and after they leave. I want to know about changes to the gardens, which are most frequented, and anything else unusual. Oh, and if anyone sees that woman again, we need to question her."

Laniel looked doubtful that it would work, but he would get the job done. Jaylen was sure of it.

"Anything else you wished to say, Laniel?"

"Only that it's good to have you back, General." Laniel grinned and salut-ed.

Jaylen returned the grin. "You did well while I was gone. I don't know if I ever thanked you for protecting my men for me. If you want to be a captain, I can make that happen."

"Thank you, but I'd rather be a soldier, sir." Laniel sniffed the air and left Jaylen by himself.

Jaylen didn't understand why Laniel would turn down a promotion, but he figured he didn't have to. Laniel was superb at what he did, and Jaylen needed individuals like him in all positions.

DESPITE BEING FREE from the Montanes, Maya still felt anxious around Skah. It didn't help that now she had to pretend like she didn't have plans to leave Ithol. Her heart raced every time she saw Skah, convinced that he knew her secrets. All the more reason to leave. Until then, she had to continue living her normal life. That meant helping Skah search for the Kindroot, as promised. Skah wasn't from Tafka. Maybe he didn't realize she knew Blackthorn personally. Besides, no one ever paid attention to the servant. Any message the other tribes would have received was that the princess had the Kindroot and maybe that she had a servant, but they wouldn't expect her to stay behind.

Maya straightened her shoulders; grateful the Korin soldiers were no longer standing guard at the entrance to the temple garden and walked through the gate. Skah was already looking underneath plants.

"Have you found him?" Maya tried to see under the rose bush he was squatting next to.

Skah jumped. "I didn't hear you coming! No, no, I haven't found him yet."

"How do you want to search? Should we stick together or split up?" Maya resisted the urge to turn around and go somewhere else, anywhere else. But she had to smell the part. Not until they had a trustworthy team, could they flee Ithol for good. It's funny how that worked. She had been content to help rebuild Ithol until she and Blackthorn decided otherwise. Now she couldn't stand being in Ithol.

"Why don't we split up? You can search to the left of the main entrance, and I'll check the gardens to the right."

Maya didn't fail to notice he took the part of the gardens that Blackthorn usually hung out in and was glad that Blackthorn wasn't anywhere near them. They both agreed it was too risky for Blackthorn to be there.

"Of course. Did you draw a picture of him for me like I asked?"

Skah reached into his pocket and pulled out a folded piece of parchment. "Here. I'm not skilled in drawing, but it should provide the basic idea."

Maya unfolded the parchment. It was the perfect likeness to Blackthorn. "Wow, this is amazing! What are you talking about? If this isn't skill, then I don't know what is!"

Skah shrugged. "It's not bad."

"May I keep this? It's so realistic. And you say he's little? He looks like a Manzanita tree except with furry leaves and little berries! Maya traced the sketch as she named each part. What color are those, or do you know?" Blackthorn would get a kick out of this.

"Yes, it's yours." Skah laughed. "I don't know his exact coloring, but if I were to guess, I'd say those berries are red and the leaves green?"

He was smart. Maya knew he knew the colors and was just lying about them. Blackthorn's leaves weren't green, they were brown and orange. His lie made him appear innocent, and that he was just there to bring him to trial.

"Thank you so much! I'm going to hang your picture on my wall." Maya smiled and searched between the rose bushes on her side of the entrance.

"Thank you for helping me. It means a lot to me."

Maya turned to look at Skah's pale face. "You're welcome."

He smiled and got to work. Maya turned towards the rose bushes, then proceeded to the drier garden with succulents and cacti. She lifted every overhanging branch and vine, looking anywhere a small tree might hide. She worked toward the outer wall and then moved up a row and worked back toward the center and so forth.

Whenever she reached the center, Skah also reached the center. They exchanged their news of finding nothing looking like a Kindroot and kept at it.

After an hour, they reached the end. Maya stood up and saw Skah nearby. It didn't take long for him to join her.

"I'm sorry, we weren't able to find your Kindroot," she said. "Are you sure he was here?" This was the moment Maya had been playing out in her head while she worked. She'd asked this question countless times in her thoughts and tried to come up with his answer, and now she was finally about to receive it.

"I know he was here. If I could have continued looking for him that first day, I'm certain I would have caught him." Skah wiped the sweat off his forehead.

"Why didn't you say something? I mean, that day we met. We would have helped you." Maya tried to look like she meant it.

"I even had him in my hands, and he slipped away."

"So, today you wanted to search the entire Aromatic Garden? If he knew you were coming, wouldn't he hide somewhere else? I mean, that's what I would do."

"You're right. But at least we know he isn't here. Now I can search the other gardens. Perhaps he moved to a different one."

"How fast can a Kindroot travel? And why hasn't anyone seen him before now?" Maya wondered out loud. Even she didn't know how fast Blackthorn could move, only that he could go wherever he wanted. The sight of Blackthorn walking was strange. For two months, she never saw him move unless someone was moving him in their hands or pockets.

"That's an excellent question. I don't know the answer. He got away in the time it took me to greet Misu."

"Hmm. Do you think it is possible for him to cross the entire city by now? It's been days since you saw him last. Do you think he left Ithol?"

"Again, I don't know the answer to that, but if we keep an eye out for unusual plant growth, perhaps we'll catch him." Skah's stomach rumbled. "We ought to eat something before broadening our search."

Maya laughed. "I know the cooks are serving up fried dranks today. Shall we?" She gestured for Skah to take the lead. Maya followed at a slower pace, still thinking about if she could have done anything differently. Skah turned and slowed down, but Maya waved him on. "I'll catch up."

He nodded and was turning the corner a moment later. For a moment, Maya was alone until two men emerged from the shadows, surrounding her.

"You're coming with us, Miss."

"Wh—"

The larger one wrapped his arm around her, covering her mouth. She tried to bite down on his hand, but it was impossible. Somehow, he closed her mouth and held it shut. Maya tried to breathe, but suddenly breathing through her nose was the most difficult thing she had ever done in her life. She watched Skah disappear around the corner and knew it was useless to fight. There was no escape. They steered her away from the temple and into the depths of the city.

Chapter 7

Blackthorn followed the fragrances through the city. He didn't have a nose, not like humans, but he could absorb scents through his leaves and roots. Unable to see far on the ground, he focused on each nearby scent. When he smelled a drank or thorny devil, he pretended to be a tiny tree. They passed right by him without the least idea he was there. When he smelled a Korin soldier, however, Blackthorn hid behind whatever barrel or cart or body he could find and reached out for other plants. He could sense them from quite a distance and made his way towards them as quickly as he could.

Following the scent of fig trees, he crossed the blood-soaked streets. He wished for a faster way to travel, but Maya was right. It would appear suspicious if she went to all the gardens prior to searching with Skah. And he needed Skah to think he had already left the city. Waiting for Ashkii to arrive was the smart thing to do, but the thought of being with Ashkii alone was undesirable.

Blackthorn's roots reached into the earth, sensing the tree's roots near the surface. Its roots were dry and brittle, as if it had suffered the effects of a fire. No doubt many of the plants throughout Ithol either caught on fire or were choked by the smoke during the last battle.

Blackthorn crept closer. Sure enough, it was in a garden. The only problem was the two men hiding in the building next to the garden. He couldn't see them, but their stench was that of Korin guards. He couldn't approach the tree. They'd smell him for sure. Instead, he dug his roots further into the ground till he reached the tree's roots and then sent life into it from his safer spot outside the garden. The figs plumped up, and the leaves turned green despite the cold in the air.

He breathed in what little sunlight forced its way in between the buildings. Then he reached out for the roots of some thyme and rosemary plants. Soon, all the plants looked and felt healthier in the little courtyard. They couldn't thank him since they didn't have souls, but Blackthorn felt useful helping them.

Lately, he'd been feeling the weight of the surrounding death. Not just the Itholeans or the Korin soldiers they were burying, nor the thorny devils and dranks, but he felt overwhelming death on the doorstep of many plants. Most weren't dead yet, but they would be soon without intervention. Would Agonya figure it out before it was too late?

She had to fix the covenant. At least, Blackthorn hoped she was the one in the prophecy. In many ways, Agonya had progressed further than he thought she would. Against all odds, she still lived and had the will to do the right thing. Being a prisoner was a problem. The urgency of escaping Ithol to go rescue Agonya pressed down on him. She needed to be free to find Dana and help his family.

Blackthorn froze. Something was wrong. He could smell it in the air.

A Kor had stepped outside of the building and was staring at the fig tree. Before Blackthorn could hide further, the Kor whirled around. "Hey, Wesa! Did you see anyone pass by?"

"Not a soul. Did you?"

"No but look at that tree!" The Kor walked in and picked a fig. He took a bite. "These figs are the best I've ever had, but they weren't here a moment ago."

"Move over. Let me try one." Wesa said, joining the first and plucking his own fig. "Mmmm. These are amazing!"

"We need to send word to the General. He asked about unusual activities. I didn't think there would be, but this..."

"Do you want to go, or do you want me to?"

"I'll go. Keep your nose up. If you smell anyone nearby, we'll need to question them. As soon as I can, I'll be back."

Wesa stood at attention and paused his search of the area. He looked in Blackthorn's direction. Was he spotted? A moment later, the soldier kept scanning the street and then back to the garden.

This was his opportunity to get away. Blackthorn retracted his roots and ran as fast as he could, one root in front of the other, bouncing off the hard ground in the opposite direction of the garden. He kept moving, hugging the walls of the buildings until he came to a dark alley. He got off the main street and peeked back at the remaining soldier.

That was close. Too close. He waited for the air to clear, then headed to find another abandoned garden.

The next garden he came to also had a couple of Korin soldiers nearby. There was something off about them. Blackthorn couldn't think what it was. Not until the fourth garden did he realize what was wrong, and only because he saw more Korin soldiers walking by. They were in uniforms, but the ones near the gardens looked like Itholeans. Blackthorn breathed a sigh of relief, grateful for his acute sense of smell that saved him from his enemies.

He continued healing the plants in the garden, satisfied that he'd figured it out. He healed the rosemary bush, a fir tree, and a honeysuckle vine... That combination of scents reminded him of Maya. It was her scent, her aroma. Maya! He needed to warn her. He'd almost forgot what she was doing.

"Maya!" he reached out to her mind. "Be careful, there are Kors disguised as Itholeans, guarding the parks throughout the city."

"Oh Blackthorn! It's too late! A couple of men ambushed me when I was leaving the temple garden to go eat the midday meal with Skah. I need your help. I don't know where they're leading me, but it's not the palace."

"Do you know what street you're on?"

"I don't."

"Picture it in your mind."

As soon as Maya showed him what she was seeing, he knew where she was. "There's something I need to do real quick, then I'll be on my way. It won't take long. If the opportunity arises, escape, but don't return to the temple. I'll find you."

Blackthorn didn't wait for her reply but let the connection break. He searched the area near Maya for anyone who could help. Ryker was close. Did he trust Ryker with his secret? He was a man that had done everything to help Maya since they met. He was kind. He was skilled at everything he did. He never lied. Blackthorn was unsure if Ryker had the ability to lie effectively, but he didn't have the luxury of guessing Ryker's thoughts. It was sufficient that he was a good friend of Maya's.

"Ryker? I don't have time for explanations. I'm a friend of Maya's and she's in trouble. Will you help?"

Ryker delayed only a second, trying to process what was happening inside his mind. "Of course. What can I do?"

Blackthorn told Ryker where she was and what she'd told him. Then, he looked around the park and noticed a rabbit enjoying the grass he'd watered earlier. Blackthorn approached the rabbit's mind, sending pictures of riding it around the city. The rabbit was hesitant but agreed. Soon Blackthorn was on its back, and they were headed towards the northern gate.

"I DON'T THINK YOU UNDERSTAND the situation."

Maya heard the yelling but couldn't comprehend it. She tried to open her eyes. They opened, but she couldn't see anything. A cloth wrapped around her head, blocking her vision. Where was she?

The same voice that woke her up calmed down but still reached Maya's ears loud and clear. "I know you are protecting it. You better tell me everything you know. To make it easy, start with your name."

"No."

Maya sat up off the dirt floor; the rope dug into her wrists. She ignored the pain. She recognized that voice. But no, it made little sense. If the voice she heard belonged to Ryker, why was he here and why didn't he reveal his identity? Ryker was no one special.

"No? Did you say no to me? You understand that I have the authority to execute you?"

Maya heard a chair scrape the floor and something made a loud thud.

"Your name. I recognize you from somewhere. But I promise you, after I'm done with you, no one will recognize you anywhere."

Maya heard Ryker gasp for air. She had to do something. The last thing she remembered was talking with Blackthorn. Oh. They were taking her somewhere. She couldn't get away. It was Ryker in the next room. He had seen her struggling to get loose. She remembered it now. Ryker had come around the corner, moved to the side of the road, until he'd seen her. Then he attacked. But he was one person against two. One engaged with Ryker while the other... the other one slammed the butt of his sword onto her head. Maya tried to touch the back of her head, but she couldn't. Her hands were tied behind her back. Even worse, her head was throbbing.

Ryker cried out in pain. Maya forced herself to think of an escape. She needed to get her hands in front of her. She pulled her legs up to her chest and tried to bounce in place, moving her arms underneath herself a little further with every bounce.

"Don't tell me your name. It's not important. Where is the Kindroot?"

The Kindroot? Maya gasped. Blackthorn was on his way to rescue her! She must warn him not to come, but she didn't know how to initiate the conversation in her head.

"Don't you smile like you're better than me!"

Maya heard something hit Ryker. He didn't cry out.

"Tell me where it is," the man demanded, and hit him again when he didn't answer. "You will tell me what I want to know."

Finally, Maya got her hands in front of her. She pushed the blindfold off. She was in a small room. There was nothing in it but herself. No furniture, rugs, rock, or anything at all except the dirt beneath her.

Maya wriggled her hands to loosen the rope, but it was no use. It only got tighter.

Ryker screamed in agony. Maya bit her lip and tried to untie her feet, but she didn't have enough strength to loosen them even a tiny bit. She leaned against the wall to help her stand up. Being on her feet somehow felt like she could fight back. Even if she couldn't walk. If she tried to take a step, she'd fall flat on her face. "Oh, Ryker!" Maya thought. "Why did you have to try to save me?"

She had to block out the violent sounds. But how? She was trapped, standing against a wall.

Whack!

Ryker groaned.

Maya tried to hop closer to the door. She did it. She hopped with every sound that came through the wall, whether it was a blow being dealt to Ryker, or his cry of pain. A few more hops and she'd reach the door. Maybe, there would be something useful to cut her free.

She stumbled and fell forward. Maya threw her hands in front and caught the wall with a thud.

Silence from the other side. Maya's heart picked up speed. She heard a door open and close. Were they leaving? Maya held as still as possible and squeezed her eyes shut.

The door to her room opened.

"Trying to escape?" The man's oily voice sounded amused.

Maya opened her eyes to see her captor.

"Here, let me help you before you hurt yourself." The man grabbed her elbow.

Maya sucked in the air that she'd been unconsciously keeping out. The smell of death overwhelmed her. She gagged and swallowed her bile. She couldn't resist the man lowering her to the ground. But she felt amused and annoyed. No, Maya didn't feel that way. The man felt that way, but somehow, she could feel what he was feeling.

Maya groaned. His emotions smothered her own. She didn't care what he was feeling. Why was this happening to her?

"See. Isn't that better?" The small man straightened, leaving Maya sitting where she started.

Maya couldn't help it. She burst out crying. All that effort wasted. And what was that sickening scent? His emotions changed at the sight of her tears. Was that hatred?

He didn't sound like he hated her. "Now, now. There's no need to cry. You see, as soon as you tell me what I want to know, I'll set you free."

Yes, he detested his need of her, a simpleton.

Maya worked up the courage to speak to the vile man. "What do you want to know?" Maybe she could soften him up. Change the way he was feeling.

The petite man smiled. He was hopeful.

"I knew you would be more reasonable than your friend. Tell me everything you know about the Kindroot in this city and where he is. Also, I would very much like to know who your friend is. I feel like I've met him before but can't remember where or how."

At the mention of her friend, Maya felt a flicker of emotion that scared her. She couldn't tell this man anything, but she needed to tell him something or he would stop playing friendly.

"Kindroot? I remember my mother sang a song about the Kindroots to me before I went to sleep."

"No." He shook his head and held up his hands to stop her. "You don't understand. I don't want to hear the old stories. Tell me about the Kindroot you're protecting. And I know you know what I'm talking about. Don't try that again."

Maya swallowed hard. If she couldn't distract him with useless information, then she couldn't tell him anything.

"Oh now, don't be like that. We had something going, the two of us. We were getting along so well. I'd hate for that to change."

"Why?" Maya squeaked.

"Why? Because you have such a lovely face, and I wouldn't want to disfigure it."

"No, why are you doing this?"

The flame extinguished. The man's feelings changed from mere annoyance to rage. His hand raised so fast; Maya didn't see it coming. Whack!

She felt the cold hard hand slap her wet cheek. The ring on his hand dug into her skin, pulling a chunk away when he took it back. Blood trickled from the wound.

"You will tell me what I want to know. I can play nice, or I can play the bad guy. It's up to you."

The sting enveloped her face. Maya looked at the man. She didn't know him, though she had a guess. This must be the man Agonya warned them about. "Aekan? That's your name, right?"

The man narrowed his eyes. "How do you know that?"

"I didn't. But now, I do."

"Who told you this?" Aekan raised his hand to hit her again.

"I've heard about you. Weren't you the one who tried and failed to capture the princess? I heard you got locked up for that."

If Maya had thought he had hated her before, she was wrong. He loathed her now. She couldn't help it. "You're back, I see, to redeem yourself. Is that it? You must prove your worth. Who are you trying to impress?"

Aekan didn't bother to reply. He hit her with all the force he could. Maya fell back, her head hit the hard packed dirt which knocked the air out of her.

"You will tell me who your friend is and where the Kindroot is. You will not presume to know me." Aekan kicked her in the stomach. "Who is that man?"

Maya gasped for breath and tried to curl up, to protect herself. He kicked her again and again. She felt satisfaction, but it wasn't her own. She wanted to cry out, to push his feelings away. "Yiska," she whispered.

"Yiska? Is that his name? Good." Aekan knelt to look her in the eyes. "Who is Yiska?"

"My cousin."

"Is he?" Aekan leaned forward and kissed her hard, so hard that it hurt, then he pushed her away. "That's hard to believe. You look nothing alike. And that means you're lying. I don't like lies."

Then the beating began. Maya's sole focus was Ryker, knowing that she had caused his torture. He didn't deserve this. But she felt as if she deserved every blow. Then again, she couldn't tell if that was her own feelings or Aekan's.

Chapter 8

A loud thud sounded behind Krillin. He spun around. Amber was sprawled out on the ground. He rushed to her side. "Are you okay?"

She nodded but didn't speak.

"Here, sit. All three of you can wait here. I'll go on ahead and see if I can find a good place for us to make our home for a while."

Sari grimaced. "I'm not sure it's a good idea to split up, even briefly."

"I won't be gone long. But you are all hurt and tired. Here, take my dagger. That way, two of you have a weapon. I'll have my bow."

Sari hesitated, then consented. "You come back straight away if you hear one of us holler."

"Yes, Mother, you know I will." The moment he said it, he regretted it. He couldn't be trusted. But he pushed down his past, turned and ran on the easiest path he could find. He always took the easy path, which is why he was on the run with his family. He should have helped the queen, but that would not have been easy.

The path he took now led him around bushes and up and over cliffs. He was about to turn around, finding nothing, when he caught a glimpse of something above and off to the side.

Krillin ran to the rocky cliff, pulled himself up and sure enough, a cave as tall as his mother was hiding in the mountainside. Krillin sniffed the air. Nothing he hadn't already seen. He moved inside the cave. The front had ample sunlight, but the back was darker. Krillin had to be sure nothing lived in it before he brought his family here. He felt the cold, wet rock walls all the way to a dead end and smelled the air. No creatures. This just might work.

Before long, Krillin was lifting Sari up the cliff, then Anya and Amber. Once they were all inside, they made their beds, and Krillin went to collect firewood. He felt better about them having three sides to a home. Fighting off any intruder would be easier. This could be a fragrant home for them, away from war and politics, a place to heal from their wounds that went deeper than the claw punctures and weariness.

Once a fire burned on the large flat rock that was the ground outside of the cave, Krillin ventured out for meat. The sun was already below the horizon. He had to hurry, or they'd go hungry.

Krillin closed his eyes and sniffed the air. Praise the patron of Fortune. There was a skunk nearby! The girls wouldn't like it, but it was meat. Krillin notched his arrow and waited.

The skunk lumbered along, unaware of its danger. Whack! Krillin killed it in one hit before it deployed its weapon of defense.

Krillin slung his bow back over his shoulder, picked up dinner and returned to the cave.

"Skunk! Eww!" Anya groaned and plugged her nose.

"Yes, skunk," Krillin laughed. "You ought to be happy I got anything at all."

"I know, it's just, why did it have to be a skunk?"

"I like it," Amber walked over to take the skunk off Krillin's hands, "I mean, I am tired of eating squirrels every night. Aren't you?"

Amber cleaned the skunk like she'd been doing it her whole life. She even cleared away the odor without releasing it into the air.

Soon, Sari was turning it on a spit above the fire. They were all relaxed, recounting the day's adventure as if it was a normal day. This is what Krillin was looking for. Family and friends to enjoy life with. He smiled and took a bite. The skunk tasted good, especially after all those squirrels. And yet, the bite he took turned sour in his mouth. It wasn't rotten meat. Krillin's mind clouded with self-doubt, convinced that happiness was beyond his reach. He was a monster and deserved to die. He should have stayed to help the queen as recompense for being a traitor and causing so many to die.

No. He was doing the right thing, protecting these three beautiful aromatic women. Krillin forced himself to smell their scents as they laughed and talked. They trusted him. They depended on him. They loved him despite his failings. Krillin swallowed and took another bite, ignoring the bitter aftertaste it left in his mouth.

THE CITY WAS ON THE horizon now. A speck growing larger and larger every day, and now Agonya could see its shape. She had visited there once before, when her mother was alive, but her memories were vague. None of them were pleasant, even though her parents had been on cordial terms with King Reid back then. Prince Lucas and his friends were bullies, telling her how inferior she was to them.

Agonya sighed and adjusted her pack as she prepared to become one day closer to that dreadful city. By her best guess, it would be another two days. What little hope she had of being rescued or escaping dwindled even further. Blackthorn had his own troubles back in Ithol. And Huren was in no condition to help plan an escape.

When she glanced around, no one else was getting ready to walk. Were they stopping here for a day? It made no sense. They stood in a barren landscape, surrounded by dirt, cactus, and other creatures Agonya had only heard about in her lessons. Apart from Korina, there was no visible sign of any town or nearby surroundings. Bannon had been warning her every day about her impending death once they arrived. Why weren't they moving? Where was her normal contingent of guards? There were only two waiting for her when she came out of her tent.

"Excuse me, sir." Agonya approached one of them. "When are we departing?"

He looked startled. "We're not. You have one day to rest and then work begins."

"What work?"

"Harvesting and processing the jojoba beans." The soldier pointed towards a bush she wasn't familiar with, or maybe it was a tree. "You better hope you don't come across a desert snake while you harvest," he smirked. "They love these trees."

"Snakes?"

"Yeah, the odorless creatures kill with one bite," the second soldier chimed in.

Agonya gasped. "They steal your scent by biting you?" She knew snakes had venom that was dangerous, but she didn't realize how easy it was for them to kill their prey.

"I think she's catching on, Lapu."

Agonya flipped her hair over her shoulder, turned, and went to find the morning meal. If the guards followed, they followed, but she didn't need to be patronized by them. It made little sense. Why wasn't she being taken to Korina? Also, the cold made it clear that it was not the time for harvesting. Not to mention all the dying plants she'd seen on their way there. This jojoba plant he'd pointed to barely looked alive. Granted, everyone knew about jojoba oil. Some of her favorite perfumes used the oil to hold the scents together. But she'd never seen the tree that produced it. Maybe they always looked half dead.

The morning meal was mush again, but with a nutty fragrance. Agonya grabbed a bowl and found a seat. What were Huren and Tanish doing? Would they let her speak with them? Probably not. Resting days were for washing clothes, healing people, and collecting supplies from the area. Despite the possibility of snakes, she was relieved to have another day without encountering her uncle. The more she thought about it, the more Agonya felt relief washing over her. She had more time. Harvesting jojoba seeds with her people sounded way better than dying.

MAYA COULDN'T MOVE. Aekan had left her on the floor of her cell. Her whole body ached. Every movement shot intense pain throughout her body. So, she laid there and let her tears run down her face. Bless the scents, the smells of death abated when Aekan shut the door behind him. Maya knew how she felt again, and it wasn't that 'she deserved what she got'. She knew that now. Those feelings had belonged to Aekan.

It was hard to feel anything anymore, like she was empty, drained of all emotions. Did Agonya feel this way after healing others? Feeling Aekan's emotions wasn't magic, was it? Maya had no other explanation for it. Agonya was the one who was born with this rare ability to use magic, not Maya. Maya was a nobody. And if this was magic, she didn't want it.

Perhaps Blackthorn had answers for her. But he shouldn't be risking his life to come answer Maya's silly questions. Maya closed her eyes and realized her eyelids didn't hurt when they moved. She opened and closed them repeatedly, as if by moving them she would send all her other pain away. Every time she closed her eyes, she pictured one of her friends. Agonya. How would they ever rescue her if they couldn't rescue themselves? Blackthorn. Was he safe? What did he need to do before he came for her? She wished she could warn him not to come rescue her, not like Ryker, who tried and failed. It was all her fault he was dragged into this. Thank the god of Fortune that Tyler and Kahlilah were safe. Was Kahlilah tending to the wounded or cooking? Misu. He must be organizing everyone, giving them tasks to complete. Brynn... Maya felt the pain again. Her throat swelled and tears burned her eyes.

She tried to block Brynn from her thoughts by thinking of Ryker. That only made it worse. How badly was Ryker hurt? Was he dead, too? She couldn't bear to think about it. He had to be alive. He was a fighter. How could Maya carry on if he died too? Not just because she had dragged him into this mess, but now she realized her growing fondness for Ryker over the last month. He was like Brynn in so many ways, always knowing what she needed and helping without asking. He was funny and easy to listen to and talk with. She knew he liked her in return. The way he looked at her... It was obvious why he tried to rescue her without stopping to think. Yet, she hadn't given him the time of day. She liked the way he smelled, and she wanted him to know that. He deserved to know why he was being tortured. If they escaped, she'd have to share everything with him and ask if he'd come to rescue Agonya.

Maya closed her eyes one last time and gave in to her body's wishes. She was so tired from everything she'd been through and couldn't open her eyes anymore. In sleep, she didn't have to feel her pain.

BLACKTHORN FROZE IN place. He didn't want to fight unless need drove him to it. So, Blackthorn watched Ashkii and the unfortunate Korin soldier disguised as an Itholean walk up to the guards from a safe distance.

One guard watched the second guard disappear inside. Ashkii snuck up behind him and raised the butt of his dagger. He aimed for the guard's head, but the Kor called out. The guard swung around. Ashkii's arm came down. The butt of the dagger hit the guard's shoulder. The guard drew his sword in the few seconds it took Ashkii to regain his footing. He kicked the errant Kor away, and the two circled each other. While they measured each other up, Blackthorn grabbed the Kor's legs out from under him and pulled him further away.

The guard made his move and slashed his sword down across Ashkii's poised arm, intending to knock the dagger from his hand. But Ashkii moved out of the way. The sword sliced through the air. Ashkii took advantage of the sword's position and moved in closer, slashing his dagger across the guard's wrists. The sword fell as Ashkii struck the guard hard on the head. The guard collapsed.

Blackthorn left his hiding spot and climbed up on Ashkii's shoulder, who cleaned his dagger, stepped over the guard, and went inside.

A hall stretched before them. The second guard met them halfway down the hall. "Where's Wesa?" he asked.

"With your friend out front," Ashkii replied.

"Is that what I think it is?" the man pointed to Blackthorn on Ashkii's shoulder.

"What? This?" And while Ashkii spoke, he stuck his dagger in the man's side. He was careful not to kill the man, but to wound him enough to get him out of the fight. Then he took the sword half-drawn from the Kor's sheath, leaving his dagger in the man to prevent his bleeding out.

They continued down the hall, past the parlor, beyond the kitchen. The hallway turned and Aekan greeted them with a smile.

"I'm thrilled you joined me. I've been looking for you, friend." Aekan stared at Blackthorn, not surprised by his presence at all and not the least bit concerned by Ashkii's.

Before either Ashkii or Blackthorn responded, four other guards stepped out of a doorway behind them. They were surrounded. Blackthorn had no choice but to fight alongside Ashkii. In his treble voice, he said, "I agree. It's about time we met."

In a single bound Blackthorn was on Aekan's face. He heard Ashkii attack the guards and so it began. Blackthorn sent pain signals into Aekan's body and wrapped his roots around him. Aekan tried to pull him off, but no matter how hard he pulled, he couldn't do it.

Blackthorn glowed brighter with power. He sent his roots to find Aekan's weapons, but Aekan already had knives in both his hands. One of them dug into Blackthorn's trunk. He recoiled and dropped to the floor. Aekan waited for Blackthorn to make the next move, not realizing that Blackthorn was healing his own wound.

The weapons were Blackthorn's first target this time. He smelled eight stashed on Aekan's body amid his layers of clothing. What else could he smell? Blackthorn reached out with his senses and smelled the rotting bodies in a room off the hallway. Then he smelled Aekan's emotions. His mind was walled off, but Aekan couldn't block his emotion, which was confidence. Blackthorn let his roots wrap around Aekan's foot. With the first touch, Blackthorn used the rotten scents around him to swap Aekan's emotions with the way he wanted him to feel: worried and a lot less confident.

Bending down, Aekan tried to get Blackthorn off him but gave up. Messing with his emotions succeeded! One of his roots found a knife and pulled it out of Aekan's boot. He tossed it to Ashkii, who had his own dagger knocked out of his hand by one of the three guards still standing.

Ashkii caught it and took down another guard by sheer surprise that he had another weapon in his hands so quickly.

Blackthorn intensified the pain signals in Aekan, bringing him to his knees. Once on his knees, Aekan was closer to Blackthorn and slashed several roots attached to him clean through. Ignoring the pain, Blackthorn discovered additional weapons, which he removed from their hiding spots.

Aekan, an excellent fighter, struggled to capture Blackthorn. Blackthorn took advantage whenever Aekan made skin contact by shooting pain into Aekan's hands, causing him to let go. Soon Aekan didn't have any weapons except his own hands. In desperation, Aekan picked Blackthorn up and tried to run past the fighting. This time, the pain knocked him unconscious. Blackthorn was free to help Ashkii.

He turned to latch onto one of the guards, but Ashkii knocked the last one out before he could help. They did it. Now to find Maya. She was in one of these rooms. Blackthorn closed his eyes to see if he could smell her. Ashkii tied up all the men they'd fought. When he was done, Blackthorn knew where they needed to go.

MAYA WOKE UP WHEN SHE heard Blackthorn's voice outside her door. She tried to sit up, but it hurt too much. So she laid there and listened to the fighting. She couldn't tell who was winning, but she clung to hope. Blackthorn had come for her and someone else was with him.

The fight continued for a long time. Maya didn't know how long, but eventually the sounds lessened until she heard a surprising voice, one she never expected to hear again.

"Which one is Maya in?" Ashkii asked.

A moment later, Maya heard the door open. Once again, the smell of death and sweat and blood washed over her. With the sickening smells came both Blackthorn and Ashkii's emotions: relieved and satisfied that they had found Maya.

Before she could process these feelings, the whole room froze. Ashkii's relief at seeing her vanished. Fear and hopelessness replaced it. Why was he afraid? Maya tried to turn her head to look at him, but pain shot through her body, reminding her of what she must look like to him.

"We're too late," he breathed.

He thought she was dead. "Not... too... late," Maya replied in between breaths. But as soon as he heard her speak, he rushed to her side. She felt his hands on her shoulders. She couldn't stop herself from crying out in pain when he moved her. Tears flowed down her bruised and bloody face, stinging as they went.

"Oh, Maya! I'm so sorry. I didn't mean to hurt you. What did they do to you?!" Ashkii finished, turning her to face him. She tried to focus on the joy of being rescued, but it couldn't block out the pain.

Ashkii was still afraid, but the relief was back. Maya was glad that Ashkii was there, a bit surprised Blackthorn had trusted him, but Blackthorn was safe. Blackthorn was right there beside her. He reached out with his roots and glowed softly. Maya felt his energy flow into her veins. It filled her up and then it was gone. Blackthorn was tired. Maya wanted to sleep herself, especially after the brief infusion of life. She had to fight the urge. Ryker was still alone in the other room. She didn't know what condition he was in.

"Ry..." Maya began.

"Shhh," Ashkii put a finger to her lips. "I'll go check on him. Blackthorn, stay with her."

Blackthorn shoved his tiredness out of the way and found fresh energy to speak in Maya's mind. "I'm sorry I didn't come sooner, but I knew I needed help."

"It's not your fault," Maya thought back. "How did you find Ashkii?"

"I meant to tell you sooner, but his mind was open, and he thought about me. When I discovered he was nearby, I convinced him to come to Ithol to help us rescue Agonya. He was already on his way to rescue her, but now he's not alone."

"I'm glad that he helped you find me, but Blackthorn, Ryker tried to save me. He was being tortured for your scent. We need to make sure he's okay."

"Maya?"

"Ryker?" Maya couldn't believe her eyes. He only had a few bruises and was walking towards her.

"Maya," he said again. "What did he do to you?"

Maya took a deep breath and winced from the pain of it. As much as she wanted to share everything with him, she couldn't force the words out.

Then he started to cry. "Why? Why would he do this to you? I don't understand." Ryker lifted her into his arms and clung to her. "I'm so sorry, Maya. I couldn't save you from this. Blackthorn told me you were in trouble, but I didn't realize... I couldn't think of anything else but stopping those men when I saw them kidnapping you. I failed."

"Don't." Maya closed her eyes, took a deep breath. Maya opened her black eyes again. She met Ryker's eyes and tried. "It's not your fault. You were amazing, not succumbing to Aekan. I'm sorry to drag you into this. It's all my fault."

"I don't understand. Maya, all I care about is that you're safe, and I'm angry at what that man did to you."

"I know." At the mention of how he felt, Maya realized there was more they needed to know. "I can feel your joy and your anger. Something happened to me. I can feel Blackthorn's contentment and tiredness. I can feel Ashkii's relief at seeing Blackthorn safe and me alive, and his empathy towards my condition."

Ryker turned to see Ashkii standing in the doorway. "You must be Ashkii, but where's Blackthorn?"

Blackthorn placed one of his roots on Ryker's arm. "I'm Blackthorn. You have my gratitude for what you did today."

Ryker started to pull away but then realized his mistake when Maya gasped. "But you're a," Ryker stuttered, "you're—"

"I'm a Kindroot. And magic is real. Now, Maya, I need to know more. You can feel our emotions?"

"Yes, but I don't understand. Why can I?"

Blackthorn thought for a moment. "It is the scent of death that allows you to feel what others feel. It is strong here. If we think about it, it has been when you are near the dead, when grief has overwhelmed you, beyond the normal."

Maya remembered. He was right. Whenever she had been overwhelmed with emotions, she had smelled death. Maya furrowed her brow. She also remembered working in the streets, carting the dead and yet most often she hadn't been affected by the stench.

"We'll have to talk about this later. Right now, we need to get you somewhere safe. The temple is no longer an option." Blackthorn touched her again and started to send what little healing power he could into her.

Ashkii spoke up from the doorway. "I'll get something that will act as a stretcher."

Maya closed her eyes, content to rest in Ryker's arms and let Blackthorn work his magic on her. It wasn't difficult to feel their emotions because she felt the same. Despite his confusion, Ryker was happy. She let it flood her mind and smiled.

JAYLEN WAS FURIOUS when he heard what happened. They were supposed to bring her to him, not Aekan.

Who was the General? Aekan? No. Jaylen was. Aekan's failure weakened his image.

"Bring them to me, now." Jaylen yelled.

The poor messenger saluted and ran from the hall as fast as he could. Jaylen regretted yelling as soon as he did it, but there was no taking it back. He paced, trying to figure out how to deal with the insubordination. They had to be punished, but Aekan was also highly regarded by the king. The king wouldn't believe a word Jaylen said against Aekan. He had to be very careful how he went about this. At least he had information Aekan didn't have.

"Sir, they're here."

"Well, bring them in." Jaylen turned to watch Aekan stumble in with his followers right behind him. Good. He had the decency to look ashamed. "I want to hear it from you."

"Fair enough. I didn't trust you, so I went behind your back and recruited these men to come straight to me if they found anything suspicious or that woman you wanted to question."

"You admit it freely? I was appointed general and governor here, and you deliberately turned my men against me. You will all have to be punished. But go on. Tell me about your encounter with the girl. Did you learn her name? Or anything else that might be useful."

Aekan looked Jaylen in the eyes and smiled. "Her name is Maya, and she is protecting the Kindroot, or rather the Kindroot is protecting her."

He recognized that name, but he couldn't recall from where. "If that is the case, why do you not have the Kindroot in custody?" Jaylen was tired of being baited. He needed to know the whole truth of it.

"Ah yes, well, there was a slight complication. When they brought the girl to me," Aekan gestured at two of the men behind him, "they also brought a man who tried to save her. His name is Ryker, which confirmed my suspicions. You see, I have seen him before... before the surrender. It wasn't until that Montane said his name that I remembered."

"What Montane?" Jaylen had to keep his voice from rising at the mere mention of the Montanes who had so spectacularly messed up his own plans to capture the princess and the Kindroot.

"I believe his name is Ashkii, sir."

"Ashkii? Are you sure?"

"Yes, do you know him?"

"I do. He has been a thorn in my side for too long. Go on, where did he come from?" He also knew who Maya was now. She had been the princess's servant, but they had buried her...

"Wesa," and this time Aekan yanked one man forward, "brought him to me, claiming he had information he wanted to share. I had no reason to think he would attack us. Montanes don't take sides."

"And yet one Montane single-handedly defeated all seven of you." Jaylen knew Ashkii was good, but he hadn't thought he was that good.

"No, he had help from the Kindroot."

"Let me get this straight. A Montane and a Kindroot took out seven of you. Either you all are rather incompetent, or they are superb."

"I'll admit some of us were pretty incompetent," Aekan glared at the men standing next to him, "but not all of us. We fought well if you don't mind me saying so."

"I do. The Kindroot slipped through your fingers like perfume on the wind." Jaylen closed in on Aekan until they were face to face. "You are going to work for me now. None of this insubordination stench. You are going to do exactly as I say. If you had in the first place, you would have known the Lord Commander sent us information on how we might capture the Kindroot and you wouldn't have failed."

"Please, tell. I'd love to know how you would have captured him." Aekan smirked.

"I need to know that you will obey me when I tell you to do something."

"Of course, my Lord. I am at your service." Aekan bowed his head but didn't sniff the air as if Jaylen wouldn't notice the small, neglected act.

"Excellent. You may have the honor of burying our remaining dead. Now, go. There is still daylight left to help you." He could tell Aekan wanted to balk at the command to dirty his nose, but he held his tongue and left with his pathetic men.

Chapter 9

The home with the tunnel below the floor, the one they had used to escape Ithol earlier that year, was being guarded. It made sense since that Korin captain had been with them when they returned to Ithol during the war. Of course, he would monitor it as the appointed Lord Governor of Ithol. Ashkii said he didn't want to use it, anyway, that it would be easier to help everyone over the wall out of view from any watch towers. That's why Maya was in an abandoned home in the eastern quarter of the city where they could gather supplies and make a plan to rescue Agonya.

She felt better after a restful night. It was comforting to almost be back to normal. The urgency to leave weighed on her. She was frustrated because her only task was to rest and guard the supplies. Maya was used to being busy that it felt strange to sit there until the others returned. But she didn't have to wait long.

There was a brief knock on the door and then Misu entered, carrying several sleeping mats and blankets tied together on his back. Ryker had insisted on telling Misu, Tyler, and Kahlilah about the Kors torturing them and that they had to leave Ithol. They, in turn, insisted on helping them prepare. Tyler wanted to go with them but there wasn't room. Maya and Blackthorn would share Ashkii's elephantus while Ryker would ride with Tse. Besides, the people here needed expert hunters and fighters to stay and help them face the dangers of Ithol. As much as Misu was an outstanding leader, he couldn't lead alone. He was older than everyone else and didn't have the strength Tyler did.

"I still can't believe anyone would want to hurt you." Misu said. "How are you today, Maya?"

Maya rose from her seat to help him take his pack off. "I'm better. My ribs don't hurt so much, and my face is healing." Thanks to Blackthorn, who was working his magic on her.

"Good. I guess they didn't get you as bad as it looked yesterday. I know you still want to leave. You're right that it's for the best."

"Oh Misu, you have been like a father to me. I'm going to miss you. I feel better knowing you're here to take care of everyone."

"Not a problem, my lady. I will miss you, too."

Tears welled up and Maya had to swallow hard.

"It's not goodbye yet. I'll be back with the next load shortly." Then Misu left Maya alone in the abandoned house.

Maya got busy sorting the supplies into four different piles. One for each of them. Her back was to the door when it burst open. Skah's blonde head popped into the room. He scanned it. Seeing Maya by herself, he marched over to her.

"I need a word with you," he hissed.

Maya immediately called for Blackthorn in her head, even though he couldn't hear her. How on earth had Skah found her? They had been careful not to let him know anything going on. Her panic must have been written all over her face because he raised his voice.

"You've been lying to me!" He spat at her.

Maya wiped his spit off her face. "What on earth makes you think that?"

Skah took a deep breath and, through gritted teeth, said, "I see it in your eyes. You know it. You lied about the Kindroot."

"I have done nothing but try to help you find this Kindroot you speak of!"

Skah stepped closer, causing Maya to step back again, but this time she could only take a half step as her back was against the wall.

"When I arrived at the dining hall, you indicated you would be right behind me. I turned back but couldn't find you anywhere. It took me a bit to figure it out, but I did."

Maya folded her arms across her chest. "Figure what out?"

"You went to warn the Kindroot that we'd be coming to look for him."

"Really? And then, when I didn't show up for the rest of that day, you didn't think to look for me? Look at me, Skah." Maya waved her hand in front of her face. "Notice anything different?"

Skah gasped and stepped back as he took in the scars overlapping scars that covered her whole face. "What happened to you?"

"Korin soldiers ambushed me on our way to eat, took me somewhere, and tortured me, asking the same questions as you."

Skah pushed her against the wall. "You admit it. You know something. Hand him over."

"You have to believe me. I don't have him. I'm telling the truth."

"I don't believe you!" Skah pinned her to the wall with one hand and reached into her pocket with the other. Maya tried to swipe his legs, but her own legs were too short.

"Help!" Maya called out.

"Quiet, Scentless One!" Skah covered her mouth and dug into one of her other pockets.

The door opened. Skah shoved Maya again before he let go and faced the newcomer.

Kahlilah emerged carrying a large basket of food and several water skins. "Get away from her."

Skah smirked. "Or what?"

Kahlilah set the basket and water skins on the ground and placed her hands on her hips. "What would your mother think of you treating women this way?"

While she spoke, Maya scooted to the left and grabbed an iron pan.

Skah saw her weapon. "Stink, woman! I came and helped you and your friends, and this is how you repay me?" He stormed out, bumping into Kahlilah on the way.

Maya watched him go, relieved that Kahlilah had come when she did. It might not have ended so well otherwise. Then she sank to the floor. Maya wiped her face. Her hand came away wet. When had she started crying?

"Did he hurt you?" Kahlilah asked once the door shut behind him.

"No, yes. He did. But not much. I hurt him. He scared me." Maya couldn't make sense of it. Her words didn't want to cooperate.

"No sense in staying on the floor. Come on now, I'll find you a nice cup of tea and you can tell me all about it." Kahlilah's strong, wrinkled hands lifted Maya off the ground.

She wasn't sure she wanted to tell her about it, but didn't dare refuse the old woman. That would hurt her feelings. Maya couldn't bear to hurt anyone else.

The table was in the other room. The old cook left Maya sitting on a bench to go heat water. What should Maya tell her? The only thing Kahlilah knew was that the Kors had tortured Maya, and that was why she was leaving. She knew nothing about Kindroots and the other battles simmering under the perfumes. If only Blackthorn were nearby or speaking with her from afar, he would tell her what to say.

Oh! She had to warn him! Skah would surely be watching the comings and goings of this place. He would see Blackthorn come back and capture him. Maya laid her head on the table. The coolness of it felt good on her hurting head.

"Now, dearie, tell me all about it." The older woman sat next to her, bringing two warm mugs of tea.

"I... I don't know what to say. Skah is mad at me for not finding the Kindroot he was looking for. He thinks I know where this Kindroot is, and that I'm not telling him. In his anger, he pushed me against the wall and searched my pockets..." Maya felt her pockets, turning their ripped seams out.

"I knew that Montane was no good. We shouldn't have welcomed him into our homes."

"Don't say that! I know he hasn't turned out to be what we thought he was, but he helped us a lot by killing all those thorny devils and helping to bury our dead."

"I don't know, Maya." Kahlilah shook her head back and forth. "That's twice in two days you've been roughed up. Where is everyone? I thought after what happened yesterday, they wouldn't leave you here by yourself."

Maya nodded. "They wanted to leave someone with me, but I insisted they get what they needed as quick as possible so we could be on our way."

"I'll stay until someone else returns. I don't trust his scent. As for the rip in your clothes, don't worry about that. Mending clothes is simple. Now, did you get hurt when he pushed you?"

"Maybe a little bruised, but that's all. Thank you, Kahlilah. I feel better already. But you can't stay here with me. You need to find Ryker and let him know that Skah visited me here."

"What if Skah comes back?"

"I'll lock the door as soon as you leave, and I've got weapons here to defend myself if it comes down to it. He took me by surprise earlier, but that won't happen again." Maya walked over to the pile of growing weapons and picked up a spear.

"If you insist, but I don't like it. Lock that door as soon as I leave." Kahlilah stood up and went to the door.

Maya watched the gray-haired woman with all her wrinkles head back to the temple. Then she bolted the door, finished her tea, and washed the mugs. She would be ready to leave as soon as the others returned, hopefully before Skah tried again.

IT WASN'T LONG BEFORE someone tried to open the door. Maya double-checked the windows to make sure they were sealed. They were. That was the first thing they did when they claimed this place. The door rattled harder. Would the bar break? Whoever it was couldn't be trusted. The others would have called out to her.

Maya went over to Ashkii's pile of supplies. He carried most of his weapons on himself, but he had a lot of weapons. She dug out a dagger and stuffed it in her boot. Then she picked up that spear again. She was no warrior, but she could swing a good solid stick if necessary.

Thud!

Something hit the roof! She'd forgotten how the Montanes were obsessed with roof hopping. But there were no natural openings on this roof. That didn't seem to matter to whoever was up there. They were banging the roof all over, looking for a weak spot. Maya tried to go as far away from the whacking as she could. Should she sneak out the front door?

Thud! A crack appeared above the table.

Maya lifted the bar and opened the door. She heard another thud in the same spot and the crack widened. Maya slipped outside. But where should she go? The moment she stepped further into the street, Skah would spot her.

Thud! Chunks of the ceiling fell to the floor as a hole opened in the roof. There was nothing for it. Maya ran as fast as her little legs would carry her, weaving between streets, not caring where she went so long as it was far away from her attacker.

"Come back here, Scentless One!" Skah yelled after her.

Maya ran faster. She turned a corner and ran smack into a Korin soldier. "Whoa! What's with the spear?" he asked.

Maya tried to pull away from him but stumbled.

The Kor caught her. "Do you need help?" he asked.

Maya stifled a cry. "There's a—a man." She pointed behind her.

The soldier swiveled Maya behind him just as Skah rounded the corner. "What's the meaning of this?"

Skah laughed, then lunged for Maya. The Kor blocked him and called out for help. Maya dropped to the ground. It was no good. She couldn't fight anyone. A group of soldiers emerged from various houses along the street. Skah was outnumbered. He raised his hands in surrender.

"You're under arrest."

Skah smiled. "Take us to your general. Let him decide who should be arrested. I'm sure he'd be very interested to know who that is." He pointed at Maya huddled on the street.

"There's no need. I'm already here."

Maya gasped. She recognized the general's voice and didn't know whom she would prefer to capture her.

"Take him away. I would speak with the girl and then decide his fate."

It happened so fast, Maya didn't realize the choice had been made for her, that she was alone on the street with the man who'd chased them through the Perfumed Pines until it was too late.

JAYLEN SAT DOWN NEXT to the frightened girl and waited.

She tried to stop crying, but her sobs made it difficult for her to breathe.

Finally, he lost his patience and lifted her head. He gasped and let his hand fall from her face. He was convinced this was the woman he'd been looking for, but her face was covered in scars. "What happened to you? Did that man do this to you?"

Maya shook her head.

"Then, who? How? Why?"

She couldn't answer because her sobs increased.

Jaylen had a sinking feeling he knew what had happened to her. The man that had been chasing her just now was a Montane. But he wasn't the only one after the Kindroot. "Aekan," he whispered.

That was enough for her to freeze in place, confirming his suspicions.

Anger boiled inside Jaylen. He hadn't realized the extent of Aekan's treachery. There was no denying it. Aekan had tortured this woman. And for what? The very Kindroot they sought came to her rescue and Aekan walked away with blood on his hands.

"I'm so sorry he did this to you. You must believe me that he did it without my permission. All I wanted was to speak with you. He went behind my back and has been punished accordingly. Though now I think his sentence was too light."

The sound of footsteps was approaching. Jaylen stood up to meet whomever it was.

Another Montane rounded the corner. This one was bigger than the other one. Jaylen wished he hadn't sent all his guards away.

But the Montane didn't attack. "Maya?"

She looked up at the sound of his voice and leapt to her feet. She ran straight into his arms.

That was odd. Why run from one Montane to another?

The man looked awkward holding her. He patted the top of her head. "Kahlilah told me what happened. Did he hurt you?"

Jaylen knew at that moment what he had to do. He couldn't keep Maya safe if he took her back to the palace, but he also couldn't be seen helping her. None of his men were here. It was the perfect alibi. "She's not safe yet. Can I trust you to protect her?

The Montane looked startled but agreed.

"I need you to fight me to make it look like you bested me."

"There's no need." Then he pushed Jaylen down and leaped onto the roof with Maya in his arms.

Jaylen watched them bound away into the distance and knew he needed to get to the bottom of this. Who was he fighting for? His king? Korina? Because if they required him to torture women like Aekan did to her, he wanted nothing to do with it.

"IS SHE OKAY?" ASHKII asked.

Tse nodded. "I think she will be okay. We should have left someone here to protect her. If it wasn't for Blackthorn, none of us would have been able to find her." Tse patted his cloak pocket where the Kindroot's leaves were poking up.

Ryker looked up from his seat next to Maya and thanked Tse again for saving her.

Maya reached up toward Tse. She didn't have to say anything for them to know what she wanted. Tse pulled Blackthorn out of his pocket and handed him to her. She hugged the tiny tree and put him in her own pocket.

"I don't understand," Ashkii said. "He just let you go?"

"No, he insisted I take her and go. He was on our side, wanting me to pretend to fight him.

"Whatever the case, we must leave soon." Ashkii gathered as much as he could carry and took it to the elephantuses waiting outside the city walls. Tse followed. Once all the supplies were transferred, they led Ryker and Maya to the wall.

Tse picked up Ryker, and Ashkii picked up Maya. Together, they jumped onto the ramparts. Then they dropped into the forest.

Ashkii couldn't help but feel elated to leave Ithol behind. They were all together. He'd done what the Kindroot asked of him. Now he was on his way to rescue Agonya.

LATELY, AGONYA FELT trapped in a cage, but today had the most fragrant scent she'd smelled in a long time. There was so much space between her and the sky, with just two guards in tow. Every few seconds, thoughts of escape crossed her mind before she dismissed them. They were two days' walk from Korina, which meant any escape she tried would fail. They could rally a huge crowd of people after Agonya in no time at all. She couldn't outrun them. Nor was she sure that she wanted to. Perhaps if she had a horse of her own or an elephantus. Oh, how she wished for the days of riding an elephantus even though her companions hadn't been trustworthy. She missed

Ashkii and Maya and Blackthorn and Brynn... It still hurt her heart every time she thought of him. She woke up often, as he was ripped from her arms. But she didn't want to think about the dead while her living friends needed her. What were Huren and Tanish doing?

Agonya kept walking through the camp. Glancing over her shoulder, she saw her guards close behind. Perhaps if she was facing away from them, they wouldn't see what she was about to do. As discretely as she could, Agonya pulled out that bottle of perfume Tanish had given her from her bag and uncorked it. The scent filled her nostrils as she breathed deeply. Then she reached out to Huren's mind.

"How are you healing?" she asked.

"Getting better every day, thanks to you," Huren replied.

"Glad to hear it."

"You sound chipper. Why the change?"

"I can hardly believe I'm down to two guards."

"Did you hear the news of building our settlements here in the desert?"

"Yes, but, Huren, why am I included with all the rest? I thought Bannon was determined to have me executed the minute we arrived in Korina. Not that I'm complaining."

"He'll have to report to the king and then receive the king's commands. It's a day's ride from here, by the looks of it. But seeing as you're only one person, I don't know why he didn't put you on a horse and take you with him. Unless there was something he wanted to find out in Korina before he takes you there." Huren fell silent.

Agonya enjoyed the silence. It felt like Huren was walking beside her past the other Itholeans sitting around campfires or washing clothes with water from the wells. She should wash her clothes too, while she had the chance.

"We need to escape now if we can." Huren interrupted her thoughts.

"Now? But I've still got two guards following my every move."

"Two is the best you can hope for. I will shake my guards. Then help you do the same."

"Even if you succeed, it's still hopeless," Agonya protested. "Riders would catch us in no time at all. If I had a horse, maybe, but even then, I don't know that I could do it alone. I'm responsible for getting these people into this mess. Should I abandon them to it as well? What kind of queen would that make me?"

"It would make you a smart queen. It is not your fault that the war came to Ithol or that we lost, but if you stay to die, then who would lead our people upon our return? You do not have an heir. Would you have Kors rule over us forever? I can go with you and Lord Tanish wouldn't hesitate, either."

Agonya bit her lip. His words were logical, and she didn't want to die like her mother, but how were they to escape?

"I can incapacitate my guards."

"But Huren, are you strong enough for that? I didn't think I healed you enough to be fighting so soon."

"I have strength enough, but you're right. If any other guards return, they could overpower me. You could cause a distraction, and I can slip away."

"Hang on a second. I'll talk with Tanish and see what he says. Be right back." Agonya released Huren's mind and sniffed the perfume again, this time recalling Tanish's aroma.

"I've been waiting for you, Your Highness."

Tanish was good. She hadn't said a word, and yet he felt her presence inside his mind. "You were expecting me?"

"We need to talk about your safety."

"Oh, I was just talking with Huren. He wants to escape. We both are down to two guards. What do you think? Is it even possible?"

"Absolutely. You are the throne's sole heir. You must escape, which is why I've already given my guards the slip and am strolling through the camp."

Agonya forced her feet to keep moving as naturally as she could. Tanish was already free!

"Now, the question is how we're going to help you and Huren lose your guards. And then we must consider that being together makes us more discoverable. We should reconvene on the edge of camp."

Leaving her people after she had surrendered tore at Agonya's insides. But they were right. She needed to escape, if it was possible. "We'll need two horses if we can manage."

"Why not three?"

"I think I ought to ride with Huren since he's still healing."

"It's decided. I'll grab the horses. You help Huren get away from his guards and head west."

"West? Why west? Wouldn't it be better to go south?"

"They'll be expecting us to go south, my dear. And if they anticipate us anticipating them, they'll think we'll go east towards the mountains. They'll never suspect we'll head further into the hot, dry, scentless, snake infested desert."

"West it is. Wait. Snake infested? I thought they were exaggerating!"

"No need to worry, your Highness. The snakes should hibernate this time of year."

Agonya shuddered at the thought of snakes, but trusted Lord Tanish to know all about them and their scents. "Okay. We'll smelif soon." Agonya left Tanish and went to find Huren.

When she entered Huren's mind, she could picture his surroundings. Granted, the entire camp looked the same. But she could follow his scent. As she made her way towards him, she filled him in on her conversation with Tanish. He agreed and would be ready when she made her distraction.

Now, what should her distraction be? She could sense Huren nearby, so she spun around, looking for anything that might help. She could make tents collapse, but that wouldn't lure the guards away. No, she'd need a fire.

Agonya kept walking. She walked near one of the fires int the camp and, before thinking it through, she grabbed a stick from it and threw it on top of a nearby tent. She looked around. Her guards stood with their mouths open before they started running towards her. She cried out, "Fire! Fire!"

Soon, there was a large crowd shielding her from view. Buckets of water were forced on her guards. They had to help extinguish the fire. Agonya smiled and slipped away.

"Good work, your Highness! One guard left to investigate the commotion. I rendered the second guard unconscious, and now I'm leaving my tent."

Agonya redirected her path eastward and then meandered through the tents. She picked up a blanket, pretending to carry it to be washed somewhere, and snagged some food along the way too.

The sun was setting just as she reached the edge of camp. Tanish and Huren were nowhere to be seen. She was hitting herself for not being more specific about where to meet when she remembered she could talk with them long distance and she could follow their scents. She did precisely that until they found one another. Tanish was true to his word and had secured two horses for them. It was now or never.

They walked the horses further away from the camp before mounting them, not wanting anyone to question them. Agonya could hardly believe their plan was working. It was too good to be true.

"YOU, THREE! STOP RIGHT there."

Agonya's heart pounded so fast she thought it might explode out of her chest when she heard the words.

"Turn around. Show me your hands."

"If we obey, our chance of escape ends right now," Huren reminded them.

"What do we do?" Agonya hissed.

"Ride with speed. Go!" Huren kicked the sides of their horse which bolted forward.

"Alert! Alert! Prisoners escaping." The guard's words rang so close to her ears. Had he closed the gap between them so fast? He was so loud.

She felt the horse move into a gallop and held on for dear life. The guard's voice fell further behind. Tanish led the way. They galloped straight away from the camp. But it was useless. The shouts were getting louder again and the sound of hooves beating the earth pounded in her ears. Huren didn't wait to consult the others but steered their horse away from Tanish. Agonya almost shouted to let him know they'd changed course, but then she realized they had more chance of escape separately than together. "I wish you both the best of luck tonight. May the Patron of Fortune be with you," she said in each of their minds.

"And with you as well, my lady." Then Tanish vanished from her sight. He must have gone behind a random bush. That's what they needed, something to block the Kors' view of them. The sun was almost below the horizon and there were plenty of jojoba plants, but they were spread out and cactus grew up between them. In fact, there were more and more cacti appearing on the ground. The horse was having trouble dodging them. They had to slow down. "Do we ditch the horse and hope they think we're still on it?"

"That's not a bad idea, Agonya." Before she could protest, Huren slowed down and pushed her from the horse, then he sped up and kept going. Agonya hit the hard packed dirt and rolled. When she pushed herself up, she hit a cactus. She did her best not to cry out as the Korin soldiers were close to riding past her now. She tried to blend in with her surroundings. Thankfully, Huren had pushed her after they passed a jojoba tree, which mostly blocked her from view. She didn't have time to be upset with him because the danger was still too close at hand.

She held her breath and stayed perfectly still as the horses went by. It worked. None of them saw her. But that meant Huren had sacrificed himself for her. She had to get as far away as possible. The moment she moved to stand; she felt the thorns in her back. She removed as many as she could reach, but there were some she couldn't get. She breathed in the scents around her and tried to push the thorns out with her magic. But that was a mistake. Now she was glowing orange while everything else around her was getting darker. She extinguished her magic and made a run for it, hoping no one had seen her.

"Over there! I saw something."

"Stink! Someone had seen her. Agonya ran, weaving around all the plants as fast as she could, which wasn't fast enough.

"Stop! We've got you surrounded."

Agonya glanced over her shoulder and saw maybe three soldiers closing in on her, but when she looked ahead again, there was Bannon gliding towards her. How on earth did he get here? He was supposed to be in Korina.

"Oh dear, dear, Agonya. What on earth possessed you to run away?" Bannon stopped his horse and dismounted. "Now, you'll have less freedom."

"Freedom?" Agonya couldn't believe her ears. "You call this freedom? Only death awaits me here. Why wouldn't I try to escape?"

"I was just negotiating your life with the king."

Agonya stepped back when Bannon approached her. She smelled guards behind her and hadn't realized how close they'd gotten. Glancing around, she didn't see any sign of Huren or Tanish. She breathed in the nutty jojoba plants as well as a citrus scent. There must be an orange tree nearby. The fragrances filled her up, and she began to glow a faint orange.

Bannon tried to grab her arm, but there was a shield around her that pushed him back. "There's nowhere for you to go. Come with me and I'll see what I can do about your freedom."

What choice did she have? Just as she was about to lower her shield, she noticed movement on the ground.

"Serpent!" a guard shouted. He swung his sword at it, but it only forced the creature to move closer to Agonya and Bannon. Dropping her shield was out of the question. Bannon drew his sword, but too late. The snake lashed out and bit his ankle. The sword fell from his hand as he fiercely grasped the snake's body, tearing it in half while screaming in pain.

When his eyes met Agonya's, they both knew the wind had changed course. His life was now in her hands. It was only a matter of time before the snake's venom spread throughout his body and killed him. He needed to ask for her help. She alone had the power to save him, and she wouldn't do it for free.

Turning to his men, Bannon commanded them to give them space so they could talk in private. As soon as they were several paces away and facing away from them, Bannon knelt before her. "Please. You can heal me if you so desire."

Agonya didn't respond. He was confident that she could heal him. However, she had doubts. She'd never healed someone who'd been poisoned. But he didn't know that. How could she use this for her benefit? It wasn't as if once he was healed, he couldn't take back any promise he made right. She would be right back where she started.

"Please. I'm begging you."

"No. I've been begging you to spare my life, to spare Huren's life, to spare all our lives from the moment we met and what have you done? The bare minimum."

"I'll do anything you ask that is within my power, your Highness."

"Since when do you acknowledge my sovereignty?"

"I'm sorry I haven't done so before now. Please, my life is in your hands. Would you let me die just because I'm your enemy? You said that you care more about the lives of others than your own life. Now my life is in your hands, your Highness. Will you save me?"

His face looked paler now. She did not know how quickly the venom would travel, but that thought gave her an idea. "I will."

She knelt beside him and rested her hand on his leg just above the bite. There were no healing scents nearby but there was plenty citrus which is what she used to create her shield. Breathing in the sweet fragrance, she let her magic flow into his leg. She could sense the venom spreading in his veins and reached her magic all the way around it so that the venom was surrounded. Then she pushed on it until her magic contained the venom to a small area around the bite and tied it off. She assessed its effectiveness by inhaling more scents and letting her magic flow back into his leg. The shield she had put in place was still there and she couldn't sense the venom in his leg anymore.

"There. I haven't healed you the way you expected. There were no scents for that, but I have contained the venom. That is as long as my magic can survive, which I imagine might not be very long if I die. You could let me go now. Say I tricked you and got away." Agonya resisted the urge to smile even though she swelled with pride at her cleverness.

"I don't think so. Your magic isn't the only thing keeping me alive. I have my king to answer to. That means you're coming with me. But thank you for what you've done for me. I will do my best to keep you alive." Bannon stood up and called his men to escort them back to camp. "For now."

That last part was so quiet, Agonya almost missed it. Her pride puffed out. What did she miss?

Chapter 10

"Go inside, miss." A soldier in a blue and gray uniform opened a simple yet beautiful cedar door and waited for her to enter.

The room had a sizable bed with an intricately carved headboard against the gray wall. To the left of the bed was a meter wide window. A small table stood to the right of the bed and the opposite wall had a wardrobe and full-length copper mirror. An armchair rested in the room's corner and across from it hung a painting. Agonya's heart skipped a beat as she stared into the eyes of her dead mother framed on the wall. What game was Bannon playing at?

Why was she in this room in the palace? Why wasn't she in a cell, especially after her attempted escape? Agonya turned to her bag and pulled her one extra dress, the white one she'd worn the night they left Ithol, out of it, and hung it on a hook next to the wardrobe. Instead of unpacking the few remaining items, she set the bag on top of the wardrobe.

She meant to sit down and rest her weary feet, but as she passed the copper mirror, she saw a complete stranger. Her hair was greasy and matted and falling out of the ponytail she'd worn most of the trip to Korina. Her face was covered in dirt, the green dress she wore was filthy too but didn't look quite so bad since it was already a darker color. A few rips and loose threads were noticeable.

There was a knock on the door before it opened. A woman entered and gave a brief nod of the head. "I'm here to make sure you get a bath and fresh clothes before you stand in front of the king. Follow me." The woman motioned to the door. She didn't wait for an answer but went back into the hall.

A bath was what Agonya needed. The warm water felt so good. Agonya might have fallen asleep in it if it weren't for the woman who added peppermint and rosemary oil to the water. Then she helped wash Agonya's long, black mane. The last time she had a bath like this was ages ago. Now that she thought about it, it was the morning of her father's funeral. Scents! She felt like a queen now that her kingdom was taken from her.

"Time's up," she said.

Of course, that feeling wouldn't last. She still had to go before King Reid and hope he wouldn't kill her. The last time she'd seen her uncle was at her mother's funeral many years ago. Back then, she didn't know his dark secret. She was just a child who was devastated to lose her mother. Uncle Reid had simply been another person related to her. Now, Agonya remembered the whole thing. She knew he was responsible for his sister's death. He didn't care that Agonya was his niece.

A large knot formed in Agonya's stomach, but it couldn't be delayed any longer. She stepped out of the bath and let the woman dry her off. A brand-new dress, not the extra one Agonya had packed for this purpose, slipped over her head. The simple, yet beautiful silvery silk dress was a perfect fit.

"This was your mother's dress."

Agonya forced a smile. "Did you know her?"

"No, but my mother served her when she lived here."

Agonya was sure Uncle Reid was not trying to be nice. This dress was a slap in the face. "Thank you for letting me wear it. It's lovely." It wasn't a lie. But by making her wear her mother's dress, Uncle Reid was saying he had the power to do to her as he did to her mother.

Back in her mother's old room, yes, her mother was all around her here. The memories flooded Agonya again. They overwhelmed her with longing for her mother to live, to be there with Agonya and to tell her what she should do.

Agonya wished her mother sat beside her now at the foot of her bed while the woman brushed her hair. She both wished and didn't wish it were Maya weaving her hair into beautiful patterns instead of this stranger. She told Maya to stay in Ithol for a reason.

Agonya hoped Maya was all right and was glad she had Blackthorn to help her with her enormous task of taking care of those left behind, and to rebuild the city. But Agonya feared it might be too much. She feared her uncle even more. Out of everything that had happened to her in the last few months, this was the worst.

The woman finished Agonya's hair, allowing her to stand up. Agonya walked to the window. She was on an upper floor of the palace, which itself stood on a hill. From her window, Agonya could see the city sprawled out below her. She could see the Itholean camp off in the distance. How many of them would succumb to snake bites? At first, when she learned they were to harvest the jojoba nuts, she thought it might be pleasant work. But after her failed attempt at escape, she wasn't so sure.

"It's time. King Reid will see you now." The stranger wiped her hands on her apron.

"Very well." Agonya turned from the window and followed her into the hallway, maybe to her death.

WHEN AGONYA SAW HER councilors waiting in the hall, she was taken aback. "Lord Huren!" Agonya cried. Was Tanish captured too? She'd thought they'd gotten away. Whew. Tanish wasn't there. That was a good sign. He escaped. A servant knocked on the large cedar doors, inlaid with gold. They opened from within. She announced Agonya, and her councilors' arrival to the king and those already present with him in the throne room.

King Reid waved them forward. Agonya led her counselors as far into the room as she dared. Reid ignored them. Instead, he continued his conversation with the Lord Commander Bannon, which they must have interrupted. "I understand. I will consider your request." Agonya's uncle rose from his throne and approached the commander, placing a hand on his shoulder.

Did Bannon explain the snake venom incident to the king?

"Great work, Bannon, you are victorious! I will not forget that." Reid clapped his hands together. "Now, I must see to my niece."

The King strode past Bannon to where Agonya stood. He grasped her hands in his large ones. "Welcome, Agonya Kate Nakai, my lovely niece. Have you found your room to be quite satisfactory?" Reid's smile broadened.

"Yes. It was very thoughtful of you to set me up in my mother's room."

"You are more than welcome. It has been way too long since we saw each other last. Indeed, I regret we are meeting again in these circumstances." Reid wrapped his arm around her shoulders and started walking her back towards the throne. "If I had known about your father's death, I would have called an immediate halt to the siege and come to speak with you. We might have been able to come to agreeable terms without all the fighting." Reid shook his head as if he cared about the lives lost.

Agonya swallowed the lump in her throat but walked with him willingly enough. He continued, "You needn't worry. You're here. And you're safe. I'll make sure nothing terrible happens to you while you are with me."

Agonya met his gray eyes. Why didn't he come out and say what he meant? She hadn't delivered the Kindroot to him and she had attempted to escape. He could not be happy to see her. His words must be hiding a threat.

"I have a present for you." Reid reached into his pocket and pulled out a bottle of cedar wood. "Here. But you mustn't use it yet. Wait until the feast tonight."

Agonya took the bottle from his hands and smelled it. "Thank you, Uncle. It smells wonderful. What is it composed of?"

"A little of this and a little of that." Reid winked at her. "You must know, it has been my intention to save you from your mother's tragic fate. While I do not wish to speak ill of Azurarus, let's just say he had his secrets. I'm so glad you're here, where you belong."

Agonya seethed at his words. He taunted her! Then a horrible thought crossed her mind. Why didn't he tell her what was in his gift? Could it be poison? "I dare not accept such a prized perfume. It is too much for your servant." Agonya bowed and held the bottle out.

Reid's jaw clenched and his cheeks grew hot. He grabbed the bottle from her hands and her elbow with his other hand and yanked her toward her counselors. "Counselors, are you not?"

Several heads nodded, and a few murmured affirmations.

"Then, council, your queen. Which of you would refuse a gift from your queen?" Reid looked each of them in the eyes. "I asked you a question," Reid barked.

Agonya groaned when Lady Velia stepped forward. "If I might, your Majesty, I have never thought of her as my queen. She is but a child and is still thinking like a child. Perhaps, your Majesty, will consider forgiving her for her foolishness."

"Forgive her, you say?" Reid stood in front of the woman and lifted her chin so he could see her black eyes stare back at him. "Yes, I think you're quite right. She is still a child. A child needs to be punished when they do something wrong, or they will never learn. Wouldn't you agree?"

"Y-yes, your Majesty, of course," Velia stammered.

"Then you will understand why I'm doing this," and letting go of Agonya's elbow, he pulled his sword from his hilt and pierced Lady Velia through. Agonya tried to hold him back, but he was too strong for her.

Reid yanked it out, ignoring his niece's feeble attempts to stop him. It was as if he couldn't hear the gasps and cries from the captives.

A servant ran forward, took the sword offered to him, and wiped it clean. Servants started to clean up the dying woman as if she were already dead, but Reid waved for them to stop, so they retreated against the wall.

"Now, I shall forgive you for your foolishness, my niece. Look at your councilor and remember why she is dying."

"How could you?" Agonya cried.

"I did it to teach you a lesson." Reid uncorked the perfume, dabbed Agonya's wrist with it, then pushed the bottle into her hands. He held his head high, accepted the clean sword offered to him, and left the throne room behind.

Oh, Lady Velia! Agonya rushed to her side. If only she had her orinberries or pine bark with her, Agonya closed her eyes anyway and laid her hands on Velia's gushing wound. All she could smell was that blasted perfume her uncle gave her, lemon and chocolate?

Agonya wanted to vomit. Instead, she swallowed the bile that came and tried again. She couldn't find her magic. There was a hole inside of her. She could do nothing!

"Help! Please. Anyone?" Agonya looked Velia in the eyes. "I'm so sorry! Can you forgive me even now?"

Velia stared back, unmoving. No words. No breath. She was gone.

Agonya felt hands pulling her away from the body. She had failed. Someone directed her into the corridor. Agonya was vaguely aware of walking back to her room. This was all her fault. She heard the door shut, collapsing where she had been deposited, and wept.

The room darkened until the only light came from beyond the door where Agonya knew her guards stood listening to her sobs.

Agonya breathed deeply and pushed herself off the floor. Her uncle was right. She needed to learn her lesson.

Agonya walked over to the table next to her bed and, sure enough, a candle sat on top. It took a minute, but Agonya found a lighter and soon had a flame.

Lady Velia. She was always making Agonya's life miserable. But she didn't deserve to die that way. Agonya wiped her sopping face with her sleeve, her mother's sleeve. Yet another person who shouldn't have died by her uncle's hand.

Agonya witnessed both, but this one she knew what she was seeing. Her uncle had no care for life at all. This room he put her in smelled of his treachery. Did he think she wouldn't remember? Or did he want her to remember?

Agonya crawled into the large soft bed, not even bothering to change out of the blood-soaked dress she wore. Then she thought of Maya. Maya and all her people. She had let them down. What had she expected? Civility? From her uncle? No, she had expected him to kill her and not her councilors.

Agonya should have known better. King Reid would never forgive her for not surrendering the Kindroot. And if her death meant the death of his lord commander, what other torture would he devise for her?

What a terrible queen she was to the Itholeans! But more than that, Agonya had a stronger fear. She thought of Reid so she could avoid thinking of the one thing in all of this that frightened her the most.

Why couldn't she heal Lady Velia?

"TIME TO GET UP," THE same woman from the day before said, and threw back her blanket, sending a chill through Agonya's body.

"What's on the schedule today?" Agonya asked the question before she realized her mistake. She wasn't at home, being woken up by Maya. She was in her uncle's prison. She belonged to him now. Whatever he wanted her to do, she had to do.

"You've been summoned to the throne room. Put this on."

Agonya caught the dress and slid it on as quickly as she could.

Within minutes, she was standing in front of the throne room doors, waiting to be admitted. This time, instead of being shown in right away, she was forced to stand there for over an hour before the door opened and her name was called. The woman stepped forward and sprayed her with the perfume King Reid gave her.

Agonya tried not to breathe in the scent, but she had to take a deep breath to keep her fear at bay. She was still alive after her meeting with him yesterday. Her heart pounded with fear, even though the situation remained unchanged. She walked in and waited for him to speak.

King Reid looked at her for so long she became uncomfortable, but her training kicked in and she stood straight-backed, waiting.

Then he broke the silence. "Where is it?"

Agonya wasn't sure how to answer, so she said nothing. If she told him where Blackthorn was, that was the end for Blackthorn. If she didn't tell him, there were any number of things he could do to make Agonya's life miserable.

"You don't have the luxury to stay quiet. I know you know where it is and you are going to tell me." Reid stood up from his throne. He descended the dais until he was right next to her.

What could Agonya do? No ideas came to her.

Wham! King Reid's hand slapped her face. Agonya almost cried out in pain, but she had to be strong.

He stroked her face where he had struck her. "Tell me, or you will regret it."

"Tell you what?" Agonya replied through clenched teeth.

"Shall I rephrase it for you? Where is Blackthorn, the Kindroot?"

She couldn't help it. When he said Blackthorn's name, she let out an audible gasp. How did he know his name?

"I knew you knew what I was talking about. Now, I have a problem." Reid walked around Agonya, studying her. "My lord commander, whom I dearly love, was supposed to bring Blackthorn to me when he returned, but he didn't. I could have him killed for his disobedience, but I kind of like him and he brought me a magnificent gift. He says that Blackthorn is just a little delayed. But you see, I can smell trouble in the air and I'm tired of having to do everything myself. I want to make him successful so that he can go on living and being my lord commander. It is rather hard to replace your lord commander, though you haven't had to do that yet. Oh, dear me, listen to me prattle on. I want to hear from you." Reid stood in front of her and cupped her face in his hands. "You know where Blackthorn is. Tell me."

"If I tell you," Agonya replied, "I will regret it for the rest of my life."

Reid let go of her face and stepped back, calculating her. "Ah yes, speaking about your life. I heard a rumor that if you die, then my lord commander will die too. Is that true? You see, if I decide he doesn't deserve to live, I could just have you killed because we both know he's the only reason you're still alive right now."

"Then, kill me. It makes no difference to me whether he lives or dies. But it does matter to me that Blackthorn should live. I will not betray him."

"Just like your mother. You know, her death was something I regretted, but now that she has been avenged, I feel like we're on the right path."

"Her death has not been avenged! Is that what you're telling your people?" Agonya gestured to the guards and a handful of noble lords and ladies watching the whole thing play out. "You killed my mother! I know. I was there."

Before she could finish talking, her uncle's fist landed in her stomach. The force of his blow knocked the air out of her and pushed her backwards. She lost her balance and fell to the floor.

"Liar! Your worthless father killed her, and you know it." Reid kicked Agonya. Then he kicked her again. "You don't deserve the hospitality I granted you! I took you into my home, treated you like family and this is how you repay me?" He began kicking her over and over.

Agonya tried to get away, but she couldn't move. She reached for her magic, but it was distant. The scent of the perfume on her was blocking her magic again. She tried to envelop herself, to protect herself from his beating, but it evaded her grasp.

"Stop!" A young man watching from the side of the room stepped forward.

Reid paused and looked up. It was his son, the Crown Prince. "Do you have a better idea of what to do with this unpleasant stench?"

The prince bowed. "Let me have her. You owe me a debt. You could give her to me to be a part of my household. I will get her to speak." He gestured to her body curled up on the cold stone. "She can't speak very well lying on the floor, getting the wind kicked out of her. It appears she's under a delusion of how her mother died. We ought to educate her. Then, when she has learned the truth, she will speak because she'll know it to be the right thing."

"Very well, Lucas. She is yours. But someone must die in her place. Her counselors failed to teach her. They will be executed tonight."

Agonya felt cold and rotten. She couldn't breathe.

Reid ignored her and kept talking. "And the Itholeans will no longer be considered prisoners of war but shall be my slaves."

Agonya broke. Her mind wouldn't cooperate. Her body refused to move. Their deaths would be her fault. All of her counselors? Huren? He was the best commander she could have hoped for. Sir Besnek and Sir Marco? She was overwhelmed by the genuine kindness they showed her while she was growing up. The others? But there was nothing she could do.

Agonya saw the prince extend his hand towards her, but she didn't grasp it.

Prince Lucas squatted next to her. "Come with me, your Highness?"

His voice was soothing. He smelled of peonies and oranges. Somehow, it didn't bother her he wore her mother's scents. She was too numb from everything else.

The prince lifted her until she was on her feet. The pain was worse standing, but she let him lead her out of the throne room. He didn't say anymore but let her hide behind her depressing thoughts all the way back to her room.

Once there, he spoke. "I'll send Tara along to help you get cleaned up and make sure you don't need a doctor."

Agonya left him at the door and went to the bed that she'd been dragged from only an hour before.

JAYLEN RAN ALL THE way back to the palace without stopping. He still couldn't believe he'd let her go. What was he thinking? The memory of the pink scars crisscrossing her once beautiful face flashed across his mind. There would never be a sufficient reason to justify what Aekan did to her. What was so important about this Kindroot, anyway? Why would his king end a war for it but say the war was about avenging his sister's death? The death of King Azurarus should have ended the war if it was about her.

"Lord Commander!" A shocked guard hurried to open the gate to let him pass through.

Jaylen went straight to the Great Hall. A Montane waited for him, and he couldn't know that Jaylen let her escape. He had to placate this man no matter how much he wanted to beat him instead. The guards opened the doors and Jaylen forced himself to ignore the Montane standing in the middle of the room.

"Where is she?" the Montane asked.

"Quick," Jaylen addressed his messenger. "Gather division two, send them to the eastern quarter before our suspects escape."

"You let her get away?" The Montane's face reddened. "After I told you not to?"

Jaylen spun on him. "Who are you to tell me what to do?" Jaylen sighed. "Forgive me. You were right about the girl, but at the time, you were the dangerous one. If you must know, I was ambushed," he lied. "Why do you think I'm sending as many men as I can to find her?"

"What's this about letting someone escape?"

Where did Aekan come from? Jaylen pinched his nose and released it before turning to face the newest arrival. "You'll have to forgive me, Aekan. I didn't realize how slippery that woman is."

"You mean Maya?" Aekan asked innocently.

"Yes, Maya. She ran right into our grasp and, like you, I couldn't keep her from slipping away. What I don't understand is how her friends keep finding her so fast."

Aekan laughed. "Really? I know precisely how."

"How?" both the Montane and Jaylen asked.

"The Kindroot can smell her."

Jaylen nodded thoughtfully. "I wonder if there's a way we can do the same to find them."

"There is a way. But first, I thought you were going to tell me what you learned about how to catch him once I showed you that I could obey orders."

Jaylen nodded and began to pace. He had been upset with Aekan for his insubordination, but now he was furious with him for what he did to Maya.

He hated himself even more for what he was about to do. "Wear protection. The Kindroot's powers are stronger if he can directly touch your skin."

"That's it?"

"That's what the lord commander said in his message. Now, if you know a way to sniff them out, tell us."

"No."

"No? Did I not just give you an order?"

"I don't know this man."

The Montane held his hand out for a smelif. "I'm so sorry. I'm Skah, a warrior of the Imka people. I came to Ithol looking for the Kindroot."

Aekan raised his eyebrows before taking the extended hand and smelling it. "You realize that if we succeed in capturing the Kindroot, we will have to take it to Korina."

"So long as I can accompany it, that is fine with me."

Aekan smiled. "Then we have much to discuss. I still don't trust you, but I am willing to collaborate with you."

"Great." Jaylen clasped his hands together. "You have your orders. Find the Kindroot and take him to Korina. I suspect he'll be leaving Ithol soon if he hasn't already. So, you should begin by packing." Jaylen couldn't be rid of these men fast enough.

"What about you, Governor General?"

"I have a city to run. I can't be chasing after a Kindroot. But I can provide whatever you might need for your trip."

Aekan nodded and led Skah out of the Great Hall.

Jaylen dismissed his guards to the hall so he could have a moment alone. Now that he'd decided helping the Kindroot was the right thing to do, he hated himself for sending those two men after him. But if they knew what he'd done, that would be the end of him. He needed to find another way to help the Kindroot. For that, he needed more information.

Chapter 11

The Elephantus ran through the edge of the Perfumed Forest. Maya tightened her grip on Chestnut's fur. She'd never ridden anything so fast in her life. It looked like they might hit the trees in front of them, but somehow, they dodged every single one. Ashkii tried to reassure her, saying they weren't as fast as horses. Was that supposed to make her feel better?

"You don't need to worry about them pursuing us. They need time to get reinforcements, but even with horses, elephantuses have superior endurance."

Maya took a chance to glance behind them. She had to peer around Ashkii to see Tse and Ryker. But looking backwards made her stomach lurch, so she went back to facing forward.

"Don't worry," Ashkii continued, "I'll smell if they fall behind."

"Yeah," Maya cleared her throat and tried again, "but what about the trail we're leaving behind us? These elephantus are not small or careful."

"That is a problem," he conceded, "but right now, speed matters most. The more distance we put between us and them, the better."

"My head tells me that you're right. That general may have let us go, but he won't hesitate to send pursuers. He has to keep up appearances."

"Then why are you afraid?"

Maya didn't think she was that transparent. "If he has to keep up appearances, that means he's going to send..." Maya held tighter to Chestnut's fur and said that dreadful name, "Aekan after us." The general knew what Aekan did to her. He even apologized for Aekan's actions, but there wasn't anything he could do to stop Aekan from chasing after her again. Her hand went to her face and traced the outline of his ring, where it had dug into her flesh, overlapping itself over and over.

"Does it hurt?"

"Not anymore." Maya sighed and, realizing her mistake, dug her hand back into Chestnut's fur.

"I'm sorry we didn't find you sooner," Ashkii said, for what must have been the hundredth time.

"It's okay."

Blackthorn joined the conversation in his high-pitched, tiny voice. "No. It's not okay. I could have come directly to you and brought Ashkii to our location using our mind connection, but I went to Ashkii first."

"But Blackthorn, if you'd come alone, Aekan would have caught you and who knows if Ashkii would have been able to rescue us then. Besides, Aekan's actions are not your fault. They are his own. I'm blessed to have you in my life. If it hadn't been for both of you, I could have died in that horrible place. Seriously, I'm okay."

They rode in silence after that. Maya tried not to watch the grass getting trampled underneath Chestnut's feet but looked up toward the trees touching the sky. The stars were appearing. They traveled far since that morning.

"How long till we reach Korina?"

"If we don't run into any problems and maintain our current pace, we should be there in about ten days."

"A lot can go wrong in ten days. Do we even have enough food?"

I won't repeat my previous mistake. Tse and I came prepared with enough to get us to Korina. That means all the supplies we gathered before leaving Ithol should cover you, Ryker, and Blackthorn."

"Oh, I won't be needing much," Blackthorn replied.

"What about the elephantuses?"

"They will eat grass along the way, and we brought food for them, too."

"Do you guys use magic to help you ride these giant, furry beasts?"

Ashkii laughed. "Not exactly. Elephantus have excellent noses, which means they can use magic to boost their speed and endurance."

Suddenly, Maya smelled something rotting nearby, and with it she felt emotions, not her own. She felt worry mingled with relief to be getting closer to Agonya. That must be how Ashkii was feeling. She also felt hopeful about the future. Was that how Blackthorn was feeling? Maya didn't have time to ponder it further because Ryker and Tse's emotions of alarm became the dominate feeling. She twisted to look at them, to see what was wrong.

"Faster, Ash," Tse called out. "We've got trouble. I spotted your father's scout in a pine."

In a moment, Ashkii's feelings shifted to hatred, but he quickly refocused on weaving through trees. Maya knew he didn't have a good relationship with his father, but where had the hatred come from?

"Are you all right?" she asked.

Ashkii didn't respond but veered Chestnut toward the river. Maya gasped as the chilly water rushed around her legs. Their progress slowed as the elephantus had to push against the current. Then Ashkii pulled a vial out of his pocket and made a call to Chestnut, who then raised his trunk and smelled the perfume Ashkii offered. Then he tossed it to Tse, and both Elephantuses increased their speed. It was as if the water wasn't there. They truly were magical beasts.

All Maya's questions about how the magic worked had to wait. Her companions' urgency to hide their trail was overwhelming her emotions.

Blackthorn tried to comfort Maya by making his emotions be calm and hopeful. "Thanks," she thought back to him.

"I remember the first time I felt the weight of other people's emotions," he said in her mind. "Practice makes it easier, especially if you can focus on someone who has the emotion you need in the moment."

But even as he spoke, the scent of the rotting animal faded into the distance, allowing Maya to focus on her own emotions again. "Why couldn't I do this a year ago?"

"Ah. My guess is that you could, but you were never smelling death a year ago."

"But I did when the king died, and his soldiers."

"The people around you likely experienced similar emotions."

Maya recalled the day she and Agonya discovered the king, and Blackthorn was right. They had both been horrified and frightened. She wondered how Agonya was feeling now. Was she feeling the same pain as Maya, scared and unsure? Would Chief Golar or the Kors keep them from reaching Agonya? Maya didn't know what would happen, but she hoped whatever they did would be enough.

AGONYA RELAXED HER grip and tried to breathe. Her contraband was tucked in the folds of her dress. She wasn't able to bring much but hoped it would suffice to keep Huren and the other councilors alive. She'd never tried to heal anyone from a distance, but that would not stop her from trying.

Prince Lucas sat next to Agonya right up front, near the square's raised platform. His father, King Reid, sat on his other side. And next to the King was a woman Agonya hadn't seen for many years. She knew her, though. Prince Lucas' mother was beautiful except for the hardness of her face. Agonya imagined it had to do with the reason they were there in the first place, but that was too generous. She was probably annoyed that she had to be there instead of doing whatever it was that she enjoyed.

Agonya tightened her grip on the yellow dress she was forced to wear. Her stomach twisted inside her. This was her punishment. Agonya was going to have to watch her councilors die, just like she hadn't been able to save Velia. She wouldn't be able to do anything to stop these deaths. She was a failure. In her head, she knew she had saved Blackthorn. But how does someone choose to save one person and forfeit the life of another? She had hoped she could save all of them.

No, she couldn't afford to think like that. Her uncle thought to teach her a lesson by making her watch the executions of the only people she'd known to help her in ruling Ithol. Yes, Agonya regretted their deaths. It was horrible, but she didn't intend to let them all die. Her magic wouldn't fail her tonight. And that was a fragrant thought.

Crowds of people gathered behind them. The balconies facing the square were full. Every available place that could be filled was filled. Lord Commander Bannon led the condemned into the square. Agonya was relieved to see that Lord Tanish had indeed gotten away. She hadn't seen him in the throne room, but she couldn't be sure he had escaped until now.

Agonya lowered her hand, which had been clutching her chest without her knowing it. The prince was looking at her. She supposed she was a novelty to him, like a new perfume for him to study. She wasn't sure what to make of him. On the one hand, he had saved her from his father. But there was something else going on. She didn't know what it was. Agonya tightened her lips and focused on her councilors' aromas as they walked by: Lord Commander Huren, Lady Tiva, Sir Marco, Sir Len, Lady Altsoba, Lady Kasa, Lord Sakima, Lord Yiska, and Lady Rebekkah at the end. Nine in all. There were others who'd been on the council, but they either died in battle or had blended in as a commoner. She had arranged that some of them pretend to be normal Itholeans of no importance before the surrender. Thankfulness filled her in that moment, that not everyone who had served her father and then her would be executed this day.

Commander Bannon ordered his soldiers to line up, one to a prisoner. Then he turned towards the king and the people beyond him. "By order of his Majesty, the king of Korina, King Reid Nayavu, I hereby order these enemies of the crown to be executed this night. They were councilors to King Azurarus Nakai and to his daughter, Queen Agonya Nakai of the Itholeans. As such, they will join their king in death, having aided the queen in surrendering falsely."

Bannon ended his speech and held out his sword towards the prisoners. It all happened so fast, Agonya rushed to retrieve her contraband without the watchful eyes of the prince and bring the berries up to her nose. She pretended to be in distress. Her earlier surprise helped with her disguise.

The familiar scents filled her mind and body and, in her haste, Agonya sent a wave of magic toward Lord Commander Huren, who was farthest from her. She squeezed her eyes shut and embraced his fragrance. It was similar to entering other people's minds. Once she was in their bodies, she could sense their wounds and smell the blood flowing from them.

Her magic rushed into his body, and Huren was healed. The soldier who'd pierced him cried out and Commander Bannon stepped up to him. Seeing that Huren lived and did not look like he was going to die, Bannon pushed him on the ground. He raised his sword and moved swiftly. Huren's head rolled onto the cobbled streets.

What had she done? There was no time to focus on that. She had to figure out a way to save at least one of them.

"Oh Princess. Tsk. Tsk. I wouldn't try that again if I were you." Prince Lucas rested his hand on her knee.

She wanted to run, to get as far away from him as she could, but the executions weren't stopping. Commander Bannon was going down the line, pronouncing them dead or cutting off their heads. Agonya re-directed the scent of orinberries and magic towards her dead friends. They were all dead.

All of them. But wait, she could sense a faint heartbeat. Agonya focused harder. It was coming from Lady Rebekkah. But Bannon had pronounced her dead. He said they were all dead. Her eyes widened in disbelief as she witnessed the miraculous opportunity to save one of her counselors. She let her tears flow for Huren and concentrated on repairing Rebekkah's wound.

"Come, walk with me." Prince Lucas rested his hand on her shoulder.

Agonya shook her head and remained as she was. She had to finish the job before it was too late.

"Take your time. I'll wait for you."

Focus. She needed him to leave her alone. Rebekkah lived. Rebekkah stirred on the ground where she lay. Agonya flew into her mind. "Don't move! I have healed you. They think you're dead! I'm sorry I couldn't heal more of you. I'll find a way to save you from the grave. For now, pretend to be dead."

"Your Highness?"

"Yes."

"How are you in my mind?"

"I can't explain. I'm being watched. Just pretend to be dead and I'll save you." Then she opened her eyes and faced her captor. "I'm ready. Thank you for waiting for me to gather myself." Agonya took the hand he offered and let him lead her away from the scents of death.

And yet, the prince was steering her towards Commander Bannon. They weren't leaving the square. "Why aren't we leaving?"

The Prince halted mid-stride. "You must deal with the consequences of your actions."

"But I didn't do anything."

"Oh, but you did. You just didn't succeed."

Before Agonya could respond, they were standing in front of the commander.

Bannon looked up as they approached. "Your Highness! What can I do for you?"

"You are to take Agonya to go bury her precious counselors. I think Huren's head will be light enough for her to carry."

BEFORE PRINCE LUCAS left Agonya in the hands of Lord Commander Bannon, he dug into his cloak and pulled out a perfume bottle. He dabbed it on her wrists and smiled. Agonya held her breath. Perhaps if she didn't breathe it in, it wouldn't affect her.

"Be good now. I expect to see you in the morning. We have much to discuss."

As soon as he walked away, Agonya wiped the perfume off her wrists and breathed. There was still a faint scent of chocolate and citrus in the air, but Agonya reached out to the other scents surrounding her. She didn't need a perfume to smell the fragrant life or rather the scent of the sweaty guards standing next to her. Bannon led her to a cart. As she watched them pile her counselors on to it, Huren's head was suddenly in her arms. She gagged and almost dropped him before she regained her composure. She would bear him to his grave. The prince thought it was a punishment to her, but she did it gladly. Huren deserved no less, and Lady Rebekkah was somewhere on the cart. Maybe Agonya could keep her from being buried alive after all.

The crowds dispersed, the further from the square they went. And any who were there parted on either side of the small group to let them pass unhindered.

All the way to the city gates, Agonya tried to heal her councilors, but healing dead people just wasn't possible. Agonya smelled all their wounds thoroughly. But even though Bannon proclaimed Lady Rebekkah dead when she wasn't, Agonya couldn't find anyone else who had survived even the tiniest bit. Her magic flowed into their cold dead bodies and came right back to her as it had left.

"See what you get for trying to play tricks?" Bannon stepped next to her. "That little stunt of yours didn't help anyone."

He was right, and he was wrong. She hadn't been able to save Huren and if she looked down at him in her arms, she would lose it. But he didn't know about Rebekkah. "How far?" she asked.

"Over that bridge and up that hill and to the left."

That wasn't time to figure out how to help her get away unnoticed. Reaching out to her councilor's mind, she asked, "Lady Rebekkah?"

"Your Highness! I can't move!"

"I'm so sorry! I wish I could get you out of there. I'm still trying to figure out a way for you to not be buried with the others." A fresh wave of tears burst out of her, causing several soldiers to glance at her outburst.

"I know you're doing the best you can, and I am grateful that you saved me, but I don't know if I can stand this much longer. Please hurry!"

Agonya wiped the tears off her face and saw Bannon looking at her. He had a curious expression on his face, as if he knew she had been having a conversation with someone, even though she'd never said a word. Agonya cried out just as he tripped over a root and fell to his knees. She noticed him favoring his good leg and had an idea.

"Are you all right, Commander?"

He straightened and glared at her while the soldiers snickered. "You realize the only reason you're not in that cart is because of me, right?"

"Ha!" Agonya didn't believe that for one second. Reid was more than willing to kill her, even if it killed his lord commander.

"You're laughing?"

"Don't you know why we're both not in that cart?"

"What are you talking about?"

"I'm talking about the fact that your king doesn't give a sniff whether you live or die. He was inclined to kill us both if it hadn't been for the crown prince."

"You've piqued my interest. What does Prince Lucas have to do with us?"

"He saved my life, decided he wanted me to be a part of his household, and by extension, he saved your life."

"He always was going after the beautiful fragrant women." Bannon shook his head.

Agonya wasn't sure how to reply to that. Did that mean her cousin wanted her as a fragrant woman? That was absurd. But what other role was she to have in his household?

"I'm going to be sick." Agonya thrust Huren's head out in front of her and threw up between her outstretched arms. She groaned. Some of it had splattered on her arms and dress.

"You'd better not do that in his presence," Bannon said. "If you don't please the prince well, he may decide you aren't worth it and kill us both."

"I could displease the prince."

Bannon glared at her then. "Do you care so little about your life?"

"Or," Agonya went on, "you can help me."

"What do you want from me? I can't help you with your duties."

"Not with those. Here. Now. I need your help, and you can help me."

"Go on."

"First, you must promise not to tell anyone else what I'm about to tell you."

"Fine. I promise."

Then Agonya reached out to his mind, not daring to risk the other soldiers hearing what she was going to say. "Lord Commander, I healed Lady Rebekkah and now I need your help to not bury her alive. It's her life or yours."

Bannon stopped in his tracks. "What is this scent? How are you speaking in my mind?" he thought back.

"It's part of what I can do. Are you going to help me or not?"

"But how could you have healed her? I made sure they were all dead, especially after you tried to heal your little commander."

"Yes, that was a mistake. But after you pronounced her dead. I checked, and she wasn't, so I healed her."

Bannon left Agonya's side and drew near the cart up ahead of them.

"How's that ankle?" Agonya prodded.

Bannon glanced back at her and spit on the ground. In her mind he said, "I will think about how to not bury your councilor, but don't expect me to be your servant. I will find a way to not be dependent on you and when I do, I will not be so accommodating."

Agonya turned with the others into the field marked by a wooden gate between two posts, with a carved falcon resting on top. They walked a little further until they came to an empty patch large enough for ten bodies. A soldier started handing out shovels. Agonya set Huren's head gingerly on the grass and then took one for herself. She was the first to dig.

The soldiers scoffed at her, giving her more strength to dig. She hadn't noticed their conversations on the way because she'd been so self-absorbed and talking with Bannon. But now that the digging had begun, their crass words made their way to Agonya's ears, deepening the wound that already ached in her chest.

Agonya shoved her spade into the ground with all her might and pried it back. The dirt and weeds tumbled to either side of her spade. She had to scoop it back on the shovel to move it aside. Then she did it all over again.

With each shovel-full, Agonya thought of the fallen men and women they were about to bury, singing a funeral song as she worked.

Finally, the hole was big enough for ten bodies to fit inside. One by one, the soldiers swung the Itholeans by their hands and feet into the ground. Agonya tried to be gentle with the heads that had been severed. Huren's was the last one she placed in the grave. She stood back and watched them finish. Thanks to Bannon's directions, Lady Rebekkah was the last one in.

"Lord Commander?" Agonya wiped the hair off her sweaty face. "May I have a moment alone with them before we cover them up?"

"I don't see why not. Dylan, what do you say?"

The prince had appointed Dylan to monitor Agonya, so he had come with them when Lucas had ordered Agonya to carry Huren's head. He shrugged his shoulders. "We'll wait by the gate."

"All right, men. You all deserve a break, anyway."

A chorus of agreement followed, and the men left their shovels and Agonya by the graveside. Agonya spoke to Lady Rebekkah in her mind and knelt on the ground. "They've got their backs turned."

And just to make sure, Agonya glanced back at the group fifty paces away. They were all talking among themselves. She couldn't see anyone watching.

"Words can't express my gratitude, your Highness!" Then Lady Rebekkah crawled out of the grave. She didn't dare stand up, in case it drew attention, but kept close to the ground, almost slithering her way to a copse of trees not too far away.

Agonya stood and started shoveling dirt back into place. "I couldn't have done it without Commander Bannon's help. I'm sure if you need it, he will help you find shelter and food. I'm afraid we won't cross paths for a very long time to come, if at all. May the god of Jedrek guide your path."

"And yours as well."

Agonya could no longer see Lady Rebekkah. The trees covered her and just in time. Some of the soldiers, seeing Agonya shoveling dirt, came and joined in.

She hadn't been able to say the proper words for a burial. She didn't have the proper scents either, so she did her best to imagine she could dump a bucket of excrement on the grave, followed by the cleansing peppermint. "May we find healing, even though these men and women can't," she thought to Lady Rebekkah.

"We will heal," Lady Rebekkah echoed Agonya's words.

Chapter 12

Agonya woke with her heart pounding in her chest. She'd dreamed that Lady Rebekkah had been caught, and she had been forced to watch her get her head cut off. Blood was everywhere. Heads severed from bodies. Agonya pinched her nose and pushed herself out of the tangle of sheets. That bed was a curse.

Breathing deeply, Agonya calmed herself with the scents in the room, the oak door, the cedar posts, the dirt and blood... Her heart raced, and she had to start over, focusing on the more comforting cedar smell of her bed. Agonya walked to the window, pulled back the curtains, and opened the shutters. Moonlight streamed into her room. It wouldn't be much longer before the moon set and the sun rose in its place. Until she would be summoned to the Crown Prince. But the darkness hadn't lifted yet.

Agonya turned away from the window and sat in her mother's old chair. Yesterday she was ready to fight, to resist her captors, but today she felt like curling up into a ball and hiding from everything. Why couldn't she have died like her mother had, protecting people? Agonya couldn't help but feel like a failure. She knew Lady Rebekkah was still out there somewhere, that she hadn't really died, but so many others had. And now, according to Bannon, all that awaited her was to be a fragrant woman for her cousin. There had to be something she could do to resist her captors. She wasn't paralyzed anymore, and she didn't want to go back to being the spoiled brat she was before her father died.

Uncurling herself, Agonya walked along the edges of the room. She ran her hand along the smooth walls until she came to the painting. Her mother looked so young and vibrant in the picture and yet, even then, her mother's eyes told a different story. There was a burden on her shoulders, but what burden did her mother have back then? Agonya thought her mother hadn't been introduced to Blackthorn until after she'd married Agonya's father.

As Agonya stared at the painting, she noticed it didn't lie completely flush against the wall. There had to be a compartment behind it, like the one in her father's chambers. Agonya slid her hand between the painting and the wall and felt around it. Her fingers found a small book and pulled it out.

Replacing the painting, Agonya took the book over to the armchair. She lit a candle and opened the dusty book. The first page read: "On the eighth day of the second month, in the thirty-first year of King Lucio, I, Princess Kanti, found the true contract."

What contract? Was this the cause of her mother's burdens? She turned the page.

Kanti's elegant script continued. "It all started about a week ago. I suppose I ought to start at the beginning. I woke up on the first, to the promise of finally meeting my betrothed, Prince Azurarus. I wasn't disappointed. He arrived an hour after the midday meal with his entourage. I watched them approach the palace from my bedroom window. When they got close enough for me to see their individual faces, I dashed downstairs to greet him properly."

Agonya paused in her reading. Oh, that contract: her parents' first meeting. It all sounded wonderful, as if her mother didn't have a care in the world. She'd heard the story from her father. So, hearing her mother's side of it was very fascinating. Agonya kept reading. She wanted to sit on her mother's lap and hear her voice, but this journal would have to suffice.

A knock sounded, waking Agonya with a start. She looked around, trying to get oriented. Her mother's journal lay on the floor. It must have slipped out of her hands while she slept. There was another knock.

Agonya rushed to return the book behind the portrait and not a moment too soon.

The same servant from the day before, the prince, had called her Tara, entered before Agonya could compose herself.

"His Royal Highness is waiting."

Agonya glanced down at her nightgown and blushed.

"Come on, let's get you dressed." Tara pushed open the wardrobe and grabbed the first dress her hand touched.

Agonya took the forest green dress and slid it on. It fit perfectly. Agonya quickly brushed her hair, then followed Tara through the palace hallways, but not the way she expected. Tara led her out of the palace to a courtyard where Prince Lucas stood talking to a stable hand.

They waited in silence until he was done.

Prince Lucas dismissed the boy and turned towards them. "Great! You're here." He welcomed them with a smile. "Thank you, Tara. You may go."

She curtsied and went back inside the palace, leaving Agonya alone with the prince.

"Walk with me. We have a busy day ahead of us," he said.

Agonya tensed. The last time he asked her to walk with him, he forced her to carry Huren's head.

"No need to be afraid. Yesterday was yesterday. Today is a brand-new day."

Was that supposed to make her feel better? He may not be holding a grudge to her defiance yesterday, but that didn't mean he wouldn't make her do other terrible things. "Where are we going?" she asked.

"I have a few errands to attend to around town, and then we're going to visit a friend of mine."

Agonya forced a smile. She didn't want to take this man's arm, but he held it out and waited for her to take it. When they left the palace grounds, a contingent of soldiers walked in front of them, keeping the people on the streets from getting too close.

"Tell me about this person you want me to meet."

Prince Lucas smiled. "I wouldn't want to spoil the surprise. No, that wouldn't be any fun." He patted her hand as they walked. "Tell me, what do you miss most about home?"

Agonya didn't answer. Had she heard him correctly? Why was he pretending to care about her? The very touch of his hand on hers made her want to run as far from him as she could. There was no way she was going to let him know her weaknesses. They were enemies.

"Go on. I hardly know anything about you, except you're exceptionally beautiful and you smell wonderful, too." Prince Lucas raised Agonya's hand to his nose.

Agonya felt the blood rushing to her cheeks. And not from impropriety, but contempt. It appeared she would have to tell him something to satisfy him. "I miss my father most." Agonya swallowed the sudden lump in her throat. Of all the things she could have told him, why did she tell him that?

"How did he die?" he asked. Then, seeing the look on her face, he quickly added, "Sorry. I knew he died, but it wasn't in battle, was it?"

"No, not in battle. An assassin."

"I heard you were attacked on the way here, but it slipped my mind until now." Prince Lucas motioned to one of the guards ahead of them. "Keep a look out for an assassin."

The guard nodded and scanned the surrounding roofs, then went to inform the other guards of the new danger.

The prince back-tracked fast. "Don't worry. You're safe. They'll sniff out an assassin before he can get within a hundred meters of us."

Agonya appreciated his concern. Apparently, her slip of the tongue wasn't all bad. Not only had he been alerted to the potential assassin, which she had forgotten about amid all the trauma of the last few days, but Prince Lucas also let her be.

She barely noticed their surroundings. Between the memory of her father's funeral and her friend trying to kill her, Agonya didn't trust herself to talk without losing her composure. She didn't dare remember when she found her father dead in his chambers. It was his resting place she pictured in her mind, among the ylang-ylang trees, next to her mother. And thinking about Ashkii... It couldn't have been him. She thought he'd changed. She'd read his mind after his first betrayal, but this was too much. They could never return to the way things were.

She followed her new tormentor through the winding streets, stopping occasionally for whatever it was the prince needed or wanted. Then, chaos broke out in the streets in front of them. Agonya heard shouting and saw fists flying. Prince Lucas halted in his tracks as his guards surrounded him.

"Don't stay here. Go stop those men," he ordered the guards. Prince Lucas turned to Agonya and whispered, "I'm so sorry. This isn't what I had in mind at all. It'll only be a moment before everything is back in order."

Everything back in order? Before Agonya could ponder this more, the guards stood between several men. About half of them looked Itholean, the half that was bloodied up and filthy. Was this how her people were being treated? But the guards were gentle with them.

Prince Lucas left Agonya's side and went to talk with the Korin masters. "What seems to be the problem?"

Agonya saw the masters lower their heads in submission to their prince.

"Speak! I asked you a question."

"We're sorry, your Highness, you had to witness this."

"I'm sure you are." Prince Lucas glared at them.

"These slaves you've blessed us with failed to do their simple chores. We need to show them their place, your Highness."

"I see." The prince rubbed his chin and turned to one of the Itholean slaves, a strong, healthy worker. "And what do you have to say about this?"

"Your Highness, please forgive us for our mistakes. It won't happen again."

"And what exactly were these mistakes of yours?"

The Itholean bowed lower before responding. "Your Highness, we assumed our work of loading and unloading our master's commodities was done, but it wasn't. We missed a whole cart load."

"An honest mistake." The prince looked at the masters. "I'm sure..."

"We forgive them for their offense, your Highness."

"There. All is forgiven." Turning to the slaves, Prince Lucas addressed them. "Do not treat their forgiveness lightly. You have been given a second chance, but it does not guarantee anymore."

The slaves mumbled their acknowledgment and various words of loyalty about not being lazy.

To the masters, he said, "Next time, we have a system set up to deal with rebellion. Use it."

The masters bowed. "Yes, your Highness."

Prince Lucas walked back to Agonya. "Shall we continue?"

"If that is your desire, your Highness." At that moment, Agonya felt like she was one of those Itholeans. And she was, even if she wasn't being treated like them. She hadn't thought specifically about her people that had come to Ithol with her, except her councilors, since the night she tried to escape the jojoba encampment.

"Please, call me Lucas. We're family."

"Erm, Lucas, would you mind if we returned to the palace? I'm not feeling too well."

"We're almost there. And I'll make sure the trip back to the palace is quicker when we go." Then he called one of the guards over. "Fetch a double palanquin."

Agonya went with the prince down a few more streets. Why did she think he would do anything different?

They arrived at a river that led out of the city. A large arch crossed over it at the wall, a bridge for the soldiers. There were two large wooden doors under the bridge that stayed shut, only opening for the occasional trader or merchant boat. Most merchants came by land. The prince and Agonya were on the land and there was no need for those gates to open. They walked up to the wall. The prince talked to a few guards, and then led her through the much smaller door.

"I thought you said we were almost there."

"We are. Come on."

The other side of the city wall was quiet except for the soothing sound of the water rushing by. There was a small path that weaved in and out of trees along the river. They followed it all the way to the confluence with Dead-end Creek. Then he took her off the path to follow the smaller of the two rivers. "We made it." Prince Lucas gestured to a large waterfall at the end of the creek. "This is the Churning Vapors Waterfall."

It was beautiful and all, but Agonya was baffled as to why he would bring her out here.

The prince motioned for his guards to stay, and then he grabbed Agonya's hand and pulled her all the way up to the falling water. The water misted and roared in her ears. She was dismayed when he kept pulling her towards the water, but then a cave appeared directly behind the waterfall. It wasn't visible until they were right up next to it.

Agonya couldn't see very far into the cave. It was too dark, but soon, Prince Lucas had a torch lit. In moments, torches all along the walls held flames. And Agonya was able to see the large cavern that opened up to them. All at once, she was amazed by the magic and horrified at what she saw.

Kindroot after Kindroot lined the walls in glass boxes. This must be Dana's stronghold. The shock of it froze Agonya in place. Prince Lucas had taken her directly to Dana. She tried to see into the recesses of the cave, but there was no sign of the woman. She heard the prince calling to her but stayed where she was. The next thing she knew, he was waving a bottle under her nose, and she was breathing in an unfamiliar scent. Whatever it was shook her out of her stupor. She felt confident and ready for whatever was to come. Agonya followed the prince deeper into the cave. There were so many Kindroots. This was Blackthorn's family. They were all caged. Was this his fate? None of them showed signs they saw Agonya enter the room. Only those nearest to Prince Lucas cowered in the corners of their little boxes.

"Please, come in, Agonya. Sit with me and we'll talk while we wait for our host to return." Lucas sat on an upturned log, patted the log next to him, and waited for Agonya to sit.

"I can't," Agonya replied, "not while these Kindroots are trapped."

"But you must know that only Dana can set them free. So, we might as well be comfortable while we wait for her."

Agonya couldn't believe what she was hearing. Did he honestly think she could hold a conversation in her enemies' lair and wait patiently for Dana to come back and enslave or kill her?

"But I insist." The prince stood up, slipped his dagger from its sheath, and pressed the tip of it into her back. "Sit."

Where had the knife come from? Agonya tried not to look too hard at the Kindroots she passed. She had to have a clear mind. But a small pile of branches caught her eye on the floor behind Lucas as she sat down. She didn't have to ask to know that they were dead Kindroots. Agonya did her best to swallow her bile and pretend she hadn't seen.

"Now, why don't you tell me where our other little friend is hiding."

"I don't know."

The prince smiled knowingly. "You can at least tell me where you parted ways. We know you didn't give him to us. I mean, what was last night all about, anyway? And we know you don't have him with you. I've heard what you've gone through to get that point across. So where and when did you part ways with your little Kindroot friend?"

Agonya hated him. He was so manipulative and smelled sweet, but underneath Prince Lucas' actions was a stink that he would never be able to wipe off. How long could she appease him without telling him what he wanted to know?

"I know that look. You're trying to invent a story, but I want the truth, and really, you want me to know the truth, too."

Agonya raised her eyebrows.

"Of course, telling me the truth means that you won't have to tell Dana the truth."

Agonya swallowed. He wanted to know where she had parted ways. She could tell him. "He was taken from me before I even returned to Ithol."

"Ooh!" the prince leaned forward. "This ought to be good. Who took him?"

"The Montanes took him from me. You really should be asking them, not me, where he is."

"I know this story! Dana told me all about it. After they took him from you, then you took him back!"

Agonya groaned inwardly. "Did she tell you the part about her trying to kill me?"

"I'm sure it wasn't personal."

"It wasn't personal?! Do you even hear yourself? Why are you defending her?"

Lucas raised his hands. "No need to get feisty. She didn't kill you, did she?"

"No but look behind you." Agonya pointed to the pile of Kindroots on the cave floor. "What do you call that?"

"I call that trying to save the world."

"For whom?"

Lucas started to reply when a raven flew into the cave and landed on his shoulder. He reached up, patted the bird's slick black feathers, and untied the note attached to its leg. "Alas, we came all this way only for something to come up and cause us to reschedule. Unfortunately, our host won't be able to join us today."

Agonya felt the relief wash through her body. She didn't have to confront Dana today. On the way back to the palace, Agonya recalled the day's events. It wasn't a complete loss. Dana not showing up was a blessing. Now, Agonya knew where Blackthorn's family was being kept and how they were being

143

kept. Now she had to find a way to rescue them. She also knew that it wasn't just her uncle in league with Dana, but her cousin absolutely belonged to Dana.

SEVERAL DAYS OF RIDING Chestnut nonstop, constantly looking over their shoulders, had them all on edge. So, when Ashkii suggested they take a break. Everyone agreed. They would remain on the alert, but they all needed to rest. Ashkii immediately went to the river. Tse gathered firewood so they could cook some of the roots his mother packed for them. Maya and Ryker went off somewhere, talking, under the guise of looking for berries. It was the wrong time of year for berries, not to mention the state of all the plants they passed. Ashkii couldn't help wishing it was him and Agonya going for a walk in the woods. Sighing, he dipped under the water's surface, as if it would wash away all his concerns for Agonya's safety, for their own safety. When he came up for air, he heard a strangled cry.

Was that Tse? Ashkii began to swim to shore. Halfway back he heard it again. This time, he knew it was Tse. It sounded urgent. Something wasn't right.

Ashkii dove for the shore, grabbed his atl and bag of bombs. Tse couldn't be too far. Ashkii dashed off in the direction he'd heard Tse's voice. Just beyond the small ridge, he saw him.

Tse was jerking about, swatting his body. It was the strangest thing Ashkii had seen him do.

"Tse?"

"Ash! They're all over! Watch o—" Tse's mouth shut tight, and his hand flew to his face. Yet it didn't touch his face. It landed on... What was that? A small creature blended in with Tse's pale face. Its quick movement caught Ashkii's eye. Soon they were all Ashkii could see. Hundreds of them flocked to Tse and now to Ashkii, too.

"Come on, Tse! We have to run!" Ashkii leaped to his friend's side, whacked creatures off with his atl and gave his friend a push back the way he came.

Ten of the little scaly creatures clung to Ashkii's bare skin. Their claws dug in deep. He had to think! Ashkii yanked them off as he ran, then he reached for a bomb. How could he possibly think straight enough to get it to work? The large spade-like leaf wrapped around Kylie's famous powder mixture that, when stimulated by their magic, caused everything to go to sleep. If he didn't figure out how to not breathe it in himself while being chased by invisible creatures, he'd fall asleep among them, normally he would use his cloak to cover his nose and mouth, but they were hanging on a bush near the river.

Tse jumped into a pine tree, but the creatures scurried right up after him. "Brilliant, Tse!" Ashkii jumped into a nearby oak, imitating his friend. He grabbed several leaves and leaped up to the next branch. Then he closed his eyes and activated the bomb. He threw it down at the hordes of creatures following them and covered his own mouth and nose with the leaves he'd grabbed.

The odor bomb slowed them down, but they didn't go to sleep! Ashkii turned to see Tse jumping from tree to tree. He was almost to his elephantus, still packed from their traveling. Ashkii followed Tse absentmindedly. He couldn't figure out why the bomb didn't work. What were these things chasing them?

The large elephantuses didn't have any creatures on them yet, but they felt their masters' fear and stomped the ground. Ashkii flew onto Chestnut and was about to retrieve his clothes when something flew past him. Ashkii turned to see what it was. Water burst into the air, spraying the creatures. They made a deep guttural sound in their throats and zipped away faster than they had been chasing them.

"The water, Tse! Into the water!" Ashkii swiped his clothes off the tree branches and galloped into the river. Chestnut wasn't fond of the water himself but obeyed without reserve. Soon the water reached Chestnut's shoulders, but there was no need to swim, so Ashkii didn't dismount. There was a chance that more invisible creatures were on the other side.

All the time they were crossing, these strange water bombs soared over their heads, stopping the full out attack. Now Ashkii looked in earnest for their savior. Indeed, none of these vicious creatures could be seen on the far bank. Ashkii's eyes meticulously scanned up and back away from the bank. Was that? Surely not!

Ashkii urged Chestnut up and out of the river and kept riding. He didn't wait to see if Tse made it across.

"Krillin? Is that you? I thought you were with the queen."

The taller man, now even skinnier, rose from behind his boulder. "Ashkii. I should shoot you again."

"What did I do this time? In my defense, last time I had no clue who you were or who you were working for. I was only defending the queen. But tell me, how did you become separated from her? I had hoped you were still with her, protecting her." Ashkii's scar on his hand started to ache the way Krillin was looking at him, as if he really would stick another arrow in it.

"Get dressed." Krillin turned to leave.

Ashkii slipped his shirt on while he spoke. "Wait! Where are you going?"

Krillin didn't turn to face Ashkii, but stopped walking away from him, ready to leave at any moment. "You're a Montane, aren't you?"

"What about it?" Ashkii straightened his pants before sliding down from his perch. It'd be easier to put them on standing up than sitting on Chestnut.

"You killed Jerky." Krillin spat on the ground and started walking away again.

"I didn't kill Jerky! I would have stopped my father's men if I could have. My people have done a great many things I wish they had not." Ashkii noticed Krillin hesitate in his movements. So, he kept talking, "I was bound and gagged, and had several guards pointing their spears and daggers at me. I have been their prisoner ever since. It wasn't until a week ago that I was able to escape."

"That doesn't make me like you. The last I saw you, your friends were open firing upon us as we fled into a tunnel." Krillin's eyes narrowed as he looked past Ashkii.

Ash spun around. He let his shoulders sag: it was just Tse. "Look, Krill, they shouldn't have killed your horvelina. They were following orders. Given the option, I would have been there to help protect Jerky and assist you in the tunnels."

"Ash, have you seen the others?" Tse said as he walked up behind them.

Ashkii's heart skipped a beat. Maya! "Where did you see them last?"

Tse frowned. "They went that way," he said, pointing away from the river.

"Who are you talking about?" Krillin turned back toward the river.

"You remember Maya, right?"

"Yes."

Before Ashkii could say any more, Krillin was running. Spotting a pile of skins nearby, Ashkii guessed they contained water. He swiftly gathered as many as he could and jumped back across the river. "Stay with the animals, Tse."

Ashkii was much quicker than Krillin as he leaped from tree to tree. "Maya! Ryker! Where are you?" he called out. How could he have forgotten about them? Despite his vow to avoid past mistakes, here he was, saving his own skin instead of helping his friends in need. "Maya!" he called again.

Blackthorn's voice sounded in his head. "We're over here." And then Blackthorn sent him an image of Maya and Ryker fighting off the creatures. Ashkii glanced around for anything that might give him a clue.

"That way!" he called out to Krillin. Then he bounded off towards what he thought looked like the right trees.

Blackthorn sent him another image of a small clearing. Ashkii could see it now. He searched briefly for the creatures and noticed them climbing his tree. He leaped to the next tree and kept going till he could see Maya and Ryker in the clearing. As quickly as he could, he pelted a water skin towards the couple. It burst on the ground in front of them. The creatures scattered. Ryker looked up and saw Ash in the tree.

"Quick, come over here and I'll lift you up out of reach," Ashkii called down to them. Ashkii started throwing water skins in a path towards himself, clearing the way.

Soon water skins were coming from the ground as well. Ashkii jumped down, grabbed Maya, checked for creatures, then leaped into an untouched tree. As quickly as he could he went back for Ryker and then Krillin.

"What now?" Krillin asked. "I can't jump from tree to tree. The cheemas are already halfway up this tree. You can't jump all of us from tree to tree quick enough."

"Cheemas?" Ashkii shook his head. He had to focus. "I can set you back on the ground and you can run back."

"Yes, Ryker should join me, and you can carry Maya between trees."

That was good. He swiftly jumped Maya to a new tree and returned for the rest. He grabbed Ryker first and took him to a spot on the ground that wasn't moving, then went back for Krillin.

Chapter 13

The river was a welcome scent, though not as much as Maya's rosemary, honeysuckle, and fir. As soon as they were all together, Krillin slung his bow across his back and tightened the straps to his bag. He still couldn't believe she was alive! He hadn't killed her after all. Scents! He had just saved her from the cheemas. Well, the Montane helped, but Krillin couldn't believe he could start rectifying the wrong he had done to her. Would she forgive him? Turning to face her, he saw her staring at him. Her scarred face was proof of his evil deeds. He thought he'd killed her when he tied her up to that tree. They'd buried her. But even as he remembered, he realized he hadn't seen her body. He had smelled her scent and seen her hair. That explained her shorter hair now. If he could repay his debt, he wanted to; he needed to. Falling on his knees, the words flowed out like an uncorked bottle of perfume.

"Forgive me, Maya. I don't know how you are still alive after what I did to you, but you have to know I never intended for you to die or to get hurt! I hope that my aide today shows how sincere I am. I owe you my life."

Then the petite woman surprised him. She walked forward and lifted his chin until his eyes met hers and she smelifed first one cheek, then the other. "Krillin, your scent is most pleasant to me. I forgive you."

How was it possible? A large lump formed in the back of his throat, and he couldn't swallow until the tears let loose. He didn't know how to stop them. He knew they were all staring at him as if he were mad, but never had he imagined she would forgive him.

"Truly, it's all right. I'm all right," she said.

Krillin breathed deeply to steady his emotions. When he blinked away the tears clouding his sight, he was met with her beautiful smile. He almost started crying again. "I don't know what to say. I don't deserve to smell your fragrance or for you to smell mine. Yours is so much better than mine."

"Stop," she said. "What exactly are you sorry for?"

"For tying you up and letting that creature attack you and give you those scars."

Maya paused and then started laughing.

"Why are you laughing? I'm so sorry that drank did that to you but also for betraying you, tying you up to that tree."

"Oh, I know," she said through tears. "But the drank that 'killed' me wasn't real. That's why I'm laughing. I'm sorry. I shouldn't have laughed. Agonya and I knew you were a traitor, along with almost everyone else who was with us, so we came up with a way for me to spy on you all. It was challenging work tricking you into thinking I was dead. Your sense of smell is amazing!"

Understanding came to Krillin. He had smelled her, not just her lingering scent on her belongings. Relief washed over him. He hadn't caused those scars. But then who or what had? All the relief he'd felt a moment ago disappeared. "But I left the princess when she needed me the most."

"And why did you do that?"

"I heard a child crying and went to investigate."

"So that's why you left," Ashkii chimed in.

Krillin stood up. He had to come completely clean, or any forgiveness he received wouldn't count. "I was also deserting the army. But like Maya said, I was already a traitor. My orders from the Kors were to get the package and kill or capture the princess if I had to and at that point, I didn't want to have anything more to do with the Kors. I am terribly sorry for not coming back to help the princess, Maya."

"I know why you did what you did, and why you stopped working for the Kors. It is enough." Maya slumped briefly, but Krillin saw it.

Why was he still blubbering? "Let me make it up to you. Come, rest with us for as long as you need. Though we do not have much, we do have shelter and food."

Ashkii grabbed Chestnut's reins and followed. "Your scent is most welcome, Krillin. We are in your debt. Thanks for helping us back there. What are those things, anyway?"

"Anya calls them cheemas, but I don't know what their actual name is. They're about as tasty as a rat. They won't bother you on this side of the river, though." Krillin pulled himself up the side of a large boulder in the ground.

Ashkii and Tse tucked in their reins so they wouldn't snag on anything while the elephantuses grazed on the almost bare forest floor. Ashkii patted Chestnut. "Guess you can't come where we're going."

The Montane's words were a punch to his gut. Krillin was glad he was the first one up the boulder, out of sight from the others, so they couldn't see his reaction. It wasn't fair that the Montane got to enjoy the company of his elephantus when the Montanes had killed his horvelina, but maybe he deserved it.

Krillin looked around, hoping to see Anya running to greet him. Her scent always calmed him. But she was nowhere to be seen. Probably off somewhere with Amber picking flowers. He sighed and headed home.

"We've got guests, Mother." Krillin leaned his bag against the cave wall, then he removed his bow from his shoulders. "This is Maya, Ashkii, Tse and..."

"Ryker," their companion said, stepping forward and offering his hand for a smelif.

Sari rose from her mat and smelled his hand. "Welcome to our humble home. Please smell the air and be at ease."

After introductions, Sari asked, "Did you bring back food?"

Krillin reached into his bag and pulled out several small fish and a few cheemas he'd snagged on the return journey.

"Excellent. I'll go get our meal started." Sari took the offering and went outside.

Despite Sari's invitation, Ashkii and Tse remained standing in the mouth of the cave after she left. Krillin ignored them and sat next to Maya and Ryker, hoping to find out more about how she survived. He was about to ask her when Ashkii sat between them.

"Look, Krillin, I know you don't like us. I am sorry about Jerky. But our meeting you again, here in the middle of nowhere, is a sign."

"I don't believe in signs." It was true enough, at least what Ashkii meant by signs. But in the back of his mind, Krillin remembered Ogi's friend. He had prophesied this outcome.

"We're trying to reach the queen before it is too late."

"Too late? I think you are already too late. We were too late to save Ithol. We were too late to do anything properly. We are too late to change anything."

"That's just it. My—the Montanes have sent an assassin to kill Queen Agonya. I cannot let that happen."

Krillin turned toward Ashkii to take a good look at the little white man deceiving himself. "She made her choice when she surrendered. She will not live even if you stop this assassin."

"You talked of being sorry about not going back to help her after you got Amber to safety. Now's your chance to prove it. Come help us help her."

"I am sorry that she was captured, and I understand she's still in danger, but what makes you think we will get there in time to be of any use?"

Maya spoke up. "Don't ask me how I know, but I know she is well guarded, being a captive and all, and I think whatever assassin may be after her will have a tough time getting access to her. We have a decent shot at getting there in time."

"Fair enough. I'm tired of the games. I have a family to look after. My Mother. My sister, Anya. And now, Amber, my friend. I will not abandon them again." Why was he explaining himself to this man? He didn't even like him. Krillin was free now, to go where he wished, to serve only those whom he wanted to serve.

Then the smellier Montane spoke. "It is not just the queen's life at stake. I know nothing of your past, but I know the reason I am helping Ashkii is that the Montanes are wrong about the Kindroots, about Queen Agonya. I will do everything in my power to stop Dana. If she is not stopped, more creatures like these cheemas will come. These plants will continue to suffer. Did you see the health of those fish you caught? They were too small already. We would be grateful for your help, but you must do what you must do."

"You sound very much like Aekan. He said the Kors would bring paradise back."

Maya flinched and pulled back into Ryker's arms.

"If you think a man like Aekan can bring back Paradise, then I don't want you to join us," Ashkii said.

"I didn't say I thought he could bring back Paradise, only that he claimed he would, just like you are claiming something fantastical." Maya seemed to retreat further and further the more they spoke. "Maya, what's wrong?"

The small, fragrant woman pulled back and didn't answer.

Ryker spoke for her. "Aekan was the one who gave her these scars. He tortured her while she was protecting what Queen Agonya was protecting."

Krillin hissed. He should have killed Aekan when he had the chance, before he had poisoned the wells, and then when he returned to Ithol and found Aekan's henchmen holding his family hostage. But he had only been focused on getting his family to safety. "I'm sorry, Maya. Aekan is an evil man. I should have stopped him, instead I helped him. It is all my fault."

"No. Krillin, you are not responsible for Aekan's actions no more than Ryker or Ashkii are. I have already forgiven you for your actions. Don't carry the weight of other people's evil deeds. But if you are sorry for what you did, for what you didn't do, help us."

"Is that the price of my forgiveness, then?" Krillin knew it was too good to be true. There was always a price.

"My forgiveness is free. But what will it take for you to forgive yourself?"

"I may never forgive myself. It seems like whatever I do leads to more harm. Besides, there is so much evil in the world. Even if we rescue the queen, it won't stop people from doing more evil."

"No, it won't. But shouldn't we try to make the world a better place to live?" Maya's scarred face stared back at him.

"What makes you think you are doing good by doing this? What one person thinks is good is bad for another."

"It doesn't matter what we think or don't think. There are basic truths that don't change. It is good to love people. It is bad to kill them. It is good to find justice. It is not so good to seek revenge. I don't think we can prove absolutely that everything we're doing is the right thing, but we have witnessed the injustices that Dana and Aekan have done and want to fight against that. Surely, that is the right thing to do."

"Tell me about these injustices."

"First, she took control of our minds to make us kill the queen. But if that isn't enough, we have been working with Dana since, well, since long before I was born." Ashkii grimaced. "From what I know, the Montanes, the very

153

first Montanes, broke away from Ithol when Dana did. They believed she was right about the Kindroots. We came over the Acrid Mountains with Jedrek, the first king of Ithol."

Krillin couldn't believe his ears. "Wait. You're telling me the Dana that took control of our minds in the meadow is the same Dana that started this war? I can't smell it."

Both Montanes nodded. "The very same."

"But how is it even possible that she is the Dana from over a thousand years ago?" Krillin straightened. He needed to pay close attention to make sure he followed their facial expressions to catch any hint of a lie.

Tse nodded to Ashkii, who continued the story. "Dana is still alive today because she uses the Kindroots' powers, or rather steals it—"

Krillin cleared his throat. "Kindroots are a myth."

"And so was using magic to infiltrate our minds," Ashkii countered.

He had a point. Krillin would have to investigate this further.

Ashkii took a deep breath and continued. "The Kindroots made a covenant, a contract, with Jedrek the first and all his people. No one except the Kindroots and Dana remember what it said. But Dana claims the Kindroots broke the contract, and we, the Montanes, agreed with her, at the time anyway. At one point in our history, we stopped helping Dana. Some thought she was the one who broke the contract. But as the years passed by, and the distance between us and Dana grew, we became vulnerable again to her deceptions. There were no Kindroots protecting the land. The dranks and horvelinas, and other animals from the Acrid Mountains, came down and attacked our villages. I imagine these "cheemas," as you call them, are also a result of the broken covenant. So, the next time Dana came to us in our homes and promised to protect us, we joined forces with her again."

"And now, she hasn't kept her word, and you are going to work against her." Krillin finished the story for him. Yes, he could see that. It was obvious, looking at the cheemas here this far down the mountain. "But why aren't the Montanes trying to stop her? Why just you two?"

"We aren't the only ones, but you're right. My father, Chief Golar, and the other chiefs are afraid of Dana. You saw what she did to your people."

Krillin cringed. He still didn't like to be associated with the Itholeans, so he returned to his previous question. "And you're sure this is the same Dana that lived in the time of Jedrek the first?" Krillin wondered how many wrinkles she must have if it were even true.

"That's what I've been told. The day she walked into camp to convince us to work with her, she was radiant. That's what Kylie says, anyway. Dana uses her olfamancy to heal herself, to extend her life." Then Ashkii took his shirt off and turned so that Krillin could see his back. "Do you see any scars on my back?"

"No." What was the point in showing his back to Krillin when there was nothing to show?

"There should be. Before we arrived in Tafka, before we met you on the road, we ran into a pack of dranks. They sprayed both my friend Brynn and I with their acid. Neither of us could walk, let alone stand up. Until the queen healed us. She did it at her own detriment, too. I'm not sure how it works, but it seems to require some sort of energy to heal. The queen drew on her own energy to heal us, which reduced her own ability to walk. She went unconscious healing us."

"Is that true?" Krillin asked Maya. "If it is, why do you have scars on your face?"

"It is true," Maya admitted. "The scars came after the queen was exiled."

Laughter floated into the cave, bouncing off the walls. They were so intent on their conversation, all of them jumped as Anya chased Amber into the cave. "Tag! You're it!"

"No fair! The cave is safe," Amber retorted before seeing their guests. Amber's eyes narrowed as she took in the newcomers. "Who are they?" She pointed at them as if they shouldn't have been there.

"Amber, these are our friends, Maya, Ryker, Ashkii and Tse."

"Are they Montanes?" Anya squeezed her hands together at the mere prospect of getting to meet a real live Montane.

"Yes, and they are sitting right here, sister. You can try asking them yourself."

"Hi." She stuck out her hand. "I'm Anya, Krillin's sister. But you already know that. I can't believe I didn't smell you before I came into the cave. I smell everyone and everything different right away. You smell like tuberose."

"It's nice to smell you too." Ashkii grinned. "If I were to tell you that you smelled like nutmeg, what would you say?"

"You're wrong. I smell like cloves."

"Ha!" The big, bodied man called Tse laughed so loud that soon everyone was laughing too.

"Enough of all the racket," Sari called from outside the cave. "Our meal is ready."

The girls ran back outside, followed by the adults, who had a little more dignity. Sari knew how to cook. Despite growing up with her cooking, Krillin was still amazed every time.

The night passed with tales, songs, and laughter. Tse even pulled out a long wooden flute and played a few tunes. The music carried them back to better days. When none of their loved ones were dead or hurt, when they didn't have to worry about where they'd get their next meal or if they would be separated again. Every time Krillin thought about the queen or about Ithol, he tried to push it from his mind and focused on the moment with these friends and family. But it kept coming back to Maya. Here was someone he had harmed, and even though she said she forgave him, he still felt like he needed to protect her. If it weren't for her, he would ignore their request for help. His family depended on him. How was he going to help both? Would his family be safer by his side, or should they go separate ways? All these questions swirled around in his head as he drifted off to sleep.

THE HARD CAVE FLOOR became harder and harder the longer Maya tried to fall asleep. It didn't help that Ryker was snoring next to her. Aekan kept intruding into her thoughts. She was aware he was nowhere close, but when Krillin mentioned his name casually that afternoon, it felt as if he was standing over her again, sneering. The memory of his scent was overpowering. Maya scrambled to her feet as quietly as she could and crept out of the cave. Just in time, too. All the contents of her evening meal reappeared at her feet. She glanced over her shoulder to see if anyone had heard her and sighed in relief when no one stirred. Smelling her vomit made her gag, but there was nothing new to throw up. She tried not to breathe in the sickening scent again, but it was no use. She'd have to clean it up.

Maya stepped gingerly over her mess, walked toward the edge of the boulder, and peered over. Chestnut and Nutmeg were curled up, fast asleep. She climbed down the best she could. As she searched for something that would help her clean up her mess, she felt an odd sensation of being sneaky. That was strange. Oh! Someone else was being sneaky. This wasn't her own emotion. Maya turned to see who it was, but a hand covered her mouth and kept her in place.

"Back up," said a raspy voice.

Maya had no choice but to do as he said. He pressed a dagger into her side while he pulled her away from the elephantus. Memories flooded her mind, and she breathed faster. She couldn't not breathe faster. She knew she needed to call out or escape quickly, but her body wouldn't cooperate.

Then Blackthorn was in her mind. "Maya, what's wrong? I smelled your vomit and now all I feel from you is fear."

Maya let out a sob, then responded to him in her mind. "They found us, Blackthorn! Wake the others and then go hide!"

"Are you hurt?"

"No. Wake the others!" The man holding her kept pulling her back until he was with his companions. They were Kors and Montanes. Maya's heart stopped when she saw Aekan and Skah standing off to the side with their arms crossed and smirks on their faces. An unfamiliar woman came over and patted her down, reaching into her pockets and pulling everything out. Not that she had much on her. The woman found Maya's knife but backed away when she got near the hem of Maya's skirt, which was still splattered with vomit.

Blackthorn was gone. She couldn't sense him in her mind anymore. Before she could react, Aekan pressed a lavender scented cloth up to her nose. "You will help me find him," he hissed in her ear.

She sucked in a breath and smelled all the scents on the cloth. Sleep crept over her no matter how hard she tried to stay awake. Her body was out of her control. Not long ago, she would have given anything to fall asleep, but now she needed to stay awaa...

Chapter 14

Jaylen could feel the tension leaving his body and could breathe the fresh air again. His job with Aekan was done. He and that Montane left the city days ago.

Now all Jaylen had to do was to govern the ruins of Ithol. Sure, it was an enormous job, but it was simple. There were no hidden agendas. Once everyone knew what they needed to do, it happened. The food supply was staying steady, thanks to the thorny devils and dranks being rounded up. Much to his surprise, the Itholeans were cooperative.

Aekan's arrival and interrogation about the Kindroot worried Jaylen. Would his previous labor be in vain? But now, he worried about the Kindroot and Maya. His skin became clammy thinking about Aekan hunting them. Jaylen hoped they had enough of a head start to evade that terrible man. The only comfort he found was that Aekan was no longer in his city harassing the other Itholeans.

His first act without Aekan hovering over his shoulder was sending out search parties to find the rest of the healthy gardens. There were more than he expected. Of course, the Itholeans didn't like him coming in and forcing them to share with the Kors, but he couldn't let one group have everything while another group was lacking. Riots sparked over the harvest from the gardens. But eventually, Jaylen hashed out a deal with their leader, an old man named Misu.

Now everything was settled, and Jaylen had time to process what had happened. Something felt off about the entire Kindroot situation. Which is why Jaylen found himself in Ithol's Perfumed Library. It was amazing how many scents were collected in this one place.

The library was separated into two sections: rows of actual perfumes of all the fragrances and rows of scrolls, tablets, and books. He started by searching the scrolls and tablets for the Kindroot histories, but they seemed to have been erased from the archives like they'd been erased from most everyone's memories. But the children's stories and songs, most of which he grew up hearing, referenced the Kindroots. They shared the same story of how the Kindroots burned a contract with Jedrek the First and how that contract was broken. Many claimed the Kindroots broke the contract, while some said Jedrek did. None of it was new information to him. Perhaps it was hopeless sorting this out. He shouldn't have come here. Aekan was gone. The princess was gone. And the Kindroot was gone.

No, Jaylen couldn't let it go. He needed to get to the bottom of this. He couldn't help but think the fact that the Kindroot was in Ithol, that he was real, meant there was truth hidden in the old stories. He just had to find it. Setting his scroll back on the shelf, he walked down the aisle. He was about to give up when he noticed a painting on the wall.

A wooden frame with thin golden lines wove throughout it and helped bring out certain plants in the painting. But it wasn't until Jaylen was standing in front of it that he realized there was no canvas. The painting was on the wall, a shallow recess inside it created a shelf big enough to hold something as small as a Kindroot.

There were no Kindroots in the painting that Jaylen could see. He was reading too much into the stupid painting. He needed real answers. Jaylen sighed and turned to leave, humming the song Maya had sung for him, a song his mother had taught him. That's when he smelled it. Turning back, he saw a tree that hadn't been there before. It had some sort of nut growing on it, and he could smell it! He closed his eyes and breathed in the nutty aroma, wishing he could share the scent with his mother and father. They could tell him what kind of tree it was. Then he opened his eyes. He gasped and stumbled backwards. He couldn't see a thing. Nothing! Where were the roof windows of the Perfumed Library? Where were the lanterns? Jaylen's heart raced. He closed his eyes again, breathed, and hoped this was all a dream.

He opened his eyes. It was no dream. Either something terrible had happened to make the sun disappear or Jaylen was no longer in the Perfumed Library. Jaylen held up his hand. He could make out its outline in the dark, so he wasn't blind. Tentatively, he stretched out his hand. There was no wall, no painting, nothing.

BLACKTHORN PANICKED. Rosemary, Honeysuckle, Fir. Maya's scent was getting further and further away. She was in trouble. Again. They all were in trouble. What would happen to their fragrances? Would they hand him over? No. He couldn't think about what might happen. He'd spent too much of his brief life thinking about what might happen. He'd made his choice when he helped rescue Maya and Ryker back in Ithol. And now they were risking their lives to help him.

Musk, tuberose, wildflower. Ashkii. Uncurling his long roots, Blackthorn reached out and grabbed Ashkii's shoulder, who immediately reached for his dagger. Blackthorn shouted into his mind, "It's me! Don't cut my roots!"

Ashkii bolted upright and grasped his head in his hands, his dagger clanging onto the cave floor.

"Shhh!" Tse growled.

Before Ashkii could respond, Krillin was on his feet with his bow and arrows in his hands.

Oops. He shouldn't have shouted. "Ashkii," Blackthorn said into his mind, "Maya is in trouble. They've found us."

The Montane leaped to his feet, followed by Tse. "There's someone out there," he whispered. The men moved quickly and quietly. Someone woke up the rest of the sleepers and soon the whole cave was packed up into bags and ready to leave.

Ow! Ryker stuffed Blackthorn into Maya's pack and slung it over his shoulder. What did Blackthorn expect? They didn't know they were hurting him. Blackthorn shook his leaves. What was he thinking? He should find out what they were up against, not thinking about his grievances. Sensing his surroundings, he reached out past the scents of the various objects in the bag with him and beyond the people in the cave. Ashkii wasn't among them.

"Ashkii, have you found Maya?" Blackthorn projected his thoughts into the Montane's mind. A minute passed.

When he answered, he responded with an image of Montanes in the trees and Korins on the ground, a few clumped together around Maya. Blackthorn could smell her again. She was fast asleep. That was odd. At lease she seemed safe for now, and Ashkii's image also showed Blackthorn the number of enemies they were facing and where they were. Blackthorn focused his energy on that direction and smelled everything he could. Lavender was in the air, but only near Maya. That was why she was sleeping. Then he reached out past the enemy camp, to either side and between it and the cave. That's when he noticed Ashkii was in danger. There was someone above him, sneaking up on him.

Before he could warn him, Blackthorn felt something he hadn't felt in an exceptionally long time, a tugging from far away. No, no, no, no. Not now. How was this even possible? He couldn't be transported! Maya needed him. Ashkii needed him. The sensation lasted for only a minute, but it was long enough to distract him from Ashkii's peril. When he regained his wits, Ashkii was already fighting the Montane in the tree, and Ryker was running for cover near the cave's entrance. Krillin and the women were nearby.

Krillin! Blackthorn had never tried to speak with Krillin in his mind, but Ashkii needed help. Sensing Krillin's aroma, he reached out and spoke to Krillin's mind.

Krillin spun around, looking for the voice. Blackthorn sighed. He needed to explain the whole mind communication thing again. Thankfully, Krillin was a quick learner and was soon on his way to help Ashkii.

A moment later Ashkii and Krillin returned with the Montane.

"Who do you have there?" Tse called out.

"Shhh," Ashkii hissed. "There are others nearby. They have Maya."

"Who has Maya?" Ryker interjected. "Where is she?"

"Calm down, lover boy," Ashkii replied. "She's not in immediate danger. There's a camp that way. Looks like Skah and Aekan teamed up."

"What do you mean, they teamed up?" Ryker asked.

"I mean, they're working together. We all know what they're after. But they will not get it."

"Aekan is here?"

Ashkii frowned and spit on the ground. "He is."

Ryker cursed and Blackthorn could sense his whole body go rigid. "You expect me to calm down when that man has Maya in his grasp!"

"Look, I know it isn't ideal, but I saw her. She's fast asleep. They aren't hurting her at this moment."

"Not ideal?! How would you feel if it were Agonya?"

"The same as you. Agonya is a captive of our enemies. Why do you think I've been pushing us so hard to get to Korina?"

That shut Ryker up long enough for Blackthorn to speak in Ashkii's mind. "Let me have a moment with your captive. I'm sure I can get him to talk."

Ashkii replied out loud. "He's all yours." Then he pushed the Montane towards Ryker.

"Wha—" Ryker began.

"Not you. Blackthorn."

The Montane's eyes widened, and he struggled to get away. Ryker steered him back into the cave and pushed him to the ground. Blackthorn emerged from the bag and approached the Montane, who let out a shriek. Ryker moved in and secured a gag around the prisoner's mouth. Then he went to guard the cave entrance.

Blackthorn wrapped his roots around the Montane's ankles, securing him even more than the rope around his wrists. Then he absorbed the man's scent and penetrated his mind. He didn't have to ask him anything. The man's mind was an open scroll for Blackthorn to read. It felt wrong to dig around someone's mind uninvited, but this man was his enemy. It was time to find out what Dana was up to.

THE KINDROOT WAS MORE of an asset than Ashkii had given him credit for. He not only alerted them to the presence of their enemies, granted in an unconventional manner, but he gave them time to prepare. Also, by letting Blackthorn take charge of their prisoner, the rest of them were free to plan their counterattack. To start, there were only seven of them, not including Blackthorn, against the thirty or so Kors and Montanes that he had spotted. But there was an advantage to having Krillin and his family on their side. They knew the terrain.

"We need a plan."

Anya perked up. "If we climb higher, there's another cave that I've only just begun exploring, but it can be guarded and once inside, there are many paths to help us confuse them."

"That's not half bad, sis."

"But won't we be trapped in a cave?" Ashkii countered.

"Not all of us need to enter the cave," Krillin said.

"Okay. I wish we had more time to think through this plan, but if we want the advantage, we can't delay. Let's move Blackthorn and our prisoner to this other cave and then split up. Tse and Krillin, you'll be with me. Ryker, I need you to stay with the women in that cave."

"But I want to fight!"

"Oh, you will. Don't worry. We want them to split up. You'll have plenty of fighting." Ashkii grinned and pulled out his daggers. Then he motioned for the captive Montane to get to his feet. Blackthorn must have seen because he unwrapped the man's legs and crawled up onto his shoulder. The Montane yelped and scrambled to his feet. Ashkii pressed the tip of his dagger into the man's back and they left the cave.

The girls were already scrambling higher and higher. Amber looked back. "They're coming!"

Sure enough. He could see Montanes leaping from the trees onto the large flat boulders where they had been moments before. Ashkii nodded at Tse, and the large man lifted their prisoner over his shoulder and leaped up the mountain past the girls. Ashkii grabbed Krillin's mother, "Pardon me," and leaped after him. Soon he was standing in a large, cavernous room. He set the older woman on her feet and looked around. Many crevices and tunnels went deeper into the mountain. No wonder they didn't sleep in this cave. Who knew what might be lurking in the shadows.

"Quick! Hide!" Tse shouted.

The girls scrambled in and showed Tse where to put their captive. Ryker stumbled in last, out of breath.

"Guard the entrance while the women get set up." Ashkii barked the order and then left the cave. The Montanes were gaining ground. Tse approached from behind and pointed down and to the left. Kors were climbing up. It was time to fight.

An arrow flew past him, hitting a Montane square in the chest. Excellent. Krillin would give them cover as they advanced on their enemies.

Ashkii nodded to Krillin in thanks and flew through the air. He flew right over a group of Montanes running for cover and landed in the midst of several Korin soldiers who didn't see him coming. Tse followed closely and spun around with a spear, knocking the Kors off the boulder. He almost knocked Ashkii off, but Ashkii was already barreling through their ranks.

AS TARA HELPED GET her ready, Agonya reminisced about Maya being by her side. Maya could have helped Agonya process what had happened the day before. Sure, she now knew where Blackthorn's family was and that they were still alive. Shouldn't that comfort her? She also knew that Lucas was working for Dana.

A chill ran down her spine. How was she supposed to accompany him to a ball that evening? His scent was foul in her nose. But she wasn't free to do whatever she wanted. She would have to put on her court act.

"There." Tara tucked a stray hair into Agonya's cascading curls and stepped back to look at her artwork.

The knock on the door came not a moment later. Tara rushed over and opened the door.

Prince Lucas was immaculate, as always, with his short, cropped hair, smooth face, and stunning red silk suit. Of course, it had to match her silky, flowing red dress. He was proclaiming his hold over her. Agonya breathed deeply and kept her calm. Reaching out, she took his hand and smelled it. There was something off about his fragrance tonight. Probably her imagination.

"Aren't you beautiful! You even smell like flowers after the rain." The prince extended his arm.

Agonya curtsied and took it. The jaded compliments and niceties were starting.

On the way, Prince Lucas jabbered on and on about how well the businesses were flourishing with the harvest of jojoba oil and that was despite the crops' low yields. Thinking about how he was being so prosperous made Agonya want to hit him. He used slaves, her people, to risk their lives so that he could have his precious oil to make his perfumes. She still couldn't figure out which scent he was wearing, and it put her on edge.

The palanquin arrived at the large gateway to the feast. Agonya tried to exit first, but the prince wouldn't let her. He had to be the first one out so he could help her, though she didn't need help. The poles rested on blocks the right height for an easy exit.

Agonya straightened up and looked beyond the prince up the broad staircase to the grandest house Agonya had seen, that wasn't a palace, and wondered which fragrance blessed the home.

Prince Lucas must have seen her surprise because he said, "My cousin on my mother's side, Sir Mato, lives here with of course his beautiful wife Tsula." Prince Lucas spread his arms to welcome a tall, slender woman who looked vaguely familiar.

Agonya watched them smelif, and then it was her turn to be introduced to the hostess. "Your smell is pleasant, my lady."

"Enough formalities, come, my dear. I'm so glad you could make it. Shall I give you the tour?"

The prince walked with them up the stairs. When they arrived in the large entryway, the prince resisted letting go of her arm before returning Tsula's smile and saying something like he'd already had the tour, but it was an excellent idea for Agonya to see the place.

"Don't take too long, cousin. You are stealing my date, you know."

"I wouldn't dream of it, your Highness." Tsula curtsied and swished Agonya away from the prince.

"Do I know you? You look familiar." Agonya couldn't help but think about where she would have seen her before.

Tsula smiled. "I don't think we've met but come. There's something I want to show you."

Agonya knew there was something familiar about her scent. She would remember eventually. But seeing as how she had escaped from the prince's side, Agonya decided Tsula could be her friend for the night.

They walked through the large foyer and, instead of following all the other guests through the large double oak doors, Agonya followed her host through a smaller entrance on the right. The halls were lined with paintings here. Some were of various people, others depicted waterfalls and nature. Agonya saw one of Tsula standing next to a man whom she could only assume was her husband and realized she was falling behind. She sped up. Af-

165

ter pointing out the restrooms and various sitting rooms along the way, Tsula turned to Agonya.

"Here we are." Tsula grinned. "My favorite room in the entire estate!" She pushed it open.

"It's beautiful!" Agonya cried.

They were in a large room. The floor was covered in dirt, rocks, and various plants. Along the back wall, water flowed down over some large boulders into a small pond lined with river rocks.

Not at all what Agonya had expected. She never would have guessed a paradise hid behind that door, and then she saw them...

Agonya's hand flew to her mouth. "How did you-know?"

"Know what, my dear? I take it that something in here means something to you more than just a pretty garden?" Tsula raised her left eyebrow at Agonya.

"Oh!" Agonya felt the blood rush to her cheeks. What was she doing? Reacting without thinking! Agonya lowered her hand. "Yes. If you must know, peonies hold a special place in my heart." But Tsula couldn't know the secrets of the peonies, could she? Ashkii had claimed the flower, and she had trusted him only for him to betray her. No. There was nothing special about peonies anymore.

"No need to feel ashamed, dear. Peonies are quite spectacular. Most girls prefer the lesser rose or daisy, but did you know peonies can live over a hundred years?"

Agonya nodded, unable to say any more.

"My parents are obsessed with them."

"Is that why you planted so many here in this room? Can you open part of the roof to let sunlight in?" Agonya tried to see where a roof window might be, but the ceiling was one piece.

"Ah!" Tsula's smile grew bigger. "Now, we're going somewhere! I like you, Lady Agonya. No wonder my cousin is infatuated with you. Let me show you." Tsula pushed a lever, and the ceiling rolled into a large scroll, coming to a rest on some rock ledges on the far wall.

How was that even possible?

Tsula barely gave her time to appreciate what had happened. "That is exactly how His Highness feels about you." She laughed, delighted.

"That's insane."

"Normally, when he brings a woman with him to a ball, he makes them serve him. They never leave his side. Sure, he hesitated when I asked to give you a tour, but he covered his response with lightheartedness. He doesn't want anyone to think about how he feels about you."

Agonya took a step back. "You do realize that I'm his slave, right?"

"That means nothing to him. I can tell by the way he looks at you and the way he tries to hide it. It's that same look that was on your face a moment ago."

It couldn't be true. He was her cousin! Yes, she had considered marrying him, but that was to bring peace between their kingdoms. Also, she barely knew him. Tsula didn't know the whole of it. There was something else behind his actions.

"Don't worry. I know how demanding he can be. You're welcome here anytime; if you need to catch a breath of fresh scents."

"That means a lot to me. Thank you."

Tsula walked over and grabbed Agonya's hands in hers. "It will take time to know him, but he is a great guy once you get past all the layers of perfume. But enough about him. I feel like I already know you. You are the talk of the town. I'm so glad the king, praise his scent, didn't execute you." Tsula's smile reached her black eyes.

Agonya smiled back. "What are they saying?"

"Oh, I don't know much, only what my brother told me."

"Your brother?"

"Now that I think of it, that's why I seem familiar to you. He claims you two have already met and that you are the reason he was promoted to general and governor of Ithol."

Governor of Ithol? But that meant... "You're Captain Jaylen Dahel's sister?!"

"Lord General Jaylen Dahel, now, thanks to you." Tsula had no idea of the emotions rushing through Agonya's body. "Come, let's get you back to the prince before he knocks down all the doors to find you."

There was no escape. The prince. Jaylen. Now Tsula. It took a moment before Agonya realized how ridiculous her thoughts were. They weren't her real enemies. Dana was the one she needed to worry about. The question that was bothering her all day formed. Where had Dana been when the prince had taken Agonya to Dana's cave? What was so important that Dana couldn't confront the one person who had been fighting her? They passed a painting of a forest. And then she knew. Blackthorn was in danger and there was nothing she could do about it.

Chapter 15

The memories flashed through the Montane's mind so fast that Blackthorn couldn't make sense of them. He saw a cave, not the one they were in. A little boy running. Soldiers prepared for battle. A woman's face. Then, without warning, Blackthorn found himself shaking. The Montane was shaking too. What could that mean? He glanced around and saw that the whole ground was shaking!

Everyone seemed frozen in place. Then, a large chunk of the rock ceiling broke away and crashed to the ground, shattering into hundreds of pieces.

"Quick! Out of the cave!" Blackthorn shouted at the top of his high-pitched voice.

"Move!" Sari shouted at the same time and grabbed the back of Anya and Amber's cloaks, pulling them closer to Blackthorn.

No! They weren't supposed to move towards him, they were supposed to get out of the cave. Blackthorn tried to move towards the exit, but the Montane grabbed onto him, holding him in place. He sent a jolt of pain into the Montane, who yelped but didn't release his grip. He sent another stronger jolt of pain, but as soon as the Montane let go, Krillin and Ryker disappeared from view and a group of Kors took their place in the cave's entrance.

"In here." Anya tugged on Sari's hand. They stepped into a convergence of tunnels.

"There's no way out," Blackthorn thought. He scrambled to the girls and hoped for a miracle.

The soldiers were still coming towards them. Skah led the pack.

"Great, just who he didn't want to see," Blackthorn thought.

But a loud rumble made them halt mid-step. Another tremor shook the ground, this time stronger and lasting longer. Several of the men retreated, but Skah and several others didn't move fast enough. The cave's ceiling collapsed, crushing them.

Large chunks of limestone and marble splintered on the ground and piled up. Sari wrapped her arms around Anya and Amber. Blackthorn climbed onto Sari's shoulder, and they huddled together for what seemed like an eternity. All he could think about was how close Skah had come to capturing him.

In reality, only a few minutes passed before the shaking and breaking stopped. They remained huddled together a moment longer, just to be sure. Then Sari stood up. "Is everyone okay? No one's hurt, right?" She bent over the girls trying to see if they'd been wounded, but Blackthorn knew she wouldn't see anything because when the ceiling caved in, it also blocked out all their light.

"I'm okay, mom. Stop poking me."

Sari sighed in relief and straightened back up.

"But what about Krillin?!" Anya whispered.

"Oh No!" Sari gasped. The walls were still caving in.

Blackthorn took a moment and breathed in all the fragrances in the air: rock dust, blood, sweat, metal, Sari, Amber, Anya, the captive Montane, and one unfortunate Kor that didn't escape or get crushed. The girls were fine, and neither the Montane nor the Kor were moving, so he reached out to Krillin's mind first. It was harder with a rock wall between them, but he could still find him. "We're safe but trapped in the cave. Are you okay?" he asked.

"Blackthorn?"

"Yes. What's going on out there?"

"The sky went dark, but many of the soldiers retreated when the ground shook."

"What does the air smell like?" Blackthorn thought he already knew the answer.

"Rotten eggs and oakmoss."

"That means Dana is nearby."

"Dana's here?!"

Blackthorn could sense Krillin's heart race. "Find the others and get everyone away from here. You need to get away before she captures you."

Blackthorn was now feeling a lot better that he was trapped inside the cave instead of within Dana's grasp.

"But Maya!"

"Maya has already been captured and is safe. If you are fighting, you may be killed in the trying to save her and that won't help anyone."

Krillin was silent for so long, Blackthorn worried. But he didn't have time to wait. He redirected his attention to the women, reassuring them that Krillin was alive and well. He neglected to mention anything about Dana, because he didn't want to frighten them anymore than they already were.

"Okay, let's find a way out," Sari said.

"How should we handle the Montane and the Kor over there?" Blackthorn wondered out loud.

"Kor?" Sari spun around to see what he was talking about.

"What's wrong, mother?"

But Sari was already feeling her way towards the man in the dark. Blackthorn scrambled to catch up with her. The man was hurt, but Blackthorn was uncertain of the extent. "Be careful," he said in Sari's mind.

"Sir?" she asked the Kor, ignoring Blackthorn's warning. "Are you okay?"

The man stirred and mumbled something. Sari and Blackthorn moved closer. Blackthorn reached out and touched the man's hand, breathing in his fragrance. From what Blackthorn sensed, the man hit his head hard, but he would heal. Noticing the sword laying nearby. Blackthorn yanked it away before the Kor discovered it and attacked them. It landed at Amber's feet, who bent down and picked it up.

"Do you know how to use that?" Blackthorn asked in his high-pitched voice.

Amber's face was shocked at being addressed by a small tree, before she regained her composure. "Krillin was teaching me a few things about fighting, but mostly from a distance."

"Hold on to it, then. We might need it if one of these guys tries to attack us."

"No. No fighting," Sari said, then leaned forward to help the Kor sit up.

"Who are you? Where am I?" the man croaked.

Blackthorn sat stunned. He must have been hit hard if he didn't remember anything. Perhaps Sari was right, and they wouldn't have to fight these men.

"I'm Sari and we're in a cave. The entrance collapsed and knocked you down. Are you hurt?"

"I don't feel hurt. Wait... I don't know who I am."

"Don't worry about that, dear," Sari said. "We'll give you a name. Do you remember anything? Your favorite scent?"

"Hmm... I like fires."

"I almost forgot!" Amber said. A moment later, the scrape of flint and steel was heard. A flicker of light showed Amber's young face, focused on lighting a torch.

"Let me help." Anya took the torch so she could use both hands to get a proper spark.

It didn't take long before it was burning and filling the enclosed space with smoke. "We can't stay here," Blackthorn said. "It'll get too smoky if we keep that thing burning."

"We can call you Smoky!" Anya chimed in.

"Smoky? I like it, and what's your name?"

"I'm Anya and this is Amber, and I don't know the Montane's name. What's your name, Montane?"

The Mons looked startled at being addressed.

Anya asked him again.

He finally mumbled an answer.

"I didn't hear. What should we call you?"

"Nakos."

"Great. Now all the introductions are done. We need to get going."

"But where are we going? We're stuck in a cave. We can start trying to dig our way out. That sword could help move all these boulders."

"No," Blackthorn interjected. "That won't work. It's too dangerous. There are a lot of tunnels here. There has to be another way out." It wasn't really a lie. It was dangerous to try to unblock a collapsed cave entrance, not to mention the possibility of more groundshakes, but Blackthorn really didn't want to make it easier for Dana to find him.

"You're right. We can't stay here," Sari said. "Everyone, gather what you can carry."

"I'm not going anywhere," Nakos said.

"Why not?" Smokey asked.

"Because you and I, we're their," he pointed at the girls and Blackthorn with his hands tied together, "enemies."

"Maybe this would turn into a fight after all," Blackthorn thought.

Sari turned to Nakos. "You don't have to be our enemy," she bent over to untie his hands, "and I won't force you to come with us, but we can't stay here. It's too dangerous for all of us."

Nakos lunged for Blackthorn, but Smokey blocked his way. "You say we're enemies, but I don't want to be. I won't let you harm them."

Nakos spit on the Kor. "Traitor."

"She just untied your hands; gave you back your freedom and you want to keep fighting? What have they done to you?"

Nakos pointed at Blackthorn, "He has been intruding on my mind and causing me pain since they captured me."

Blackthorn shook his leaves. "You were trying to kidnap me. I was defending myself and couldn't let you report back to your captain my location. Sari shouldn't have untied your hands, but I'll overlook it if you allow us to leave. Do you smell my fragrance?"

Looking between Sari, the Kor, the girls, and finally to Blackthorn, Nakos raised his hands in surrender. Smokey relaxed and collected the bags left in the cave prior to the fighting. Nakos even helped gather the supplies and headed deeper into the cave with them. Blackthorn was sure he was only going along because he didn't want to lose sight of his precious Kindroot.

"DON'T PANIC," KRILLIN told himself. That Kindroot said his family was safe. They were unharmed, except that they were trapped in a cave, and Krillin couldn't get them out.

A sword thrust at him, interrupting his thoughts. Krillin ducked and rolled toward his attacker, sweeping him off his feet. Then he kept moving. He didn't have time to stay and fight, nor did he want to. He needed to get to Ryker and the others before it was too late. Dana was here! But it was difficult to see in the magical darkness. His eyes weren't adjusting quick enough. If only he could jump into the trees like the Montanes. Anger boiled inside him. Anger at them for coming and ruining everything he'd worked for these last months. Anger at these people attacking him. He smelled an attacker behind him, spun around and released his poised arrow. Anger at being separated from his family.

Wait. Dana's fragrances were affecting him. His family was safe. He needed to clear his mind. Relaxing his bow, Krillin pulled a vial out of his pocket and uncorked it. The pine, lavender, and mint perfume refreshed him immediately. He didn't feel angry anymore, only worried that he wouldn't be fast enough to help rescue Maya. Yes, he deserved whatever might happen to him, but Maya, no matter what Blackthorn said about saving himself, she was innocent, and he was going to rescue her. Krillin prepped his bow with another arrow and breathed deeply through his nose. He didn't need to see to take down his enemies. He could smell exactly where they were. It was just like target practice back in Ithol.

He could smell Ryker still fighting by his side. Sensing two Montanes flying through the air towards Ryker, Krillin took aim and released an arrow. Within seconds, his second arrow was notched, and he brought down the other man. Ryker was not a bad fighter. He wielded his sword masterfully. In the time it took Krillin to shoot the Montanes, Ryker eliminated two Kors of his own. But there were more. Krillin closed his eyes, breathed in the nearby aromas, and froze. He had been so focused on helping Ryker he didn't realize there was a group converging on him.

As quick as he could, Krillin sent more arrows into their ranks, one after the other. Then they were too close to shoot arrows. He dropped his bow and pulled out a water bomb from earlier. Why not? Krillin threw it at the men. As soon as the water bomb exploded, cursing pierced the darkness. Then Ryker was there fighting the disoriented soldiers. Krillin pulled out his daggers and placed his back against Ryker's. Together, they fought until there were no more soldiers to fight.

Exhausted, Krillin wanted to sink to the ground and rest, but their task wasn't done. "Come, let's find the others."

Ryker nodded in agreement, even though he looked ready to drop.

"What about your mother and sisters?"

Oh. Krillin didn't realize Ryker was concerned about his family. "They are well."

"But how do you know?" Ryker insisted.

"The Kindroot told me. He also reminded me who has the power to cause groundshakes and this oppressive darkness." Krillin waved his hand through the air to prove his point. "But why aren't you affected by her fragrances?"

"Um... why aren't you affected?" Ryker asked.

Fair enough. "I was prepared with my own scents to counteract hers. Ever since she tried to control me several months ago, I've been walking around with this." Krillin pulled out his vial and showed its vague outline to Ryker. "What about you?" Krillin asked again.

"Oh." Ryker was silent for a long time before he finally answered. "The truth is, I can't smell them."

Krillin stumbled. What?! "You can't smell them?"

Ryker got defensive, so Krillin quickly added, "That's awesome! You're immune to Dana's mind control! You have a superpower. Together, we can totally win."

Krillin could hear the smile in his response. "Then we'd better go see if Ashkii and Tse need help."

ADRENALINE PUMPED THROUGH Ashkii's body, allowing him to block the Kors' swords with ease, often surprising them from behind. Out of the corner of his eye, he saw two Kors ganging up on him, so he flipped backwards over them, stabbing his daggers into both of their backs as he landed. Then he pointed the daggers down and yanked them out. Kicking off the dying soldiers, he flew onto a branch. From that height, he saw Krillin and Ryker next to the cave's mouth beating back the Montanes. They wouldn't last for long against that many. Already he could see soldiers getting past them into the cave. But he couldn't leave Tse to go to their aid. Glancing back to the ground, he watched his friend swinging his spear in wide arcs. Ashkii reached into his bag and pulled out a palantia bomb.

"Tse!" he called. Then he hurled the bomb down to the ground. Tse leaped up at the exact moment the palantia leaves opened. The concoction of scents released, and the nearby Kors slumped to the ground.

Ashkii pointed toward the cave and leaped to the next tree. Midway through the air, everything became darker.

"Sticks." he muttered. He knew what that meant. "Hold your breath Tse!" he yelled. Then he crashed into the tree he was aiming for. As soon as he regained his balance, Ashkii pinned his cloak across his face. It wouldn't keep all the scents out, but it would give him time. Before he could do anything else, Tse crashed into him, almost knocking him off the branch.

"Ouch!"

"Sorry!"

Crack.

"Quick, up another level." Ashkii made his decision. Not knowing if there were soldiers waiting for them down below, he grabbed Tse's hand and they leaped upward, holding their free hands above their heads. As soon as they made contact with the branch above, they let go of each other and grabbed onto the tree.

Then the tree shook. The branch they had been standing on moments before broke off and fell to the ground. A loud crash of stone on stone told Ashkii the branch wasn't the only thing falling to the ground. They pulled themselves up as quickly as they could until they were seated on the branch. The tree was still shaking, but less violently.

"What do we do?" Tse asked. "I think the whole ground is shaking."

"We wait. It can't last forever. Dana is causing this. She expects panic and wants us to go down in the confusion.

"Ash, if Dana is here, we can't wait it out. We must confront her."

"Are you out of your mind? She's too powerful for us."

"Yeah, but it would be the last thing she expects from us."

Tse had a point. They should confront her. Isn't that their goal this whole time? Ashkii didn't feel ready. "Or... we could leave."

Tse gasped. "What about Maya? And the others?"

Ashkii grimaced. He couldn't leave them. He'd already been that person to them. Doing it again would not win him favor with Agonya. "Yeah, my nose was clogged just now, but I can smell you are right. We have to confront her. I just don't know how. If we wait here, she will find us. If we help Krillin and Ryker, she'll find us, and she would be that much closer to Blackthorn. We need to go for Maya first."

"Okay, but how do we find her when we can't see the tree we're sitting in?"

Ashkii wondered if he could remember the way. He doubted Maya had moved since he'd seen her at the start. Even as he thought about it, his eyes adjusted to the darkness. He could see the tree they were standing in, the outline of it.

"Follow my scent. I know the way." Ashkii stood up, smelled the distance to the next tree, and jumped. He waited for Tse, then he leaped to the next tree. It wasn't as hard as he thought it would be. Slowly, they retraced the path in his memories. They didn't want anyone to notice them. The whole point of this was to have the element of surprise.

Finally, they arrived back where Ashkii's day had begun. He did a quick scent check for any concealed Montanes. But he didn't sense anyone. So, he returned his focus to the ground. Maya was still there, lying on the ground with two guards standing over her. Although she looked as if she were a few meters from her earlier spot. No. He must be remembering it wrong. At least they found her.

"You take the one on the right. I'll take the other one," Tse hissed.

They leaped down with their daggers in hand.

MAYA'S DREAMS WERE conflicting emotions and images. She tried to focus on something, anything. There was something she was missing. Her instinct was to spin around to see what was creeping up on her. She repressed the urge and instead turned slowly around. There was nothing behind her, not even the ground or trees or buildings. Where was she? What was she doing here? Why did it smell of rotten eggs? She felt pleased with herself. Things were going the way she wanted them to.

No. Maya shook her head. How could she feel that way when she didn't even know what was happening? Was she sensing someone else's feelings, like what she had done before with Aekan? But whose? There was no one in sight.

The feeling of being annoyed tugged at Maya's insides. Was that her own feelings at not knowing what was going on? She also felt concentration on... a cave? This made no sense. And yet there was something familiar about a cave.

Oh! She had been in a cave with her friends. They were trying to rescue Agonya and save Blackthorn. But she couldn't sleep. Was she sleeping now?

A feeling of satisfaction washed over her. Finally, sleep came to her. She had wanted to sleep on the softer dirt. But she hadn't fallen asleep. They were under attack! Why did she feel so calm? She needed to warn Ryker...

Oh. She couldn't warn him because she'd been captured. But where was she? She needed to wake up.

Maya felt the ground beneath her. Were those pine needles? Something was poking her face. She turned over and was about to sit up when a fresh wave of lavender and neroli orange washed over her and she felt so sleepy. She just needed to sleep. Why was she trying to wake up? It didn't seem important anymore. But it was important. She knew that for sure. Maya struggled to stay awake, as awake as she had been, but it felt like a load of bricks was weighing her down.

Eww! Rotten eggs, again! Maya tried to bury her nose in the ground. But with the rotten stench came memories. Someone else's memories of her! She had already woken up and fought. She had almost escaped, but Dana had stepped in and, and whatever Dana had done made the ground shake, and Maya had fallen. Dana's soldiers had tackled her and put her to sleep.

This revelation did nothing to help Maya keep fighting. With Dana preventing her escape, there was no hope. She should give in and let the calming lavender lull her deeper into sleep. But Dana was here! All the more reason she needed to wake up and escape. Was Ryker safe? He was probably coming to rescue her. He was sure to be captured or killed. No. Maya couldn't think about that possibility. She had to believe he was safe. He had Krillin and Ashkii and Tse and Blackthorn to help protect him. And Blackthorn had known! He must have given them enough warning to evade capture.

Just as she came to this conclusion, she smelled something familiar. Something comforting. A feeling of relief washed over her, but it wasn't her own relief. Ashkii had come to rescue her! Maya used that knowledge to overcome the brick wall of sleep and forced her body to move.

She opened her eyes. It was dark. Why was it dark? It didn't matter; she told herself. She just had to focus on his musky scent. That would help. She didn't know why it would help, but she knew it would make it easier to sit up, and it did.

"Maya, stay where you are," Tse said.

A moment of fighting passed, and then she felt someone lifting her off the ground.

"Are you hurt?"

Maya didn't know. She tested her arms and legs. "I don't think so. Just groggy. I feel like there's a weight on my chest." She was surprised her voice worked.

"You have hold of her, Tse?"

"Yeah."

"Let's go up."

Maya felt the sensation of falling and then rushing upwards. They were in the trees. The air was clearer up here. She could think much more clearly. The words rushed out of her. "Guys, Dana is here! She caused a groundshake. Is Ryker okay? What about Blackthorn? How did you find me? Why isn't Dana striking us down right now? Last time she knocked me to the ground before I could go five feet."

"Whoa!" Ashkii interrupted. "Slow down. We'll answer your questions, but we're not out of danger yet."

"Ash, do you see that?" Tse said, shifting Maya closer to the trunk of the tree.

"What is it?" she asked.

Ashkii responded so quietly and vehemently, she almost didn't hear him. "Cheemas!"

Chapter 16

Her chest constricted as Tsula led Agonya back to the feast. She'd tried to reach Blackthorn in her mind, but she couldn't find him. Had Dana already captured him and placed him in a glass cage? Her chest constricted even tighter. Breathe. She had to breathe. Tsula was leading her into the ballroom.

"We do things a little backward," Tsula said. "Everyone grabs a plate and serves themselves. We have servants who will bring you a drink of your choice, but they don't serve the food."

Agonya looked up to see what she was talking about. A series of long tables lined the wall. They were laden with all sorts of foods which smelled amazing! She picked a few of the sides that Tsula put on her plate. Then she saw the fried dumplings. While loading her plate with dumplings, she heard his voice from behind.

"Aha!"

Agonya jumped. A dumpling and some peas rolled off her plate. "Prince Lucas! You startled me."

"Finally, I learned something about my mysterious cousin. But what does she do? Jump like a startled rabbit."

"You must forgive her, your Majesty." Tsula came back down the table. "But you do appear to be hunting."

"I admit that I have been on the lookout for your return. And now I know Agonya likes fried dumplings. Excellent work. Come, let us find a table." Prince Lucas guided the women away from the food tables.

Agonya's plate wobbled again, but she kept everything on her plate this time.

"Here, Agonya, I'd like you to meet Sir Mato, Tsula's husband. Sir Mato, meet my lovely companion, Agonya."

"He does not lie, my Lady except in his understatement. You are much more than a lovely companion. Come, have a seat at my table." Sir Mato gestured for them all to take a seat.

The two men resembled one another. Agonya kept looking from one to the other. The only differences she could see were that Prince Lucas had smooth, olive-toned skin, while Sir Mato's had a few scars around his left ear. And Sir Mato's hair was long, pulled back into a ponytail while Prince Lucas kept his hair short.

"I've actually been waiting for your invitation, Mato, simply so I could show her off to you."

"Ah, but we've met before. Don't you remember? When we were little brats."

Agonya racked her brain. What on earth could he be talking about? She'd only met Prince Lucas a handful of times before their parents went separate ways.

"Oh, yeah!" Prince Lucas popped a dumpling from Agonya's plate into his mouth. "We played a trick on her. She had no idea!"

Agonya hesitated. "Wait. You were the one who was showing me around Korina? I thought you were Prince Lucas, but it was really you."

"That's a nice way of putting it." Prince Lucas plucked another dumpling off her untouched plate.

"Would you please stop eating my food? You could get some of your own, you know." Agonya scooted her plate further away from him.

Prince Lucas raised his hand. A moment later, a servant approached the table. "The lady requires another plate of fried dumplings."

"Of course, your Highness."

Agonya tried to protest, but the Itholean servant was already gone. What must he think of her? Agonya couldn't believe the prince. Making it seem like she was the one making demands when all she'd done was ask him to be polite.

"There. Now I can eat all the fried dumplings off your plate that I like."

"As you wish, your Highness." Agonya pushed the whole plate in front of him and folded her hands in her lap. This evening couldn't end soon enough. She longed to be in her room, far away from Prince Lucas and Sir Mato. No, not her room. She would rather be with Blackthorn, fighting Dana, trying to protect her friends.

The servant returned with a fresh plate of dumplings. Agonya tried to catch his eye to say sorry about it, but he kept his head down. "May I do anything else for your Highness?"

"That will be all." Prince Lucas ignored the plate Agonya put in front of him and plucked another dumpling off the new plate in front of Agonya. "Tell me, Mato, what's been happening around here? Did I hear you're having trouble?"

"It's nothing, really. Some slaves thought they could be their own master, but we put a stop to it."

A chill ran down Agonya's back. What did he mean by "put a stop to it"? She had the sinking feeling that whatever he meant, it wasn't good. And Sir Mato said it as though nothing had happened.

"Very good. If you need anything, all you have to do is ask," Lucas replied.

Agonya scooted her chair back, but Prince Lucas rested his hand on top of hers. The man was insufferable. Yet, what choice did she have but to sit and pretend everything was okay?

Then, as if he was reading her mind, Lucas turned to face her more fully. "What's the matter?"

He couldn't be in her mind. She would feel his presence if he were. So, she smiled sweetly and replied, "Oh, you wouldn't want me to bore you with all my troubles."

"You could never bore me."

Sir Mato suppressed a laugh.

Lucas glared at his cousin, then turned back to Agonya. "Pay him no mind. Tell me what is bothering you."

What should she say? She couldn't tell him he was her problem. "If it's okay with you," Agonya uncrossed her legs and then recrossed them the other way. "I need a moment in the ladies' room." Agonya withdrew her hand from his.

The prince's smile tightened but remained in place. "Don't take too long."

The people were a blur to her as she rushed out of the room, out of sight. She sighed in relief when she reached the hallway. It was empty. Agonya started towards the ladies' room. She remembered Tsula pointing it out on her tour earlier. Just as she was about to turn the corner, Agonya noticed movement behind her. Someone was following her. Of course, he wouldn't let her go alone.

She pushed open the door, but instead of going in, she hurried around the next corner. Did she lose her tail? Agonya needed to be alone, to think properly. She had to find that room Tsula had shown her.

After two wrong turns, she finally found the garden room. The running water soothed Agonya's nerves. She found a log near the base of the waterfall and sat down.

The fragrance of the peonies in the room helped clear Agonya's mind. Sir Mato had said he'd taken care of a problem with the slaves. Had he killed them or beaten them? The way that servant had looked at him made Agonya's stomach twist inside her. She had caused this.

The hurt and the pain filled Agonya's mind. She wanted to scream. Every time Agonya thought she was doing the right thing, people continued to suffer and die all around her. She wished the feast were over and she could curl up in her bed. But she knew the moment she did, she would wish for the morning to come so she wouldn't have to relive her nightmares.

She had to do something. Something that would help fix the damage she'd caused. But when she tried to heal Huren, she had gotten him killed. Yes, she saved Lady Rebekkah, but that was... That was the key! Her work required a more nuanced approach. What better time than now when she didn't have anyone watching her?

Agonya breathed in the sandalwood perfume Prince Lucas had sprayed her with before the feast and closed her eyes. She remembered the servant who brought her the dumplings, his fragrance, and tried to find him in her mind.

He was talking to someone. "How bad is she? ... What? Can I not go to her?"

Agonya could hear what he asked but couldn't hear the reply. This woman must have been the one Sir Mato spoke about. Could she find her on her own and heal her?

"I thought I'd find you here." Tsula pushed open the door to Agonya's sanctuary and held it open. "Prince Lucas won't wait much longer, you know."

Agonya sighed. There had to be a way to help that woman, but it would have to wait. Her time alone was done. "Lead the way." Agonya rose from her perch and walked toward the deceitfully friendly face. Then she had an idea. "Tsula?"

"Yes?"

"Would it be all right? Would you invite me to visit you tomorrow?"

Tsula's eyes lit up. "Of course! I would love to have you over for tea."

THE SILKY DRESS LIFTED and spread out in a circle around Agonya as Prince Lucas twirled her around to the music. He lightly pulled on her hand to bring her closer. "I realize why you're upset with me."

"You do?" Agonya focused on her feet not tripping on invisible roots. She had to. She couldn't afford to let the prince distract her. If he did, she was sure to fall. And not just onto the floor, but emotionally, too. Blackthorn was in danger, her people suffered, and she was dancing as if there wasn't a care in the world.

"I was callous about Sir Mato's troubles."

Agonya ducked under his outstretched arm. "No, you were very sensitive towards Sir Mato."

"I meant... well, you know what I meant." The prince pulled Agonya out of the center of the room.

No, Agonya did not know what he meant.

"Sir Mato's servants–" the prince began.

"Slaves," Agonya interrupted.

Prince Lucas looked around at the other couples dancing before nodding. "Slaves, well, they were out of line."

Agonya raised her eyebrows but remained silent. What was he playing at?

"Mato shouldn't have dealt with them like that."

"Like what? What exactly did he do?"

Prince Lucas grabbed Agonya's elbow and started walking towards the balcony. "You know what he had to do. You would have done the same if they were your slaves."

Agonya scoffed. "You're making a lot of assumptions. First, I would never have slaves. That's not who I am. Second, if I did have slaves, I would treat them like I treat my servants. With respect and understanding."

The prince sighed and rubbed the bridge of his nose while still holding her elbow. "I'll talk to him about it."

"If you're sorry about it, help me. Let me see how bad they're hurt. I can heal them."

"You realize what you're asking?"

"Yes." Agonya tried to remove her elbow from his grip, but he held on. "Please, let go of me."

His grip tightened momentarily, then he released her as they stepped outside. "I want to help you, Agonya. I really do, but you keep fighting me." Lucas clenched his fists and then loosened each finger deliberately. "I can't. I am the prince, and you have no rights here. Did you forget you are my slave? The Itholeans lost the war. You lost the war. It's because of your foolishness that they are slaves now. We were willing to help them assimilate into the cities here in Korina, but you didn't hold up your end of the bargain."

Agonya strode to the railing and turned her back on him. She didn't need to hear about her crimes. She knew them all too well. Despite the hardened mask she'd been putting on all evening, a traitor tear escaped. It slid down her cheek in silence.

"Let's talk about it." Prince Lucas stepped next to her. "You want to heal slaves who were beaten because they disobeyed their master? If I allowed this, what consequences might happen?"

Agonya shook her long black curls and bit her lip. She didn't dare say a word for fear the rest of the tears building up inside her betrayed her, too.

He went on, oblivious to the emotions bubbling up inside her. "Other slaves would hear of it and assume there are no repercussions for disobedience and then some might end up dead instead of just beaten. Or we swear everyone to silence. You heal them, and then you hear of other disobedient slaves. What do you do then? You can't heal them all."

He was right. She couldn't heal them all. She wasn't even sure if she could heal these few in Sir Mato's service.

"I heard what you did on your way to Korina. That is simply amazing. I've never heard of anyone being able to heal as many as you healed. You know the answer, don't you?"

Agonya breathed in through her nose and faced him, her mask back in place. "You want me to hand over Blackthorn."

"Yes." He smiled a gentle smile.

His heady smell of anise clouded her mind. Agonya stepped away and breathed in the night air. She tried to pick out the fragrances of the various plants growing in the garden below. "I can't do that," she said once her mind had cleared.

"It's simple—"

"No. It's not." Agonya checked herself. She couldn't afford to yell at the man who held her freedom in his hands.

"No. It's not simple," she tried again. "You are the crown prince. You, of all people, should know that nothing is that simple. You said you want to talk about it. Well, what happens if I sacrifice Blackthorn's life for my people?"

"You wouldn't be sacrificing his life. We don't want to kill him." Lucas laughed. "To think, this has all been a misunderstanding." The prince smacked his forehead. "He is the key, Agonya. With his help. Yes, we only want his help. With his help, we can heal the world. You'd be saving more than a people from a life of slavery. You'd be saving us all. Did you hear me talking about the low crop yields? Our plants are dying. With Blackthorn's help, we can fix that."

Agonya could tell he genuinely believed what he said. "You're right. That's not the impression I got. If you're not collaborating with her, why bring me to see Dana? You would give her Blackthorn? You would give the woman who enslaved his entire family, the woman who can't control which creatures come down from the Arid Mountains, the woman who hides, who sends others to steal what she wants, the last free Kindroot."

Or the woman who was capturing Blackthorn at this very moment. Agonya didn't want to think about what Dana was doing.

"You've got her wrong. Dana is a wonderful person. I wish she had been there earlier. She could have told you herself who she really is and explained to you how this is a good thing."

Dread filled Agonya's insides. She had to close her eyes. Dana was a Monster. She had no desire to be near her. And yet, she needed to know her enemy in order to protect her friends.

"Think about it. I will take you to meet her once she returns. Come, it's getting chilly out here."

Agonya had no choice but to follow him back inside, where cheerful banter and singing voices echoed in the great hall. These sounds and the smells lingering from the feast clashed with Agonya's feelings. They had no clue what they were celebrating. Prince Lucas might appear righteous, but that's all it was, a facade. Her friends' lives were in jeopardy because of him.

CHEEMAS RUSHED UP THE tree towards Maya and all she could think about was if Ryker was okay. Before she could process what was happening, Tse slung her onto his back like a sack of dirty laundry and jumped. Maya screamed and held on tight.

The moment they landed. Maya demanded to be set down.

Tse shook his head. "We need to get away as fast as we can."

"There's too many of them," Ashkii added.

"Okay, but where can we go?" Maya asked. "Our friends are somewhere nearby and we're just going to leave them?"

"We need water."

"No, we need to get out of here, Ash. Water will not stop Dana."

"But it will stop the cheemas. Didn't we just agree that we need to confront Dana? If we're ever going to confront her, we will have to do it no matter what she floats our way, whether it's cheemas, dranks, or thorny devils. And Maya's right. Our friends are back there. We can't abandon them."

Maya couldn't help but wonder how they were going to find them. She didn't even know where she was, not really. How long had she been asleep? It was morning when she'd been captured in front of the caves, and now it was dark.

"Follow me," Ashkii said.

This time Maya held on tight and squeezed her eyes shut before Tse leaped into the air. He also didn't stop at the next tree, but they kept changing trees. Maya had to trust their sense of direction. The only comforting thought was that they found her, so maybe they knew where to go.

When they started to descend, Maya's heart raced. Being in the trees felt safer than being on the ground. She knew they were headed to the river and that water would protect them from cheemas, but it didn't feel safe.

"Stay here. I want to see if Krillin and Ryker are still fighting."

"We should stay together," Maya protested.

"Maya, if we all go, there's a higher chance of being seen."

She protested again, but Ashkii kept talking. "And if I am seen, you two will still be safe."

"He's right, Maya." Tse said. "Let's make water bombs while Ashkii looks for our friends."

"Why only Ryker and Krillin? Where are the others?"

Ashkii shared a look with Tse before answering. "There was a ground-shake."

"I know, I felt it."

"The cave opening collapsed."

"What?! We have to go save them!"

"Shhh. Stink. Now they know where we are."

The cheemas came so fast, Maya didn't have time to react. How could she have been so stupid? Several cheemas dropped from the trees onto her shoulders. They dug their claws into her. Maya jumped into the cold, rushing water. No more cheemas came for her, but three still clung to her. She tried to pry them off, but their claws dug in deeper. Maya dunked her entire body under the water. The cheemas let go the moment the water touched them. Maya grabbed them and tossed them further down the river.

When she could finally look for her friends, she saw Ashkii and Tse also coming up out of the water, but they weren't alone. They were fighting Korin soldiers. What should she do? Maya was not a fighter. Her eyes glanced toward the shore. She couldn't see any enemies.

A tremendous splash sprayed Maya's face. As she wiped the water away, she caught a powerful scent nearby. It was awful! But with it came an awareness of other people's emotions and a blood lust from hundreds of creatures. Maya gasped. When she looked closer at the bank, she saw movement from the cheemas climbing over each other, all vying to get closer to her but not wanting to touch the water. The emotions were overwhelming. She felt trapped, like a load of bricks was crushing her.

"Give it up," a chilling voice spoke into the darkness. "You're surrounded."

Suddenly, Maya felt angry and helpless. She was angry that she was helpless. They should surrender. There was no escape. But then, Maya realized Dana hadn't found Blackthorn yet. If she had, she wouldn't be calling for them to surrender. She'd have killed them already. She also realized that these emotions were not her own.

Then the unimaginable happened. Ryker strolled right up to Dana.

Where had he come from? Why wasn't he prevented from getting too close?

Dana looked as surprised as Maya was. But she recovered quicker than Maya. A huge grin broke out on her face. "You've made a good choice, young man."

"What choice do you think that I've made?" Ryker replied.

Dana paused and frowned. Then Ryker pushed a sword through her belly.

What was he thinking?!

It took only a second before Dana laughed. She yanked his sword out and immediately began to heal. "You think you can kill me?" she laughed again.

Maya gasped. The cheemas next to Dana had stopped moving. But no one else seemed to notice. And Ryker didn't look fazed at all. An arrow flew, hitting Dana directly in the heart.

Now she looked annoyed. While she went to remove the arrow, Ryker raised his sword and swung for her neck. Dana glowed orange, and Ryker's sword bounced off an invisible shield. He stumbled and rolled to avoid Dana's attack. More arrows shot towards Dana. One after the other. This time, none of them came close.

Maya could feel her anger boiling. Dana was about to annihilate Ryker! Maya had to do something and quickly! Focusing all of her own emotions and the emotions of everyone else that had been piling on top of her, making her immobilized, Maya pushed with all the strength she had and flung Dana's emotions off. It was liberating. She stood up taller and called to Ryker, but he couldn't hear her in the middle of all the chaos that had suddenly exploded.

Whatever Maya had done, it was affecting all the cheemas who were now attacking the remaining Montane and Korin soldiers. Soon, they were running for the water. Dana screamed and looked directly at Maya, but whatever emotion Dana was trying to smother Maya with never reached her.

Ashkii and Tse were by her side, lifting her out of the water. Then Ryker was by their sides. The ground shook. Nothing needed to be said. The two Montanes lifted Ryker and Maya into the trees. To Maya's surprise, Krillin was already there. They began their escape, with Tse carrying both Ryker and Maya while Ashkii carried Krillin. Dana screamed in frustration and the trees began to shake.

Chapter 17

The vibrations were faint, but Blackthorn felt them deep inside the earth. The waves he felt from the hard ground were strong enough to catch his attention.

Several minutes of distant vibrations frightened Blackthorn. He searched his memories for the previous groundshake, not the one that trapped them earlier, but the one before, from a hundred years ago. He hadn't been near that one, nor did he find out what caused it. Blackthorn thought about the storms Dana made recently and how far her power stretched. This last groundshake was definitely Dana's work, but why were the groundshakes still happening? Surely her purpose for them was complete with the capture of his friends. Unless they hadn't been captured yet.

"Did you feel it?" he asked the group.

"Feel what?" Anya asked.

"The groundshake?"

"Another one? Are you certain?" Sari turned to face him.

"I'm positive," Blackthorn said. He shook his branches to show how much the ground shook. "Back where we came from, the groundshake was smaller than before."

"How do you know? I mean, I didn't feel a thing," Amber said.

"I can smell it and feel it on the ground. Like how I knew about Smokey before we saw him. I can gauge distance, simply from the vibrations people or groundshakes make." Blackthorn hadn't thought about it before Sari made him say it out loud, but he had calculated the distance of the groundshake already in the back of his mind. "This one is across the river we crossed to escape the cheemas."

Sari gasped. "But Krillin! He's out there. Is he in trouble?"

"If he's in trouble," Blackthorn interrupted, "we're too far away to do anything about it."

"We've got to go back."

"What are we going to do? Dig our way out of the cave? It's too dangerous. Besides, I know Krillin isn't near Da—," he almost said Dana, but if Sari knew Dana was nearby, she would insist on digging their way out, "the cheemas," he lied. "I'm pretty sure if he is in trouble, he'll be able to handle it."

"What about the others?" Anya asked.

"Ryker is with Krillin. I'm not sure about the Montanes, but they could be in the trees and it's harder to feel them when they aren't touching the ground." The lies came easily. Blackthorn would not make it any easier for Dana to find him, and that meant Krillin's family couldn't go back. Sure, the last time he'd paid attention to where Krillin was, he was with Ryker, but that didn't guarantee they were still together.

Sari opened her mouth to speak and then closed it.

Amber gasped and sat next to Blackthorn. "But Blackthorn! You can show us the way out of here!"

Everyone started talking at once. Blackthorn was grateful for the babble because he didn't know how to escape this maze. There was nothing for him to search for that would tell him which way to go, and he didn't know how to tell them that. The tunnels all smelled the same.

"Come on," Anya said, smiling. Then she scooped him up and put him on her shoulder. "Which way, Leader?"

"Sensing people and groundshakes doesn't mean I know where to go," he mumbled too quietly for them to hear.

"That way." Blackthorn pointed his roots to the left, directly away from the groundshake, and hoped it would lead them out.

THE NEXT DAY, AGONYA was back at Tsula's home. The house was empty compared to the night before, when fifty guests roamed the halls. One of her perpetual guards, Deepak, stood next to Agonya in the entrance while they waited to be shown to the parlor. He was a little too close for comfort, but Agonya did her best to ignore him. She thought the prince would not allow her to visit Tsula for tea, but he had let her come despite their argument the night before.

Tsula rounded the corner ahead of the servant who'd let them in. "Agonya! I'm so glad you could make it."

Tsula's smile warmed Agonya's heart, and she found herself returning the smile. "Your invitation was exactly what I needed this morning."

"Shall we?" Tsula waved for Agonya to join her as she walked back the way she'd come. "I'm excited for you to try my latest tea! I grew the leaves myself and haven't shared it with anyone apart from my husband."

"Ooh! What's it called?"

"There's no name yet. I grafted a clipping I got from a cocoa plant into my peppermint and the results are fabulous. I love the smells they make, both individually and together."

Now, Agonya was curious to try this new tea. The cocoa plant was supposed to lift your spirits. And peppermint was supposed to help refresh oneself. The combination, well, that was just what Agonya needed.

The parlor was as inviting as this tea sounded. Agonya followed Tsula to the plush sofas, while Deepak followed Tsula's servant to the edge of the room by the large windows.

"Last night, you mentioned your family. Would you tell me about them?" Agonya crossed her legs under her floor length dress.

"You know my youngest brother already. Jaylen happens to be my favorite brother of the three that I have."

Jaylen was her favorite brother? Agonya felt very weary. She liked Tsula but Jaylen...

Not pausing to take a breath, Tsula continued explaining her family to Agonya. "And my mother loves to work with animals of all sorts. That's why their estate is on the edge of the city. She wanted enough land for her companions to roam. My father is a harvester; he's the one who taught me the plant names and how to graft them together."

"And what do your other brothers do?"

"Chaska, the oldest, is also a harvester like my father. He has been so busy of late since the crops are failing. They need to cover more ground than usual.

Minco oversees training the king's koliimuses." Tsula reached for the teacup offered by a servant. "Here's the tea I told you about."

Agonya took the cup from Tsula and brought it to her nose. "The fragrance is so refreshing and comforting!"

Tsula took a cup for herself and together they drank. Agonya pushed her weariness of Jaylen from her mind and tried to enjoy Tsula's company. She was easy to talk to. Agonya found herself telling Tsula about her own mother and father, both of whom were dead now. She had no siblings to speak of. She was telling Tsula about her best friend, Maya, omitting the part about her being a servant, when a knock came at the door.

A young woman rushed forward and opened the door. "My lady, Minco is here." Then she stepped aside, and a man, who looked like Jaylen but with many scars all over his forearms and minus Jaylen's height, walked in.

"Sorry to interrupt. May I have a moment, Tsula? Alone."

Tsula nodded to the servants who disappeared out the way her brother had come. "You too, Deepak."

"Beg your pardon, my lady. I have strict orders to stay with Agonya."

"I understand. I will be with her. And will vouch for her. Go on, now." Tsula stood from her resting place.

"Sorry, sister, but I must insist that the Itholean princess leave too." The man shifted from one foot to the other.

Agonya rose. "It's okay. I'll go with Deepak."

"Very well."

Deepak held the door for her, and they stepped into the hall. Where should she go? Part of her still wanted to heal those Itholeans, but she knew Prince Lucas was right about it being worse for her people. So, she wandered the halls. Maybe she should return to that wonderful room from the night before.

Agonya started walking, and Deepak followed. She turned into a smaller corridor and kept going. After several more turns, Agonya was thoroughly lost.

Deepak cleared his throat.

Agonya turned. "Yes?"

"We should return to the main part of the house."

His reluctance to let her keep going made her think his instructions included keeping Agonya out of certain places. Like the servants' corridors. Should she insist on exploring them?

In her moment of uncertainty, Deepak moved between her and what she could only guess were the servants' rooms. So much for that idea. Agonya turned and retraced their steps. Closing her eyes, she attempted to identify the scents hidden behind each closed door. She didn't know what she was looking for, but it was good practice for her to decipher various fragrances. It reminded her of when she was searching for orinberries to heal herself.

They turned another corner, and a new scent caught her attention. Agonya gagged. Her hand flew to her nose and pinched it shut. Deepak tried to usher her beyond the opened door, but Agonya also smelled life in that room. Emotions burst inside her, and she pushed past her guard and rushed into the room. Deepak was too startled to stop her.

Crossing the dimly lit room, Agonya noticed several beds. Was this a sick room? Where was the healer? The person on the bed in the far corner was unrecognizable from all the wounds covering the face. If she had to guess, this woman was the Itholean slave that Mato had "taken care of". What else would cause these wounds? Now Agonya knew he had the slave beaten to the point of death.

Agonya couldn't help herself. She knelt beside the girl and laid her hands on her bloody face. Bracing herself for the stench that was about to assault her, Agonya breathed in and channeled her magic into the woman. By the time Deepak had caught up to her and started pulling her away, the woman's wounds were healing. The infection was disappearing, and the cuts were closing.

"You can't be in here." Deepak said, drawing her away from the Itholean.

"Please," Agonya begged, "Let me heal her!"

It was no use. Deepak was much stronger than her. He lifted her off the ground and slung her over his shoulder. Halfway back to the parlor, Agonya took control of her emotions and asked to be put back down.

"I don't think so."

"Please. I won't try to go back. Let me walk with dignity."

"Fine." Deepak lowered her to the ground.

Agonya straightened up and continued walking back to Tsula, even though her mind was back with that Itholean dying on that bed. She'd known she wasn't allowed to heal her. Why had she done it? It was as if she had felt her pain as her own.

The return trip was much faster. The door opened just as they reached it and Tsula's brother walked out.

"Ah! Come on in. Sorry about that. We had a family matter to discuss." Tsula joined Agonya in the hallway. "What happened to you?" Tsula said, taking a step back.

"I'm so sorry," Agonya began.

"We passed a room with a rotten scent to it," Deepak interrupted.

Tsula nodded in understanding. "Come inside and have some more tea. You'll feel better in no time."

Deepak shook his head and held his arm out to stop Agonya from entering. "That's not all that happened."

Tsula's eyes widened.

"I didn't realize where we were when she ran past me. She went straight to the Itholean on the far bed and started healing her. As soon as I realized what was happening, I stopped her."

Tsula motioned for a servant, instructing her to prevent her brother's departure. Then she turned to Agonya. "You shouldn't have interfered."

"I know. I don't know what came over me. Please forgive me." Agonya bowed her head and hoped the prince wouldn't hear of her disobedience.

"Let's walk. Shall we?"

Agonya nodded and followed Tsula back the way they'd come. What was Tsula going to do to her? Agonya knew Tsula was Jaylen's sister, but she liked her. The silence was torture. Was Tsula upset with her?

Tsula told Deepak to stay in the hall with Agonya, then she disappeared into the awful room. A moment later, Tsula burst back through the door, breathless. "How, by all the smells above, did you do that?"

"Do what? Exactly?" Agonya didn't think she'd done anything extraordinary.

"You saved her! She's completely healed!"

"What?! I mean, I began to heal her, but Deepak took me away before I could finish."

Tsula grinned at her and pulled her back down the hall. She didn't go to the parlor, but to the foyer of the enormous house. Her brother leaned against one of the pillars with his arms crossed. He was annoyed at being asked to wait.

Agonya followed Tsula over to him and listened as Tsula explained what Agonya had done. He raised his left eyebrow, the same way Tsula liked to raise her left eyebrow, when he appraised Agonya.

"Do you think she can help? I know you wanted to keep this in the family, but I think she might be able to make a change."

"Okay. Let her try." Then he turned and walked outside.

"Um. Did I miss something?" Agonya asked.

"That family matter we were discussing, well, it's my father. He's not doing well. We would like it if you would come and heal him."

Agonya saw the hope in her eyes and had a bad feeling about this. "I don't know if I can."

"It's okay if you can't. Will you at least try? I mean, what you did today is absolutely amazing."

Agonya felt the blood rush to her cheeks. "I will try, but I don't want to disappoint you if I am unable to help."

"I appreciate that. Is there anything you will need to heal my father?"

Agonya's shoulders relaxed. Maybe she wasn't in trouble after all. Tsula wanted her help. "I'll need perfumes that have the healing scents like orinberries, peppermint, and sandalwood."

"Done. I'll make arrangements with the prince. I'm sure he won't mind if I borrow you again." Tsula hugged Agonya without warning.

When she was released, Agonya stepped back and smiled at this woman who wanted her help, even though she was an Itholean slave. "I'll be ready whenever you call. You know I'll do my best. I can't guarantee that I'll be able to help, but I will try." Not only would she be healing someone when there were so many she couldn't heal, but it would be another way to escape her cousin's presence one more day.

Chapter 18

Water was all Jaylen wanted. Two days had passed since his arrival, and he still hadn't figured out where he was or how he was going to get back to the palace in Ithol. Using old torches from brackets on the wall, he'd explored what looked like an animal burrow, except all the walkways were large enough for humans. There were dead plants everywhere. And none of them were edible. Jaylen's throat was parched, and he felt weak. He needed to find water and food soon. He pried his foot off the dirt and moved it forward. Then the other foot. There had to be a way out.

Rounding the next corner, Jaylen walked into a large room with a pecan tree growing in the center. It was alive! Sunlight filtered through the ceiling slits. Jaylen rushed to the tree, but when he got closer, he noticed other nuts on the tree, not just pecans. Since when did more than one type of nut grow on one tree? Despite Jaylen's desire to pick and eat the nuts, he was too terrified to try. The tree looked ancient and untouched for an extremely long time. Then he noticed a waterfall trickling into a small pond in the corner. Jaylen changed course and found himself scooping up the water and drinking it. The water felt so nice sliding down his throat. The sweetness refreshed him in a way that water never had. He kept drinking until his hunger pangs became stronger than his thirst.

He turned to the tree and thought about eating the nuts again, but now that he'd had water, he could think more clearly. That tree was definitely magical.

Even as he thought about it, Jaylen knew this place was connected to the Kindroots. Was it their home? Where had they all disappeared to? Was Blackthorn truly the last of his people? Jaylen had been thinking about the Kindroots when he appeared here. But why did he come here now? Lots of people were thinking about the Kindroots all the time. Why wasn't this place filled with all of them? Jaylen breathed in the refreshing nutty aroma of the tree and remembered the scent he'd smelled in the library.

Wait. He was back in the library! The tree was gone. The painting on the wall was in front of him now. Was the painting a door that could only be unlocked by this particular scent? Jaylen had so many questions but even as he stared at the wall, someone started shouting behind him.

He sighed, still wishing for more water, but it was time to face his commanders. He was the Governor General, after all, and they were probably wondering where he'd been. What was he going to tell them? This felt like a secret too big to share. Jaylen needed to know more before he trusted anyone else with this discovery.

A moment later, Laniel came jogging into the library. "Sir, are you okay? Where have you been?"

Thank the patrons, Laniel was the one to greet him. "I—" Jaylen cleared his throat. "I need water."

Laniel reached to his side and removed his skins from his belt. Jaylen took it and gulped it down. His thirst was easing, though his throat still hurt. "Do you have food? I'm starving."

Laniel nodded and waved to the men rushing in. "Bring the general food!" he barked. Motioning to Jaylen, he directed him to a secluded corner table away from the growing crowd in the hall.

Jaylen did his best to focus on his friend. Laniel needed to know his general was okay. "Thank you. It's been two days not knowing where I am or how the hell to get back. Just before I—" Jaylen hesitated. How should he say it? "I found my way back here, I found water, but not enough. I think I'm just tired. But tell me, Laniel, how has the city been? Any complications while I was gone?"

"No, sir. Everything has been running smoothly except the fact that you've been missing. We've searched the entire city and palace, and no one knows anything. So, when that servant saw you standing here in the library, he panicked instead of approaching you and finding out your state."

"Don't be too hard on him. I'm glad he found you and brought you to me. We've been through a lot together and I know I can trust you. Are you sure you don't want a promotion?" He really did trust Laniel, who had been there for him during the war. Laniel had been the brains behind the tunnels that collapsed the city walls. Laniel had taken care of his men, looked out for them. Should he tell Laniel what had happened to him? Jaylen didn't know.

"I don't want to be promoted. Logan is doing fine as a captain. But you know that. Why do you keep asking me?"

"Because I need someone I can trust in a position of authority. I know I can trust Logan, but it's not the same."

"Speaking of Logan, he'll be here soon. I know he'll want to speak with you directly."

The fresh bread and roasted meat and squash came before Logan did. Jaylen smelled them coming and then they were on a plate in front of him. He barely heard the commotion as the servant weaved through the crowd. Instead, he breathed in the aromatic smells and felt like he'd already eaten the food, even though it was still on his plate. He took one bite and then couldn't stop himself from inhaling the rest. He was going to be sick from eating so quickly, but he was just too hungry, and the food was too good.

The curious onlookers dispersed when they realized they wouldn't get a speech from their mysterious general and governor.

"Where was I last seen?"

"There were several locations people said they saw you, but no one knew the exact location you disappeared."

"Good. Let's keep it that way."

"We could give them a false lead," Laniel said.

Jaylen grinned. It was good to be back and to have Laniel on his side. They had a lot to figure out.

"I CAN'T BELIEVE SHE let us go!" Ryker said for the millionth time. "Why do you think that is?"

Maya had wondered about that, too. She was still unnerved by the way Dana had looked at her. No, it was more of a glare. Was Dana upset by something Maya did?

"I don't know," Krillin replied. "It all happened so fast. She was about to chop off your head when something triggered all her soldiers and cheemas to go crazy."

Oh. Maya had been so focused on not wanting Ryker to die that she had—what? Pushed everyone else's emotions off of her. Right after chaos broke out, they were able to escape. Was it connected? Had Maya caused the chaos?

"It looked like Dana's magic backfired. She lost control of the cheemas, not to mention that groundshake she did while we were escaping." Ashkii noted.

Tse fell back to walk next to Ryker. "I felt a mix of anger, confusion, and fear, stronger than ever before."

"Now that you mention it. So did I," Ryker said. "Maya, it felt like the way you described feeling other people's emotions. Is that how you felt when..."

Maya knew he hadn't realized what he was saying, and he stopped himself from finishing the thought, but it still hurt remembering what Aekan had done to her, to them. "Maybe. I... think I did something, but I don't know how or what I did."

Ashkii stopped in his tracks, causing Ryker to run into him. He turned to face her. "What do you mean?"

Everyone waited for her answer, and she felt embarrassed to have spoken up. These men were incredibly skilled at everything they did. The very thought that she had done something that none of them could do was terrifying. "Well, it probably wasn't anything I did."

"Stop," Ryker said. "You always sell yourself short. Tell us what happened."

Maya took a deep breath and told them all about when she'd been captured and forced to sleep. She told them about the emotions she'd felt and how she tried to break away from them and then her small successes, once before Ashkii and Tse had found her and then again when they had. She told them about the overwhelming emotions she'd felt by the river and then seeing Ryker about to die and pushing all of those emotions off herself so she could go to him. Heat rushed to her cheeks at that admission, and then she started crying.

"Hey, hey." Ryker wiped the tears from her face. "It's okay. I'm okay."

"Do you realize what this means?" Ashkii asked. "I mean, if you did, by all the scents, work this magic."

201

Maya shook her head.

"It means you can do olfamancy, too. It means it is more common than I thought it was."

They started walking again.

"Also, how did you control so much power without being paralyzed like Agonya was?"

No one answered his question. No one knew. But they all wondered.

Maya was exhausted now that she thought about it; but the exertion to push all those emotions away and the adrenaline from their flight had kept her going. They'd been traveling for an entire day since the incident and hadn't stopped to rest. Tse had carried her between trees until they finally abandoned the search for their elephantuses. They got as far from Dana as fast as they could before Maya had to walk on her own. So, maybe she would be fine. Maya reminded herself that Agonya had combined her magic with Blackthorn's, and that amount of power had been what paralyzed her. When she used her magic without Blackthorn's help, she seemed to be fine.

"How much further to Korina?" Maya asked after another hour of walking.

"Not far now," Ashkii assured her.

Maya felt relief at hearing his words. Each step she took seemed heavier and heavier to her. Maybe she was worrying too much, and it was all in her head. But maybe not.

THE STREETS OF KORINA were not what Ashkii expected. Memories of the first time he entered Ithol now flashed across his mind. Korina had the same markets and, of course, many of the same people, now that the Itholeans were in exile here. The only difference was in the layout of the streets. He liked the windy streets of Korina compared to Ithol's boxlike design.

Now, where would his brother hide out?

"If I know Kilchii, he's going to stick to the outer edges of the city." Ashkii followed the curving road, not more than a few streets beyond the western gates.

Tse followed. "Even if he is, which I don't know, Ash, he might have prepared for you to follow him. Not to mention, this place is enormous! How are we going to locate him?"

Ashkii replied from beneath his leather hood. "Oh, trust me. He'll want to be close to the city wall, so he can escape if the need arises. This is also why we left Krillin, Ryker, and Maya outside the city. If he slips away, Krillin will smell him." Ashkii paused when he came to the next intersection. The street leading into the city was nearly straight. He could see the palace rise higher than the other buildings around it. The street had a gradual incline towards the center of the city.

Agonya was in there somewhere. It took all of Ashkii's willpower not to go straight to her. He had to scope out the situation and find his brother. The possibility of Agonya being dead was too real. He wasn't even sure his brother was still in the city.

As if Tse could read his mind, he said, "Don't worry. We would know if she were dead."

Ashkii sighed and kept walking. The noise from a public house drew Ashkii forward. They needed to start somewhere and, having just survived a fight with the most powerful evil being, a nice place to sit and eavesdrop on the unsuspecting, smelled delightful.

"Come on. A nice mug of ale and some food will help us think."

The public house was full. Some Itholean women and men were dancing on the raised platform. Ashkii walked past tables of couples and tables of soldiers, keeping his head down, until he found the perfect table in the center of the room. He slid onto the hard-backed chair. He couldn't see everyone, but he could hear most of them. And he could see the door. The serving ladies bustled around their table as they went back and forth between the kitchen and the tables.

Tse sat so he could watch the kitchen exit. "He's not here, Ash."

Ashkii smiled. Tse liked to state the obvious, and Ashkii found it lightened his mood. "The question is, Tse, has he ever been here before, or more likely, do these lovely people have valuable information for us?"

Tse held up his hand. A server came over. "How can I help you, sir?"

"Two ales please and a loaf of bread." Tse slapped a handful of chips on the table.

She smiled, scooped up the chips, and disappeared to the kitchens.

"You said you needed some ale to help you think."

"I think you overpaid her."

"It might come in handy later when we need a quick escape."

A moment later, she reappeared with two foaming mugs and a loaf of bread. "The Patron of Fortune must be smiling at you. Cook just took a fresh batch from the oven. Can I get you anything else?"

"If you have it, some information might be nice. You see, we're travelers and arrived today. Do you have any recommendations for where to stay?" Tse returned her smile.

"Yes, I can see you're not from around here. You're not Itholean either. That's good for you. Half the city loves the influx of slaves, and the other half, well, let's say they preferred the way things were."

Ashkii cut in. "And which do you prefer, miss?"

The lady shrugged. "I don't mind the extra help. But I could do without the fights."

"Fights? Are the Itholeans chaffing under their new masters?"

"Yes, and no. People are more upset about the Itholean princess who wasn't executed, with her councilors."

Ashkii's heartbeat quickened. She wasn't dead. Finding his brother quickly was now more important than ever. "And they're worried she's a threat? Why wasn't she executed?"

"No one really knows, sir. I hear she's got the prince under a spell."

Ashkii's hood slid back, and the words slipped out of his mouth before he could hold them back, "But she's a slave, like the rest of them." Of course, he knew what awaited her here, but he still didn't want to think of her with anyone other than himself.

The lady stared at Ashkii in horror before she glanced away. She turned back to Ashkii and Tse. "Excuse me, I've got some other customers to attend to. You should talk to Peta. Just ask around and you'll find him."

"Way to shut her up, Ash."

Ashkii was confused. She seemed willing enough to talk. Why the sudden change?

His gaze followed the woman, who didn't go to the waiting customers but went straight to the master of the house. They exchanged brief words and then the master, who was not a small man, headed their way.

"I told you not to come back," he said.

"I've never been here before. We've been traveling and arrived this morning."

"That's a lie. Why are you asking about the princess again? You should know better. Last time you started asking questions, a riot broke out. Get out!" The man pointed to the exit.

Ashkii gulped the rest of his ale down quickly and tucked the loaf in his cloak. "As you wish. I meant no offense."

"You, too, sir." The master waited for Tse to stand up.

Ashkii wrapped his cloak tighter as he left the public house. At least he learned something from the brief visit inside. "Not bad, eh, Tse? He was here."

"Yes, but why? He's not covering his tracks very well. I thought he didn't want to be noticed. Not only was he seen, but he's been remembered too." Tse took the broken half of the loaf Ashkii held out to him.

"She did give us a name."

"A trap more like it. Why would she be free with her information and then decide to report us?"

"She didn't recognize me right away. If you were paying attention, you would have seen she was willing until she saw me with my hood down. Yes, she gave us a name, but she gave it after she'd seen my face. That means whoever this guy is has dealt with my brother. It's a good place to begin."

Tse let it drop and together they approached various people in the streets. Most everyone remembered the riot, but hardly anyone recognized Ashkii.

"Peta, you say? Sure, go down this street. You'll reach the corner with the blacksmith, then turn right. Take the second left. You'll find Peta."

Ashkii thought the man who gave him directions didn't know what he was talking about because they walked for an hour before they saw a blacksmith shop. They turned and turned again.

"Great. A dead end." Tse threw up his hands in frustration. No one was nearby to even ask about Peta.

Ashkii couldn't give up. Stepping up to the only door in the alley, he knocked.

No answer.

He knocked again. No answer, not even the faintest smell of someone behind the door reached Ashkii's nose. He tried to push it open, but it wouldn't budge.

"The sun's setting, Ash. We better leave before they lock the gates."

"Hmm?" Ashkii looked up at his friend. "Very well."

Maya and Ryker greeted them back at the camp. Ashkii would have gone straight to Chestnut with half his bread, but Chestnut wasn't there. "Where are you, old boy?" Ashkii sighed and plopped down on his makeshift bed. He was too impatient. Now that they were at Korina, Ashkii wanted to rescue Agonya and get out, but they couldn't do that. Not until they found his brother and stopped him. Ashkii would have to wait. He could wait now that he knew Agonya still lived.

KRILLIN REACHED FOR the lowest branch of a maple tree. He needed to climb up to keep watch while the others slept. He looked at his companions. They were still awake.

"Ash?" Krillin asked. "I understand you're tired, but we must discuss our plan."

The Montane groaned and sat back up. "Can't this wait until morning?"

Krillin let go of the branch and turned to face him. "No, I don't think it can. We're all still shook up from our encounter with Dana and feel vulnerable here."

Maya and Ryker got up from their beds and joined Krillin. "I would feel safer inside the city." Maya agreed.

"But I already told you we need to stay out here to ensure my brother doesn't come this way."

Krillin rolled his eyes. "Really? Cause I thought we were here to rescue the queen. Why do we need to watch out for him? If he's leaving the city, that's a good thing, right?"

"If he's leaving the city, he accomplished his goal."

"Ahh. You're worried that he already has. But didn't you tell us she's still alive?"

"Yeah. Now can I go to sleep?"

"We have to get closer to the palace to ensure her safety."

"He's right, Ash," Tse chimed in. "And we need a plan to get her out of there. When Kilchii makes his move, we need to be nearby. It makes more sense than being out here, exposed."

"Is that how everyone feels?" Ashkii grumbled.

Krillin grinned when the others all nodded their agreement.

"Fine. Now that we have that figured out, we'll find a place in the city tomorrow. The rest can wait." Ashkii laid back down and turned away from Krillin.

"Thanks for talking it through," Krillin mumbled. Maybe the conversation could have waited, but he was frustrated that he was here, while his family was trapped in the mountain. He knew they were safe, thanks to that Kindroot creature, but he still felt helpless. Surely, Ashkii would feel better being closer to Agonya. Krillin sighed and climbed up into the old maple tree. He was on first watch because he napped while Ashkii and Tse did their reconnaissance trip into the city.

The lights from the city were all out, except for the lights along the wall. But they were far enough away that Krillin couldn't smell the guards. There was no one within a hundred meters besides his companions and a few squirrels. It was going to be a long, boring night.

Chapter 19

The day's events kept repeating in Agonya's mind. How had she healed that Itholean slave so quickly? It wasn't until she healed Huren and Lady Rebekkah from a distance that she even knew she was capable of it. The prince was sure to hear of her disobedience. Then what? Oh. It was no use. Agonya wouldn't be able to sleep with those scents floating around in her mind. Rising from her bed, Agonya retrieved her mother's journal. Perhaps she could learn something useful from it.

Opening the cover, Agonya began to read.

> The third day after I met Prince Azurarus, a feast was scheduled for all the nobility to celebrate our engagement. It was a feast like no other. Not that I've attended many feasts. I wasn't old enough until this last year when I turned of age. But that's not the point.

Agonya crossed the small room and curled up in the armchair. This was much better than thinking about her own problems. She felt like her mother was sitting next to her, telling her story in person.

> The food was delicious and smelled of the most amazing herbs. Although, the women I sat with didn't appreciate it as much as I did. They laughed at me, calling me a child. That was fine. They really weren't that bad, but the longing to sneak away with Prince Azurarus put me on edge. Eventually, after the plates were cleaned up, and the guests moved to the gardens to talk, dance, and listen to the musicians, Prince Azurarus found me.

I showed him the less traveled paths in the garden. We had the most amazing time together, laughing and talking. He even kissed me.

Several hours later, we heard someone coming near us. We hid behind the hedges and waited, though we knew we ought to return to the party. It was for us, after all.

As the newcomers drew closer, we heard their voices and recognized them. They belonged to my parents and their closest advisors. Even now, I'm reeling just thinking about what they said.

'Don't worry, darling! I'm sure Kanti will find him for us in no time. They are quite ridiculously infatuated with each other, you know.'

'I saw them dart off together earlier. Probably think they're being sneaky.'

'Yes, well, like I said, Kanti will find the Kindroot for us and bring him to us. Prince Azurarus already trusts her.'

At that moment, our eyes locked onto each other. I tried to convey my confusion to him, but the hurt on his face was more than I can bear to remember.

My parents kept walking and soon we couldn't hear what they were saying. I looked back to Azurarus, but he had vanished. He left me without waiting for my explanation. I didn't know what I should do: should I go after him, beg him to listen, or follow my parents? I decided to follow my parents. I would talk to him later. I didn't know what my parents were plotting, and now I needed to discover the truth. What other nefarious plans did they have that required me to do their bidding?

Keeping in the shadows, I found them just as they were entering the palace through one of the secret passageways. I gave them plenty of space before I followed through the hidden door.

They wound through the passages for a little while before they pushed open the disguised door of my father's office. I couldn't enter the room without being spotted, so I made sure the door didn't close completely behind them.

They talked more about their plans to convince me to betray my betrothed and argued when they should let me in on the plan, before or after the marriage. During their arguing, my mother pulled out an odd scroll. I heard them say it was some sort of contract and they talked about how to fulfill it. It was my luck though that someone came pounding on the office door, pleading for my father to come quickly. They abandoned the scroll on his desk and went to investigate the disturbance.

I snuck into the room and read the scroll. I cannot tell you how upset I am about it. But more than anything, I knew I had to break off the engagement before they could use me to their own ends. It was the worst realization of my life. I wanted to be Prince Azurarus' wife. I was ready to go live in Ithol, the City of Paradise. I couldn't do that to him. He deserved better.

I returned to the garden through the secret passages. That's when I learned what had caused the disturbance. Prince Azurarus had been in a fight with my half-brother, Reid. It took four guards to separate them, and even more to keep them from going at it again. I didn't get a chance to speak with him again that night, nor the next. I kept to my room whenever I wasn't required to be somewhere else. And whenever we were together, he wouldn't even look me in the eye. I couldn't say anything because other people always surrounded us, whether they were servants or family.

Agonya closed her eyes and breathed deeply. She was in almost the exact predicament of what her mother was in. Prince Lucas wanted Agonya to divulge the whereabouts of Blackthorn.

Agonya had to figure out what to do. It sounded like her mother and father would never marry, but she knew they had married. They were her parents, after all. Why did Prince Lucas want Agonya in his household? Bannon said he wanted her as a fragrant woman, but the prince had left her alone other than to bring her to feasts. Tsula said he desired more than a fragrant woman. He couldn't want to marry her, could he? How would he react upon learning what she did at Tsula's? He should have known by now, but she hadn't seen him since her return.

If she gave Lucas what he wanted, would she be able to convince him to set her people free, or would she only jeopardize Blackthorn's safety? No, he wouldn't set them free unless she betrayed Blackthorn. There was no compromising with him.

Agonya couldn't stand it anymore. She set the book on the table next to her chair and went to the window. She pushed the curtains aside and opened the shutters. The cold air came in, giving her goosebumps on her arms. A storm was coming. Perhaps the first snowstorm of the season. It was a pity they would have to seal the window shut for the winter.

Gazing outside brought Agonya comfort, despite the lack of anything noteworthy to see. Just a few distant torches bobbing along the streets. Agonya let the curtains fall into place. Looking out the window would change nothing. What she really needed was more information. Was Blackthorn safe? She tried to reach out to his mind, but her magic wasn't working. She'd used too much of it for healing that Itholean earlier. But how was she supposed to sleep not knowing? Regardless, she needed to try to sleep again.

ALL NIGHT LONG, AGONYA kept returning to her mother's journal. She felt a deep connection with her mother, reading her thoughts from the past. Now, she was paying the consequences for not sleeping. She could barely stay awake in her palanquin. Agonya rubbed her eyes and sat up. The Dahel's estate was on the edge of town. They must be getting close.

She peaked out of the curtains. Some kids chased each other around a potato cart. The owner looked ready to kill the first one to knock anything over. But the kids were careful. Agonya smiled, allowing the curtain to fall into place.

Her days as a child disappeared when her mother died. That's when her father disappeared, too. Agonya never saw him after that, except at meals and feasts where he spoke with important people. Agonya sighed and rubbed her eyes again. Had she not been a young child when her mother died, she might have understood her father better, and not have rebelled so much.

The palanquin halted. The bearers lowered it to the ground. Dylan, the balding guard, pulled the curtains open so she could get out. Deepak was still there along with Peta, but it looked like Dylan oversaw her today. She stepped out and greeted Tsula. It was Tsula's father's life on the line. Agonya would do her best to heal him with only the limited knowledge she had of healing people. She didn't know what was making this woman's father sick.

"Come. I'll introduce you to my parents." Tsula led Agonya towards the strange one level house. Her guards followed close behind.

They entered a room that Agonya didn't have a name for. The large room, although filled with furniture, was empty of anyone but themselves. It was not a parlor, although it shared characteristics of one. Tsula guided them out of the fascinating room into the gardens behind the house.

"We brought father out here for some fresh air. He's down this path." Tsula gestured to the wide mossy path lined by tall trees and delicate roses on either side.

"This is beautiful." Agonya admired the simplicity and yet romantic feel of the garden, even with the frailty of the plants. For indeed, several of the rose petals were wilting and riddled with holes. The trees' bark cracked and peeled, like sunburned skin. Yet the air was the crisp coolness that foreshadows the long, frosty nights to come. "I see where you got your sense of decoration from."

Agonya followed Tsula around a corner and saw a large circular patio paved with large, flat stones. Several wooden chairs sat in the sun. They weren't upright like normal chairs. But the backs were angled so that Tsula's father was partly reclining.

"This is my father, Lord Tashunka. My mother, Lady Kasa. We're all so grateful for you to come help us."

"My pleasure." Agonya approached the old man and pulled up one of the strange chairs to sit next to him. "Sir, I'm Qu — I'm Agonya and I would like to help you, but I don't know if I can. Will you tell me more about what ails you?"

Lady Kasa stepped forward. "He can't speak. It's been a gradual decline. If you had come last week, he would have answered your questions, even if only haltingly."

"When did this start?"

"When we went to the market, I went to go look for supplies and when I returned, there was an old lady with a shawl speaking with my husband. I waited for her to leave, and then I returned to his side. I asked him what she wanted. He didn't know who I was talking about. That was about two months ago. And ever since then, his muscles have been getting weaker and weaker."

How horrible! Agonya had to control her emotions. But two months? And who was that lady? Agonya thought she knew. This smelled of magic. Glancing up at Tsula, she asked, "Would you have some hot water brought out to us? And is there a place for a fire?"

"Yes, of course. Anything you need." Tsula turned to an Itholean servant and gave the request. Then she crossed to the middle of the pavement, where there was a table about knee high. There, she removed a thin slice of wood that was the top of the table, exposing a circle of river rocks beneath. She carefully placed the tabletop to the side and gestured for the guards to help build a fire inside the circle of rocks.

Agonya felt as weak as Lord Tashunka looked. She regretted staying up all night, but her attempts to sleep were unsuccessful. She kept wondering what had happened to the Itholean she'd healed. And now she was expected to heal Tsula's father, one of the most honored men in Korina. And because of her stupidity, she was exhausted. Breathing deeply, Agonya smelled the plants nearby and felt a burst of energy.

She turned her attention back to Lord Tashunka. "How are you today? I hope all is well."

Tashunka's head moved ever so slightly, but Agonya knew that to mean he was well, apart from his obvious ailment.

How was she going to help him? Was he cursed? Poisoned? Agonya wasn't a healer, not in the strictest sense of the word.

Once the fire was no longer roaring but had nice red-hot coals, Agonya selected some oils Tsula had set up on a nearby chair. "Would you bring him closer to the fire, Peta and Dylan?"

The guards looked startled at being addressed but obliged. Standing on either end of the chair, they lifted him up, chair and all, and moved him next to the fire.

Agonya poured pine oil and some orinberry powder on the coals and breathed the scents in, focusing on Tashunka. But the moment she felt the power nearing his body, it turned away as if there was a barrier between him and the rest of the world. The barrier reminded Agonya of the mind barriers the Montanes used to block others from entering their minds. Agonya tried to gather his smell in her mind, but it, too, was trapped behind the wall. He didn't have a fragrance, or maybe she was too tired to smell it.

She opened her eyes and saw Tsula and Kasa watching from their chairs. "What fragrance would you say your father and husband has?"

Tsula frowned. "What do you mean? Can't you smell him?"

Lady Kasa smiled and answered, "He smells of grain on a warm summer day."

Agonya searched the incense on the chair until she found what she was looking for. She tossed the stick on the fire. It smelled of neroli oranges with a hint of lemongrass, not quite the grain scent she needed. Agonya bit her lip and tried to conjure up Tashunka's natural aroma. Then, she coaxed the blend of berry, pine, and neroli scents towards Tashunka. This time, the barrier cracked. Agonya forced her magic through the opening and the whole barrier yielded to her will. She would need to work quickly. Her own strength was fading fast.

With her eyes closed, Agonya laid her hands on his head and worked the scents through his nose and down into his body. All his muscles were tight and unbending. So, she focused on his tongue. If she could loosen his tongue, then maybe he could speak.

"Miss?" a young girl stood beside Agonya holding a large pot of hot water.

"Thank you, place it on the ground right there." Agonya closed her eyes and drifted back to Tashunka. Slowly, she felt his tongue loosen until, finally; he let out a cry of joy.

Lady Kasa snapped her eyes on her husband, as did everyone else in the small circle.

"Father!" Tsula rushed to his side. "Please tell me you can speak."

Tashunka didn't smile, but he did speak. "I can. Thank you, your Highness."

Agonya blushed. "No need to call me that, sir. I no longer have that title. I wish I could do more for you."

"Oh, but you have. It is I who wishes I could tell you more."

"Can you tell me about that woman you met two months ago?"

"I can't. I don't even remember such a lady. My wife is the one who remembers her."

"That lady may be the key to unlocking this curse on you. I do not know how to undo it myself, and I'm afraid, my Lord, that your tongue will tighten again before too long."

"I feel it already."

The shadows faded into the sun's light. Agonya breathed in the scents from the fire and began again. She heard Tsula send the servants to retrieve the midday meal, and to Agonya's surprise, her guards went with them. She loosened his tongue even more and tried to heal all the muscles in his face and neck.

"Would it be all right if I spoke to you another way?"

"You needn't ask. All your help is a blessing here, your Highness."

Good. This would make things easier. Agonya glanced at the others in the garden. There was no hiding what she was about to do. But she didn't think they would give her secret away.

So, she spoke in his mind. "Lord Tashunka, I don't like to speak in others' minds if I don't have to, but since you said it was okay, I want to know if I can search your mind?"

"I don't know how this is possible, but yes, of course," he answered in his mind.

215

Agonya nodded and sifted through the memories he had of that day. His question about how she was doing this kept popping to the front of his mind, so Agonya smiled and answered. "A friend of mine taught me."

"Please pardon my persistence, but your capability to do this is truly extraordinary. How did your friend learn?"

Agonya wasn't sure how to answer him. Most people knew about Kindroots from children's stories, so maybe she could make it seem like this knowledge was passed down in a story. "I'm uncertain of the origins, but I think it has to do with the Kindroots from long ago."

At the mention of Kindroots, Tashunka gasped. "Kindroots? There's something about that word, but I can't put my finger on it."

Agonya pressed forward. This could be the key. "Are you referring to the old stories, or is it something else that you know?" If he had additional knowledge, it was crucial to learn it now.

"I think it's something else. I can't remember..."

Agonya drew in the scents again and guided them through Tashunka's memories, pressing at the seams. She broke through! An old lady with a black shawl appeared at his booth.

"May I help you?" he asked.

"I believe you can. You've heard the stories of the Kindroots?" Her voice didn't sound old.

"Yes, everyone knows those."

"I knew you could help." The old woman looked satisfied. "You see, I have this minor problem..." The memory faded and Agonya couldn't see any more of it.

"I remembered that!" Lord Tashunka's voice cracked.

"That's great! I wish we could have seen more of that memory, but that took all my strength. I need to rest, as do you. I'll be back as soon as I can. If you remember anything, anything at all, tell your wife or have someone write it down."

"I will," he said. Then Tashunka's mouth twitched. Agonya thought perhaps he was trying to smile. "Be careful." Tears welled up in his eyes as he spoke. "I'm afraid."

Lady Kasa rushed over to his side. "Don't be afraid, my love. We'll find a way to heal you." Turning towards Agonya, she said, "How can I ever repay you?"

Agonya brushed her loose hair behind her ear. "It isn't much. I'm afraid it won't last."

"I don't understand."

"There's a curse on your husband, and I don't know how to lift it. In order to loosen his tongue, I had to use all my strength. Already, his tongue tightens." Agonya placed her hand on Lady Kasa's back. "Don't despair. We will find a way." If there was anything Agonya wanted to believe, it was this. Because it wasn't Prince Lucas or King Reid that started all this, though they certainly weren't innocent.

Tsula held out her hand for Agonya. "You look like you're about to fall over. Let's get you home and let these two lovers talk while they can."

Chapter 20

"I keep trying to see her. Do you think we're too late?" Ashkii squinted as if that would help him see her better from so far away. Out of the corner of his eye, he saw Tse shake his head. Ashkii ignored his friend and turned his attention back to Agonya's window. No light shone behind it. Either she was in bed, asleep, or not in her room.

"You don't need to check on her. It's your brother we need to find. You saw her for yourself leaving the palace and returning a few hours later. You know she's alive and has four guards with her everywhere she goes."

"Weren't you with all the others saying we need to focus on rescuing her instead of finding my brother?"

"Yeah, but now that we've established she's alive and we have a plan, we need to make sure Kilchii doesn't mess it up."

Ashkii couldn't help but stare at the dark window in the palace and hope for a glimpse of her beautiful face. It remained dark. His shoulders slumped.

"Agonya is alive, Ash."

"I know," Ashkii mumbled.

"I know you know," Tse laughed. "You're smitten with her."

Ashkii stood up. "It sounds like you've got this under control. I'm going to check out the other gates."

"Ha! Admit it. You're stalking the girl." Tse slapped his leg.

"If I'm stalking her, then what are you doing?"

"Me?" Tse tried to look innocent. "I'm watching your back, Chief. How long do you want to be out here?"

Ashkii smiled. He knew Tse was teasing him. But he appreciated his loyalty. "I'll go around the entire palace and when I return, we'll decide how much longer. But one of us should watch her window at all times, especially now that we have a place nearby."

"I'll be here when you get back, Chief." Tse settled back onto the roof.

Ashkii rolled his eyes. Tse called him chief, but that path for him was long gone. He only ever followed Kilchii when it should have been the other way around. Tse was a good man. He would protect her if he saw anything. So, Ashkii set off to patrol the edges of the palace.

"What are you planning, brother?" he thought, as he kept out of sight. Ashkii scanned the distant rooftops, but there were no shadows out of place. The only shadows to be seen were of the guards next to the gate. "Why haven't you attacked already?"

Ashkii waited for the guards to look the other way. Then he leaped to the next roof, landing without the slightest sound. He loved the hunt. Problem was, so did his brother. At least Ashkii had the advantage of his brother, not knowing he was being hunted. Surprise was his only hope of stopping Kilchii. And he had to stop him. Ashkii didn't want to consider the alternative.

Because Tse was right. Ashkii liked Agonya more than as a friend. He would be devastated if she died. He wished he'd made Tse do the perimeter check, so he could have stayed and possibly caught a glimpse of her restlessness that he'd seen the previous night and the night before that.

Ashkii scanned the area. No one else seemed to be losing sleep, except perhaps the guards. Not even a stray cat could be smelled.

Ashkii leaped to the next roof. Scanned. Leaped. Scanned. And leaped again. He paused at each of the gates to make sure he wasn't missing anything, then continued around the wall.

The urge to breach the wall and go to her room was overwhelming. He could speak with her in less than four minutes. Hear her voice. Smell her fragrance. What he wouldn't give to be near her again.

He was so intent on remembering her; he didn't realize he was getting ready to leap onto the palace wall itself. His foot slipped on a loose tile and flew out from under him. He landed on his back.

He waited a moment to see if anyone inside heard him fall.

All was quiet. They must not have woken.

Ashkii sighed with relief and stood, careful not to slip on any other loose tiles. He turned away from the palace wall and continued his predetermined route. Soon Tse appeared, and they were standing next to each other.

"I saw her standing in the window again," he said.

Ashkii's blond head snapped to the window. Then his hand flew up to his neck. Smells, that hurt! He must have pulled something with his quick movements. Not to mention, the window was dark, and the princess was nowhere to be seen.

"There was nothing in my search. No sign of him or anything else. How did she look?"

"Like she does every night, Ash. She stares out the window at who knows what and then disappears behind her curtains. She's too far away to see her facial expressions, so unless you want to get closer, you're going to have to be content knowing she's still alive."

Ashkii moved closer to Tse. "Perhaps we do need to get closer."

Tse backed up. "Uh-uh. No way! If we get caught. If someone sees us, even if we're not caught, we lose the advantage. I was only saying you should be content."

"But I'm not content, Tse." Ashkii ran his fingers through his wavy hair. "He's out there, biding his time. We have yet to find him. Our only lead was a dead end. It's possible we don't have any surprises on our side."

"Why hasn't he come for us?" Tse countered.

"Shh." Ashkii crouched down and watched the gates open.

Tse squatted next to Ashkii. And they waited.

A short man, dressed in all black, walked through the gate, followed by five others. Not toward the palace, but away from it. Ashkii couldn't believe he had allowed himself to be so caught up in their conversation that he hadn't seen this man leave the palace and cross the courtyard. Had this man spotted them on the roofs?

It was too risky to stay here. Ashkii gave Tse the signal, and they retreated. They would take turns on watch until they had a plan to rescue her.

THE SAFETY OF THE INN'S walls made Maya feel like she was back in Ithol with Agonya. Her new magical powers reminded her where she was. The emotions of everyone in the building weighed her down. The walls helped to dampen their feelings and made Maya feel less exposed, but Dana's glare still haunted her. She couldn't explain it right to Ryker. He had offered to get the supplies for her, but Maya couldn't let him handle everything. He had his own job to do. It was her job to replenish their supplies. As much as she wanted to stay inside, she couldn't. Most of their supplies were lost in the cave or with the elephantuses.

Maya reached for the handle. Why was it hard to open the door? It was ridiculous. Maya was more than capable of shopping. She extended her arm and touched the handle. Her chest tightened, and she couldn't move until it loosened. All the others were off doing their part. Ryker was out there, scouting for more information. That thought gave Maya the courage to open the door and step outside.

They were on the third floor of the inn, the very top because Ashkii insisted on being near the roof. It made sense for him, since he preferred to travel through the air. Maya clutched her bag and descended the stairs. She remembered passing a market on their way to the inn the day before, so she headed that direction.

Korina wasn't that different from Ithol. Maya pretended she was back home, shopping for Agonya. In a sense, she was shopping for Agonya, if their plan to rescue her worked.

Maya took her time going from stall to stall, making note of the high expenses. They couldn't afford everything they needed. Food was essential and so were the perfumes Krillin had asked for, but new clothes would have to wait. Maya returned the hand knitted scarf to the rack and went to move on.

"Maya?"

Her heart raced, but that voice compelled her to turn. "Lord Tanish?"

"It is you! I didn't recognize you. What happened to your face? And what are you doing here? I thought you were still... there." Lord Tanish glanced over his shoulders, but no one was paying attention to them.

"I was, but well, it's a long story. How are you here? I thought all the councilors had been..."

"Her majesty helped me escape before we reached Korina. But I still have to be careful. I go by Yari now. Thankfully, I was able to purchase this stall. Do you want to come and eat our midday meal together? There's much I want to discuss with you."

Maya had to contain the pure joy she was feeling. Lord Tanish was alive! And he'd been living in Korina near the palace. Had he been keeping an eye on Agonya? He could give them all sorts of information that would help them. She nodded and followed him into the back, away from listening ears.

"HEY, GUYS!" MAYA BURST into the room.

"Whoa!" Tse looked up from sharpening his daggers. "Look who won a bottle of perfume!"

Maya blushed. "Where's Ryker?"

"On duty watching Agonya," Ashkii reminded her.

"Oh, right." Maya's shoulders slumped. She went to her bed and started pulling out the supplies she'd gathered. "You'll never guess who I ran into on the streets."

"Did you manage to get everything on our list?" Krillin asked, stepping over to look at what she was doing.

Maya grinned. "You should feel how confused you all are right now. It's great."

"Yeah, until one of us decides to toss you out the window. What are you so worked up about?" Tse said with a laugh.

"Who did you meet?" Ashkii asked.

"Yari," she said.

"Who's Yari," Krillin asked.

"Lord Tanish, but now he's going by Yari."

"Lord Tanish?" Ashkii rubbed his chin. "Wasn't he one of Agonya's priests?"

"Yes! And he escaped before they reached Korina. He helped me gather all these supplies and even better, he's been keeping an eye on Agonya from the little shop that he bought."

All three men stared at her, dumbfounded.

"I told him I wanted him to meet you all and invited him for the evening meal."

"You told him where we're staying?" Ashkii croaked.

Maya felt his horror and realized why he was so upset. "It's going to be okay, Ash. Remember that little thing I can do? I knew exactly what he was feeling the entire time I was with him, and he is loyal to Agonya. Believe me,

I know he is. You don't have to be afraid. Also, you should know he's bringing a guest."

"What?! Maya, you can't just go around telling strangers where we are and what we're doing. You didn't tell him what we're doing, did you?"

"Of course not! But we ought to tell him when he comes."

"Who's coming with him?" Krillin asked.

"Lady Rebekkah," Maya replied, as if they all knew who she was. That was okay. Maya didn't mind explaining it all to them. It was their first good news in a long while. "Lady Rebekkah also goes by a different name now, ever since King Reid tried to execute her."

Tse started laughing.

"Why are you laughing?" Maya demanded.

"It's just so unbelievable that of all the people you came across today, you ran into two people that you knew when you worked for Agonya and that they have escaped and survived execution."

Maya felt it when Ashkii figured it out. "She did this, didn't she?"

"Agonya doesn't know about us, but she spoke with Lord Tanish after she'd saved Lady Rebekkah. He found Lady Rebekkah and they've been working together ever since, sticking close to the queen in case she needed them."

"Yes," Ashkii said, "She did this. She always does this. Don't you see? That's why we're here, too. She loves people, and that's why she made such a wonderful queen. People are drawn to her because of who she is."

Maya couldn't help but agree with him. Agonya was the reason they were all there. Agonya saw value in all of them, including herself. There were times Maya didn't feel up to the task, but this is why she stuck with it, because Agonya loved her, and she loved Agonya. But this went beyond a feeling of love for one another. They were also here because of Blackthorn. She hadn't quite understood why Agonya loved him so much, but after spending the last few months together, she understood. Blackthorn was like Agonya. He loved the people he knew, even the ones he didn't know, and both Agonya and Blackthorn needed their help.

HOW MANY DAYS SINCE the groundshake? The sun's light couldn't reach into the heart of the mountain to let them know how many days it'd been. Indeed, they were without any light now. It seemed like they were going straight through the mountain, but they could be going in circles for all they knew. It wasn't often for Blackthorn to lose track of things. Was this how humans felt all the time? The only signs that time was passing came from his growing hunger and thirst, minimal for him, but significant to his companions, who needed frequent meals. It was good they began their trek with food, as minimal as it was, because they had already slept and woken a handful of times, though for how long none of them knew. Not even Blackthorn, who stood watch while they slept. If they hadn't had anything to eat, they would be struggling to keep moving.

Blackthorn sat on Anya's shoulders and let his roots touch either side of the tunnel. It was easier to smell and feel a thing if he was touching it. They walked in the dark like that for a little way. There were no side paths, so they went straight. Then Blackthorn smelled something different. He whipped his roots ahead and blocked Amber from going further.

Amber pushed his roots aside and dug in her bag for the flint and steel. She struck it. There was an opening to the right. She crept closer and struck it again. "Dead end," she croaked out. They needed to find water soon. Blackthorn's healing capabilities were limited.

Hastily, they passed the narrow opening, and Blackthorn extended his roots to grasp the opposite side of the wall. It felt cold and jagged.

They walked in silence. Their throats too parched to speak. The wall curved slightly away from them and Amber followed it. How much longer before they found the light of day again? Blackthorn had lived to see many things, but being trapped inside a dark cave without food or water with Krillin's family and a Kor and a Montane wasn't something he could have predicted. Avoiding Dana was an easy decision back then. He might have made a different choice if he'd known they would have to cross through the entire mountain.

Blackthorn breathed in the stale air. Water! It had to be nearby. He could smell the moisture in the air, but where was it coming from? The wall was dry. Blackthorn felt for the next opening. Then he breathed in the new air and froze. He didn't reach to block the path this time, instead his roots flew to the sword on Amber's waist. Amber felt his movement and grabbed it out from under his roots.

Blackthorn couldn't see the thorny devil, but he could smell it. He reached out to Amber's mind and told her exactly what they were facing and where he was. Amber's hands trembled.

"Here, let me," Smokey said, stepping forward.

Amber didn't resist but let Smokey take the sword. The Kor was a well-trained soldier even if he remembered nothing from his past. He didn't hesitate but lunged forward and plunged the sword through the top of the thorny devil's head where it slept. The thorny devil let out a dying screech. Smokey yanked the sword out, and the devil's head fell back to the cold stone with a thunk. The Kor waved to the girls to go ahead of him. Blackthorn felt relief. That could have been a lot worse.

That's when Blackthorn noticed the others. Smokey gasped when he heard several low growls a moment later. There were lots of them. And now they were all angry.

"Run!" he hissed. Smokey swung the sword up and blocked one, jumping towards him. The sword clanged against the hard scales. The Montane stepped up beside Smokey and helped push the devil back.

"Ahh!" Amber cried out, "Pit!"

Too late. Anya ran into Sari, who knocked Amber forward. She cried out again. This time Blackthorn could hear her voice falling through the air. He shot his roots out and wrapped them around Amber's waist just as she slipped over the edge. He pulled her up. Then he turned to face the thorny devils at their backs. They couldn't run this time.

Smokey and Nakos blocked the thorny devils in the side tunnel as long as they could, but soon the devils forced them to back up. Blackthorn unwrapped his roots from Amber now that she was stable and leaped off Anya's shoulders and onto Nakos' shoulder. From there, he extended his roots to the closest attacking devil and sent a jolt of pain into the creature. The devil stumbled and Smokey stabbed it with the sword. He did his best to help the soldiers kill the devils. Together, they incapacitated and stabbed the devils one after the other. Sometimes their sword and daggers bounced off its scales, but when they got through the armor, they dug their daggers in and ripped it upward or downward. The thorny devil's growls echoed off the walls.

Fortunately, the cave narrowed here. No more than two of the waist-high creatures could reach them at a time. Blackthorn felt drained. They were weak from no food, but he had no choice but to trip the devils with his roots, tying them up and sending pain into them to keep them from getting too close. He heard Anya cry out in pain. As soon as Smokey killed the devil he was holding, Blackthorn rushed to her side and sent immense pain into the devil.

The devil let go of her ankle and turned toward Nakos, who thrust his daggers forward into the devil's eyes. It screamed and backed away. Then they were gone. There were no more devils attacking them. Blackthorn lowered himself to Anya's side. Sari was already there, tying a piece of her dress around Anya's leg. He couldn't really see them, but he heard her movements.

"I'm sorry, Anya." Blackthorn said.

"Not your fault." Anya managed between sharp breaths.

Blackthorn shook his leaves. "I should have thought through our decision to find another way out versus digging our way out, but I was so focused on keeping out of Dana's reach—"

"Dana?" Sari gasped.

Oops. They hadn't known Dana was there. "I'm sorry. I should have told you Dana was the one who caused the groundshake."

"And you let us abandon Krillin to her? You said he was safe!"

"He was safe. I could tell he wasn't near Dana. You're right, I should have informed you. Look where we are now. I didn't mean for any of you to get hurt. Let me see if I can heal Anya's leg." Blackthorn breathed in Anya's fragrance and focused on her injury. He was so drained, but he sent his magic into her ankle and started the healing process. "I did what I can for now. I need to rest before I can heal it anymore."

Sari sat back. "Can you stand, Anya?"

"Help me."

Smokey sheathed his sword and lifted her as gently as he could. She tried to put weight on her injured leg and winced.

Amber struck the flint and steel. Blackthorn turned to see her standing next to the pit. She struck it again. This time, he saw a small path circling the edge of the pit. How were they going to cross it with Anya's injury? They were too weak. They required food and water, among other things. Amber made the light again. This time, Blackthorn noticed the dead thorny devils and smiled. He could solve one of their problems, after all. Then he set to work explaining his plan to harvest its meat.

RAW, THORNY DEVIL MEAT was not edible, but they were too exhausted to figure out how to cook it after their fight. So, despite the cold and their hunger, Blackthorn helped them sleep. While they slept, he kept guard and thought of ways to get a fire going to cook their food. Eventually, he crept away from the warmth of his sleeping companions to explore.

He tried to remember the warm sun on his bark and leaves. Being in this dark, dank cave made him feel more trapped than ever. He resolved to find a way out.

Blackthorn sighed and headed for the ledge. He felt his way along the skinny path and did his best not to fall into the gaping hole to his right. Each step was slow and deliberate. He didn't even know if the other side would go anywhere. It could be another dead end. But he had to try. They couldn't stay here for the rest of their lives, or their lives would be very short indeed.

On the other side, Blackthorn did his best to hurry. He needed to ensure it was safe for before he risked Anya trying to cross over. The wide, straight path allowed two people to walk side by side. Seeing a tunnel diverge from his path, Blackthorn halted.

Confident that it wasn't a dead end and there were no more evil creatures waiting to attack them, Blackthorn returned to the humans. They were awake and working on cutting up more thorny devil meat when he got back. Blackthorn squatted next to them. A small pile of thinly sliced meat lay in between them. The meat had little fat, but enough for his purpose. Blackthorn sifted through the meat for a fattier piece. Then he reached into Nakos' bag and pulled out an empty perfume bottle.

"Here, hold this."

Anya took the bottle from him.

Blackthorn held the meat up over the bottle. "Amber, strike the flint and stone underneath the meat."

Amber kept striking them together until they saw the fat start to liquefy. Little by little, drop by drop, the fat rolled off the meat down into the bottle. It was painstakingly slow, but they all knew what it meant. They kept at it for several hours. Slice after slice. They took turns between striking the flint and steel and slicing meat.

At last, they had a full bottle of fat. Sari held out the stick they'd used for their torch. But what wick could they use? Blackthorn could only see the clothes they wore, and they were not enough to protect them from the cold.

"Smokey, I think if we had some of your cloak, we could use it to get our torch to last longer." He hated to ask, but knew it was their best option. The cloak was the best quality of weaving since it was guard material.

Smokey nodded and cut several inches off the bottom and wrapped it around the end of the stick. Then he poured some of the fat on it. He waited, allowing the fat to soak in, and poured more fat on it. It had to be soaked all the way through, or it wouldn't last long.

Finally, Blackthorn let Anya do the honors of lighting the torch. The fire was so brilliant to their eyes!

Sari was the first to speak. "We'd better cook some of this meat, now that we have a fire."

The tasks never ended. Once they overcame one obstacle, another appeared. But Blackthorn knew the tasks were necessary and was grateful that they could do them at all. He didn't mind all the food and fat preparations because it delayed the problem of getting Anya across that tiny ledge.

Chapter 21

The initial burst of curiosity about his disappearance died down after a couple of days. The people were more relieved to be free from looking for him than they were about discovering his whereabouts. Which made it easier for him to justify another disappearance. This time, Jaylen would be prepared. Whatever that place was was important. More important than any task he'd ever had. And he didn't want to draw attention to it until he knew more.

Logan was easy enough to work with. Jaylen even trusted him. But Logan had been irate when Jaylen finally returned and wouldn't tell him where he'd been. If Logan had more authority than Jaylen, things might have turned out differently, but Logan was under Jaylen's authority, so Jaylen placated him by telling him it was a secret scent that he couldn't talk about.

Laniel, however, handled Jaylen's disappearance rather well. He didn't like that Jaylen promoted him to be the captain of his guard. But he understood why Jaylen needed him in that position. He wouldn't have to answer to anyone but Jaylen. It was a compromise. Jaylen promoted Laniel, but just to oversee six soldiers on Jaylen's personal guard, not an entire division.

Walking into the Great Hall, Jaylen spotted Logan giving orders to the captains for the day. He waited for him to finish and then approached.

"Hey Logan, remember that secret scent I'm working on?"

Logan grunted.

"I'll be working on it all day today and maybe the next few days. Think you can handle Ithol while I'm gone?"

"Of course. Who do you think I am?"

"I didn't mean it that way. You're great at what you do. I just wanted to give you that warning I promised."

"I know." Logan admitted.

"Then why are you so upset?"

"I've worked with you for a long time and even though you gave me this promotion, I still feel like you don't trust me, and I want you to trust me like you trust Laniel."

"You're jealous? Of my relationship with Laniel? You realize that you have the bigger promotion than Laniel, right?"

"Yeah, but..."

"But you are the perfect person for this job, and Laniel is the perfect person for the job I gave him. So far, I'm very pleased with the work you've both done. Don't make me regret putting you in charge."

"I won't, sir." Logan saluted Jaylen like they used to do back on the field.

Jaylen accepted the salute and left Logan in the Great Hall. Perhaps he'd been too hard on him. He was a good man. If Jaylen discovered anything useful, he would try to include both Logan and Laniel.

Laniel waited for him in the hall. "Are you ready, sir?"

"Yes. Let's go."

THE THORNY DEVIL WAS cooked and stored in their bulging bags along with a couple of perfume bottles filled with fat. They were ready. Amber went first with Blackthorn on her shoulder. Then Smokey started across, with Anya clinging to his back. Nakos went next and then Sari followed with the torch held high. Blackthorn's leaves quivered faster the further from the main cave floor they went, but he kept his roots from shaking so he didn't frighten the others any more than they already were. One. Two. Three. Four steps. Twenty-nine steps. Then Amber stepped onto the other side. They turned and waited for the others to cross. As soon as Smokey got close enough, Blackthorn reached out and grabbed his waist, helping him and Anya up onto the solid ground.

He felt the tension leave his body as soon as Anya was lowered to the ground. "Can you walk?" Smokey asked.

"Yes. You can't carry me the whole time. If I have someone to lean on..."

"Lean on me. The tunnel is wide enough for us to walk together.

Smokey and Anya took the lead. Before they knew it, they were further than Blackthorn had scouted. They turned a corner, and the stench of dead fish hit Blackthorn. He partially retracted his roots, resisting the overwhelming urge to fully do so. The smell was unbearable.

"Are you okay, Blackthorn?" Amber asked.

Blackthorn couldn't reply. His vision fuzzed. When he opened his eyes, something was different. He couldn't quite make out what it was. Amber's voice was gone. Despite being surrounded, he was alone on the cave floor. There was another light up ahead. He started toward it and heard voices but couldn't make out what they were saying.

As he approached, he heard a woman speaking. "Jay, dear, this isn't right. That beggar may have had a vision but, really?"

"Trust me, Korina, I know there's a way through these mountains. I can feel it."

"You can feel it? Ha!"

Jay? Korina? Those names were familiar to Blackthorn. He moved forward to ask them which side of the mountain they'd come from. Their accents weren't hard to understand, but it had been a long time since he'd heard it.

When he rounded the corner, he saw Jay and Korina talking in what appeared to be a vast domed opening in the cave. Not only were their names familiar, but they looked familiar too. A small pond lay behind them, and hundreds of people lined the walls, spilling into the tunnel on the other side of the room.

"Excuse me." Blackthorn spoke in his high-pitched voice.

"Yes, I feel it. Don't you worry, I know you wanted to go with Jed and his group but, I know what Monsters lie in his path. This is the safer way." The man spoke to the woman as if Blackthorn had said nothing at all, as if he wasn't there, and then it clicked. This was a vision of the past. Jed must be Jedrek the first.

"Didn't you see that pit you nearly fell into?" The woman pointed to the tunnel the people were emerging from.

"I didn't fall in, did I?" Jay waved his hands in the air. "That's nothing compared to what your precious Jed is going to face!"

Korina flushed and turned away from Jay, who kept talking.

"I know why you desired to go with him."

"You know nothing!"

Blackthorn watched and listened to them fight and wondered why he was seeing this vision. Suddenly, the vision vanished without a trace.

He heard Sari speaking to him.

"Blackthorn, wake up." Then he felt the icy touch of her hand. He turned towards the sound of her voice.

"Blackthorn. You're awake." Anya's bubbly voice made him smile.

"What happened?" Sari asked.

Blackthorn shook out his branches. "I had a vision. There were people arguing. Many people were standing around a pond. A pond. Come on!" Blackthorn tried to jump onto Anya's shoulder but got tangled up and had to slow down to untwist his roots. "I'm pretty sure the vision was of the past. If it was accurate, there's water up ahead."

Blackthorn felt the breath of life, knowing that water was close. He was sure of it. He simply followed the smell of rotten fish. Why hadn't he made the connection before when he first smelled the fish? Blackthorn wanted to go faster, but he could only go as fast as Smokey was going, since he was helping Anya.

They rounded the bend.

Before them was the same cavern he had seen moments before. The empty scene only had a small pond with dead fish on its surface. Blackthorn moved forward, but Anya tripped. Her hand slipped from Smokey's arm, and she fell to the ground. Blackthorn went down with her. As they were recovering, he noticed a silver chain under her foot. He tugged on it and lifted her foot for it to come loose.

"Here, Anya." Sari knelt next to her daughter and helped her sit up. "Drink some water."

Blackthorn saw Sari help Anya drink from their wooden bowl. However, his gaze remained fixed on the necklace in his grasp. He knew the delicate curve of the silver, crisscrossing each other. A seam ran the length of the side, just like Agonya's mother's necklace. He pried it open. Inside lay a tiny pad. The pad had a faint smell of something salty. Possibly something fishy? He probably smelled the rotting fish in the water.

"Ooh!" Amber sidled up to Blackthorn and squatted down to get a better look.

"And who is its owner?" Blackthorn wondered.

"That's a good sign, right? The owned must have found a way out!"

"Our entrance wasn't blocked when this person came through here. There's something about it..." His eyes glazed over as he trailed off and another vision hit him.

Korina rubbed the necklace at her throat as she walked. A blend of salt and... and fish? Drifted over to where he sat. Blackthorn usually avoided the scent of fish, but it wasn't exactly fish. Fish was the closest smell he could think of to describe it.

None of them seemed to notice him. It seemed so real. They were the same people, but the place was different. Sunlight pierced through the darkness behind them and then faded in the direction they walked.

No one seemed to care that they were leaving the sun behind. Korina didn't even seem to pay attention to where they were going. Her mind was so obviously somewhere else. Just like Blackthorn's. He ambled towards the light. When he reached the bend in the path, the people were still walking through, but Blackthorn was blocked by an invisible wall.

He turned back and watched the procession move further into the dark and resigned himself to follow. Whatever this vision was must be important, because it had found him. Just as he caught up to the beautiful woman lost in thought, he realized that none of this was familiar to him and yet there was light! That meant there was another way out. If he followed them, perhaps they could find the way out when he woke from the vision.

"Korina," another woman shorter and plainer than Korina spoke from her other side.

"Hmm."

The woman lowered her voice. "Don't worry about her. She'll be safe."

Korina looked up to see who had heard the woman speak. "Shh! You can't talk about that! If word gets back to him..."

The woman gave a small laugh. "Who? Jay? He's at the front leading the way."

"But someone could tell him."

"I don't think they will. Look, Korina, I'm only saying the girl will be fine. Jed will protect her."

"I know. I just wish I was with her." Korina straightened her shoulders and looked forward.

They walked through the cave, but the light didn't diminish as Blackthorn had expected. He looked around and saw that several torches were lit. Of course, they would have torches. Blackthorn paid attention to every twist and turn of the cave.

"Blackthorn! Wake up!" A frantic voice grew in the back of his mind. Blackthorn strained to hear it.

"Blackthorn! She's hurt! Please!"

He gave a start. Amber's face was in his way, tears streaking down her cheeks.

"Blackthorn! Please, wake up!"

"I'm awake," he said, shaking his branches. "What's the matter?"

"It's Anya. She passed out after she drank the water."

Blackthorn found Anya laying on the ground a short distance away. Sari was bent over her daughter, weeping. One look at Anya's pale face and Blackthorn knew as surely as Amber and Sari knew she was on the brink of death. He didn't stop to question how it came about but went to her and tried to heal her. Someone picked them both up and ran towards the tunnel on the far side of the pond. Blackthorn called out the fork they should take and focused on Anya's tiny little body. Poison raced through her veins. He tried to draw it out of her.

He heard Sari and Amber call to them to wait, but Blackthorn told Smokey to keep going. They would find a way out and get help. The others would follow. They were following. They couldn't afford to wait, to be cautious. Not now.

THE PAINTING ON THE wall looked exactly the same as before. Why would it change? It was a ridiculous thought, but Jaylen couldn't help but wonder if the magic would have changed it when he wasn't looking. It hadn't.

Laniel walked up to him. "Sir, there's no one else here."

"Thank you. Stand guard at the door. Don't let anyone in. If I'm gone past the evening meal, lock the library and you can rotate the guards to stand watch."

"You have your water and food?"

Jaylen patted his bag. "I'm not making that mistake twice."

"See you soon, sir." Laniel saluted and walked toward the library doors.

Jaylen turned to face the painting on the wall. He could pick out the tree now that he knew what to look for. He took a deep breath through his nose but detected no scent. Why couldn't he smell the tree? What did he do the previous time?

He'd been looking at the painting, imagining a Kindroot sitting on the sill blending in and then he had hummed a song his mother had taught him when he was little! The excitement built up. Jaylen hummed and sure enough, he saw the nut on the tree in the painting and could smell its beautiful fragrance. He breathed it in more deeply, closing his eyes, and when he opened his eyes, he was not in the library anymore.

Jaylen grinned and looked for the torches on the walls. There was one right next to him. He lit it and pulled it out of its bracket. His grin faded when he realized he was exactly where he'd entered before. It had taken him two days to find the tree, but he had been confused and didn't know what he was doing. There was still a mystery to this place, and Jaylen wasn't going to waste time exploring side tunnels.

He threw his cloak over his shoulder and walked forward, retracing his steps to an intersection of tunnels. Which way should he go? Jaylen examined the walls, searching for a scent to guide him. He couldn't detect any out-of-place scents. Then he noticed markings on the walls. They were all trees, but not the same tree. Which one was the one he wanted?

The tree on the corner going straight ahead had something resembling a fruit on it, or perhaps a nut? He tried smelling it for clues. This place was magical, controlled by scents. Aha! The tree smelled of citrus. Turning to another tree, Jaylen sniffed it and moved to the next until he found the one that had a nutty scent to it. He took the tunnel to the right.

Now that he knew what to look for, navigating these tunnels didn't seem so daunting. It was still several hours of walking before Jaylen noticed there were lines beneath the trees. The lines were decreasing at each new intersection. Why didn't he find any other trees last time? Had he gone in circles without knowing it?

Then he turned a corner and there it was. The tree was beautiful. But now that he'd found it, what was he supposed to do? He was getting hungry, so Jaylen sat down and pulled out some cheese and bread and thought about everything he knew about Kindroots. Someone high in the ranks of the Korin military knew about Kindroots. Why else would they be ordered to target the princess of Ithol? Her words to him had a plausibility he didn't want to admit. She'd told him Kindroots were the true reason for this fight. That was obvious in hindsight. But why was she protecting them? Why were his people going to war to find them and under the pretense of justice?

There were so many questions that needed answers. For instance, how long had this feud been going on? Jaylen tried to remember the history he'd been taught in school. If the reason for going to war with Ithol was about Kindroots and not their Princess Kanti's murder, what else might be a lie? No, he didn't have time to figure that out. That wasn't why he was in a place that appeared to be the Kindroots' home. There was one particular Kindroot everyone was hoping to smell. And Jaylen knew that Kindroot was working with Princess Agonya and her handmaiden, Maya, but not with his commanders. He could work with that.

Laniel and Logan followed him because they trusted him as their general. This Kindroot must trust the Itholean princess, at least more than the people Jaylen was working for. This was a dangerous thought. Despite his decision to not be a part of whatever Aekan was doing, but to aid the Kindroot, betraying his loyalty to the king proved challenging. Jaylen frowned. Why was he still feeling loyal to King Reid? Was Jaylen as shallow as only wanting glory for himself? He knew the answer to that. He hadn't been concerned with true justice. Jaylen had only wanted to out-scent his brothers. He wanted to prove himself, and this was how he could do it. He had done it. But at what cost?

Maya's face, once beautiful, now scarred, flashed in his mind. The queen, clothed in pure white, walked with confidence between the thorny devils and dranks away from her city... The cost was too great. He needed to retrain his instincts.

Jaylen stood up and wiped the crumbs off his general's cloak. There was something magical about Kindroots. How did it work? And what had happened to them all? Was this Blackthorn the last of the Kindroots? As he stared at the tree in front of him, he understood King Reid's ill intentions with the Kindroot. Jaylen wished he hadn't hunted Blackthorn. He needed to fix this.

"If I can do anything to help you, Blackthorn, I will do it," Jaylen vowed. His next breath was filled with the fragrances of the nuts on the tree. He closed his eyes and felt a tugging in his stomach. It got stronger and when he opened his eyes, he wasn't back in the library.

THE LIGHT BLINDED BLACKTHORN as he rounded the bend and felt so good at the same time. The tunnel opened up, revealing, a large arch to the outside world. But what he saw and smelled was unlike anything he'd ever seen before. There were no trees, or dry ground, only the edge of the cave and water that stretched on for as far as he could see. It smelled of salt. Did the water have its own scent?

How on earth was he going to save Anya? Smokey took a tentative step forward and dropped to his knees.

"There's nowhere to go," he whispered. "I'm so sorry, Anya."

Blackthorn climbed off her shoulder and felt dirt beneath him. He soaked up the sunlight and the nutrients within the ground. They might be trapped on a cliff, but now that Blackthorn could smell fresh air and absorb the sun's light, he could heal Anya himself.

Sari and Amber walked up behind them and gazed out at the endless water, and then Sari turned and embraced her limp daughter in her arms.

Digging deeper, Blackthorn sensed their surroundings. The water was deep, so deep that the ground had to drop far before it flattened out again and extend into the distance.

"Sari, Blackthorn, look!" Amber stood at the edge where the rock met the water.

Blackthorn moved back onto the rock and over to where Amber was. She was pointing to the side of the cave. The sight of so much water had overwhelmed Blackthorn he hadn't bothered to see the outside of the cave. Wet rocks scattered their way along the cliff and then they were like steps but not carved by a man. Blackthorn started to glow.

"There's hope after all," Sari said.

Amber led the way across the slippery rocks, and then they climbed. Blackthorn wrapped his roots around Anya's shoulder, pulling himself up to rest there. Then he continued healing her while they climbed up the side of the cave. The land stretched out behind them and followed the water in a straight line.

"A city!" Amber jumped up and down with delight.

Was this the city Jedrek the first came from? Parts of the old tales came back to him, and he remembered something called a sea that was vast and unmeasured and knew that was what the water was called. Maybe he would find some answers here. Then the tugging began again.

It was irresistible this time. Blackthorn didn't have time to tell Sari what was happening before he found himself transported back home. He could feel the Kor's emotions and read his thoughts, but still retreated into the depths of the Spring Beech tree as soon as he could move again. He knew this Kor and didn't trust him one bit. How in all the scents did that man find this place and use the magic to call Blackthorn home? What did this mean? What should he do? Was Anya going to die? No. Her healing had begun and there was a city nearby them. A healer would live there. Blackthorn took a moment to breathe in the refreshing scents of his home, and then he cried.

Chapter 22

The view from the roof was decent, even if Ashkii would have liked a closer vantage point to the palace. But Krillin didn't care what Ashkii wanted. The palace grounds were visible in one direction, and in the other, the markets. It was a suitable location. Krillin turned towards the streets.

"They're late," he thought to himself. It made him feel anxious. Any number of things could go wrong. Had they been betrayed? The streets below were getting emptier as everyone went to their homes, except for a few shoppers. Krillin sniffed the air, picking out each scent floating by. He should be able to smell them coming. Lord Tanish was a familiar scent from when he reported to Aekan. He had spied on Tanish, after all.

The priest turned out okay as far as nobles go, but Krillin still didn't care for the man. He represented everything Krillin hated about his own people. Krillin had to stop thinking like that. Dana didn't care who she hurt in order to get her way, and it sounded like Lord Tanish did care, according to Maya anyway, and Krillin trusted Maya. She was one of the best people he knew.

Lord Tanish's aroma finally caught Krillin's attention, and he turned to see the man approaching from the side. A lady was with him. He didn't recognize her from this distance, but he had probably seen her in Ithol from time to time. Krillin opened the door to the roof and climbed inside.

"They're almost here," he said.

There was a shuffling of boxes and crates as everyone got ready. A moment later, the door opened, and Maya walked in, talking with Lord Tanish.

"Come on in," she was saying. "Your scents are pleasing."

"Of course. I'm so glad that you all are here. The queen's life is at more risk every day she's trapped in that palace."

Ashkii stepped forward and smelled their guests the Itholean way before asking, "What do you mean? Why is it getting worse?"

"I've heard rumors about what the prince is planning." Lord Tanish frowned.

"Please, let's sit and eat, then we can talk," Maya said, gesturing to the table.

Krillin sat facing the door, positioned at the far end of the table. He wanted no surprises. "Why were you late?" he asked as soon as everyone was seated.

Lord Tanish glanced at the woman sitting next to him. She shifted in her seat. "That was my fault," she said.

"And you are?" Krillin had to ask, even though Maya had already told them who she was.

"Oh, forgive me. I used to be one of Her Majesty's councilors."

"Lady Rebekkah," Maya said in agreement.

"Please, as Yari has need for anonymity, so do I. Call me by my new name, Annika."

"All right, Annika. Why were you late?"

"While returning to the shop, I encountered a palace servant. She told me about that rumor Yari mentioned. While she was serving the prince his midday meal, she heard him talking to someone she didn't know. The prince mentioned taking the ex-princess to see someone who was probably going to kill her."

"Hold up," Ashkii raised his hands in protest. "How do you know this servant? Why would she tell you this?"

"Don't worry. Tara knows nothing. We became friends and occasionally meet up to hang out and chat. She was bursting to tell me her news because she hates the princess and ever since the princess has been in Prince Lucas' household, he's forced Tara to serve the princess whenever he doesn't need her..." Annika blushed and looked at all of their waiting faces. "Tara thinks the king should have executed the princess along with all her councilors, but she has no idea that I was one of those executed councilors."

"So, news of the princess dying is exciting to this person?" Krillin asked.

"Oh, she wishes she could watch the princess die herself and is disappointed that the prince is planning on making it look like an accident."

Ashkii stood up and started for the roof.

"Where are you going?" Maya asked.

"We have to get her out of there right now!"

"Ashkii," Tse said. "Stop. We will rescue her, but we will not go in there unprepared."

Krillin nodded at Tse in appreciation. Tse was good for Ashkii, who could be hot-headed at times.

Ashkii breathed out his frustration and returned to the table.

"If it's at all a comfort to you," Yari said, "I have people watching all the exits from the palace, so we will know when she leaves to meet this person."

"How soon will we know?" Krillin asked. "I mean, your people may see her leaving, but how fast can they let us know?"

"I want to know how soon we can get her out of there."

"Should we rescue her from the palace, or would it be easier to intercept her on the way?" Ryker spoke up from his corner of the table.

That was good. Krillin liked the way Ryker thought. "We can totally get her while she's en route, if, coming back to my original question, we can quickly know when she leaves the palace"

Lord Tanish ripped off a chunk of bread before answering. "In the past, I've known within a few minutes that she'd left, but that doesn't mean it might not take longer. It depends on which exit she takes."

"I think we need to focus on the palace." Ashkii took a swig of his ale. "We know where it is, we're close by, we have the skills needed to get her out."

"I agree," Tse said. "We don't know where the prince will take Agonya, so we would have to catch up to them, and that makes it rather hard to ambush them."

"But if we wait until she's out of the palace walls, we won't alert the entire palace guards to what we're doing." Krillin countered.

"I think we need to be prepared to rescue her either way," Maya said. "Lord Tan—Yari is right. The longer Agonya remains in the palace, the greater the danger to her life."

"Not to mention my brother," Ashkii said in a hushed tone.

Krillin looked at the food on his plate. He wasn't hungry, but he knew he should eat something. Breathing in the fresh aroma of the bread, he thought about Ashkii's relationship with his brother and couldn't imagine having to fight his sister. "I still think Ryker is right. Our best bet is to get her on the move."

"Yeah, we can make sure we know when she leaves and gauge which direction they go. I don't think it'll be too hard to figure out which direction they're going and set up ahead of them on the path." Ryker looked excited about the prospect.

Maya shook her head. "Yari, would it be possible for one of us to get into the palace?"

"Ooh!" Annika exclaimed. "You could totally get into the palace, Maya. Tara was just trying to convince me to come work with her. I can recommend you to her and she would totally accept you." Annika swished down her drink and stood up. "I'll go and ask her now."

"Wait!" Maya said. "First, we need a plan. If I can enter the palace as Lady—Annika suggests, I'll learn when the prince will act and may have an opportunity to warn Agonya and ensure her safety."

Ashkii nodded.

"Of course he liked that plan," Krillin thought. "Ashkii would do anything to be the one inside the palace but would settle for Maya."

"Okay, but how will that help us get her out?" Ryker asked. "Won't it only make it harder, because then we'd have to make sure you get out again too, Maya?"

"I disagree with you there, Ryker," Krillin said. "Maya's presence inside is a tremendous advantage, and no one has to know she's there. It wouldn't be hard for an ordinary servant to leave."

Ryker didn't look convinced, but he wouldn't be happy no matter where Maya was. Krillin looked at Annika, still standing. "You should go talk with this Tara and find out if it's at all possible for Maya to work in the palace."

She looked at Maya questioningly.

"Yes, anything you can do is much appreciated." Then Maya turned to Yari. "I'm so glad I ran into you at the market. You've already given us more than we can repay. Thank you for keeping us informed of Agonya's movements. That will be a huge help."

Yari nodded and stood to join Annika. "You know where to find us if you need anything else."

After the door closed behind them, Ryker rushed to Maya's side. "Are you sure about this?" He grasped her face in his hands. She smiled up at him, and Krillin looked away.

"Don't worry. I will know if anything is amiss before they can discover me. I'll get out. You just need to do your job."

"Which is?" Ryker asked.

"First, stay alive. Second, help get Agonya out, of course. I'm sure the prince will try to use magic to stop you once he realizes what's happening. You may be the key to disarming the prince and getting Agonya."

"She's right," Ashkii said. "Krillin will sniff out the guards and soldiers and let us know how many we're up against and where they are. Tse and I take care of the guards while you confront the prince."

"Let's hope Dana doesn't show up," Krillin said.

Everyone turned to look at him. Maya nodded. "If we prevent Agonya from reaching the prince's destination, then Dana won't get involved."

"She's the person the prince is taking Agonya to, isn't she?" Krillin connected the scents in his mind. It made sense. Naturally, the prince partnered with Dana, who would be furious following her unsuccessful attempt to retrieve Blackthorn from the cave.

"We need to get Agonya out and get her out fast," Ashkii said for the hundredth time.

Krillin agreed. They all knew it. They needed to get Agonya to safety before they could face that evil woman.

LADY REBEKKAH HAD BEEN right. Tara hired Maya solely because Annika vouched for her. As soon as Tara received permission to hire Maya, she gave Maya a tour of where she would work and introduced her to the short man she would work with. He wasn't one to talk, so they mostly scrubbed floors in silence. Even when Maya tried to engage him in conversation, he only gave one-word answers or grunted.

Maya gave up trying to gather information from him and tried to memorize the halls they were cleaning and all the rooms they entered. The morning dragged on, and Maya only ever saw other servants. It was much like working in Ithol's palace, where servants were invisible, unless they were like Tara, who was assigned to the prince. Maya didn't know Tara other than she was a talker and had gushed over the prince and how if Maya did well, she might be promoted to come serve with her. Maya couldn't afford to work her way up the hierarchy. Agonya couldn't afford her to. So, while she scrubbed the floors, Maya thought of ways to contact Agonya. Part of her wondered if Ryker was right. Would she be of any use in here? The chances of glimpsing Agonya were slim.

It wasn't until Tara came to escort them to the midday meal that Maya saw anything of interest. On their way to the kitchens, they passed guards at the foot of a staircase. Tara nodded at them and kept walking without saying a word. Maya wouldn't have noticed the exchange except for the change of mood in Tara. It was fleeting but smelled like a flicker of anger and worry before Tara refocused on work. Maya made a note of the staircase. She knew Agonya's room was on the second floor. Could it be near her room? Tara didn't like Agonya, so maybe that was why she'd felt angry? Maya knew she was making a lot of assumptions, but it was a possibility, especially after what Lady Rebekkah had said about Tara hating Agonya. She finished processing Tara's emotions and entered the kitchen.

The meal was cold, but good. Maya ate in silence while the other servants laughed and joked and told stories from their days. There was nothing of real importance in what they said, and their emotions all smelled the same. That is until someone started throwing up in a trash pail. Maya hurried to console the servant, but upon looking up, everyone else had vanished. When had they left? Was she so self-absorbed that she didn't notice them going back to their jobs? Maya thought back to the emotions she'd smelled along the way and realized that the other servants had been there when the woman started throwing up, but they hadn't wanted to smell the sickness, so they'd rushed to get back to work.

"Are you okay?" Maya asked.

The girl nodded and tried to sit up. Maya anticipated her movements and assisted her. "Thank you. I don't know what came over me."

"Here." Maya offered a clean towel to the woman. "You still don't look too well. Are you sure you're okay?"

Before she could answer, Tara returned.

"Where is everyone?" Tara demanded and looked at the sick servant, whom Maya was comforting.

"They left," she said and then covered her mouth and nose.

Tara gasped. "Oh Theia, you smell retched! Are you okay?"

The servant nodded and started to stand, but she quickly bent over the pail again without replying.

"What happened? Did you feel unwell before coming to work today?"

"I assure you; I was well when I arrived. I think it was something I ate."

Tara blanched and glared at the cooks. "What exactly did you eat?"

"I was taste-testing the princess' food."

"The princess? Are you sure? It wasn't His Highness' food?"

"I'm sure. See," the servant gestured at the food tray, "I sampled the soup, but felt sick before taking it upstairs."

Tara walked over and held the bowl of soup up to her nose. "Who made this?"

Tara faced the shocked cooks.

"I asked you a question and I demand an answer!"

The cooks searched each other's faces. Then one of them cleared his throat. "Um, I think whoever made that soup isn't here anymore. I recall a tall, skinny man working on the soup earlier, but no one here matches that description."

Tara walked over to the cooks and examined everything they were working on until she found the soup pot. There was no one standing next to it. Then she pointed to the cook who'd spoken, "You, come test the soup."

The cook shuddered but obeyed. Nothing happened. Tara turned to leave, and then the cook began throwing up. Tara jumped out of the way. Then the cook fell to the floor.

Maya could feel the fear shoot through everyone in the room. Someone had poisoned that soup.

Tara started shouting orders. "Take him to the healer. You, go with him! Don't throw out the soup! We need it. Someone get the captain on duty!"

Once everyone had obeyed, Tara turned back toward the tray of food. Maya could sense Tara was at war with herself. On the one scent, Maya knew Tara wanted to poison the princess, but on the other, everyone in that room knew the food was bad, so she couldn't.

"What am I going to do now?" Tara whispered to herself.

"I can help," Maya said.

Tara looked Maya over from head to toe. "How do I know you didn't poison the princess' food?"

"I haven't had the opportunity. Kabes has been with me all morning. I didn't go near that pot or this tray until I was trying to comfort Theia."

"All right. I had to ask. Get a new tray of food for the Itholean. Test all of it, then you can take it up those stairs we passed earlier. If the soldiers give you a hard time, tell them Tara sent you. Go straight to the princess' room, then return here. Do you understand?"

Maya nodded and got to work, throwing out the tainted food. While grabbing the last of the food for Agonya, the captain barged into the kitchen, demanding an explanation. Maya hurried out of the room. She didn't want to be there for the fallout.

Once she was out of the room, she let her feelings surface and smiled. The attempted poisoning of Agonya was concerning, but this was a stroke of luck! The Patron of Fortune had surely scented her today by allowing her to go to Agonya and by herself.

Two soldiers still guarded the staircase. She tried to pass by them without saying a word, but they blocked her way.

"Who are you?"

Maya tried to breathe normally even though her heart rate was speeding up. "I'm Maya. Tara sent me to deliver this food to the Itholean princess."

"Where's Tara?"

"In the kitchens, the person who taste tests the princess' food got sick."

"Very well. Be quick."

Maya nodded and rushed up the stairs as fast as she dared.

AGONYA PACED BACK AND forth in her tiny room, worried about Lord Tashunka. Why had Dana cursed him? How had she been able to wipe his memories? Agonya tried to replay the memory she'd recovered in his mind, but there was nothing in it that could help her figure it out.

The knock on the door gave Agonya a start. She knew that knock. But she hadn't heard that knock since... no, that was impossible. The door opened and in walked Maya. Agonya couldn't believe her eyes! She turned to her friend, ready to embrace her, but froze when she saw Maya's expression. Maya motioned ever so slightly to the guards a few paces away. Of course, they shouldn't know that Agonya's dearest friend was in the room. But how could Agonya keep quiet at a time like this? She wanted to rush over and give her friend a proper hug and smell her fragrance.

It took all her self-control to stay indifferent. "Put the food over there," Agonya said.

Maya smiled and walked toward the table in the far corner. When she got close enough to Agonya, Maya whispered, "Speak in my mind."

Oh, right! Why didn't Agonya think of that? Breathing in Maya's fragrance, she spoke in her mind. "Maya! How are you here? Why aren't you in Ithol? What happened to your face? Are you here by yourself? How did you find me?" The questions kept flooding Agonya's mind.

Maya kept walking as slowly as she dared. "I must go, but we can still talk even if I'm not present, right?"

"Of course! Don't you remember?"

"I know. I just wanted to make sure." Then Maya set the tray on the table Agonya had indicated. "I know you have a lot of questions. I will do my best to answer them quickly." Then she turned and left Agonya standing where she'd been when she entered. The door closed and her friend disappeared.

"Maya, it's so wonderful to smell you again! I feel as if I'm going to cry."

"I know! Me too. But like you said, we have a lot of questions to answer. I'm not sure where to begin except that now you know I'm here and I'm not alone."

Agonya was instantly relieved to know Maya had support. Was Blackthorn with her?

"No, Blackthorn got separated from me."

"What?! I trusted you to take care of him."

"I know, I know. Just let me tell you what happened. He is safe. At least, that's what he told us."

Agonya smoothed her dress and listened while Maya told her what she knew. It didn't surprise her that the prince thought Dana would kill her when he brought Agonya back to Dana's cave. When Maya told her about being tortured by Aekan, Agonya wanted to cry. But remembered a conversation the prince had had the previous day.

"But Maya, you know Aekan is in the palace, right?"

"What? Oh. I should have figured that out. Don't worry. I'll be careful."

Agonya shook her head. "But he knows what you look like, and your scars stand out, and you gave them your real name? You have to leave now."

"I'll be gone after today. Hopefully, now that you know we're here to rescue you, you can warn us when the prince takes you to Dana and share knowledge about the guards and the palace grounds."

"Yes, I can do this. But I'm still worried about you."

"Don't worry about me. I'm worried about you! Someone just tried to poison you! It wasn't the prince, or Tara wouldn't have been surprised."

"I'll be more careful and test all my food before eating it. But neither the servant nor cook died according to you, right? They just got sick. I can heal myself if I need to." Agonya looked at the food on her tray. She hadn't touched it yet. Her excitement at seeing Maya made her forget all about her hunger.

"The cook may have died. He was rushed off to a healer, carried by several people. Please be careful. I have to focus now. Maybe you can reestablish our mind link every hour or so?"

"Of course! It's no problem. It doesn't even matter if my cousin is in the room. He won't know, unless... Oh, Maya, he has this perfume that negates my powers! If you don't hear from me regularly, he might be using that on me."

"That's good to know. If I don't hear from you, I will assume he's taking you to Dana. But I can't talk anymore. Tara is approaching me."

Maya's beautiful voice went silent. Agonya sighed and went to get her food. But when she picked up the cheese, she burst into tears. Smelling Maya again was the most wonderful gift she'd ever been given. And it happened so fast. All the stress and loneliness Agonya had experienced since her separation from Maya flowed out of her in a flood of tears. Almost an entire hour passed before Agonya regained her composure. She'd better check in with Maya.

Remembering Maya's scent almost brought on a fresh wave of tears, but Agonya stopped herself and focused on finding Maya's mind.

"Maya?"

"I'm here. Tara said the cook survived and shared a suspect description, but the guards haven't found him."

"What did he look like?"

"Pale-skinned, tall, skinny, wavy blond hair."

"Oh, no." Agonya groaned.

"What is it?"

"You realize who that sounds like?"

It took a minute before Maya realized who she was talking about. "They're probably not checking the roofs."

"How could Ashkii betray me like this?"

"What? Ashkii? He would never poison you. He loves you too much."

"But I saw him when he stabbed me with a dagger."

"He stabbed you with a dagger? Ashkii? When?"

"On the way here to Korina."

"That wasn't Ashkii. He has a twin brother. That's why Ashkii escaped from his father. He wanted to come protect you from his brother, who was sent to kill you."

How was that possible? The assassin had looked exactly like Ashkii. He didn't just resemble Ashkii like Sir Mato resembled Prince Lucas. No, they looked exactly the same. Agonya took a deep breath and smelled all the fragrances in her room. There was an orange on her tray, along with cheese and bread, things that would be harder to poison. And then she remembered. Agonya already knew Ashkii wasn't the assassin. Blackthorn had told her that Ashkii was helping him in Ithol. What was happening to her mind?

"Maya, I knew it wasn't Ashkii. I just remembered that I knew. I'm so confused. Why didn't I remember that? It's almost like what happened to Lord Tashunka..."

"Lord Tashunka? Who's that?" Maya asked.

"Do you remember that Korin Captain?"

"You mean General Jaylen Dahel?"

"Yes, he was promoted. Lord Tashunka is his father."

"What?! How do you know him?"

It was Agonya's turn to launch into her story of meeting Lady Tsula and healing people. Agonya could smell that Maya was listening, even though she said little. An interesting phenomenon was happening in the back of her mind while she talked. Agonya could see where Maya was and what she was doing. There was a short older man working alongside her as they scrubbed floors and dusted paintings.

"Yesterday when I went to heal him, I couldn't smell his aroma, but with the help of his wife I found some scents that allowed me to see one of his forgotten memories. But why is this happening to me?"

"I think," Maya spoke up, "I want to know why it was information about Ashkii that you forgot? That is more important. If you've been cursed, like Lord Tashunka, to forget something that happened, that means there's something someone doesn't want you to know."

"You're right. I should write down important memories I don't want to lose."

"That's a good idea." Maya said and straightened up from her task. "I'm done here. Check in again soon."

In an instant, Agonya found herself alone, with only her thoughts for company. This time, she wouldn't have a complete breakdown. She had a lot to ponder. Not about being cursed but, there was something Maya said about Ashkii that made it sound like he had feelings for her. Could that be true? It was a silly thing to wonder when her priority should be escaping and staying alive.

Ashkii had betrayed her time and time again. He did not have feelings for her. Yet Maya had said he'd wanted to help, that his father had forced him to abandon her. Why was his brother trying to kill her? Ashkii's brother had been the assassin this whole time?! But that meant he was the one who had killed her father. And Ashkii knew it. How had she forgotten about the assassin that had killed her father? And the assassin that nearly killed her? Why hadn't he chopped off her head like he'd done to her father? She'd been so focused on other things, trivial things like how to behave around her cousin when she should have been more concerned about him plotting to kill her. Not to mention the Montanes wanting her dead, too.

Agonya remained powerless, despite knowing all that.

Her only option was to be alert and fully prepared. Agonya smelled the bread on her tray. It smelled normal, so she took a bite. She knew Maya had tested it, but she didn't know if there was magic involved. It tasted fine.

Chapter 23

The nights were getting colder. Ashkii was accustomed to the cold, so this was not freezing to him. He didn't mind keeping watch on the roof while Tse warmed up, circulating the palace grounds. A few distant clouds dotted the sky. Where Ashkii sat, he couldn't see them. Besides, he had to make sure she was well. He'd heard Maya's reports.

Jealousy burned inside him, knowing how close Maya had been to her. Now that Agonya knew they were trying to rescue her, she checked in with Maya regularly. Why hadn't she tried to talk with him? He knew the answer. She didn't feel the same way about him as he did for her. And why would she? All he'd ever done to her was hurt and betray her.

Ashkii scanned the roofs for any visitors and then the wall. He needed to make sure Kilchii didn't slip past him. Since Maya witnessed the poisoning, there was no sign of him. He knew his brother was not done. The soup was intended to weaken the princess, making it easier to kill her. That meant Kilchii would kill her tonight. Not to mention, the guards had a description of him, which meant Ashkii had to stay out of sight. They were identical twins. Kilchii probably allowed himself to be identified to ensure Ashkii's capture. But if Kilchii did that, he knew Ashkii was here. Ashkii's neck hairs stood up and he spun around. Was he being watched?

Only a few stragglers roamed the empty streets, heading towards their beds. And, of course, the guards kept watch at their posts.

Ashkii saw movement out of the corner of his eye. He turned and smiled. The shutters on her window were being opened. There she was, radiant as always. She didn't have that melancholy look that she usually had. It was more frustration than anything else. Ashkii could tell, even from this distance. Having carried her for so long through the Perfumed Pines and studying her, he knew she was trying to figure something out.

She didn't stay in the window long, though. But it was long enough for Ashkii to know he'd let his guard down. He knew that smell, and it was way too close for comfort.

"Hello, brother," Ashkii said. When he turned around, Kilchii stood half a meter away.

"Hello, brother. Out for an evening stroll?"

"It is a beautiful night, but I know why you're here. I've been waiting for you. Figured it was easier than tracking you down in the city." Whatever surprise he'd had was long gone. But Kilchii didn't know Ashkii had friends.

"Thinking about taking the glory for yourself? Or was there another purpose for being here?"

"I came to inform you about the contract we burned with the princess, which you might not know about yet. I thought it best to let you know before you kill her."

"A contract? What contract?" Kilchii moved next to Ashkii and searched for the window.

"We became her ally. She's more powerful than you know."

"Ha! She's nothing compared to Dana. Look at her! She didn't last more than a few months on her throne. Me killing her will do her a favor."

"Oh, that's why you've failed to kill her twice." Ashkii smirked.

"You're right. The first time she survived, caught me off guard. I should have gone for her head like I did for her father. As for the second time, I wasn't trying to kill her. I knew it wouldn't work." Kilchii paused. "Besides, I already knew about said 'contract' by then."

Ashkii reached for his hidden knife. If Kilchii knew, that meant he knew Ashkii wasn't here on father's orders.

"Relax, brother. Father said I should expect you. He also said you would try to stop me from fulfilling my orders. I urge you to come with me. Help me. Yes, she has power. I'll grant you that. Two would be better than one."

Ashkii didn't know how to respond. Should he accompany him and then betray his brother once there or prevent him here before he even got close to her? Now that he thought about it, it was obvious.

"Thanks for the offer, but I can't. I can't allow you to hurt her."

"Do you have feelings for her? Such a pity." Kilchii turned towards Ashkii with his own knife in hand.

They faced each other, ready to fight. Each the mirror image of the other, though very different in scent.

Kilchii took the first move, dashing forward and slashing his knife down. Ashkii met Kilchii's knife with his own. Kilchii kept going, using his momentum to push his knife further to the side and down. Ashkii twisted out of the way and stuck out his foot, tripping his brother who recovered quickly.

This time Ashkii wasn't ready. Kilchii twirled towards Ashkii and even though Ashkii met Kilchii's knife again, Kilchii grabbed Ashkii's arm with his free hand and twisted his wrist so that Ashkii had to let go of his knife. "Come, brother, you've forgotten your family. We shouldn't be fighting."

Ashkii tried to lunge for the dropped knife. Kilchii merely kicked it off the roof. "Oops."

Ashkii looked around him. There! A cracked tile. He had to keep Kilchii talking long enough. "You know as well as I do that Dana has failed us. She does not keep her promises. Why do you still fight for her?"

"She only reminded us of our own failure. Believe me when I say I will not fail tonight."

Ashkii stepped back, turning slightly toward the tile. "Don't you think we were on the wrong side to begin with? We only joined her because she threatened us."

Kilchii mocked Ashkii. "But she's our family. Are you going to abandon us all for an exiled queen, all because you fancy her?"

"She's also family to that exiled queen." Ashkii pretended to stumble as he backed up. He snatched up the loose tile and pushed back up.

Kilchii met Ashkii's tile with his knife. Ashkii tilted the tile just right, so the knife got lodged in another crack. "Yes. I love her, and I won't let you take her from me." Ashkii yanked the knife out of Kilchii's hands, throwing the tile and knife off the roof. Ashkii dodged Kilchii's grasp but tripped on another loose tile. Kilchii took advantage and dug his knee into Ashkii's back. Ashkii tried to roll out from under him but couldn't move.

"Don't do this, Kil!"

Kilchii ripped the bottom of Ashkii's cloak and gagged him. Then he yanked Ashkii's arms out from under him. Ashkii tried to grasp any part of Kilchii's body that he could, but a cord wrapped around one wrist, then the other. Soon his legs were bound too.

Kilchii straightened. "I hope you enjoy the show." Then he dropped off the roof to retrieve his dagger before darting off into the distance.

Ashkii was being forced to face her window, to watch his brother murder Agonya. He was helpless to prevent it. How could this happen? He'd prepared to stop his brother, to protect Agonya, yet her life was almost over because he hadn't been good enough. If only Tse would return, then he might have a shot at saving her.

That hope dwindled though as Kilchii's dark form leaped onto her windowsill flawlessly. He looked back at Ashkii, still sitting exactly as he left him. Then an arrow struck him. Kilchii cried out and leaped away as fast as he could go. Ashkii couldn't decide whether to grin or cry. Krillin had arrived for his shift and smelled Kilchii.

AGONYA COULDN'T FALL asleep, not after everything that had happened that day. After Maya had surprised her, Prince Lucas had come to her room. Having heard of the assassination attempt, he feigned care for her well-being, assuring her she would be better protected from now on. The poisoned food didn't even reach her room! How could they be better than stopping it in its tracks? What he really meant was that he would know everything she did. She'd told Maya about the extra guards. To think that Maya had come for her, and that Lord Tanish and Lady Rebekkah had been watching out for her, too!

Agonya rolled over. As she did, the curtains moved. Someone was out there. As quietly as she could, she slipped out of bed and crept towards the window. She scanned the room for anything she could use to defend herself.

There was a cry of pain. Rushing to the window, Agonya saw a cloaked figure leaping into the darkness. There were shouts from below. The assassin had been spotted.

Agonya leaned further out to see what was going on and gasped. There was blood on the windowsill. He must have been wounded. Agonya was incredibly grateful at that moment for the numerous people watching over her.

The commotion grew louder and soon guards were bursting into her room.

Agonya let out a scream.

"Come with us, please."

Agonya lowered her hand from her chest and followed the guards out of the room. "Maya!" she said in her mind.

There was no response. Was she sleeping? Agonya would have to talk with one of the others. Wanting to avoid Ashkii's mind, she contacted Krillin.

"Your Highness?"

"I'm sorry to jump into your thoughts so suddenly. Maya wasn't answering—"

Krillin cut her off. "I know. I shot the man trying to enter your room through the window."

"You did that? Oh, how can I thank you?"

"Where are you being taken?"

"I'm not sure, maybe to see Prince Lucas. We are going in that direction."

"Okay. Let me know when you arrive. I have to go find the others."

Agonya was right. Dylan spoke quietly with the guards in front of the prince's door. One of them knocked and entered. A moment later, the doors swung open and Agonya was ushered in.

"Well, well, well. You can't get enough excitement for one day. You simply had to try to be killed twice. Come on in. I think you'll be safe in here."

Ugh. This guy was revolting to her. Everything about him compelled her to get as far away from him as possible.

Prince Lucas walked towards her, and she stepped back without thinking. He raised his hands. "I won't hurt you."

Agonya closed her eyes. She didn't trust herself to say anything good, so she said nothing. She was still focusing on breathing normally when she smelled his aroma of anise, lavender, and sweet orange right next to her and felt his arm wrap around her shoulder. He pulled her further into the room, instructing the soldiers to guard the hall.

The sound of feet shuffling out the door filled Agonya with dread. Until it dawned on her, she didn't have to be alone with this man. Reaching out to Krillin's mind, she let him know where she was.

"Are you in danger?"

"I'm not sure. But I don't enjoy being alone with him. Will you stay with me? We don't have to talk. I will feel safer if I know I can talk with someone if I need to."

She could sense Krillin's hesitation, but he agreed to her request.

"Come rest." The prince led her to his bed.

Agonya shook her head. "I don't want to rest."

"I insist. I'll even sleep in the chair."

Before Agonya could protest further, he picked her up and placed her on the bed. Agonya got back out. "I told you I don't want to rest."

"Suit yourself." the prince shrugged and climbed into the bed. "But you're going to want sleep before tomorrow."

"Why? What's happening tomorrow?"

"You'll find out. Goodnight, Princess."

Agonya started pacing. His weird hints could only mean one thing. "Krillin, he's taking me to see Dana tomorrow."

THEY ALL GATHERED AROUND the table in their room at the inn. Ashkii desperately wanted to be on the roof, especially given the recent events, but it was too risky. Every soldier on duty was on alert, patrolling the palace walls. Watching her room was pointless without her in it. Kilchii wasn't coming back tonight. Ashkii was sure of it.

Maya stretched and rubbed her eyes. Krillin nodded, even though no one had said anything. He must be responding to something Agonya said. Ashkii hated waiting for him to tell them all what was happening, but be-grudgingly admitted if it hadn't been for Krillin, she might not have survived the night.

"She thinks he will take her to see Dana tomorrow."

"We must rescue her tonight," Ashkii said.

"How?" Krillin countered.

"I don't know!" Ashkii yelled.

"Shh!" everyone said at once.

"Sorry. I'm frustrated. How long have we been in Korina? What have we accomplished?" Ashkii glared at each of them, although he knew they were all doing their best. Maybe he should rescue her on his own. He wouldn't have to worry about anyone else getting caught, just himself.

"We protected her from your brother tonight," Krillin said.

It was true. They had done something, but Ashkii had wanted to have Agonya by his side, riding away from this wretched place.

"I have an idea, but you won't like it," Ryker said.

"What?"

"Well, you do look a lot like your brother, right? Which is why you've been keeping a low profile."

Ashkii did not like the direction this was going.

Ryker sat up straighter and said, "You can cause a distraction and draw the troops out of the palace so we can get in and get Agonya out."

"No. Absolutely not."

"Why not, Ash?" Tse asked.

Ashkii groaned. Not Tse too. Why didn't they grasp his necessity to be there?

"Why not?" Tse asked again.

"You all need me in there."

"No, we don't. You're an exceptional fighter and have certain advantages that we do not. Though I also have the agility that you have, your greatest asset right now is exactly what Ryker said. The guards are looking for the assassin as we speak. This is the best time to give them what they want. Kilchii is out of the picture for tonight, so all we have to do is eliminate the guards and deal with the prince."

"A prince who has powers to make you forget things," Maya reminded them.

"We don't know that for sure," Ryker said.

"Agonya says he's finally asleep," Krillin added.

"Do we even know where the prince's room is?"

"I think I can find it. I haven't had much time to learn the halls of the palace, but I know where he's not, and Agonya can help us. She knows where it is." Maya shifted in her seat. "I agree. We should do it tonight."

Ashkii looked at all his friends. Tse could jump Agonya out of danger if need be and he was a decent fighter if it came down to that. Ryker could resist the prince's magic if he had any. Krillin had an amazing sense of smell and could help them know what they were up against once they got close. As much as he hated it, he knew they were right. "Okay. Once you're in place, I'll cause a distraction so you can get in and get out."

They all stood up and gathered their supplies. It was a good thing they had multiple weapons and backups of those weapons. Lord Tanish had really come through for them. Ashkii watched Maya and Ryker leave first. Then, a few minutes later, Tse and Krillin left. He waited a little longer and then went up on the roof. If he was going to cause a commotion, it would be in the skies.

AGONYA SNUCK OVER TO one of Prince Lucas' windows to look outside. She wasn't exactly sure where it was in relation to the gardens. Was there anything distinctive to help? Krillin had filled her in on the plan, and she was supposed to help them find her. She wished she had frankincense to calm her nerves, but she couldn't risk waking the prince up. Lifting the heavy curtain, she heard movement behind her. As slowly as she could, she kept the curtain pulled back and turned to face her cousin. He looked asleep. But he was facing away from her. That meant he couldn't be watching her. That was a relief.

She turned back to the window and saw behind the curtains, her heart plummeted in her chest. There were shutters locked in place and not just with a bar securing it. Great. She needed a key to unlock it. Her friends were on their way.

"Krillin, we can't use the window. At least not until I can find a key to unlock the shutters."

"Tell Ashkii. He can break it open during his distraction."

"But wouldn't that wake up the prince?"

"How many guards are outside the room?"

"Ten, maybe more. I'm not sure."

"Look for the key and let the others know the situation. I'm only near Tse, so you'll have to let the others know."

Agonya let the curtain drop back into place and started pacing again. This time trying to look for places the prince kept his keys. She had a bad feeling they were hanging around his neck. While she walked, she informed

Maya of the new development. Maya and Ryker were almost to the palace gate, hoping to sneak in when Ashkii caused his distraction.

Then, she reluctantly reached out to Ashkii's mind. "The window is shuttered and locked," she said, not bothering for the proper greetings.

"Agonya?"

"Who else?"

"It's so good to hear your voice."

Agonya frowned and noticed something odd about the prince's desk. When she didn't respond, he spoke again.

"I'm so sorry for everything! I wanted to help you, but I couldn't. My father—"

"Everyone is in place," Agonya interrupted him. She already knew what he was going to tell her.

He was silent for a moment. "I know you want nothing to do with me after what I did to you. I'm begging you to forgive me. And I know I've already had a second chance from you, but I didn't want to betray you that second time. I was tied up and unable to stop my father from doing what he did. I know that may be difficult to believe. But I'm going to be here for you, no matter what. If I get captured again tonight, I'm going to escape so that I can protect you, unlike my failure to escape from my father."

"Don't make promises you can't keep," Agonya retorted. "They're waiting for your distraction."

"I found your shuttered window. See you soon."

Agonya waited to hear Ashkii's distraction, but all was silent. And then she heard shouts from far away. "That wasn't my window," Agonya whispered in his mind.

"Yeah, I figured that out, but either way, it's causing all the guards to come after me. Can't talk."

Agonya let him go fight or flee the guards, whichever he wanted to do. She really hoped he got away.

"Maya, he made his distraction."

"Yeah, there are several guards leaving the palace now. Oh, Krillin is here. Gotta go."

Agonya wished she could see what was happening like she'd seen earlier with Maya cleaning the palace. Instead, she paced back and forth across the prince's rugs and hoped he wouldn't be alerted. It was no use. A moment later, she could hear the guards arguing in the hallway. One of them burst into the room. He saw her standing there in her nightgown and looked at the prince asleep on the bed.

"Your Highness! There's been another attack."

He sat up so fast, Agonya thought he might keep falling forward, but he didn't.

"Where? How long ago?"

"Your father's room. I came as soon as it happened."

Lucas scrambled out of bed and donned his clothes. "I'll have to go to my father's aid. I didn't want to have to do this, but I have no other choice. Lock her in the cell. I don't want to let her out of my sight, and the cell will keep her safe."

Before Agonya could think of anything to say, she was being dragged out of the room and down a large spiral staircase. This was not what they'd planned. And the way he'd said "the cell" worried her.

Chapter 24

He felt like an idiot, but he couldn't dwell on it. His task was to lure the guards away from the palace. So, Ashkii tricked them by letting a group of them force him to fight before leading them deeper into the city, only to let another group gain on him and have to turn and fight them off too.

Why did he have to pick the wrong shuttered window? He should have used his senses. Of course, there would be multiple windows shuttered. And he picked the king's! At least it achieved his purpose. Too bad he didn't see Agonya before he had to flee. He was an idiot. Of course, he had to make that mistake in front of her. He couldn't get anything right when it came to Agonya.

He glanced behind him. Fewer soldiers chased him now, but they were gaining on him. Ashkii slowed and waited for them to be in range before he launched backward, landing in the middle of them and swinging his daggers in a circle. The blades sliced through several layers of padding the soldiers had on before they fought back.

Without time for weapons, they lunged for him, but Ashkii used their bodies to launch into the sky. He landed on a roof and watched them stare up at him. Grinning, he jumped down outside of the group. The soldier deflected his dagger, but Ashkii kept moving to the next soldier, whom he stabbed in the side. When she cried out in pain, Ashkii jumped back onto the roof in shock. It wasn't that she was a woman. There were many fine women soldiers he knew, but her voice sounded like Agonya's voice. He'd been hoping to hear Agonya's voice ever since he messed up, but she'd gone silent as soon as she didn't have to talk to him.

The soldiers were yelling at him, goading him to come down and fight, but he had no desire to kill them, so he threw an odor bomb at them and kept moving. It was time to disappear and reunite with the others. Ashkii ran to the opposite side of the roof and leaped to the ground. With the Kors preoccupied with the sky, he took to the streets.

He removed his cloak and stuffed it in his bag, pulling out a cap to hide his Montane hair. Then he hid his weapons in his bag, except for the spear, which was impossible to hide without ditching it into an alley somewhere. He would not take that risk. Too many things could go wrong, and he needed every advantage he could get. Ashkii continued to walk the streets, making his way back toward the palace. He didn't know if they succeeded or not, but he hoped they would meet him at the inn.

There were shouts a couple streets over. Ashkii turned to see what the commotion was. Soldiers were coming his way. His heart raced, and it took all his willpower not to pull out a dagger or shield. He stepped to the side to let them pass. It was a good thing he hadn't gone on the defense because they ran right past him.

Ashkii heaved a sigh of relief and continued on his way. The sky was lightening with the rising of the sun. The longest night of his life and it wasn't over yet. It wouldn't be over until he knew Agonya was safe.

WHEN THE PALACE GATE closed behind the last soldier, Maya, Ryker, and Krillin were still on the outside. There had been no way to get in when everyone was leaving, and the gate was not left unguarded. But Krillin assured them Tse would get them in.

"I knew you'd be trapped out here," Krillin said. "So, I convinced Tse of this new plan." He gestured up.

Maya glanced toward the sky and saw someone leaping through the air. That had to be Tse. They heard a slight commotion on the other side of the gate, and then it opened.

"Quick! Come in!" Tse motioned for them to enter.

Maya rushed inside with the others, noticing the guards laying off to the side, unconscious. "Should we tie them up?"

"There's no time. We have to get Agonya out as quickly as possible. Which way, Maya?"

Oh right. She was the only one of them who'd been inside the palace walls since they arrived. Walking as fast as she could, she led them inside the palace. As soon as they arrived at the staircase to Agonya's room, Maya felt Agonya linking their minds.

"I'm being taken to a cell. Prince Lucas took most of the guards with him. I'm back to having only four guards. They're leading me down a skinny corridor I haven't been in before, but I think we are nearing the kitchens."

Maya nodded and kept walking past the stairs. She knew where the kitchen was. Everyone followed her. "There are four guards taking Agonya to a cell," Maya told the others.

"I smell them, down that hall," Krillin said and pointed to the right.

"How do you know it's them?" Maya asked.

"I can also smell peonies, cinnamon, and myrrh, which can only mean Her Highness is with them."

"We can wait here and ambush them," Ryker suggested.

"Good idea."

A moment later, Agonya spoke in Maya's mind. "We're turning. There's a secret door in the wall, behind a painting of King Reid's father, my mother's father."

"We can't wait here. They're not coming this way anymore. Come on." Maya led the way down the hall.

"They went that way," Krillin said, taking the lead.

"Look! That's the painting Agonya told me about. Do you see how it opens?"

Ryker stepped closer and felt along the edge of the painting. "Aha, here." His finger slipped behind the painting and soon it was swinging outward.

Tse held up a torch he'd found in the hall and led them through the skinny passageway. It turned and descended beneath the palace.

At the bottom of the stairs, there was only one way to go, so they picked up their pace. Tse's small torch emitted a faint light for them to see their surroundings. Several times Maya tripped over her own feet. The torch should have been at the back so that its light would guide everyone in front, but she did her best to keep up.

Agonya gave Maya fleeting directions as they made their way forward through the passages. Turn right here, go straight, turn left. A few minutes later, they came to another intersection, but Agonya was silent.

"Which way, Maya?" Tse asked.

"I don't know." Maya said, breathing deeply to calm her nerves.

"That smell!" Krillin hissed.

"I smell it too," Maya said.

"What does it smell like? Ryker asked.

"Death." Krillin and Maya said simultaneously.

She could feel all their emotions stronger than she normally did, except for the one person she wanted to feel. Where had Agonya disappeared to? How far had they come?

"We have to pick a path. Should we split up?"

"No."

"We need to see what is causing that smell," Maya said.

"But Agonya."

"I know. She may have gone this way. We don't know, so it doesn't matter which way we go until we know which way she went. We know she's being taken to a cell, and what else would cause that stench but people who've died in cells?" The moment she said it, she knew she was right. Maya gagged, thinking about it.

"Maya!" Ryker had his arm around her before she could fall to the floor.

She took a moment to steady herself. "I'm fine, but we need to go that way."

"Let's go then. We're losing time standing here," Krillin said. "We can't be late."

"Be careful. There are still four guards to deal with."

They hurried as best as they could. It worried Maya why she couldn't hear Agonya in her mind anymore.

Krillin tapped on Tse's shoulder and held his finger to his lips for them to be quiet. Then he pointed down the tunnel and held up four fingers. "We must be close to the guards," Maya thought. She could sense their serious mood. Whatever instructions they had received had put the guards on alert.

"Leave the torch here," Krillin whispered.

Tse found a bracket on the dirt wall and placed the torch in it, still lit, but it wouldn't give them away when they approached the guards.

Maya did her best to keep close to Ryker. She could sense his nervousness, but he was also confident, which was what she needed. There was a flicker of light. Maya hoped Agonya was still with those guards.

Krillin pulled out an arrow and notched it in his bow. Tse saw him and pulled out a smoke bomb. Krillin motioned for him to go first.

Maya covered her face with her scarf.

Tse threw the bomb, and the light dimmed as the smoke filled the tunnel. There were cries of alarm as the guards were thrown into chaos. Krillin let his arrow fly through the narrow space and hit one of the guards, trying to flee the smoke. Maya knew it hit its mark because she could feel the guard's pain. Drowsiness took over the guards' emotions and soon they were on the ground fast asleep, without Maya or the others having to fight them.

"I can't smell her highness," Krillin said, still in a whisper.

"What? But those were the same guards, right?"

Krillin thought for a moment. "Yes, they are the same scents we followed through the painting."

"Don't worry, Maya," Tse said, "If Agonya were hurt or dead, we would still sense her aroma, but since we can't smell her at all, I think something is blocking her scent." Then he covered his own face and started walking forward.

Krillin followed, then turned around and disappeared. It took a moment, and he was back with their torch.

The closer they got to the guards, the harder it was for Maya to breathe, but she focused on Ryker's calmness and slowed her heart back to normal, though the urge to vomit kept getting stronger as the smell of death grew closer.

DEATH PERMEATED THE passage. Agonya tried to breathe through her mouth instead of her nose, but it was hard. She rarely breathed through her mouth and her body didn't like it. One of the guards pushed her forward.

"Where are you taking me?" she demanded.

The guards scoffed. "You heard His Highness. Don't speak, or you might end up like one of these." He waved his torch to the side.

That's when Agonya saw the source of the stench. Dead bodies stacked one on top of the other in the rooms to the sides of the tunnel. Her body convulsed, and she vomited.

"Eww!" Dylan jumped away from her, letting her fall to the floor. Then Deepak was there, lifting her from the floor. "Keep moving," he barked. Then he shoved her past the room of death.

"How can you be so callous?" Agonya cried. "Who are these people?"

"You want to know who they are?" Deepak said. "Here, take a closer look." Then he dragged her back to the previous room and pushed her inside.

Agonya's whole body shook with silent sobs. Then there was light illuminating the bodies. She cried out as she recognized the Itholean she had tried to heal at Tsula's house. "No, no, no" It couldn't be. She didn't understand. How could Tsula do such a thing? How could anyone do such a thing? The woman was healed, but now she was dead. She couldn't move and she couldn't stop her body from shaking. The body underneath the woman was also Itholean. The closer she looked, the more she knew they were all her people. What was happening? She knew they were slaves but this?! This was not what she had agreed to!

"Why did you show her?" Dylan groaned. "Now look at her! She won't stop wailing."

Was that sound coming from her? Agonya wasn't sure.

One of the other guards spoke next. "You can carry her, since you showed her."

Deepak laughed. "At least now she'll be easy to handle."

Agonya felt something wet on her nose and her body stopped shaking. The terrible sounds became quieter too.

"That's better, isn't it?"

Then, arms wrapped around her and tossed her over a shoulder. She couldn't stop him. She felt empty. There was no magic inside her, not even a desire to fight. She dangled there, her hair reaching to the floor.

Before she knew it, she was being tossed onto the floor. She looked up, but it was too late. The horror of where she was made her try to stand. It was hopeless. There was no escape from her glass prison. Agonya banged on the glass anyway, trying to break through, but nothing happened. She tried to warn Maya, but their connection was lost. There was no magic getting in or out of the glass. She was trapped. Her body slumped to the ground, and she cried until there were no more tears. Her whole life was one big lament. There were too many people to mourn. Her people had fallen from paradise. She'd known paradise had left them, but this made it more real. What was the point of it all?

The guards outside of her glass cage pointed at her and laughed. They didn't care what happened to her. They were in their own paradise, whatever that meant. She knew this was the wrong way to think. Somewhere in the back of her mind, she knew Blackthorn was safe. Agonya was glad he wasn't here, but she didn't feel glad. All she felt was empty and grief beyond anything she'd ever known.

Chapter 25

The smoke cloud swirled around them, but their scarves protected them, unlike the guards. Maya could still detect it, but the scent of death was stronger. Its strength immobilized her. She couldn't cling to Ryker's emotions anymore to help her. The scents crushed her, and she fell to the floor.

"Maya! What's wrong?" Ryker squatted next to her.

In between short breaths, Maya conveyed what was happening. Ryker nodded, even though she knew he didn't understand. No one could understand.

"I'll stay with you," he said.

"No! Help the others find Agonya. These scents have no hold on you."

"Are you sure?"

"We're almost there. Look, here's one of the guards laying a few feet away. She can't be far." Maya couldn't believe how the guards had fallen in the smoke when the stench of death was so much stronger.

To prove her words, Krillin called out from further ahead, "I found her."

Ryker let his fingers linger on Maya's shoulders before he went to Krillin and Tse's side. Only their feet were visible from where she lay, since the smoke from the odor bomb was rising to the top of the tunnel. She could also feel relief and frustration among their combined feelings and wondered what the problem was.

There was a banging, and Maya knew Agonya was in the prince's cell, and she knew why Agonya had gone silent. Glass. That was the sound of glass, which was still a new concept to Maya, but she knew about the cage that had held Blackthorn captive. How did the prince acquire enough glass to make a cage large enough to fit Agonya? Maya didn't have a clue.

The banging continued, but the glass was indestructible. And the gross scent of death still weighed her body down. Where was it coming from? The scent was all around her. The sickening smell forced her friends' emotions on her, and she knew they weren't making any progress. Maya tried to think of how to help them open the cage. "Is there a door?" she called out.

"No, it's smooth all over," Ryker replied.

One of the soldiers stirred.

"Krillin! The guards!" Maya panicked.

He was there in an instant, tying the guard's hands and feet together while Tse and Ryker did the same to the two other guards. Krillin was the fastest, so he tied up the fourth.

"Hey! Check the guards for a key or a clue on how to open the cage," Krillin said as he started rifling through the last guard's pockets.

The new adrenaline in the others gave Maya the boost she needed to move again. She crawled to the first guard Krillin had tied up and searched his clothing. He had a vial of perfume and a white square cloth in his pockets.

That was odd.

He only had perfume on him, nothing else. No weapon that she could find. Maybe she had missed the weapons. She searched again but found nothing.

"What did you find, Maya?" Ryker asked.

"Did you find a weapon?"

"A weapon?" Ryker stopped in his tracks. "I forgot to look for one. Wait." He dashed back to the soldier he'd searched. When he returned, he was empty-handed.

"What's the matter?" Krillin asked.

Maya jumped. She hadn't seen him come over. "There are no weapons," she said, recovering herself.

"The guy I searched had a sword," Tse said, walking over to join them.

"Are you sure?" Krillin asked.

But even as he said it, Maya knew he hadn't found a weapon on his soldier, either.

"What else did you find?" Ryker asked.

Maya held up the perfume and cloth. "This is everything."

"Here, let me smell it," Krillin said.

"Wait! That cloth is wet. I think it has whatever is in that vial on it."

Krillin reached for the perfume and the cloth but didn't bring it to his nose. "Ugh! That scent is awful!" He stuffed the items into a deep pocket of his cloak. "I don't understand," Krillin said. "How could these items help the guards in their duties? At least one of them had a sword, but why not the others? Mine only had a blank parchment, quill, and ink."

"I got a piece of parchment with something written on it," Ryker said.

"What does it say?" Tse asked.

Ryker unrolled the parchment. "FRAGRANCES. Citrus. Pineapple."

"That's all? But what does that mean?" Krillin wondered. "Pineapple is a type of citrus."

Maya gasped. "Blackthorn told me about Fragrances! There's magic surrounding that cage."

"I don't think the magic was used on the cage," Tse said.

"What do you mean?" Maya asked.

"I mean, the magic was used on Agonya."

"Oh." Maya tried to stand up and found she could do it.

"What does citrus do?" Ryker asked.

"I don't know," Maya said, her shoulders slumping.

Krillin was the one who spoke next. "I think citrus might heal, but that doesn't make sense."

Tse shook his head. "No, citrus is a fruit, but it differs from the scent of orinberries."

"You're right. But then what?"

Maya held up her fingers and named what they'd found. "One guard had perfume, another had instructions, another was able to send a message, and the other had a sword." It made no sense to her. The guards needed each other, and if one of them was missing, they wouldn't be able to do their jobs. "Krillin, what scent was on the cloth?"

"Not citrus," he said at once. "Well, there might have been a bottom scent of neroli, but the upper note was chocolate. I did not like the smell of it at all."

"Guys, we can't stay here. If we don't leave soon, we'll be trapped here," Ryker said.

"But how do we get Agonya out?" Maya asked.

"Can we lift the whole cage?" Tse asked.

"No, there's no way we could carry it through these skinny tunnels."

"But how did it get in here?"

Maya pressed her way through the air toward the cage. She had to stop and breathe several times before moving forward again, but she made it.

Agonya was curled up on the ground. "What's the matter with her?"

"I think she's asleep."

"But her eyes are open," Maya countered. She crouched on the ground next to Agonya and tried to meet her friend's eyes, but Agonya just stared ahead. "Agonya! Can you hear me? It's me, Maya. I'm here." There was no response. Maya got closer to the ground and smelled the dirt beneath her. Her mind cleared, and she knew what they must do. "Guys! Bring me that sword!"

They were already by her side, curious about what she was doing, so Tse gave her the sword. Maya shoved it into the ground and started digging. "We can dig under the cage!"

Ryker grinned and pulled out his own daggers to help with the digging effort.

It took longer than she'd have liked. Maya tried to use the sword as a lever to push the cage over, but she wasn't strong enough.

"Let me," Krillin and Tse said together and laughed. With their hands on the hilt, they pushed down with all their might on the sword. The cage moved, then stopped. It wouldn't budge because the top of the cage was pushing against the top of the tunnel.

"It's not enough," Maya said. "There's not enough space to get her out."

"Then we keep digging," Ryker said.

They set to work, digging around the edges of the whole cage, which dropped as the ground gave way beneath it. Maya welcomed these new feelings and dug faster.

THE DISTANT GROUND vibrations didn't register in her mind as something of importance. Agonya sensed them but ignored them. She didn't understand this new feeling that was overwhelming her. She'd thought she'd known what grief was when she lost her mother and then her father, even when she lost her ability to walk. But this. This was different. She felt numb because it was too painful to allow herself to feel even the tiniest bit. She laid motionless in her cage and pushed all thoughts about what she'd seen to the recesses of her mind.

Bang. Bang. Bang.

The noise was vaguely interesting only because it distracted her from her thoughts, but Agonya couldn't move or bother to see what caused it. There were voices too, somewhere above her, but what was the point?

The woman's face was burned into her memory and was all she could see. It wasn't even about Tsula's betrayal that hurt. Agonya had let her people become subjects to another king, thinking that would be preferable than them dying in the fight. Ha! How wrong she'd been. Whatever this was was no normal war. As if war was normal to begin with. She'd even known this war involved magic, but this? Agonya did not know anyone could be this terrible. Was Dana using her people as... as something to be discarded after they failed her experiments? And what about King Reid and Prince Lucas? Clearly, they were involved with Dana's plan and yet they put up this farce of being righteous. Were they so invested in Dana's quest for knowledge and power that they didn't care who lived and who died?

Agonya's body shuddered at that last thought. Was she going to be next? Oh, Agonya was going to be the best one of them all. Agonya relished the thought of the pain she would be forced to endure because she deserved it. Her whole time here in Korina, she'd known she was a failure, but now she knew she deserved whatever scent came her way.

Tap. Tap.

"Agonya? Can you hear me? It's me, Maya. I'm here." The voice was faint and Agonya couldn't bring herself to search for it. It might be Maya, but it was more likely that her punishment was beginning because Maya wouldn't want to talk to her if she'd known what Agonya had done.

"Guys, bring me that sword!"

Hmm. That was odd. Agonya thought a sword would be too quick. She did not want to die like her father with her head chopped off, at least not immediately. She wanted to suffer, then, at the very end, if they wanted to sever her nose from her soul, then so be it. How could the god of Jedrek be good after what she'd witnessed? Why didn't he stop this evil? If it didn't matter to him, why would it matter if her soul was severed from the scents forever?

The ground shook again and the glass in front of her shifted. She could see people trying to move it, but didn't care who they were. Let them come.

"It's not enough," Maya's voice said. "There's not enough space to get her out."

"Then we keep digging," a new voice replied.

Agonya felt like crying then. Maya's voice was so real. She knew it was a trick, and the torment was beginning, but she didn't want Maya to suffer. She shouldn't be here.

There were more scraping noises as the surrounding dirt lifted into the air. Breathing was getting harder because of the dust in her face, but she didn't move. Agonya deserved way worse than breathing in dirt. It was unclear how long they had been digging in the dirt. But her cage eventually disappeared. She didn't bother to look up even then.

Someone was kneeling in front of her, brushing her hair out of her face? No. This must be part of the test, a trick.

Then she felt arms around her, lifting her off the ground. The stench of death hit her stronger this time. Her fears were confirmed. There was nothing left for Agonya.

She heard talking and then they were moving. She was moving with them. Someone was carrying her. It didn't matter where. She was done fighting. None of it mattered anymore.

"WHAT'S WRONG WITH HER?" Maya asked.

Krillin glanced at the woman in his arms. She was unresponsive, and he thought he knew what it meant. "I think she's in shock. She has the sickness of battle. I've witnessed soldiers like her, encountering war for the first time or for an extended period.

"Maya, it's going to be okay," Ryker tried to comfort the petite woman.

He was a fool. What he said meant nothing. The men and women he'd seen with this sickness didn't recover. This entire mission was a failure. They came to save a queen that was supposed to help them, and they had recovered someone completely different. Whoever this person was would not help them. Krillin made a mistake coming with them. He should have tried to find his family. That was exactly what he would do as soon as this was all over.

But for now, he followed Tse through the maze of underground tunnels. Perhaps these tunnels had an exit that wasn't in the palace. Someone needed to go back for Ashkii, if Her Highness couldn't break free of whatever had its hold on her long enough to do that mind talking thing.

"We found it," Tse said.

The next turn revealed stairs leading up to a door. Who knew what was on the other side.

All was silent. Krillin braced himself for whatever was there. Tse pushed it open.

It was difficult to see with Tse blocking his view, but no one else was in sight. Krillin could smell people, and city streets and everything that came with it. Fresh bread permeated the air. Krillin clung to the aromatic scent. It was refreshing after a long night of escaping the palace. He followed Tse outside and turned toward the bread.

"Kril? What are you doing? Can you tell where we are?"

Krillin did a quick spin. They were in a house. The stairs deposited them in a simple room and pointed them towards the rest of the house. The bread was coming from another room, one closer to the city streets and to the right of them.

"There's no way to know which house we are in or where it is, but its scent means we're in Korina. And we're not alone. Someone made bread in the room next to us," Krillin whispered.

"I'll go investigate," Ryker volunteered, then took off through the rest of the house. He was back in a moment, offering them chunks of fresh bread. "There's no one here," he said. He took a bite of his bread and motioned for them to follow.

Ryker poked his head out the front door and quickly retreated, falling into Maya, who was standing behind him. The door swung open from the outside and Krillin could smell their welcoming party. Krillin slipped back into the room they'd arrived in and set Agonya on the ground. He was going to need his bow and arrows.

ASHKII COULD SEE THEIR inn when Lord Tanish stepped out in front of him.

"It's not safe." Tanish pointed to where he had been heading.

Ashkii glanced over his shoulder and then let Lord Tanish drag him into the shadows.

"I watched them enter the inn after your distraction put those guards on alert. Many pursued you, but this group came here. The prince was with them."

"The prince? Are you sure?"

"Yes. They knew where you've been hiding out."

"But how?"

"I suspect the owner of that inn overheard one of you talking or thought you looked suspicious."

"How many are up there? Do you know?" Ashkii couldn't help thinking about everything they'd left in their room. Could it be used against them? Could it be replaced?

"I don't know. The moment I saw them, I hid myself. But I did see them entering that building. The prince is hard to miss."

Ashkii had to do some quick thinking. He had to hear what they were saying, but he couldn't risk them slipping away while he tried to get close enough. "Can you keep watch for me?"

"I can, but there's no way I can let you know they're leaving and if I followed them, you wouldn't be able to find me."

"I only need you to stay and watch. I will know soon if they leave and will find you. If you can point me in the direction they go, then I'll be able to follow." Ashkii didn't wait for an answer but jumped onto the roof. He tried to be as quick and quiet as he could while he raced along the roofs. The close rooftops allowed him to avoid loud thumps while leaping.

Once he was in position, he laid flat on the roof and pressed his ear to the roof's door. He could hear boots walking around and voices, but he couldn't understand what they were saying. Soon, the boots departed. They were on the move. Ashkii waited a moment more and then opened the door. There was no one inside. He lowered himself and looked around the room. Everything was strewn across the floor. The table was flipped, the pillows were ripped open, it was a mess. Ashkii was ready to leave when he noticed something beneath the table. He bent to pick it up and found the map Maya had drawn of the palace.

The prince wasn't dumb. He would realize Ashkii was a diversion for the others to enter the palace. The question was what he would do about it. Ashkii had to find Tanish and see where the prince was going. Ashkii let the air flow around him on his way back out. He didn't bother being quiet but made his way to Lord Tanish as fast as he could.

"They went that way," Tanish said, gesturing away from the palace.

Ashkii didn't know if that was a good thing or not, but at least they wouldn't be trapped in the palace. Ashkii nodded in thanks and took off as fast as he dared. He didn't want to be spotted, so he stayed low.

The soldiers with the prince didn't look behind themselves. They had no clue they were being followed. Near the edge of the city, the prince motioned for his soldiers to get into position. Ashkii watched some climb up ladders onto the surrounding buildings. There would be no surprises.

"Sticks!" There was a scout headed his way. Ashkii opened the water barrel he was hiding behind. It was full. He went to the next and climbed inside. He didn't think he'd been seen. The scout kept walking right by the barrel without pausing. Ashkii let out his breath as soon as she was gone. He carefully slid the lid off the barrel, peeking out to see the prince near a home's door.

What was the prince waiting for? The whole situation bothered Ashkii, even though it made no sense to him. There was something obvious he missed. The door to the house opened, a soldier came out and reported to the prince. But he'd left the door open, and Ashkii got a glimpse inside. It was a typical home, but he now knew what he'd been missing!

This was exactly like the tunnels in Ithol, where it exited into a house like this one. Was there a palace tunnel leading here? Were the others in it? But how would the prince know to expect them? Oh. The prince knew Agonya was the reason they were at the inn. If they were successful, then they would come out that door or return to the palace. If Ashkii was honest with himself, there was no reason to return to the palace if there was a chance they could escape another way.

How much time did he have? Should he wait and see what happened? Or start eliminating the prince's guards. If he was caught, that would be the end. His friends didn't know they were about to be ambushed. And he couldn't be caught when Agonya needed him again. No, he would wait and watch for his opportunity to make a difference this time.

Chapter 26

The sun pushed the darkness to the edges of the buildings. Its rays didn't help the restless soldiers in their wait. But Ashkii felt its warmth. If they saw him now, those soldiers would catch him in a minute. He needed to blend in. Ashkii pulled out his cloak. It didn't matter what he was wearing now. If he was seen, it was over. He pulled out his daggers and made sure his spear was easy to grab off his back.

The prince spoke, and the soldiers stood taller. They were grinning. Only one thing could get that reaction. Ashkii checked the status of the Kors and crouched at the ready, breathing in the scents of the street. He would start with the archers and work his way toward the prince.

The door cracked open and shut. Ashkii didn't wait to see what followed but leaped onto the roof. No one noticed him. They were focused on the house. He crept to the first archer and stabbed him from behind, muffling any sound by covering his mouth. Ashkii made sure the man was dead before advancing to the next archer.

There was a commotion on the streets, but Ashkii focused on his next target standing tall on the next roof. The prince's voice rose above the rest of the sudden chaos. "Come out. We've got you surrounded."

There was a reply Ashkii couldn't hear, so he kept moving. He was almost there when the archer smelled him coming and spun on the spot. But she was too late. Ashkii plunged his dagger into her chest, and she let out a cry of pain. Several soldiers glanced up and saw him. Soon, they were shouting and pointing.

An arrow scraped Ashkii's cloak on its way past him. Rolling to the side, he kicked the archer off the roof, still clutching his daggers. Blood dripped off the tips. Two down, two more to go. Another arrow soared towards him, so he bent his knees and jumped over it. Dodging arrows became a maze, yet

Ashkii's advantage was his ability to fly like the arrows. He closed the distance in three jumps. The archer was in the middle of reloading his bow when Ashkii kicked him. The fourth archer shot another arrow. Ashkii grabbed the archer he'd kicked to the roof and put him between himself and the arrow. The arrow struck, pushing the dead archer into Ashkii's chest. He let go and jumped back before he was pushed to the ground. When he turned to the last archer, the soldier was retreating. He scooped up the fallen bow and arrows and ran to the edge of the roof. He took aim and breathed in the soldier's scent.

RYKER PUSHED MAYA BACK into the first room as soldiers came inside the house. Spotting Krillin with his bow drawn, she dropped to the floor. He let the arrow loose. It shot past Ryker and hit a Kor, trying to enter the house.

"We're surrounded," Ryker said.

"What did you expect? We left enough evidence behind us."

Maya couldn't focus on what they were saying. The Kors had found them, and she needed to do something, anything. Breathing in, she smelled the sickening scent of death mixed with the smell of sweaty soldiers and the aromatic bread. She'd avoided using her magic because the stench of death was so strong, but out of the tunnel, the scent was one of many scents, and she knew she could handle it. She felt the raw emotions of everyone in the room and outside the house. What she didn't anticipate was a powerful emotion emanating from the floor. An overwhelming sense of despair and indifference.

Without thinking, Maya rushed to her friend's side while the others fought for their lives.

"Agonya. Can you hear me?"

Agonya didn't reply, but Maya felt a spike of emotion. That was something. Before, there had been glass between them, blocking Maya from using her powers. There was nothing in their way now except the Kors trying to kill them.

"Agonya, why are you so sad?"

There was no response.

"You know how much I love you, right? I'm so glad we found you in time. Do you remember yesterday when I brought you your food? I knew your joy at seeing me and I had that same joy. Where did it go?"

Fear. Disbelief. Confusion.

Her emotions made no sense. "Agonya, it's me, Maya, your friend. You're safe now. Well, you're with us and we need your help."

At the word "help", Maya felt Agonya fall further into despair. Did she think she couldn't help? For as long as Maya knew Agonya, she'd always helped those who were in need. Why would the mention of it cause her so much distress now?

Ryker's voice broke through the chaos. "We need to go."

"She's not responding," Maya called back.

Then Tse was at her side, picking up Agonya and moving toward the door. Maya followed and made the mistake of glancing over her shoulder. More Kors were charging up the stairs.

"This way!" Ryker shouted.

She burst out of the house and threw her hands in front of her face. The sun was blinding. The prolonged darkness made it painful for her to be outside. She felt someone grab her arms and pull her. Was it Krillin? Then he lifted her off the ground. She didn't care who was carrying her. No, that was Agonya's emotions.

Maya blinked and rubbed her eyes. She opened them and could see again. Krillin carried her. Tse had Agonya, and Ryker ran next to them. They were running, passing soldier after soldier. Rushing through the streets, Maya recognized an awful presence getting stronger and knew Dana was there.

THE ARCHER DODGED ASHKII'S arrow and retreated into a group of soldiers on the street. Ashkii assessed the situation from his perch on the roof and saw soldiers fighting their way into the house with little success. He glanced at the archer just in time. An arrow shot through the air straight for his head. Rolling to the side, Ashkii jumped down and attacked the soldiers with his daggers. Fighting them was not as easy as the ones that had chased him before. Ashkii felt the tip of a sword hit his back, so he ducked and rolled into the soldier in front of him. Halfway through his roll, he stuck out his leg, causing the soldier that had been behind him to trip forward and accidentally stab his fellow soldier.

Now Ashkii was stuck. Someone grabbed his leg and pulled him out from under the wounded soldier. He twisted to see who it was and saw a sword descending on him. Trying to free his leg from the Kor's grip, he tried to knock the sword out of the way, but it pierced his side instead. Pain shot through him, and he struggled to think. The sword yanked out, and Ashkii rolled to his knees. Another sword came towards him, so he used all his strength and jumped into the sky. He was out of reach for a split second before he was falling back towards the ground, towards the raised swords. He gauged his fall to his advantage, but it was hard. Where could he go?

The Kors were closing in. He threw one dagger at the man below him and another at the one next to him. They dropped their swords and Ashkii landed unharmed. His side screamed at him. Blood oozed out of his wound. He swiftly grabbed one of his stray daggers and launched himself away from the soldiers. He was reluctant to leave his other dagger, but it was impossible to retrieve. Landing on the nearest roof, he retreated out of sight of the soldiers. The risk of being shot at by that archer was too high.

Ashkii pulled a scarf from his bag and wrapped it around his waist, stuffing it into his wound. That should stop the flow of blood. Then he took a swig from his water skin before he turned back to the battle. Tse had pushed his way out of the house. Where was the prince?

The others rushed out behind Tse. Ashkii could finally breathe a sigh of relief. Agonya was with them. But there were soldiers everywhere. She wasn't safe yet. He raced toward the soldiers charging his friends, but pulled his side and knew he wouldn't last long. So, he changed course and headed to intercept them on their flight path.

"STOP!" MAYA SAID. THERE was no point in wasting their energy running when escape was impossible.

"We can't stop," Krillin said between breaths.

"Dana's here. There is no running." Maya felt the fear spike in Krillin, but he kept running.

It didn't matter, he would stop eventually. They reached a fork in the road. When they turned right, Dana blocked their path. They tried to turn left, but Prince Lucas stood in the center of that street. Next to him stood a man that could only be Ashkii's brother with a scarf wrapped around his waist. The resemblance was amazing. No wonder Agonya thought Ashkii had attacked her. They slowed to a stop. A glance over Krillin's shoulder told Maya the soldiers were closing in on them. They were trapped.

Krillin set Maya on the ground, and she turned to face the beautiful woman, blocking them at every turn. Dana smiled, but the emotion behind the smile made Maya shudder.

"Why do you keep running?" Dana broke the silence. Then she glided up to Agonya, feigning care. "Are you hurt?" she asked.

Agonya made no reply. And Dana reached out and put her hands on Agonya's face. Tse tried to pull back, but Dana moved with him. Maya could sense energy enter Agonya, but her feelings didn't change. More energy transferred from Dana to Agonya. Agonya's eyes popped open, but she didn't ask to be put down. She looked at Dana, nodded, and shut her eyes again. The indifference to seeing this woman who had caused so much pain baffled Maya. How could Agonya not care about Dana's presence?

Maya pushed past Ryker and stepped up to Dana, trying to squeeze between them. "Leave her alone!"

Dana stepped back to better see Maya, who was significantly shorter than her. "I remember you. You're the woman who resisted my emotions. That was quite impressive. I'd be happy to take you on. I could teach you how to control it instead of flinging it into the wind."

Maya couldn't believe what she was hearing. Dana wanted to teach her magic? "I don't think you understand. I'm not here to learn from you. I'm here because I love my friend, and I don't want you to hurt her."

"Don't bother me with that nonsense. I'm not here to hurt your friend."

Maya scoffed. "But all you do is hurt people. You don't care about anyone!"

"Enough!" Dana yelled. Then she lowered her voice and stood straighter. "You don't know me, but I know enough about you, so step aside."

Ryker reached out and touched Maya's hand. She wanted to fight, even though she knew she should back down. That thought snapped Maya out of it. Whose feelings was she channeling? Maya never wanted to fight anyone and believed everyone deserved a chance to be heard.

"I'm not sure what got into me, but I'm curious why you're so interested in Agonya."

"You don't want to know my story."

"But I do."

"Of course you do." Dana's voice dripped honey. "Once you understand, I'm sure we'll become the best of friends."

"No, we will never be close friends, but I want to understand who you are and why you're doing these things."

"Nice try." Then Dana pushed Maya out of her way. "Set her down," she ordered Tse.

He obeyed. Agonya looked at Dana. "What do you want?" she asked.

Dana grinned. "I want you to help me. Come, let us return to my home and we can talk in comfort."

Agonya nodded and followed Dana away from the others. Maya was helpless to stop her. She just stood there and watched. The soldiers who'd been standing nearby the entire confrontation moved forward. Maya felt Ryker grab her hand, and they turned to face their other enemies. They were surrounded again.

ASHKII COULDN'T BELIEVE his eyes. She gave up without a fight! What was she doing? What had Dana done to her? He acted without thinking and rushed to Agonya's side. As soon as he landed next to her, he grabbed her waist and fled onto the next roof. She didn't protest, so he kept going. His body filled with pain, but he had to ignore it. They needed to distance themselves from Dana as much as possible. He would not let Agonya slip away from him again.

"Where do you think you're going?" Kilchii rose through the air and landed in front of him.

Ashkii changed course but didn't slow. His brother wouldn't stop him.

"You think you can outrun me?" Kilchii laughed. He was standing in front of him again. Kilchii moved forward in a crouch and slipped his daggers out, ready for a fight.

As much as Ashkii wanted to keep running, he knew he couldn't outrun his brother. Especially since Kilchii wasn't carrying anyone. "Agonya, I will get you to safety just as soon as I deal with my brother," he said fervently and then let go of her.

"Your Highness, come here and I can take you back to Dana. No fight needed."

Agonya moved towards Kilchii, but Ashkii couldn't let her. He grabbed her hand. "Don't do this!" he pleaded. "Please!"

She looked at him and kept walking. He walked with her. "I've been a terrible friend, but you can't give up on me now! I'm here. I've been fighting for you, and you're going to throw our sacrifices away?"

"Ashkii?" Agonya looked from one brother to the next.

"Yes, it's me," they both said together.

"Let me go."

Her voice jarred him. She hadn't said anything to him since the diversion, and this is what she said? She said it without emotion. Was she severed from all the scents? Ashkii didn't know who this person was. Agonya would never willingly go to Dana. Despite her dislike for him, she never treated people in such a manner. Something had to be wrong with her. And then he knew magic was involved. He didn't know what it was, but he had to keep fighting.

ASHKII LEFT KRILLIN with no choice when he flew away with Agonya. Krillin knew what Ashkii's actions meant, so he was the first to act. Locking in on the soldiers' aromas, he started shooting arrows. He shot the soldiers who were closest first, before everyone had time to process what happened.

The battle began as first one soldier, then another fell to the ground. Tse rushed toward them and Ryker confronted the prince while Ashkii's brother leaped on the roof to pursue the princess. Krillin used their buffer to keep shooting soldiers: three, four, five. Reload. Six, seven, eight on the ground.

They kept coming. Tse did his best to hold them back, but a couple got around him, and Krillin was forced to drop his bow and pull out his sword. If these were his final moments, he would die defending his friends. How did Dana know they were rescuing Agonya? Was it the guards they knocked out but didn't kill? There were too many soldiers for it to be a simple reaction to some guards being knocked out.

There was no time to ask questions he didn't have answers to. A sword came in from the right. He parried it and kept moving so he could block the next sword coming within reach. He fought with everything he had. If any of his companions survived, then it would be worth it. It wasn't about saving everyone, and it wasn't about protecting his family, either. Even if they all died here, he knew it was worth it. He knew that now. It was about doing the right thing. That included saving lives, and if that required killing the ones trying to take lives, that was what he would do.

Wham! A soldier slammed into Krillin, trying to knock him over, but Krillin kept moving and twisted to the side, letting the soldier fall towards the street. Another soldier was there, and they clashed swords. The fallen soldier stood up and joined the second one, approaching Krillin from behind. He did his best to smell their scents, their weapons' scents, and somehow, he managed to dodge every blow. While they recovered from their failed attacks, Krillin sliced their legs and pushed past them to the other soldiers still advancing. If he died, an obstacle to those doing evil, he was doing the right thing. Every minute blocking their enemies was a minute well spent.

MAYA WATCHED THE BATTLE begin and felt... What did she feel? Too many emotions crammed inside her. Feeling everyone else's emotions wasn't enough. She needed to do something more. Her friends fought for their lives. So she turned toward the one who hadn't been engaged by her friends. Dana remained where Ashkii and Agonya left her, inhaling the scents of a vial. Maya couldn't fight Dana. She was the worst person for Maya to fight against, but all her friends were engaged with their own enemies. Without thinking it through, Maya ran towards Dana and knocked the vial out of her hands.

Dana's hands found Maya's neck and squeezed. "That cost me quite a lot, child. You will pay for that."

Maya's feet lifted off the ground. Dana was too strong! Maya swung her feet, getting in a lucky kick to Dana's gut. Dana's hands loosened long enough for Maya to wrench them away from her neck. But then she fell to the ground. Pain shot through her ankle as she gasped for air. She had to keep moving. Dana was lunging for her. Maya tried to roll out of the way, but Dana was quick. Her hands wrapped around Maya's legs and pulled.

The pain in her ankle intensified and Maya cried out. What had she been thinking? Maya was no good in a fight. Everyone knew it. Maya had no training. She was small and weak. But now she had no choice. Maya reached for the dagger in her pocket and when Dana pulled her close enough, Maya pulled it out and stabbed in the general direction of her attacker. She didn't know where she was stabbing or if she would hit anything.

She didn't hit anything.

Breathing in Dana's aroma, she stabbed again. This time it was like her arms moved on their own accord and she hit her mark. Dana pushed Maya, who flew through the air, leaving the dagger in Dana's chest.

Maya hit the ground and rolled. When she looked up, she saw the man responsible for her pain these last months walking towards her. Her eyes flicked to his hands, and she saw the metal rings that had beaten her face again and again. He noticed and grinned. She froze. All her insides seized up and she couldn't breathe. She'd been wrong. Dana wasn't the worst. Aekan was coming for her.

Chapter 27

Blackthorn couldn't remember the last time he'd cried, but he thought it was right after Dana took his family. Since then, he had done his best not to remember their scents, their leaves, berries, or anything else about them. But he couldn't avoid it here. He was home, and they were not. But how was it possible? He thought it had been sealed up. How many times had he attempted to return, only to fail time and time again? Now a Kor brought him here? And not just any Kor, Jaylen Dahel, of all people!

What would happen to Anya, Sari, and Amber? Would they find the help they needed? Would Nakos hurt them now that Blackthorn wasn't there to protect them? No, Smokey wouldn't let him.

"Blackthorn?" the Kor said again. "Is that you? Are you... crying?"

He ignored the Kor as a fresh wave of grief washed over him. Anya had to be fine. He tried to stop it, to breathe in the scent of the King of Nuts, but it only made it worse.

"How?" he managed to squeak out.

Somehow, the Kor understood. "I'm not sure," he said. "Once you departed from Ithol, I had time to reflect on everything that had happened since I left home."

Was the Kor trying to say he had a change of heart? This man who had ruthlessly pursued Blackthorn through the Perfumed Pines and obeyed Dana's every command? Surely, he couldn't have changed sides.

When Blackthorn said nothing, the Kor continued his story.

"I wanted to know who was telling the truth because I realized it came down to conflicting claims. I knew they couldn't all be right because they all claimed the others were wrong."

Blackthorn's curiosity got the better of him. It was rare when he met a human who could recognize the lies they grew up believing for what they were. Oh, everyone became aware of the deception, at some point, in their lives, but they choose to remain blind to the truth or were apathetic.

"That doesn't explain how you found my home or how you summoned me here when I was on the other side of the Acrid Mountains."

"Wait! You were where?" the Kor threw his hands in the air and continued to pace beneath the tree.

"The other side of the Acrid Mountains." Thoughts of Anya dying flashed across his mind. He reminded himself that he had already done what he could for her, that she would get the help she needed. "Forget about that," he said to himself as much as he said it to the Kor. "No one in a millennium has stepped foot in this place until now." Blackthorn lowered himself beneath the branches.

The Kor stopped in his tracks and looked at him. Oh great. He was going to ogle at the Kindroot. But then he nodded and continued pacing. Hmm. Maybe not.

"You're right. We can't be distracted."

"Distracted from what?" Blackthorn asked. This conversation kept getting weirder and weirder.

"When I first found this place, quite by accident, I almost died because I didn't have any food or water for days before I found my way out of here."

The way he said it was matter of fact.

"I have food this time, but it won't last forever. Not to mention my liege wants your roots on his table."

King Reid's name caused Blackthorn to retreat into the safety of the tree.

"Don't worry. I will not give you to him. I think that's why I was able to find this place, and you, too. What is this place, anyway?"

"This is my home. Who else knows about it?" Blackthorn wasn't sure he wanted the answer, but he had to ask.

"Laniel sort of knows, but he doesn't know anything about Kindroots. He knows I'm here and is making sure no one misses me while I'm not at the palace. I was hoping you could tell me how this all works. This tree is a big part of the magic, but I don't know how it transported me here or why."

"How did you come back the second time?" Teaching Jaylen olfamancy was the last thing Blackthorn wanted to do.

"Do you think it was my desire to help you, combined with the scent of this tree? Oh, and maybe a song my mother taught me when I was little. Twice, I found myself in the Scented Library near a painting. I was transported here, not to this room, but elsewhere. Only after discovering this room, could I return to the library. But I don't understand it. What is it about this tree? About that song? About my belief in you?"

The Kor's words were confusing, but Blackthorn was unsure how things worked after such a long absence. He'd been under the impression it wouldn't work anymore. Blackthorn swung to the ground. He let his roots dig deep into the dirt and braced himself for the scents he was about to smell. His emotions were raw, and he wasn't even sure if this Kor deserved to know his secrets. He breathed in all the scents of home. Peonies, Resin, Apples, even the Gross and Rotten scents from plants decaying perpetually for longer than Blackthorn had been alive. There were other scents like an Aromatic cocoa, the Nutty scents from this tree, Citrus, the Ether scent of fermented wine and sulfur rising from the volcanic ground, and Spearmint. All ten were still here. They brought healing and clarity to Blackthorn.

"Yes, you're right. You must be blessed by the god of Jedrek to have the ability to use the nutty fragrance to transport yourself and then me here."

"What? You think I controlled this magic?"

"There's no other explanation. This tree is just a tree. It doesn't have a mind of its own to summon you here. The secret of FRAGRANCES has been concealed for years, yet you are the fifth person to uncover it."

The Kor tried to protest that he had discovered nothing, but Blackthorn needed to test his intentions. "First, olfamancy is dangerous."

"What do you mean?"

"I mean, you can die using it, and you can kill others using it. It is dangerous."

The Kor gaped at him. "Well, I realized my mistake when I came here without food or water, but that's not what you're talking about, is it?"

"No, though, that is worth thinking about. I'm talking about how the queen almost died using it, and how her mother, your princess, did die using it."

"Wait, I thought the queen said King Reid killed his sister, not this magic."

Blackthorn shook his leaves in frustration. "You could say that I killed her, too."

"What do you mean? That they're both true? How is that possible?" The Kor sat next to Blackthorn and waited for an answer.

Time was scarce, but Blackthorn sensed that the Kor needed to hear the whole story before he would be able to move on. "King Reid came to Ithol looking for me. Kanti knew his intentions towards me, so she refused to grant his request. When she refused, he attacked her. Instead of saving herself, she sacrificed herself to save me by using olfamancy to transport me to safety. She used too much too quickly and died, but not before her brother stabbed her through. So, yes, she died because she wasn't careful while using olfamancy and yes, her brother killed her. And yes, I killed her too because it was me he wanted, not her and I let her protect me. I even helped her, and you know how I said she used too much too quickly? Well, I gave her power a boost to help her, and now she's dead."

"Oh, I'm sorry. I didn't know." The Kor stumbled over his words of repentance, but he was sincere.

"Thank you." Blackthorn studied the Kor. "Would you sacrifice yourself, like Kanti, to protect the innocent or prioritize your own safety?"

The Kor nodded to show he'd heard Blackthorn and then took his time thinking about his answer. That was a positive sign that he was taking this seriously. If the Kor had automatically declared he would be self-sacrificing, Blackthorn would abandon him and search for Anya.

"I'm not sure what I would do," the Kor said. "In the past, I saved myself when presented with the choice. I want to say that I'm a different person now, that I would put others before myself, but I don't think I will know until my life is in danger again."

"That's good enough. I will teach you what I know. You must promise me you will do your best to value other's lives more than your own."

The Kor wiped his hands through his hair and held them up to Blackthorn. "I promise by my scent that I will do my best to value the lives of others over my own, and I will do the best I can to protect them."

Blackthorn shook his leaves in satisfaction. Helping the Kor may enable him to assist Anya, Agonya, and the others. Blackthorn breathed in the Kor's scent and began his first lesson explaining FRAGRANCES to Jaylen.

THE SCENT OF CARDAMOM and rose oil should have been pleasant, but all they triggered memories of her torturer. Aekan approached her, but Maya was frozen in place, unable to move, to think.

"No boasts for me today. Maya?"

So, he knew her name now. She opened her mouth to speak, but no sound came out. Maya remembered goading this man, doing everything she could not to give him what he wanted, but now she was speechless. How had she been so bold in Ithol?

"That's okay, sweetheart. I'll do the boasting this time." He smirked.

Then his feet were in front of her face. She felt him grab her cloak and pull her up.

She tried to stand, but her legs were like a sack of flour.

He stroked the scars on her face. She couldn't pull away from him.

"Interesting," he said, even though he didn't sound interested.

Ryker's voice cried out over the sounds of fighting, and Maya could finally move. She glanced in Ryker's direction and saw him getting up from the ground with his daggers in hand. The prince was advancing on him with a grin on his face. Her heart wrenched inside her, and she knew where her strength had come from before. She had needed to protect Ryker, and she hadn't loved him then like she did now.

Maya's feet found the dirt, and she looked up at Aekan. "What's so interesting?" she asked, only slightly curious.

"I was looking forward to ending your pathetic life, but I have instructions you are to be preserved." He shook his head and turned her around to bind her hands together.

Maya used the motion to keep twisting until she was no longer in his grasp. Halfway through her turn she saw Dana leaping onto the roof that Ashkii had disappeared on to with Agonya. There was no time to think. The moment she slipped from his grasp, he lunged for her. His arms tried to encircle her, but she knew she had to get away. Agonya was being pursued by Dana. And Ryker, her dear Ryker, was fighting for his life while she did what? Listen to this man talk? Maya stepped further out of his reach, but he followed, and soon she was running.

"There's the spark, I remember," he called after her.

Then he was tackling her to the ground. She tried to squirm her way free, but he was too strong. He pushed her face into the dirt. She tried to breathe, but all she did was inhale dust. Off to the side were horse droppings. The smell was awful, but it was also what she needed. She could sense Aekan's confidence and joy at beating her grow stronger as he tied her wrists together. She could also sense Krillin's struggle to continue fighting soldier after soldier. He was getting tired. The soldiers were filled with the lust for battle and kept coming even though none of them were succeeding at killing him.

Aekan yanked her to her feet and pushed her away from the battle. Maya tried to think. "You will not win," she blurted out.

"I've already won."

"Then why are they still fighting?" Maya asked, doing her best to point towards the soldiers behind them.

"I don't care. They're not my problem."

"But I am your problem, right? Why me? Why am I more important than my friends?"

Aekan responded by dragging her further from the fight. That was not good. She couldn't be separated from her friends, but his superior strength pushed her further away from them with each passing moment. She needed to make him more irritated than he already was, if she was going to have a chance.

Concentrating as hard as she could, Maya felt Krillin's emotions and blocked out all the rest. He was exhausted, so she tried to help him feel energized. She started by drawing away his exhaustion into herself and giving him her energy and resolve in return. She couldn't actually see Krillin because Aekan was blocking her view, but she felt completely exhausted. It must be working. How had Krillin still been standing? Maya felt her body pull her towards the ground.

Aekan cursed. "Stand up, woman!" he hissed through his teeth.

There were cries of alarm coming from the Korin soldiers, making Aekan spin to see what was happening. Maya watched his eyes bulge and his nostrils flare in anger and disbelief. "What should I do?" he asked.

Who was he talking to? Oh. Maya knew it the moment his hands dropped her, and she fell to the ground. Dana was speaking in his mind. Aekan turned back and ran to join the fight.

Exhaustion flooded her body, and she couldn't find the strength to stand. It was so hard to think straight. Agonya. Krillin, Tse, Ryker. They were in danger. Dana was concerned about Maya's magical abilities, but maybe also Krillin's fighting skills? Maya absorbed the sickening scents from the ground and focused on the soldiers attacking her friends. They were filled with rage and adrenaline. She inhaled again, this time noticing the scents of the wooden buildings around her. Then she manipulated the Kors' emotions. Their strength and energy were hers, and her exhaustion became theirs.

Filled with the strength of many men, Maya broke the rope binding her hands. This strength was incredible. She couldn't have possibly become stronger, could she? Maya jumped to her feet and faced the battle. Krillin was amazing. The soldiers fell before him. Even Aekan was struggling to reach the fight. But Tse! Maya focused on the Montane and gave him some of her strength and energy. Soon he was helping Krillin take down the Kors.

Aekan was stronger than the other soldiers she'd transferred exhaustion to and was almost upon Krillin when she turned her attention back to him. She had to stop him. Maya chased the man who had caused her so much pain, calling out Krillin's name. She couldn't dwell on the past. Aekan couldn't be allowed to keep hurting people. Maya sped up.

"Krillin! Watch out!"

Hearing her shout, Aekan turned to face her. "I thought I'd taken care of you, but you keep coming back for more."

"And every time you remain intent on stealing other people's scents." Then, without thinking it through, Maya ducked under his arms, and with the strength that remained, she tackled him to the ground.

KRILLIN HEARD HIS NAME and spun around. Maya was tackling someone to the ground. Someone who would have killed him if she hadn't been there. In that instant, he understood the sudden strength to keep fighting.

He underestimated this tiny woman. But even so, watching her wrestle with this man was tough.

Then he saw the man's face. It was Aekan.

"Maya, move!" Krillin pointed his sword down at the man who had ruined his life. He wanted to kill Aekan.

"No! Go!" she yelled. "Help Ryker."

Tse heard her, ran down the street, and was soon fighting the prince with Ryker. Krillin stood immobile. He couldn't let her fight Aekan by herself.

"What are you waiting for?"

Krillin bent down and disarmed Aekan of all his weapons. "You need my help."

"Then help me bind him," she said.

Bind him? What good would that do?

Maya was already pulling rope out of Aekan's bag.

Krillin did not want to tie the man up. He wanted to kill him! But Maya had saved Krillin's life. So, he helped her.

SOMETHING ROLLED OUT of Aekan's bag when she grabbed the rope. Maya finished tying him up with Krillin's help, then picked it up. It was a vial.

Aekan groaned and tried to break free, but her knot held fast.

"It's my turn to ask the questions," Maya said.

He glared at her.

"First, what's in here?" Maya held the vial out where Aekan could see it.

He spit on the ground.

"Either you don't know, or you don't want to tell me. Do you want to smell it for me? Then, you will know." Maya started to uncork the vial, but Aekan stopped her.

"Don't!"

"Why?"

"Please," he was begging her.

What wasn't he saying? Maya was familiar with being questioned. She had to think of things to satisfy her questioner without giving him the tools he needed to defeat her. Aekan must be doing that now their roles were reversed. She tried to breathe in the sickening scents so she could sense his emotions. His emotions couldn't lie to her. But when the scents came, she couldn't tap into her magic. Did Agonya feel this way after she used her powers to heal people? Maya did too much.

"Give it to me."

Maya started. She'd known Krillin was there but had forgotten about him. She held it out to him. He started to uncork it and lift it to his nose, but Maya didn't know what would happen if he was allowed to finish.

"Stop!"

Krillin hesitated.

"We don't know what those scents will do to you."

"They're just scents, Maya. Someone has to work magic for them to affect me. Besides, I will not put the perfume on me."

"Why not make him smell it?"

"What if it strengthens him somehow? No, we can't risk him using the scents against us."

Krillin had a point. They couldn't afford to think it through.

"Okay. Do it."

Aekan struggled to get free, which was a good sign he didn't want Krillin to smell it.

Maya watched Aekan as Krillin breathed in the scents. The moment it was done, Aekan grinned and Maya felt the pit of her stomach drop in horror. What did she agree to?!

Krillin seemed normal, but then Aekan spoke.

"Krillin, quick! Untie me before she kills me!"

Maya heard his words, but they made little sense.

Krillin bent down to untie Aekan, and Maya panicked. "Krillin! What are you doing?"

"I'm unsure how you know my name, but I won't allow you to kill him."

"Don't you remember me? Maya. Aekan just tried to kill you! I saved you from him."

The next thing Maya knew, Aekan was free, and she was being tied up and slung over Krillin's shoulders. What was in the vial that made Krillin forget his and her identities? Blackthorn could explain it to her. He would know what was going on.

"YOU'RE A FAST LEARNER," Blackthorn said.

"I wish I had more time for you to teach me," Jaylen replied. "I still have this nagging feeling that Agonya is in trouble."

"You were the one who insisted on returning to Ithol to check on things. But now that you're back, we can try speaking with Agonya in her mind," Blackthorn reminded him.

"Perhaps you can, but I lack the skill. I can only initiate the conversation if I'm looking at the person."

"Sure, you can. You just haven't tried it yet."

Jaylen shook his head. "The only person I've tried this with is you. Besides, what good would it do? It's not like we can help her from here. Can we?"

Blackthorn ignored his student and ambled out of the room. "No, don't follow me. Try to speak with me in my mind while you're not looking at me."

"But you didn't answer my questions?"

"I will, when you figure it out." Then Blackthorn reached for the roots on the ceilings and swung through the hallways as fast as he could. The rush of flying through the air was freeing.

He landed in the Aromatic room and waited. It smelled of honey and maple and vanilla and fresh warm bread all at once. Several minutes went by and Jaylen was still silent. Jaylen's impressive achievements made Blackthorn confident of his telepathic abilities. How long should he give him? The more he thought about it, he increasingly noticed his mistake.

Blackthorn reached out to Jaylen's mind. "We need to switch places."

"What do you mean? Can't I do this from anywhere?"

"Because you're still learning, it's best if you're in the Aromatic room. It's filled with the fragrance that facilitates telepathic communication. You're still in the Nutty room, which allows for transportation like how you transported me to yourself."

"I'm on my way."

Blackthorn didn't need Jaylen to tell him that. He could see what Jaylen was seeing in his mind. "Turn right. Go straight. Not that way," Blackthorn said, leaving the room and meeting Jaylen in the hall.

"Enter," Blackthorn said aloud, ending the mental link. "Wait a couple minutes before trying to speak in my mind. Focus on the scents in this room. Learn to recognize them."

Jaylen grinned when he walked in. "I like this room. What's it called?"

"It's the Aromatic room. No more questions until you can ask me in my mind." Then Blackthorn returned to the Nutty room.

This time, it didn't take long for Jaylen to enter Blackthorn's mind.

"Blackthorn? Can you hear me?"

"Yes. Good work."

"Wait. Really? It worked?"

"Yes, it worked. You wanted to know the purpose of speaking with Agonya, right?"

"Yeah."

"For one, we can find out if she's okay and how close to danger she is. That will give us time to find a way to assist her. Maybe she can point us to others nearby who can help. What do we know already?"

Jaylen took his time thinking before he replied. "According to you, we know that Prince Lucas kept King Reid from killing her, but he also has a way of keeping her from using magic. And I know she broke her covenant with them and it's only a matter of time before they kill her."

"And Maya, Ashkii, Tse, Krillin and Ryker are on their way to help rescue her," Blackthorn added. "Maybe they're already there."

"Maybe she doesn't know they're trying to rescue her. We could let her know," Jaylen added.

"Maybe they already rescued her, and they don't need our help."

"Wouldn't her Majesty contact you to let you know if she had escaped?"

Blackthorn shook his leaves. "It's better to assume she's still in danger."

"I still can't believe I'm doing this."

"Well, it's time. Picture Agonya in your mind, remember her scent if you can." Blackthorn let the memory of Agonya's floral, resinous, and aromatic aroma flood his mind.

"How did you do that? I can smell her and yet, I haven't been near her since the night she surrendered!"

"Take her aroma and focus on finding her. I'll leave your mind now so you can contact her."

Blackthorn returned to his own mind and went to be near Jaylen. He was going to need Blackthorn's help.

Chapter 28

Agonya stood motionless. Ashkii's brother lunged forward, but Ash ducked and rolled to the side. Or was it Ashkii who lunged and his brother who ducked? She heard one of them suck in a deep breath. Somewhere in the back of her mind, she realized he was wounded. He didn't let it slow him down, but was behind his brother before Kilchii could recover from the lunge. Ashkii knocked his brother's feet out from under him.

"Stop fighting for her," Ashkii hissed.

"I could say the same thing to you."

"I'm not fighting for an evil sorceress."

"Is that how you think of me?" Dana's smooth voice broke through their concentration. "I'm not evil."

Kilchii straightened up out of his crouch and stood like a soldier ready for his orders.

Ashkii remained ready for an attack but moved closer to Agonya. She could smell his scent. He had a pleasant fragrance. Agonya had forgotten his musky scent until now. It was obvious how to distinguish them.

"Then what do you call this?" Ashkii asked, interrupting her thoughts. "Killing innocent people for more power?"

"I'm not doing any of this for my power. There are more important things in life that require protection."

"What? You're doing this for love? You do not know what love is."

Dana stepped closer. Her nostrils flared. "You have no idea what you're talking about. Would you kill your brother to protect the woman you love?"

Before Ashkii could react, his brother stood by Agonya's side. His steel tipped dagger pressed into her neck. The coolness of the blade didn't bother her. No, it felt nice. She almost wished he would let it slip, but it didn't matter either way. She would die one day and until then, she would keep living.

"Let her go." Ashkii reached out towards Agonya but didn't move closer.

"No. I quite like how this is turning out," Dana said. Then she turned away as if to leave.

Agonya saw why immediately. Three people were climbing onto the roof.

"Release her," Tse said, "and maybe I'll let your little prince go free too."

Dana's smile faded as she took in the newcomers. Agonya didn't see how it changed anything. So Tse and Ryker defeated the prince and came to help Ashkii rescue her. It was pointless. Even if they helped Ashkii defeat his brother, they wouldn't be able to overpower Dana. And if somehow, they were able to escape, there was no doubt that Dana would catch up with them. In the meantime, more and more people would die in her place.

"Dana doesn't want me dead yet, or I'd be dead already," Agonya found herself saying. Why had she said that? "But she will kill you if you try to take me away from her."

"We're not leaving you," Ashkii interjected.

There was pain in his voice. That was odd.

"Oh, but you will," an oily voice said from behind Agonya. "You will leave whether or not you want to. Dead or alive."

"Now, now, Aekan. We don't need to be so heartless," Dana crowed. "I'm not evil, like some say I am. They can come along. We'll make it one big party. What do you say, Krillin? Are you going to protect us from these awful people?"

"I won't let them hurt you."

"Krillin!" Ashkii exclaimed. "What happened to you?"

"Maya!" Ryker raced across the roof and tried to take Maya from Krillin's shoulder.

"I don't know who you are, but this woman must be brought to trial. She was going to kill this man. I can't let you take her."

Ryker stumbled back.

None of it made any sense to Agonya. What did it matter if Krillin switched sides again? She stopped paying attention to what they were saying and wondered why she hadn't surrendered sooner. All of this could have been averted.

"Your Majesty?" This voice was faint. Were they talking to her? No, whoever it was must be addressing the prince.

She tried to focus on the people gathered on the roof but the voice didn't belong to any of them.

"Can you hear me?"

"Yes," she said.

Everyone turned to look at her. There was a glint of something in Dana's eyes, but Agonya didn't know what it meant.

"This is Jaylen, do you remember me? I mean, I'm the guy who chased you all the way to Tafka and back to Ithol."

Then Agonya knew he was speaking in her mind. And he was speaking to her, not the prince. That's why everyone had turned towards her. They hadn't heard the question.

"Why are you in my mind," she thought back.

"You convinced me to reconsider. I want to help you if I can."

"You can't."

"What? What do you mean?"

"I mean, you can't help me. It's too late. Dana has won and will continue winning no matter what we do," she thought back.

"But..."

Agonya ignored the rest of whatever he was going to say. It didn't matter. They were all going to die. The only question now was who would die first.

"SHE WON'T TALK TO ME," Jaylen said. What little she said sounded like she'd resigned to her fate, which did not sound like the woman he knew.

Blackthorn rested his roots on Jaylen's foot. "Maybe we should talk to Maya."

"I don't think I can, I'm exhausted from trying to talk with her Majesty." Even as Jaylen spoke, he could feel Blackthorn healing him, replenishing his strength.

"Tell me everything that happened."

"I sensed her mind, like I do when I know I've entered your mind. She was faint though. I could barely feel her. I told her who I was, and that I wanted to help, but she said I couldn't help. That it was too late like she was ready to die."

After a lengthy silence, Blackthorn spoke. "She's in more trouble than we thought. I spoke with Maya. She said they failed to rescue Agonya. They're all in trouble. Someone is about to die."

"What can we do about it?" Jaylen asked. "If what you say is true, there's no time to send help."

"No, but we can bring them to us. We can help them once they are here."

Jaylen stared at the Kindroot. There was no way. He didn't know how he brought Blackthorn here, how was he supposed to transport all of them?

"Quick, to the Nutty room!" Blackthorn swung through the air and vanished from the Aroma room.

Jaylen pushed himself off the ground and ran after him.

ASHKII COULDN'T BELIEVE his luck. How had he failed so horribly? Again. Agonya stood there limp and uncaring, not bothered at all by the dagger pressed into her neck. He wanted to scream. He couldn't kill his brother, and he couldn't let his brother kill Agonya. What else could he do though? Maybe he could slow his brother down, distract him long enough to get Agonya out of his grip.

"There is a solution, Ash. You know what it is, don't you?"

Ashkii glared at Dana. How dare she read his mind! How dare she threaten all of their lives, hold Agonya hostage, and make her think there was no hope left so she wouldn't fight back!

"All you have to do is surrender. There's no need for violence."

Ashkii crouched instinctively at her words. He positioned his dagger toward her. No violence?! Ha! All Dana did was kill people who got in her way.

Dana sighed and leaped behind him. Ashkii tried to spin around to face her, but she was too fast. He felt her yank his hands behind him, knocking his dagger to the roof. Then she secured his wrists together with a rope.

"There. Now, as for you two," Dana stepped around him and faced Tse and Ryker, "will you come peacefully, or do you require persuasion, too?"

Ashkii shook his head and pleaded with Tse not to surrender. Their chances of fighting improved, if they were free. But then Maya spoke up from her place on Krillin's shoulder.

"It's okay. Ryker, do what she says."

Ashkii groaned. What was Maya thinking?! Ashkii tried to get his hands loose, but Dana whirled on him and glared at him with those icy eyes of hers.

"I could kill you right here, right now, but I was hoping..." she trailed off.

That was foreboding. But he resigned himself to the fact that they had failed miserably. "If you truly don't want violence then, take that dagger off Agonya's neck," he retorted.

Dana nodded at Kilchii who slipped his dagger back in its sheath. Then she guided everyone off the roof and through the city streets. Once on the ground, the Korin soldiers, who survived, surrounded the prisoners and escorted them down the street.

Ashkii tried to see where they were going but the Kors blocked his view. He had a feeling they weren't headed to the palace. His hope for escape along the way dwindled with each step.

They followed the city's river upstream until they reached the city wall. The bridge to the wall was lined with soldiers. Dana bypassed the docks beneath the bridge and spoke with the guards, who let them out of the city.

Now Ashkii was really worried. They were going somewhere without witnesses. Ashkii glanced at the oaks and cottonwoods growing along the river. The path led under their branches. Maybe he could jump into one of them.

"Don't even think about it," Prince Lucas snarled in his ear.

Ashkii ignored the prince and kept walking. He wasn't going to say the prince was right, but it was pointless to jump to safety when the others couldn't do the same. Currently, they were all together, and that was to their advantage.

"Hey! Where'd she go?"

Ashkii turned to see who had spoken. It was a guard on the opposite side of the group.

"Where'd who go?" another replied.

"The small one."

Ashkii saw Agonya walking ahead of him. Ryker and Tse were behind him. Krillin was walking with the guards. But where was Maya?

Suddenly, guards were calling out and the entire party came to a stop. Dana returned to investigate the commotion. Before anyone could do or say anything else, Agonya gasped. Every head looked at her and then she disappeared!

Ashkii's heart skipped a beat. What was this new magic? He had never encountered people vanishing into thin air. His gaze fixed on Dana, but she wasn't the culprit. She looked just as surprised as everyone else.

Soon, Krillin disappeared too. The chaos and confusion of the soldiers increased. Then Tse and Ryker disappeared, one after the other. Only Ashkii was left. Then he felt a tugging inside him. The last thing he saw was a triumphant smile on Dana's face and then she was gone.

MAYA KNEW WHAT BLACKTHORN was going to do, but she wasn't prepared for it. The tugging sensation was unlike anything she'd felt before and then complete blackness. She lost track of time in the darkness until her feet found solid ground once more. When she opened her eyes, a large tree glowed before her. The walls of the room were made from dirt, and roots could be seen weaving in and out. She tried to take a step and fell towards the ground. A hand reached out and caught her.

"Are you all right?"

Looking up, Maya saw the man who had tried to capture her. He stood to her side, still holding her elbow. Her immediate response was to release her arm from his grip. He noticed and let go.

"Sorry."

"It's okay. I know you're trying to help, but after everything you've done to me, I couldn't help it."

Then a familiar high-pitched voice spoke. "I know how you feel. I felt the same way when Jaylen pulled me here."

Relief flooded Maya's body, and she breathed in her friend's aroma. She'd forgotten what he'd smelled like because it was all the scents at once. Then she remembered her friends.

"Agonya! Ryker! The others!" Her heart pounded in her chest again and she had to sit down.

Jaylen squared his shoulders. "I don't know my limits, but I will try to bring them all here. But first, let me cut your wrists free."

Oh. Maya felt ashamed. She knew the cost of magic, and that he had just done the impossible by bringing her here. "Thank you."

"You can do it," Blackthorn said. "Remember I'm here with you too, helping. You're not alone. Let's focus on bringing them back one at a time."

"Please, start with Agonya. There's something wrong with her. And if you can't bring her, then someone needs to stay by her side."

Jaylen nodded and held onto Blackthorn's roots. All Maya could do was wait. A moment later, they were both aglow with light and Agonya stood in front of them. Maya's heart lurched in her chest at the sight of her. "Agonya!"

Agonya looked up and gasped.

"What's the matter?" Maya felt the joy from a moment ago evaporate as she took in Agonya's countenance.

"What have you done?" Agonya whispered. "What have you done? We're all going to die. They're all dead."

Jaylen's eyes met Maya's, and they both rushed to Agonya's side.

"What do you mean, we're all going to die?" Jaylen asked.

Maya didn't wait for a reply but threw her arms around her friend. Agonya was safe. There would be time to figure out what had happened to her, why she was so hopeless. Tears welled up and ran down Maya's face. "Come. Sit. We can talk in a moment."

Jaylen let her lead Agonya to the edge of the room, but she could see the worry in his face. "Are you sure this is a good idea?" he asked.

Maya nodded. "Please, if you can bring the others here."

Jaylen nodded and turned back toward Blackthorn. Together they brought the rest of the crew into the Nutty room. Ashkii was the last to arrive.

Agonya sat beside Maya, rocking and muttering the same words. "We're all going to die. We're all going to die."

Ashkii's head whipped around till he found her. His face was ghostly pale.

Maya took a deep breath and rose to her feet. "Thank you, Jaylen, Blackthorn, for saving us."

Ryker rushed to her side and scooped her into his arms. "You're safe. We're all safe." He laughed.

Krillin frowned but didn't move.

Ashkii tore his eyes from Agonya and shook his head. "We're not safe." he whispered. "None of us are. Somehow, I don't know how, but this was precisely what she wanted."

Everyone stared at him in disbelief.

Then, Jaylen collapsed to the ground. She watched him fall but couldn't go to him. The only thing Maya could think was Dana couldn't possibly find them here. Ashkii was wrong. He had to be wrong. This place was nowhere near Dana, and there was a magic to this place that made her feel like she was finally home.

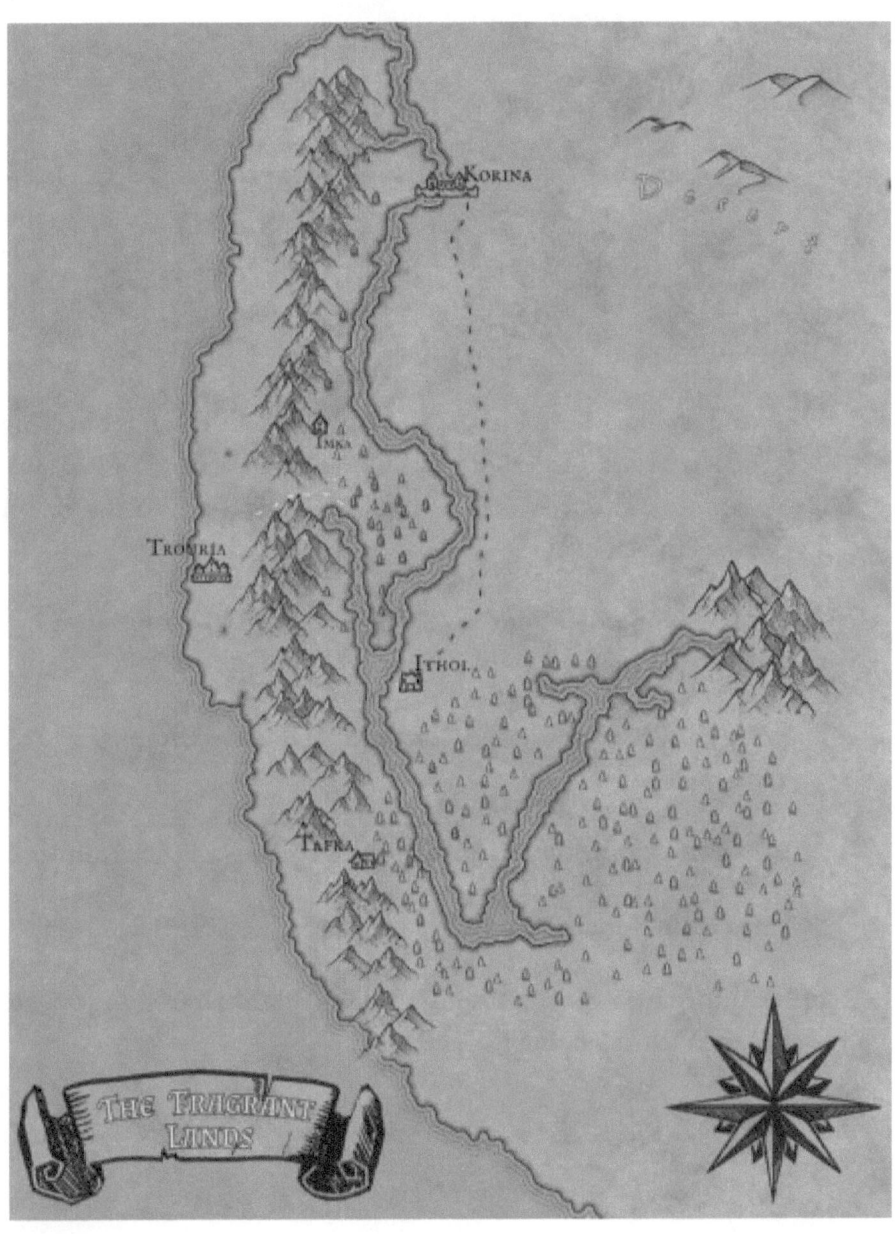

Character Lists

I tholeans:

Queen Agonya Kate Nakai (ah-GOHN-yah), daughter of King Azurarus Nakai (deceased) and Queen Kanti Nakai (deceased). No longer the queen of the Itholeans but a slave to the Korin Crown Prince Lucas.

Lord Commander Huren, Commander of the Itholean army, and a counselor for Queen Agonya

Lord Tanish, a priest and counselor for Queen Agonya. AKA **Yari**

Lady Rebekkah, a counselor for Queen Agonya. AKA **Annika**

Maya Klah, Queen Agonya's hand-maiden and best friend

Krillin Bahe a former Itholean soldier who betrayed his people and then left the fight all together.

Sari Bahe, Krillin's mother

Anya Bahe, Krillin's younger sister

Amber, an orphan and friend of Krillin and his family

Misu, an elderly man who helps Maya rebuild Ithol.

Kahlilah, previously the head cook in the Itholean palace, now helping Maya rebuild Ithol.

Tyler, best friends with Ryker, helping rebuild Ithol

Ryker, best friends with Tyler, helping rebuild Ithol

King Azurarus, Itholean king killed by a Montane assassin.

Brynn, Ashkii's Itholean friend who died at the end of Scents of War.

Korins:

Lord General Jaylen Dahel was promoted from being a captain in the Korin army to being a general and the temporary governor of Ithol after the war.

Captain Logan, one of Jaylen's soldiers from Scents of War, promoted to captain when Jaylen was promoted to general

Laniel, one of Jaylen's soldiers from Scents of War, still working for him in Ithol

Lord Commander Bannon, commander of the Korin army

Aekan Firikyi (ay-kin), a Korin spy and warrior. Krillin reported to him when he was a traitor.

King Reid Nayavu (reed), king of Korina, half-brother of Agonya's mother

Prince Lucas, the heir to Korina's throne, son of King Reid, friends with Dana

Dylan and Peta, Agonya's guards

Lady Tsula (t-su-la), Jaylen's sister and wife of Prince Lucas' cousin Sir Mato

Chaska and Minco, Jaylen's brothers

Sir Mato, Prince Lucas' cousin

Lord Tashunka Dahel, Jaylen's father, cursed by Dana

Tara, Prince Lucas' head servant

Montanes:

Ashkii (ash-kee), heir to the chief of Tafka, "friend" of Agonya's father

Tse (t-say), Ashkii's friend from Tafka

Chief Golar, chief of Tafka and Ashkii's father

Kilchii (kil-chee), Ashkii's twin brother

Skah, a warrior from the Imka tribe

Sorceress Dana, daughter of Jedrek the first and his brother's wife, Korina, over a thousand years old

Blackthorn, ancient Kindroot, magical tree-like creature that can fit in your pocket

Magical Creatures:

Elephantus (bear/elefant)- pack animal

Kollimus (mouse/hound)- Kolli for short, good at sniffing out people and objects

Drank (dragon/skunk)- squirts acid out of its mouth

Thorny Devil (lion-sized lizard)- large spikes covering its scaly body

Horvelina (horse/javelina)- mostly wild but sometimes used by skilled people as pack animals

Cheema (magical chameleon)- invisible to most, weakness is water

Acknowledgements

To my incredible readers who have been so patient these last two years for me to get this next book out and published, Thank You! Thank you for keeping me going, asking me how the writing is going (Harvey Benton and Randal Ball), being excited for me at each stepping stone, and understanding that life gets in the way of schedules sometimes. I can't wait to dive into the next and final chapter of The Fragrant Trilogy. Thank you for reading!

I want to thank all my writing friends who have motivated me to write or edit or do whatever I needed to do when I needed to do it. You were always there for advice, encouragement, and friendly company. That includes all my peeps in the Ink & Quill discord group and in the Fiction Frenzy Writing Challenge discord group. I especially want to thank Dr. Karen Renner and Dr. Lisa Hardy for checking up on me and not just about my writing goals, but for making sure all of me was doing well.

More importantly, a huge thank you to all my beta readers for Scents of Exile! To my first beta reader, Daniel Pitrowiski, who helped me think through the plot of my story before it was done. I can't tell you, Dan, how much you helped me get through the toughest part of editing this book. There was a mental challenge much like Agonya's (at the end of the book) that I was struggling with, and you sent your magic my way and helped me break through that wall, which involved breaking the original plot into all its different blocks and rearranging them into something beautiful. I also need to thank Kelly, Faramir, Brandon Hoffman, Taylor Hopper, Autumn Montoya, and Jamie Paul for your timely feedback, helping me perfect my completed story. Your help was invaluable to me.

Another thanks go to Jamie Paul and Gary Groenewold for helping me with the cover design! You're the best!

A huge thanks go to Brandon Hoffman for translating the map in my mind onto paper! It looks amazing!

Thank you to Hannah Clark and Laura Ball for being my walking partners the last couple of years. You kept me from turning into stone in my writing chair and always got me talking about my book and my progress.

Thank you to Sara Lorance, my best friend, who not only writes with me but gets me out of my bubble and into the real world where I can keep learning about what real life is all about and about who the world is made up of: what people like, dislike, dream of, struggle with, how they view the world and the list goes on.

Finally, I want to thank my family for their continued support. Ryan, you are the absolute best partner I could have asked for! I didn't even know to ask for you and yet here you are going above and beyond, loving me despite all my failures. Thank you for all our writing dates at 4 am and all the other ones too. You're amazing! Thank you to my children, Oliver, Phillip, and Jeremy, for supporting me, understanding when I'm not here to make your lunch or pick you up from school. You all have grown so much this last year as independent people finding your way in the world. I'm so proud of you all. You are the people that make my home a home worth returning to again and again. But even this home that I know and love is only a shadow of my true home in heaven.

Don't miss out!

Visit the website below and you can sign up to receive emails whenever J. L. Guyer publishes a new book. There's no charge and no obligation.

https://books2read.com/r/B-A-WUNV-MVLAF

BOOKS 2 READ

Connecting independent readers to independent writers.

About the Author

J. L. Guyer currently lives with her family of boys in Flagstaff, Arizona where she received her Bachelor of Arts in English from Northern Arizona University. She loves writing, reading, being outdoors, and napping.

You can learn more at her website, www.jlguyer.com, or find her on social media: Facebook @J. L. Guyer and on Twitter @JLGuyer1.

www.ingramcontent.com/pod-product-compliance
Lightning Source LLC
Chambersburg PA
CBHW032242010726
47494CB00002B/594